Praise for *The Naked Gentleman*

"Hilarity reigns as a queen of love and laughter crafts another "naked" book designed to keep you smiling. This delicious romance blends MacKenzie's hallmark humor with a cast of unforgettable characters."—Kathe Robin, *Romantic Times*

"What a great series! Funny, spicy, and romantic."—Jane Bowers, *Romance Reviews Today*

Praise for *The Naked Earl*

"Naked, noble, and irresistible—who could resist one of Sally MacKenzie's heroes?"—Eloisa James, *New York Times* bestselling author

"Providing plenty of heat and hilarity, MacKenzie has great fun shepherding this boisterous party toward its happy ending; readers will be glad they RSVPed."—*Publishers Weekly*

"The latest in MacKenzie's delectably sensual *Naked* historical Regencies series has plenty of sexy sizzle and charming wit."—*Booklist*

Praise for *The Naked Marquis*

"*The Naked Marquis* is an endearing confection of sweetness and sensuality, the romance equivalent of chocolate cake . . . every page is an irresistible delight!"—Lisa Kleypas, *New York Times* bestselling author

"With a delightfully quirky cast of characters and heated bedroom encounters, MacKenzie's latest *Naked* novel delivers a humorous, sprightly romance."—*Romantic Times*

"*The Naked Marquis* is a delicious indulgence. Treat yourself!"—*Once Upon a Romance*

EVER SO LIGHTLY

He silenced her with his fingertips. Lord Dawson removed his glove; his skin was warm and slightly rough as he stilled her lips and then slowly traced their outline.

What was he doing? Why did her lips feel suddenly swollen? Grace parted them slightly.

His lips touched hers as lightly as his fingers had. The briefest brush and then brush again . . .

Also by Sally MacKenzie

THE NAKED DUKE

THE NAKED MARQUIS

THE NAKED EARL

THE NAKED GENTLEMAN

"The Naked Laird"
(novella from LORDS OF DESIRE)

Published by Zebra Books

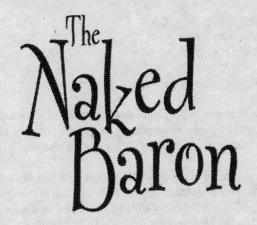

The Naked Baron

SALLY MACKENZIE

ZEBRA BOOKS
Kensington Publishing Corp.
http://www.kensingtonbooks.com

ZEBRA BOOKS are published by

Kensington Publishing Corp.
119 West 40th Street
New York, NY 10018

All Kensington titles, imprints, and distributed lines are available at special quantity discounts for bulk purchases for sales promotion, premiums, fund-raising, educational, or institutional use.

Special book excerpts or customized printings can also be created to fit specific needs. For details, write or phone the office of the Kensington Special Sales Manager: Attn. Special Sales Department. Kensington Publishing Corp., 119 West 40th Street, New York, NY 10018. Phone: 1-800-221-2647.

Zebra and the Z logo Reg. U.S. Pat. & TM Off.

ISBN-13: 978-1-4201-0253-6
ISBN-10: 1-4201-0253-2

First Printing: May 2009
10 9 8 7 6 5 4 3 2 1

Printed in the United States of America

*This one's for my agent, Jessica Faust,
and my editor, Hilary Sares*

And, as always, for Kevin

Chapter 1

Lady Grace Belmont stepped through the wide double doors into the Duke of Alvord's ballroom.

Dear God.

She froze on the small landing. Hundreds of candles lit hundreds of faces—and she'd swear every single face was turned toward her. Men in precisely fitted black coats and snowy white cravats raised their quizzing glasses. Brilliantly-gowned women, plumes bobbing, fans shielding their lips, tittered and whispered.

Dear, dear God. She couldn't escape fast enough—except she couldn't escape at all. A gaggle of elderly women blocked the stairs.

Blast! Grace swallowed and clenched her hands. She tried to take a deep breath, but the air was too thick with the scent of candle wax, perfume, and infrequently washed bodies. Black dots swam before her eyes. Was she going to swoon? *That* would be an even more entertaining spectacle for the duke's guests—the Amazon from Devon, all five feet nine inches and eleven stone of her, collapsing into an ignominious heap—a very *large* ignominious heap—on the ballroom floor. What a lovely way to begin her first—and last—London Season.

"Isn't it splendid?"

"What?" Grace looked down at her petite, ethereally beautiful aunt, Lady Oxbury.

"The ballroom, the guests . . . isn't it all splendid?" Aunt Kate almost glowed with pleasure. "It reminds me of my own come-out. The room is much the same, but the gentlemen then all wore lace and velvet, of course. They were as colorful as—perhaps more colorful than—the ladies." She sighed, smiling wistfully. "I was completely enchanted."

Enchanted? Enchantment was not one of the emotions swirling through Grace's gut at the moment. Nausea—well, nausea was not precisely an emotion. Terror, mortification, self-consciousness, anger . . . there was a lively stew brewing inside her, but enchantment was not one of the ingredients—it wasn't even one of the seasonings.

"You were only seventeen," Grace said, "and lovely. I am twenty-five and large."

"Grace!" Aunt Kate frowned at her. "Don't say that. You are quite regal."

"Regal." How Grace detested that word! It was uttered kindly by tiny women like her aunt, women who made her feel like a female Gargantua simply by standing next to her. Unless one were actually of royal lineage, regal was merely a synonym for large.

"Yes, regal. You are very striking. Don't you see how the gentlemen are admiring you?"

They were certainly admiring one specific part of her. "They are staring, Aunt Kate. That is not the same thing at all."

"Nonsense. They are all struck by your beauty." Aunt

Kate smiled, but the curve of her lips looked strained. "However, if you keep scowling like that, you will scare them all off."

One can only hope. "Aunt, can't you see where all those quizzing glances are directed? Those men aren't studying my expression; they are examining my bos—"

"Grace!" Her aunt fanned her face and glanced quickly to either side. "Mind what you say. You are not at Standen any longer."

No, she wasn't at Standen, was she? And she had only herself to blame. If she'd kept her tongue between her teeth when her aunt had arrived and proposed this hare-brained trip, she'd be home now, curled up with a good book in the drawing room, pretending to listen to Papa discourse on crop rotation and drainage issues.

The thought didn't give her the feeling of contentment she expected.

She suppressed a sigh. Of course it didn't. Life at Standen had been comfortable while Papa had mostly ignored her. Now, however . . . for the last year he'd become obsessed with the need to marry her off.

The elderly ladies had managed to navigate the first step. Now they were struggling with the second. Was it going to take them all evening to reach the floor?

Grace swallowed her annoyance. If only she'd done the same at Standen, but how *could* she have kept her temper in check when Papa had gone on and on about what a laughingstock she'd be if she appeared at the Season's events? She couldn't. So she'd let her temper slip its rein, and it had bolted, taking her good sense with it.

She blew out a short, impatient breath, causing the tendrils that had worked themselves free of her coiffure to float briefly in front of her eyes, and glanced back down at her aunt.

Aunt Kate looked as if she would like to wrap her elegant fingers around her neck in exasperation.

"You are in a pucker over nothing, Grace. Didn't you notice in the receiving line that Miss Hamilton was almost as tall as you? And I'm sure there are other ladies present as"—Aunt Kate blushed and coughed slightly—"well endowed." She patted Grace's arm. "Your father is an idiot. There will be plenty of gentlemen eager to pay you court."

That was highly unlikely, but there was no need to argue the point. "You know I'm not here to find a husband, Aunt Kate. Papa has already arranged everything with Mr. Parker-Roth. I just came to attend a few parties and see the London sights." *And enjoy my last gasp of freedom before I give my life over to John.*

"But do you truly want to marry this neighbor, Grace?"

"Er . . ." She didn't, but she was resigned to her fate. She couldn't live at Standen forever—and marrying for love was a fairy tale reserved to Minerva Press novels. "I'm content with Papa's choice. After all, didn't he choose Oxbury for you? And you had over twenty years of marital harmony."

Aunt Kate's face suddenly assumed the oddest expression, almost as if she'd taken a bite of stewed eels and couldn't decide whether to swallow or spit it out.

"Ah . . . er . . . yes." Aunt Kate cleared her throat. "But I do think you might wish—you really might wish—to look around, Grace. Mr. Parker-Roth may be a pearl beyond price, but how will you know unless you see what else is available? I, at least, had a brief Season."

"Well . . ."

"You can't go home like a beaten dog with your tail

between your legs and give your father the pleasure of saying he told you so."

"True." This *was* her only chance to see London. She should enjoy the experience. She would think of the male population as simply another sight to see, like London Bridge or Westminster Abbey. "I suppose there would be no harm in looking."

"Exactly." Aunt Kate smiled. "And there is so much to look at." She made a small, graceful gesture encompassing the ballroom. "You have all of society at your feet."

"Until these ladies finally move and we descend to join the crush." There was hope. The women had reached the final stair.

Kate's smile widened. "Indeed. So take a moment to survey the scene. I see a number of tall gentlemen, don't you?"

"Perhaps." There did seem to be one or two men above average height, though it was difficult to be certain from this vantage point.

"Perhaps? Of a surety. Look at the man by the ficus over there. Or the one by the windows. Or those two gentlemen by the . . . by the—oh, dear God." Aunt Kate turned as white as a sheet and gripped Grace's arm hard enough to leave marks.

"What is it? What's the matter?"

Aunt Kate was staring at one of two men standing by a clump of potted palms. The fellow was tall with dark hair, graying slightly at the temples. Distinguished looking—not alarming in the slightest. What could be the matter with—

Grace's gaze traveled to his companion.

Oh.

Her heart began to thud; heat flooded her face. For a moment she forgot to breathe.

This gentleman was even taller and roughly twelve years younger. His black coat stretched tight across impossibly broad shoulders, and his hair, dark blond and slightly longer than fashionable, waved back from a broad forehead. He had deep-set eyes, high cheekbones, a straight nose, firm mouth . . . and was that a cleft in his chin?

He was staring at her, but not in the highly obnoxious fashion of the other men. Oh, no. She met his gaze and felt a jolt of . . . something. The feeling fluttered down to lodge low in her belly.

What was the matter with her? Could the sooty London air be affecting her constitution? She'd never before felt this heat, this heaviness in—

She flushed. Could he tell?

A corner of his mouth turned up in a half smile. He could tell.

Aunt Kate's fingers dug farther into Grace's arm and her voice sounded slightly strangled. "I . . . I need to go to the ladies' retiring room," she said. "Now!"

"Damn, this ballroom is crowded." David Wilton, Baron Dawson, grabbed two glasses of champagne from a passing footman and retreated to the relatively quiet spot he'd found by some potted palms. "I can hardly breathe or hear myself think, there are so many people."

"Welcome to London and the *ton*." His uncle plucked one of the glasses from his hand and took a hearty swallow. "Now you know why I abhor the place, though this gathering may be even more of a squeeze than usual. The *on dit* is everyone's here to see Alvord's American houseguest—and to see how Alvord's cousin reacts to her."

David grunted and sipped his champagne. Gossip! London must be as bad as—no, worse than—the country. This was his first trip to Town for the Season—and his last, if he had anything to say to the matter. He wouldn't be here now if he didn't need a wife. But he did, and he couldn't choose a woman from the country. He'd grown up with all the females around his estate; he wasn't able to conjure up the slightest spark of desire in his heart— or other organ—for any of them.

He surveyed the blushing debutantes in their virginal white gowns. Faugh! What a collection of silly young geese.

"See anything—I mean, anyone—you like, nephew?"

"No." David swallowed, trying to rid his voice of annoyance. "Not yet, at least. But we've just arrived. Perhaps the more attractive ladies—the somewhat more mature women—have yet to make their appearance." He bloody well hoped these fluttering young girls weren't all society had to offer this Season. He didn't have forever. Yes, he was only thirty-one and had been a baron for just a year, but life was fragile and death too unexpected. He knew his responsibility. He needed to see to the succession.

Even his devil-may-care father had attended to that before splitting his head open on a rock.

"What about that girl? She'd be a pleasant sight over the breakfast table—or over rumpled bed sheets."

David looked at the young woman in question—a blonde in a crimson gown with an exceedingly small bodice. The girl noticed their attention and fluttered her fan.

"I don't think so." The chit was far too short and thin for his taste. "Do you suppose her mantua maker ran out of fabric before she finished that dress?"

"Perhaps." His uncle Alex's voice held a salacious note.

David frowned. "The girl's young enough to be your daughter."

Alex's jaw tightened; something—sorrow, pain?—flickered in his eyes, but it was gone so quickly, David couldn't be sure he'd seen anything but a shadow from the candlelight.

"A man can look, can't he?" Alex waggled his eyebrows in a distinctly lascivious fashion. "Admire beauty in all its manifestations?"

"Especially when the chit has two very lovely manifestations almost leaping from her gown."

"Especially then."

David laughed. "Behave yourself, uncle."

Alex scowled. "I am sick to death of behaving myself. I haven't been to Town in over twenty years. If I choose to celebrate with a little misbehavior, who the hell will care?"

"Surely you don't intend to take after my disreputable father at this late date?" David hoped the alarm he felt wasn't reflected in his voice.

"Perhaps I will. Luke's life may have been short, but it was intense. He knew what he wanted and he took it."

"But—"

"Mr. Wilton! Oh, Mr. Wilton! I say, can it really be you?"

"Wha—?" They both turned. An elderly woman with a cane and elaborately powdered hair was hobbling toward them as quickly as she could.

"Oh, God," Alex muttered. "Lady Leighton. I thought she'd been put to bed with a shovel."

David bit back a laugh. "She looks very much alive—and delighted to see you."

"God only knows why."

Lady Leighton grabbed Alex's arm as soon she got

close enough. "About time you came back to Town, Mr. Wilton. It's been so long, I hardly recognized you."

"Ah."

David turned his laugh into a cough. Poor Uncle Alex was apparently rendered speechless by Lady Leighton's enthusiasm.

The lady frowned and turned her grip into a pat. "I want to tell you I was so sorry to hear of your parents' passing."

A muscle jumped in Alex's cheek. Bloody hell. This time David was certain what he saw in his uncle's eyes—that stricken, bleak look was sadly all too familiar. When would Alex realize he was not responsible for Grandda's and Grandmamma's deaths?

David cleared his throat.

Lady Leighton turned her attention to him. "And who might this be?" She put up a hand as David opened his mouth to reply. "No, don't tell me—the resemblance is too great. Lord Dawson, correct?"

Damn. Was everyone going to see his ignoble father in his face? That was a trial he'd not anticipated when he'd mentally listed all the reasons not to come to Town. He inclined his head as unenthusiastically as he could manage. Perhaps the woman would take the hint and drop the subject.

No such luck. Lady Leighton thumped her cane on the floor. "Just as I thought. Luke's son. Does everyone tell you you're very like your father, my lord?"

David's stomach clenched. *No, thank God.* "I've been told I resemble him physically." He had tried his entire life to ensure that was the only way he resembled the man.

"Ah." She nodded. "Not a scapegrace, eh? Well, for all his faults, Luke Wilton was charming." She shook her head, sending a flurry of hair powder drifting down to her ample bosom. "Such a senseless tragedy."

She looked back at Alex. "And such a tragedy Standen insisted on thrusting a spoke in your wheel all those years later, Mr. Wilton. I hope this visit to Town means you've finally got over your disappointment? It's not too late to find a nice girl and start your nursery, you know. You can't be much above forty."

"Ah. Er."

She patted his arm again. "It is time to get on with your life, sir. Past time. Some woman will have you—you'll see." She turned back to David. "And are you in London to go shopping on the Marriage Mart as well, my lord? Very good. I like a man who recognizes his duty and gets down to business." She laughed. "Should I wager which of you will be the first to produce an heir?"

"Ah." It was David's turn to be less than coherent.

"I don't need to tell you—" she said.

He and Alex both shook their heads.

"—but—" Blessedly, Lady Leighton stopped and waved at someone. "Oh, there's Mrs. Fallwell. I have something of a very particular nature to say to her. I hope you don't mind if I run off?"

"No, please—" Alex said.

"Don't let us keep you." David said.

"Well, then." Lady Leighton squeezed both their arms. "Good luck with the ladies, my dear fellows," she said before she toddled off to accost Mrs. Fallwell.

"Thank God." They looked at each other and laughed.

"I never thought I'd be grateful for Mrs. Fallwell's presence on this planet." Alex took another long swallow of champagne. "She's a gabble-grinder of the first order, you know."

"Hmm." David studied his uncle. "What did Lady Leighton mean about your 'disappointment'? About Standen putting a spoke in your wheel?"

Alex's ears turned red. "I have no idea." He gulped the rest of his champagne and grabbed another glass from a passing footman.

"Is there something you haven't told me?"

"I can't think of anything." Alex stared into his champagne glass.

Why wouldn't his uncle meet his eyes? "Lady Leighton seemed quite—Damn!"

"Damn?" That made Alex look up.

"Yes. The Addison twins are here." David glanced around, looking for a suitable hiding place.

Alex gave a low whistle. "So they've tracked you all the way to London. Very impressive." He chuckled. "I'd say one of the Misses Addison plans to bag herself a baron."

"Not *this* baron." Those palms might conceal him. And look—a splendidly stout pillar as well.

"Don't be so certain. You'd best tread carefully if you don't want to stumble into parson's mousetrap."

David didn't bother to reply, he was too busy putting as many barriers as he could between himself and the Addisons. There was nothing so terribly wrong with the girls, besides the fact that he'd known them since they were in leading strings. Some man would be delighted to wed one of them, but not he. He couldn't tell them apart for one thing. Confuse his wife with her sister? That would be exceedingly awkward. And they were both far too scraggy.

He peeked around the pillar. They hadn't seen him, thank God. He watched their bony backsides move past. It was not an inspiring sight.

Were all young women today small and angular? Surely not! There must be some female who would be a good match for a man his size. He was built on a different scale than the usual, just like Grandda had been—and Grandda had found Grandmamma.

Ah. He closed his eyes. He still felt a heavy melancholy when he thought of them, but at least now it was only a dull ache and not the overwhelming, almost physical pain it had been. True, they had both been over seventy, but they'd still been healthy, vigorous, more alive than many people half their age—until their blasted carriage had slid into the big oak at the bottom of the hill between Clifton Hall, Alex's estate, and Riverview.

They should have stayed the night with Alex. Alex had urged them to. It was dark and rainy. But Grandda was as stubborn as a mule—Grandmamma, too—and they both liked to sleep in their own bed.

And now they were both dead.

Life was indeed fragile—a gift that could be taken back at any moment. He must wed—and bed—someone soon. He would not have the title die with him.

But he didn't want to wed one of these stick-figure girls. No, he wanted a woman with some meat on her bones. A soft armful—a woman with full breasts and hips who made a comfortable bed herself—sweet, yielding, warm. No, not warm—hot. A woman with a body that made a man forget his own name.

A woman like the one who'd just entered the ballroom.

Zounds! He straightened and closed his mouth. He did not care to appear the complete gape-seed if she should look in his direction.

She was beautiful. Tall, much taller than the older woman at her side, with glorious, wonderful, lusciously full curves. The neck of her gown was, sadly, too high—it covered far too much of her lovely porcelain skin. He would love to touch that skin with his fingers and lips and tongue. Mmm.

And her hair? Also lovely. It was gathered high on her head, a few tendrils escaping to frame her face. His fingers twitched to burrow through that silky mass, freeing the copper-colored length to tumble over her shoulders. Her naked shoulders.

Her naked breasts.

Could they be as large as they looked?

She took a step; turned to talk to her companion. The skirt of her dress pulled tight for a moment, outlining her hips and long, long legs.

Bloody hell, he was almost panting.

Who was she? Perhaps Alex knew. "Alex."

"What is it?" Alex glanced over his shoulder. "Are you still hiding?"

"No. The Addisons are on the other side of the room. But come here, will you? I've got a question for you."

"Very well." Alex stepped around the palms. "Always glad to be of service, of course."

David gestured toward the ballroom entrance. "Who is that woman?"

"Which woman? Surely you aren't interested in one of the elderly ladies tottering down the stairs?"

"Of course not, you cabbage-head. It's the tall, beautiful girl on the landing I'm asking about."

"Oh." Alex raised his eyes. "How should I know? She must have been in leading strings—if she was even born—last time I was in London."

"So you have no idea who she is?" Damn. David felt a stab of disappointment.

"No." Alex raised an eyebrow. "Why are you so anxious to identify the chit? Has she stolen something of yours that you need to alert the Bow Street Runners about?"

Yes. My heart.

God, he hadn't said that aloud had he? No, Alex was still looking at him with that faintly amused expression. If he'd spoken it, the man's jaw would be on the floor.

And it wasn't true in any event. Yes, one of his organs was definitely engaged—and wished to be much more intimately engaged—but it wasn't his heart.

"Of course not. It's just that I've decided . . ." David cleared his throat. "That is, I believe the lady would make an excellent baroness."

"*What*?" Now Alex's jaw did drop, and he sloshed champagne on his waistcoat. "Are you daft?"

"No." David might not know the woman's name, but he knew he wanted her. She was the first woman he'd seen who'd provoked any, er . . . interest in him at all. In fact his interest was so great it threatened to become embarrassing.

She wouldn't be crushed in his bed. He might need to be gentle with her sensibilities, but her body would fit his perfectly. He took a mouthful of champagne, but he barely tasted it. Regrettably, his body was all too anxious to see exactly how well they would fit. He'd best find a way to control his raging interest before he made her acquaintance. She might be more than a little startled if he fell on her like a lust-driven schoolboy.

Her companion had stepped forward so her profile was now visible. David nodded at her. "Perhaps you know that woman, then. I imagine she must be the girl's mother."

"I don't know why you think I—" Alex looked up at the woman and stiffened. "No." He sounded oddly agitated. "I wouldn't . . . she's rather . . . she looks—" He made a strangling sound.

"What's the matter?" Alex was reacting damn peculiarly. David studied the older woman. She wasn't doing anything unusual—just looking around the ballroom. Her gaze came to Alex . . . Her mouth fell open, her eyes grew wide, and all the color drained from her face. She grabbed her daughter's arm.

Ah, the daughter. She was looking at him now, and a very attractive flush swept up her neck to cover her cheeks. Did it also sweep down her body? How fervently he wished he could see . . .

He could almost feel her eyes on his shoulders, his face. Her tongue slipped out to moisten her lips.

He'd seen women look at him before. This girl wanted him. She probably didn't know that yet . . . she was far too innocent to recognize what she was feeling, but he would be more than happy—dashed delighted!—to explain it all to her. In detail. In lovely, hot, wet, slow detail.

"Bloody hell," Alex murmured. It couldn't be. Alex squeezed his eyes shut and then opened them again.

It was. Damn. It *was* Kate.

After all these years, he was in the same room as Lady Kate Belmont—except now she was the Countess of Oxbury.

But Oxbury was dead, had been dead a year. He'd died around the same time as Mama and Da.

Kate had closed her mouth and was turning away, her hand grasping the arm of . . . her daughter?

No, that wasn't her daughter. It couldn't be. He'd kept track. She and Oxbury had had no children. No sons—the title had passed to Oxbury's cousin—but no daughters, either.

He was embarrassed to admit it, but it had always comforted him that Kate had had no children with Oxbury. He snorted. Did he think her relationship with her husband had been platonic? Unlikely, though Oxbury had been thirty years older than she.

He watched her walk off with the girl. She was still very pale.

David grabbed his arm again. "You *do* know the pair. Can you introduce me?"

"No!" Kate would have nothing to do with him or with David—with any Wilton. And the girl . . . she must be a relative. Kate's brother, the Earl of Standen, had had a daughter . . .

Even worse.

David was scowling at him. Alex took a calming breath. "The older woman is the Earl of Oxbury's widow."

"And the girl? They are obviously together. They must be related in some way—the age difference is too great for them to be merely friends. Yet if the matron is the Countess of Oxbury . . ."

"She is definitely the countess. I think the girl must be her niece—the Earl of Standen's daughter." *The bloody bastard.*

"So, can you introduce me?"

"No." Approach Kate? She would probably spit on him.

"Why not? You obviously know Lady Oxbury."

"I *knew* Lady Oxbury. I doubt she'd recognize me now."

David choked on his champagne. "Oh, I'd say she definitely recognizes you, Uncle Alex."

Why the hell was David grinning at him? "I meant *recognize*. She'll give me the cut direct if I try to speak to her."

"I don't think so. Introduce me," David said. "I may not be quite as lofty as an earl, but my barony is an old, respected one. I—"

"You have not been attending. Clear your mind of lust. This has nothing to do with you. Did you not hear the girl's father's name? She is the daughter of the Earl of *Standen*."

"So? I can—oh." David's arrested expression would have been comical in other circumstances.

"Exactly. Standen. The man whom your mother, Lady Harriet, jilted to run off with your father. I assure you, the Earl of Standen hates all Wiltons. He will not—he will never—consider your suit."

David considered Alex's slightly strident tone, flushed face, and set jaw.

The Earl of Standen's daughter . . . damn. That *was* a problem, but not an insurmountable one, surely? He'd never met Standen, but the man couldn't be a complete idiot. He must have moved on from those long ago events—he'd married, had a daughter.

"Surely Standen has got over his disappointment," David said.

Alex snorted. "The earl has got over nothing."

"But the scandal was more than thirty years ago. From what Grandmamma said, the earl should be falling on his knees every night and thanking God he *didn't* get buckled to mama. She was much too young and too wild to suit him."

Alex shrugged. "I can assure you the earl harbors no good thoughts concerning our family. He'd drag his sister naked down St. James's Street before he'd give his consent for a Belmont to marry a Wilton."

"How do you know that?"

"He told me so himself," Alex said, his voice more bitter than David had ever heard it, "twenty-three years ago when I asked to marry his sister."

Chapter 2

"Are you certain you're all right, Aunt Kate?"

"Ah. Oh. Er . . ." She certainly was *not* all right. Thank God the retiring room was empty. Her loss of composure was bad enough—at least she was not enacting a spectacle for an interested audience.

She had to get hold of her emotions before she went back out into the ballroom.

Kate clasped her hands and tried to stop gulping air. If only she could loosen her stays. She should never have had Marie, her maid, lace them so tightly, but she'd stupidly wanted to look young again, slim and virginal and seventeen. Impossible. Marie could tighten her stays until the strings broke, she'd still have lines at the corner of her eyes, threads of gray in her hair . . .

She wasn't seventeen any longer. Alex must have been shocked—horrified—to see how she'd aged.

Oh, Alex . . .

Kate moaned slightly. Breathe in through her nose; out through her mouth. In. Out. Stop panicking.

"Here, try your vinaigrette." Grace waved the small, aromatic box under Kate's nose.

"No, I—ah!" Kate's head snapped up as she inhaled the pungent scent.

"Do you feel better?"

"Ah." No, she was just more aware of how miserable she felt. Could she spend the entire evening here in the retiring room?

Definitely not. She was Grace's chaperone. She had to go out into the . . .

Breathe.

Grace was still waving the vinaigrette in her face. Kate snatched it from her and snapped it shut.

Most likely Alex—Mr. Wilton—hadn't even noticed her entrance, didn't remember her or the unfortunate incidents of her long-ago Season, had absolutely no recollection of that mortifying scene in this very garden . . .

"Ohh." She covered her face with her hands.

"Aunt Kate, you sound like you're in pain."

"No, no, I'm fine." She waved the hand with the vinaigrette in Grace's direction.

Had Alex noticed her arrival? She'd been too shocked to see, let alone comprehend, his expression.

"What *is* the problem?" Grace said. "Is there something . . . odd about those two men?"

Two men? There were two men? Kate tried to clear some of her distress from her mind. Oh, yes—the other man—the younger one who looked so like Alex. He must be Alex's nephew, the product of the first Wilton-Belmont scandal.

Why in God's name was Alex here anyway? He should be safely in the country. What infernal coincidence had sent him to London precisely when she'd chosen to come?

His parents had died around the same time as Oxbury. Perhaps that was it. Death did have a way of making one reevaluate one's life. Oxbury's passing had certainly forced her to do some soul searching.

"Aunt Kate . . ."

Kate flushed. She had barely admitted it to herself, but she had thought . . . only in a general way, of course . . . that while Grace was looking for a husband, she might also take a glance around the London ballrooms. Oh, not for another husband—though Oxbury's heir was certainly making living in the dower house miserable—but for . . .

Well, she *was* a widow, and widows were allowed—almost expected to take—certain . . . liberties. She'd considered . . .

But she had never expected to see Alex.

Twenty-three years ago, she'd been eager for excitement and surprises. She'd had her head full of silly dreams of handsome men and stolen kisses. Of love and marriage. Of happily ever after.

She was wiser now. She knew life might hold contentment, if one worked hard and had a modicum of luck, but happily ever after? That was only for fairy tales.

But Alex was here. Could it be . . . was it possible . . . ?

"Aunt Kate, what *is* the matter with you? Are you ill? Do you need to leave?"

Yes, yes. She needed to leave—leave this ball, leave London. Go home where it was safe, where she could hide.

But she couldn't hide. Oxbury, with its comforting, orderly house and neatly trimmed lawns, wasn't her home any longer, and if she fled Town, Grace would have to go with her. She'd miss her Season and her chance to find a husband of her own choosing.

She would not let Grace be forced by circumstances—by Standen—to make the same mistake she'd made . . . not if she could help it.

"Aunt Kate!" Grace had resorted to shaking her shoulder.

"What?" Kate blinked and looked up. A very worried expression twisted Grace's features.

"Should we send someone to fetch the carriage?"

"No. No, of course not." Kate moistened her lips and smoothed her skirt with hands that didn't shake very much at all. "I am perfectly fine."

Grace opened her mouth, but Kate put up a hand to stop the words she knew were coming.

"No, truly. I am fine. I had a brief attack of nerves, that's all." She forced a smile. "It has been many years since I've stepped into a London ballroom. I was momentarily overcome, but I have recovered." She stood and shook out her skirts. "Come, let's go back to the ballroom."

Grace crossed her arms. "Not until you explain what just happened."

Kate wished Grace wouldn't loom in such a disconcerting fashion. "I have just explained. I lost my composure briefly."

Grace's left eyebrow flew up so she looked just like her father at his most skeptical. Kate had always hated that expression on Standen. Since their parents had died when she was young, she'd seen that look growing up more times than she cared to consider. At least it was better than the cold, haughty expression he assumed when he was furious—as he had been the last time she'd been in London.

"I may be new to Town, Aunt Kate, but I am not a complete flat. You've been remarkably calm this whole trip. I cannot think even a ballroom full of the *ton* could set you to quaking—especially as your nervous attack did not commence until you saw the tall, older gentleman by the potted palms. Who is he?" Grace grinned. "And, more importantly, who is his companion?"

Oh, dear. Grace's eyes were sparkling. This would never do. Of all the men in London—of all the men in the world—this was the one man Grace could never have.

"I'm not certain." Kate tried to leave, but Grace caught her arm.

"Who do you think they are?"

Kate sighed. Grace obviously wasn't going to let her leave without giving her an answer. "I haven't seen the older man in years, and I've never met the younger, but, well, I believe . . ."

"Yes?" Grace's nostrils flared and her jaw clenched. If she *were* her father, she'd start shouting now. "Who are they, Aunt Kate?"

"I believe the older gentleman is Mr. Alexander Wilton and the younger is Mr. Wilton's nephew, Baron Dawson."

"Oh." Grace blinked.

Kate felt slightly relieved. At least Grace appeared to be aware of the problem. She should only require a small word of warning to avoid the men. "I assume your father has mentioned the family?"

"Occasionally." Grace bit her lip. Yes, she'd heard Papa mention the baron—this baron's grandfather. Usually it was "that bloody Dawson" followed by a detailed condemnation of the man and his family, past, present, and future. She'd made the mistake once of asking Papa why he disliked Lord Dawson so much. She'd never got a clear answer, only more curses and then tight-lipped silence.

The old baron died a year ago, shortly after Lord Oxbury. That was also when Papa decided she needed to marry John. She'd thought the impetus for his matrimonial mania had been Lord Oxbury's demise, but now she wasn't so sure.

"Why does Papa dislike the Wiltons so, Aunt Kate? It's not as though they are our neighbors. As far as I know, Papa has never met the two gentlemen who are here tonight. Or is it only the old baron he detests? I've asked him, but he won't say."

Of course he wouldn't say, Kate thought, and he especially wouldn't tell his daughter. It was not Kate's place to reveal Standen's secrets—and she didn't relish discussing her own past indiscretions, either. "It's enough for you to know you must avoid these men."

Grace's brows snapped down. She looked extremely mulish—another expression she'd got from her father. "That's ridiculous. If you can't—or won't—tell me what the problem is, then I'll just have to ask Lord Dawson." Grace lifted her left eyebrow again. "I assume he knows?"

"Ahh." Grace wouldn't have the temerity to ask the baron, would she? "I don't know what Lord Dawson knows or doesn't know. It makes no difference. It is not the sort of conversation you can have in a ballroom full of gossips."

Grace shrugged. "Then I'll find a more private location for my questions—the garden, perhaps."

"No!" The last time a Wilton had escorted a Belmont into the Duke of Alvord's garden . . . Kate pressed her hand to her bosom. Was her heart pounding with embarrassment or . . . ?

Embarrassment, certainly. Definitely. Without a doubt. She had no desire to reenact that painful evening.

Though it hadn't been painful until later, when Standen had called her into his study. Her time in the garden with Alex had been special—a cherished memory she would keep locked away in her heart forever.

But Grace must not be making any memories with

the current baron. "You know you cannot go into the garden with a man."

Grace shrugged again. Was that a spark of defiance in her eye? "Of course, I won't do anything truly scandalous, Aunt Kate. And John won't be swayed by silly London gossip."

"Mr. Parker-Roth might not pay attention to London gossip, but the rest of the *ton* will. Do you wish to have your Season end before it begins?"

"I wish to find out what this secret is that you and Papa have been keeping from me."

"Grace, I—"

Two women came into the retiring room.

". . . and then did you see how Lady Charlotte glared at the Colonial?" the short, round one said. "I never— oh!" She stopped and stared at Kate. Her eyes widened. "Is that . . . can it be . . . Lady Kate Belmont? I mean, Lady Oxbury?"

"Y-yes, I'm Lady Oxbury. And you are . . . ?"

"Don't you know me, Kate?" The woman laughed. "I realize I've gained a few pounds with all my babies, but I had hoped I was still recognizable. We made our come-out together, remember? Hid by the ficus trees at the Wainwright ball, too shy to speak to anyone. I was miserable when you left Town so abruptly."

Kate blinked. "Prudence? Prudence Cartland?"

"The same, except now I'm Lady Delton. And this is my friend, Mrs. Neddingham."

"Delighted to make your acquaintance, Mrs. Neddingham. Please let me introduce my niece, Lady Grace." Kate could not stop smiling as she chatted with the women. She'd never expected—though now that she thought of it, she should have—that she'd know anyone in London. She did remember shy little Prudence—and now that she knew who it was, she could see the young girl she'd shared her come-out with in the broader, older lines of this matron. What other old acquaintances would she find in the ballroom—besides Alex, that is?

Alex. Oh, dear. And Alex's nephew. She must be certain Grace kept clear of him. The girl had looked far too interested in Dawson. If she were truly attracted to the baron—no, Fate could not be so cruel.

"It was lovely to see you again, Prudence, and to meet you, Mrs. Neddingham, but Grace and I must—" Kate looked to her right. Grace had been there just a moment ago, hadn't she? She wasn't there now nor was she anywhere she could see in this small room.

"Looking for your niece, Kate?" Prudence laughed. "I'm afraid she got bored listening to us old women reminisce. She left a good ten minutes ago."

Lady Luck in the guise of Mrs. Neddingham and Lady Delton had certainly smiled upon her, Grace thought as she slipped out of the ladies' retiring room. Now she could find Lord Dawson without first having to brangle with Aunt Kate. She was determined to discover why Papa held the baron's family in such aversion—and why Aunt Kate had fled when she'd seen Mr. Wilton.

If there were skeletons in her family closet, she wished to meet them, especially as they seemed to be pushing her down the church aisle toward Mr. Parker-Roth.

The ballroom was even more crowded than when she'd arrived. Couples filled the center of the room, making their way through the figures of the dance while knots of turbaned chaperones gossiped and giggling debutantes darted glances at the young bucks lining the walls. The din of all the voices almost drowned out the orchestra, and the competing smells of perfume, pomade, and, well, bodies were truly suffocating now that she was down in the midst of them.

Where was Lord Dawson? He should not be hard to locate—he was one of the tallest men in the room. There was his uncle, still by the potted palms. And the baron? Ah! He was standing by a ficus tree near the doors to the garden.

She felt the same jolt seeing him now as she had when she'd been standing on the ballroom landing, and this time he wasn't even looking at her. What was it about him that started this convocation of butterflies in her stomach? Not that the sensation was confined to her middle. Oh, no. She felt a fluttering in her chest as well as—she blushed—other, unmentionable places.

Were all the women in the room similarly affected? How could they not be—though no one else appeared to be staring at him as she was.

They should be staring. If this room were a painting, Lord Dawson would be the subject. Everyone else, all the other men, women, everything surrounding him was incidental, background and setting for him.

He stood quiet and alert, alone. Would he look her way? She felt breathless with anticipation—

Silly. She was not going to stand here waiting for him to notice her. She needed to speak to him; she could not leave that conversation to chance. She started to make her way around the room's perimeter, but she couldn't move quickly enough. She watched him slip outside.

No matter; she would follow him. She would not be deterred by something so minor as a few plants and the evening sky, no matter what Aunt Kate said. Aunt Kate was a chaperone—it was her duty to worry. She was old enough to make her own decisions.

She sidestepped an elderly woman with a cane and an excess of plumes, avoided the eye of a portly gentleman, and reached the door.

Had Lady Oxbury and her niece left the ball? He'd looked for them the last ten minutes and had seen no sign of either of them.

David resisted the urge to take out his timepiece once more. He'd been getting far too many interested looks from Alvord's guests—particularly those of the feminine persuasion; he didn't wish to cause everyone to speculate why he kept pulling his watch out of his pocket. Best to try for patience. If they hadn't left—and God, he hoped they hadn't—they would have to appear in the ballroom eventually.

He stepped to the other side of a ficus tree to avoid a very intent-looking mama and her debutante daughter.

He should not be avoiding them—he should be speaking to them and to all the other ladies in the room. He should not be concentrating on Standen's daughter. Alex was right—life would be much simpler if he could find a pleasant woman without a history linked to his blasted father.

Yes, he liked Lady Oxbury's niece's appearance— Zounds, how he liked her appearance! He was growing shockingly enthusiastic just thinking of her appearance . . . but he hadn't met her. She might smell of garlic or have a voice as shrill as a fishmonger's wife.

He forced himself to look around the ballroom. There were plenty of matrimonial candidates present. They all had two eyes, a nose, a mouth, a quantity of hair arranged in ringlets and curls. Not one made his . . . ahem . . . heart leap.

He was as bad as a hound that had caught the scent of a fox. Lady Oxbury's niece was all he could think about.

If only she weren't the Earl of Standen's daughter. Or if only her father were a reasonable man. Did Standen actually blame him for Lady Harriet's death? Impossible. Many women died in childbirth. Hadn't Standen's wife died trying to birth the man's stillborn heir?

And surely Standen didn't hold him accountable for his father's actions? People might think he looked like Luke Wilton, but no one had ever blamed him for causing his parents' elopement.

He snorted. He could have caused it, he supposed, but he'd always been given to understand he'd yet to be conceived when the young couple had made their dash for the border—though they'd certainly not wasted any time in seeing to his creation.

Or did Standen simply consider him bad seed from bad seed?

Anger coursed through his gut. The bloody fool. If anyone had a right to bear a grudge, it was him—but he didn't blame Standen for his father's death. He didn't blame anyone, though if there were guilt to be apportioned, he'd lay some on the doorstep of Lord Wordham, his mother's father. If the man hadn't tried to force his daughter to wed Standen, the whole sorry train of events would not have been put in motion.

He relaxed his jaw, unclenching his teeth. Lord Wordham was dead; it was useless to expend any more anger on him.

He would just have to persuade Standen he was the perfect husband for his daughter. He should be able to do it—he'd lived his entire life proving to the world he was nothing like Luke Wilton.

He allowed himself another glance at his watch. Where

could the ladies have gone? There was still no sign of them. He might have to concede defeat for tonight. But he would search for them again at the next gathering. He looked forward to it—and that in itself was something to celebrate. He hadn't looked forward to anything since his grandparents' damn carriage accident.

He closed his eyes briefly. He was definitely doing better. He'd finally accepted the fact Grandda and Grand-mamma were gone. He'd accepted that he was now baron and needed to attend to those duties—all those duties.

He smiled. And tonight he'd made the next step. He no longer just accepted the need for a wife and heir, he looked forward to winning the wife and getting the heir.

Another debutante and marriage-minded mama were heading his way. He should talk to them; dance with the girl . . .

He couldn't. He stepped out the door to the garden.

Where was Grace? Kate scanned the ballroom. Music spilled over her and, despite her need to find her niece, Kate's heart lifted. She used to love to dance. She watched the couples gliding around the room, waltzing. It was scandalous, men and women touching each other like that. Completely scandalous.

What if the waltz had been danced when she'd had her come-out? What would it have been like to have waltzed with Alex all those years ago?

Regret darkened her heart like the sooty London air. She saw him still standing by the palms. He was looking at her . . .

She looked away. She had to find Grace. She couldn't think about Alex and the past.

She couldn't think about anything else.

* * *

She was still beautiful.

Alex took another gulp of champagne. He much appreciated Alvord's verdant decorating scheme. This vase of flowers, for example, was very strategically placed among the potted palms. His skin-tight breeches left nothing to the imagination, making painfully clear to any casual observer exactly where *his* imagination had strayed.

Painfully clear, yes—with the emphasis on pain. He had to think of something other than Kate. There was little hope he could ease this ache tonight.

But if he could—

It was very, *very* fortunate the floral arrangement before him was a splendidly bushy collection of vegetation.

He squeezed his eyes shut briefly, but that didn't stop the memories. Twenty-three years ago, at a ball given by the previous Duke of Alvord, he'd asked Kate to marry him. He'd known who she was, yet he'd still let himself fall in love with her. He grimaced. Could he have been any more mutton-headed?

No. It was not possible—unless he surpassed himself tonight.

He looked at Kate again. She was standing alone by the windows to the terrace now, fanning herself. Standen's daughter had vanished.

Tsk, tsk, Kate. You need to be more vigilant. You know what can happen in the duke's garden.

Madness. He'd taken Kate into Alvord's garden all those years ago and had asked her to marry him. It had been the only spontaneous, daring thing he'd ever done in his life. She'd said yes, even though, as he learned later, she was already engaged to Oxbury.

And then he had kissed her. It had been a rather chaste kiss. She'd been a virgin, after all, and he, not much more than one.

He smiled slightly. God, how that kiss had haunted him. It had been awkward and short, barely more than a brushing of lips, but full of longing and possibilities. A promise of future passion—a promise sadly unfulfilled. The next morning when he'd called to ask for Kate's hand, Standen had let him know in no uncertain terms that hell would freeze over before a Wilton would marry a Belmont. Kate had already been packed off to the country.

He hadn't seen her since—until tonight.

She was a widow now. Perhaps she missed male companionship . . .

He took another swallow of champagne. He could use some liquid courage.

He'd swear she hadn't changed at all. She still looked as fragile, as sylphlike, as she had that first Season.

Would she go with him into the garden? Would she let him kiss her again? But this time the kiss he gave her wouldn't be in the least bit chaste—it would be wet and hot and carnal.

He downed the rest of his champagne, hid the glass in the greenery, and stepped out of the palm fronds. It was time to put his hopes to the test.

Kate looked at the window. The candlelight and dancing couples were reflected splendidly, but as for the terrace outside . . . She couldn't see a thing unless she stuck her nose to the glass and cupped her hands around her eyes to block the light from the ballroom.

She should go find Grace. The girl must be out on the terrace—she was nowhere to be found in the ballroom.

How could Grace ignore Kate's pointed warnings? Didn't she understand the danger? Yes, she was significantly older than most debutantes, but this *was* her first London Season. It would not be hard for her to put a foot wrong, especially as she seemed to think her age and size exempted her from society's rules.

Kate knew all too well what could happen in the Duke of Alvord's garden.

Dear heaven. Just the thought of the garden brought so many memories flooding back. Memories and . . . sensations.

She plied her fan vigorously. She should stop trying to delude herself. She hadn't gone out looking for Grace because she hoped by staying in the ballroom Alex might approach her. She was being terribly irresponsible. And pitiful.

Her stays were much too tight. She would listen to Marie from now on and forget her silly notions of appearing youthful. She tried to draw a deeper breath.

She'd like to escape the crush herself—and the decidedly stuffy air, she thought, wrinkling her nose. She'd like to go into the garden with Alex—

No! Not with—most certainly not.

Dear God, would this evening never end? She was so hot and uncomfortable—and everyone was talking about her. Oh, Prudence had been very friendly, but there had been a touch of pity in her old friend's eyes. And why not? Prudence had a house full of children and Kate had . . . nothing.

She glanced around the room—and saw Alex.

She whipped her eyes away and pretended to look out the window again. Would he ask her to dance or, worse, stroll in the garden?

She moved her fan faster.

He must have had innumerable conquests these twenty-three years while she'd been busy being a good wife—well, a wife—to her husband—her much older husband.

Oh God, he was coming her way.

She should join the other chaperones. There was safety in numbers. She glanced at the knot of older women. They were darting looks at her and Alex and whispering behind their fans.

No, she wouldn't join the chaperones.

She watched Alex's reflection. He was coming closer . . .

She moistened her lips. Her stomach shivered. Her heart, even her—She blushed and fanned more vigorously still. Tendrils of hair flew about her face.

Even the secret place between her legs, the place Oxbury had entered frequently in the early days of their marriage when there was still hope she could bear him an heir and not so frequently later—not at all in the last months when he'd been so sick—even that place shivered.

It was as if she'd been asleep all these years and now she was waking.

"Lady Oxbury?"

He was standing right behind her. She turned slowly to face him. She stared at his white waistcoat. Her mouth was as dry as dust. She couldn't speak.

"Lady Oxbury, are you all right?"

She tried to breathe, but the damn stays were too confining. "I . . ." She managed to raise her eyes from his chest to his lips.

His mouth was firm, serious, his lips narrow . . .

Did she remember how they felt? She would swear that she did. Their light, brief touch, brushing over her mouth, had ignited a fire that had smoldered for twenty-three years.

She met his eyes—

Ahh. Heat flared in those blue depths. His gaze was so intent.

She moistened her lips again.

The embers of that old fire were bursting back into life. The conflagration would incinerate her if she were not careful.

Did she want to be careful?

Was she a moth, flying to her death, or a phoenix, reborn by flame?

"Come with me into the garden, Kate." His voice, low, full of promise, melted any whisper of resistance her conscience might muster.

That wasn't all it melted. Her lips, her breasts, ached for his touch; the secret place throbbed, wept for him.

Heat swept up her cheeks. She had been faithful to Oxbury all the years they were wed and the long year since his death. Was she a light skirt, then, to so easily consider going into the garden with this man?

No. This was not any man—this was Alex.

Moth or phoenix, suicide or rebirth, it didn't much matter. She was going out into the garden with Alex, even if she had to drag him into the bushes herself.

Chapter 3

The terrace was markedly cooler, quieter—and darker. The ballroom candles cast only very small circles of light from the door and windows. There were lanterns, yes, but they seemed to create more shadows than they dispelled—if the murmurings Grace heard were any indication, a number of couples were delighted to take advantage of the dim light.

She should go back inside. Now that she considered the matter, she realized it would be rather awkward to try to initiate a discussion with the baron out here. They had never been introduced, after all. Lord Dawson probably had no idea who she was.

She flushed, remembering how he'd looked at her when she'd stood on the ballroom landing. His eyes had seared a path straight to her soul, if her soul was located—

Oh! The place low in her . . . well, that place throbbed again. It could not be her soul—it was far too physical.

"Pardon me, but are you going out, miss?"

"What? Oh, er . . ." She was blocking the door, wasn't she? A short, balding man wished to get through—a short, balding man who was now drooling on her bodice.

She stepped back quickly and caught her heel in her hem.

"Ack!" She flung out her hands to recover her balance, but it was hopeless. She was going down. She would indeed end in an ignominious heap, but at least not in the middle of the ballroom—"Oh!"

A pair of strong arms caught her and hauled her up against a rock-hard chest.

"Are you all right?" The voice was warm, deep, concerned—but with a hint of laughter.

"Ah." She blinked up at her rescuer—Lord Dawson, of course. "Er."

She couldn't form a coherent sentence—she couldn't think. She'd never been so close to a man before. A host of sensations overwhelmed her: the hard strength of Lord Dawson's arms holding her as if she weighed nothing; the rough texture of his coat against her cheek; the clean scent of his linen and . . . him.

She felt small. She had *never* felt small. Even as a child, she'd towered over the other girls and most of the boys. The feeling was completely disorienting.

She concentrated on Lord Dawson's face, but that didn't help. If anything, such a close inspection caused her heart to pound harder and her poor brain to drift further into its stupor.

He *did* have a slight cleft in his chin. And a dimple in his cheek. And long, dark lashes framing his eyes . . .

His teeth were white and even in the shadows. Was he laughing at her? It wouldn't be odd if he were. She was gaping up at him like a complete ninny.

"*Are* you all right?" The laughter was more pronounced, but there was a different undertone now. The heat was back in his eyes.

"Has she swooned, Dawson? Should I send someone for help?"

"I don't believe that will be necessary, Delton."

Good God, what was she thinking? Lingering in Lord Dawson's arms was bad enough, but lingering on the Duke of Alvord's terrace with an interested group of spectators gathered round, one of whom must be the husband of Aunt Kate's friend—She didn't need her aunt to point out she was flirting with social suicide.

Grace struggled to right herself. Lord Dawson released her, but kept a steadying hand on her elbow. She should shake him off, but she did still feel a trifle in need of support.

She straightened her skirt and lifted her chin. "I'm fine, sir. Thank you for your concern."

"I'm so sorry, miss. I . . ." Delton shrugged. He was clearly uncertain what he'd done to cause this particular disaster. Not surprising. He had merely been trying to pass through a doorway. It was unfortunate her bosom was on level with his face, but that was not his doing.

"Please, don't give it another thought," Grace said. "It was my fault completely."

Lord Dawson squeezed her elbow. "Ah, but a lady is never at fault, is she, Delton?"

"No, indeed. I take full responsibility."

"No, no. I should not have lingered in the doorway."

David smiled slightly. Was Standen's daughter going to argue with Delton? He'd best get the girl off the terrace. They were beginning to gather a crowd.

His smile widened. He'd be delighted to take her into the garden and begin his courtship. Very delighted. How fortunate he'd been standing in exactly the right place when the lady had stumbled.

Mmm—very fortunate. Just as he'd expected, she was

an entrancing armful. He'd been hard pressed not to steal a kiss in front of Delton and all their interested onlookers. With luck and skill, he might be able to steal one in the foliage. The lady had not been struggling to get out of his arms. No, she'd seemed quite content to remain there.

He stepped back slightly, a little behind the girl and closer to the garden stairs.

He definitely needed to retreat to the leafage—his enthusiasm was becoming a bit too apparent. He grinned. Fortunately, he could hide behind the lady's skirts.

And he needed to discover her given name. He could not keep thinking of her as Standen's daughter.

"Well, no harm done," he said, interrupting the polite, but pointless apologies. "Now, if you'll excuse us, Delton? I believe the lady would benefit from a calming stroll through the garden, don't you?"

"Yes, indeed. Don't let me delay you a moment longer. Just came out to blow a cloud, don't you know? I'll step out of the way then. So sorry for the accident. Do enjoy your walk—the greenery is very soothing."

"But—"

Surely the girl wasn't going to keep protesting her fault in the silly contretemps? Delton shot him a pleading look. He agreed. Someone needed to take the young lady in hand, and he was more than happy to be that person. He had his hand on her already. He exerted a slight pressure and directed her toward the garden steps.

"We are attracting a small bit of attention, my dear," he murmured. "I cannot think you will like that."

"Oh." The girl glanced around the terrace.

"A few moments admiring Alvord's plantings will give you time to compose yourself and give the witnesses to our little—our very minor—scene time to lose whatever interest they have in you and your activities."

Her brows lowered into a frown. "But isn't walking in the garden scandalous?"

"Not at all. Do you think the Duke of Alvord would have lanterns hung along his garden paths if walking there were scandalous?" Of course, David did not intend to stay on the paths the entire time, but there was no need to mention that.

"Oh. No, I suppose you are correct."

Aunt Kate would not approve, Grace thought as she descended the steps on Lord Dawson's arm. Ha—there was an understatement! She had explicitly told Grace not to go into the garden with the baron. But Aunt Kate was overly nervous, and the baron had a valid point. If strolling amongst the plants was so daring, the duke would not have tempted his guests with lantern-lit walkways.

Grace needed to talk to the man—she'd come out on the terrace with that specific goal. The privacy of such a perambulation would be perfect for getting to the bottom of her father's strange antipathy and Aunt Kate's odd nervous attack.

She would behave perfectly respectably, and Lord Dawson wouldn't offer her anything but conversation. Men never did.

But if he did . . .

She glanced up at the baron and felt a small frisson, a tiny shiver of excitement.

They turned left at the bottom of the stairs and followed the path toward the main section of the garden, leaving the ball's light and crowds behind. A slight breeze brushed Grace's cheek. She could almost believe they were in the country now. Almost, but not quite. This was London after all, and London was never really quiet. The noise of the street—the creak and jingle of harnesses, the rattle of wheels on cobbles, the shouts of the coachmen—

blended with the drone of conversation drifting from the open ballroom windows.

They strolled past a rustic bench and paused by a small fountain with a statue of Pan capering in its center. Water cascaded from the god's pipes and splashed merrily from a multitude of fishes' mouths.

Lord Dawson wandered over to the far side of the fountain to examine a fish that wasn't spouting. Grace followed him. The vegetation was especially overgrown here—they were almost in a small bower. If John were present, he'd be giving her a lecture on every leaf and twig. She sincerely hoped Lord Dawson was not a botanist.

"Is that a trout?" A stupid question—it was just a stone decoration. It could be a whale for all she cared.

The baron shrugged. "I don't know. I'm not much interested in fish." He smiled and turned to face her. Somehow her hand had ended up in his—and his was missing its glove. "But I am very interested in you. Will you gift me with your name? My Uncle Alex didn't know it, and I cannot keep calling you Standen's daughter or Lady Oxbury's niece." He rubbed his thumb over her palm.

"Oh, ah." Another, larger shiver of excitement teased her. She cleared her throat. "Grace—my name is Lady Grace."

He brushed a strand of hair back from her face. "And I am David Wilton, Baron Dawson of Riverview." His voice deepened. "I am very, very glad to meet you, Lady Grace."

Grace withdrew her hand and gave the man a cautious look. They were secluded here, but not completely hidden. Anyone passing by on the walkway could see them, if they looked. Lord Dawson appeared relaxed and pleasant—not at all predatory.

She was in no danger. It was perfectly safe to take advantage of the moment and ask about her father—and her aunt.

Her hand still tingled from the motion of his thumb on her palm. She rubbed it against her skirt.

And what if something besides information was exchanged?

She moistened her lips. If such an opportunity presented itself . . . well, she would be daring and enjoy her brief window of freedom.

She was twenty-five; she had never in all those years done anything the least bit scandalous. She was too old and sensible to allow herself to be led into complete ruin. There were hundreds of people nearby; if she became alarmed, she had a sturdy pair of lungs.

David watched thoughts of caution flit over Grace's face. He should not take advantage of her, she was so innocent. She had followed him so trustingly.

But how could he not take advantage? It was dark, and they were in this sheltered spot. He would not hurt her. His intentions were only honorable.

Hmm. Perhaps it depended on how one defined honorable. He would not take her beyond the point of no return, but he would take her as close to that point as she—and the vertical nature of their encounter—would allow. And he meant marriage, of course. He definitely meant marriage.

A few creative uses for this splendid fountain popped into his imagination, but he suppressed them. Lady Grace was a virgin, and there were hundreds of the *haut ton* just yards away in the ballroom—as well as a few walking in the garden, no doubt. Once they were wed, once he'd accustomed her to marital relations, then they could attempt more inventive activities.

Grace looked serious, as if she meant to get down to business—and not the business he would most like to get down to.

"I came out on the terrace looking for you, Lord Dawson."

"You did? How splendid—and please call me David."

Her eyes widened. "I couldn't possibly. I hardly know you."

"Oh, you will know me much better shortly."

She flushed as best he could tell in this dim light.

"I—"

"Shh." He stepped closer. "Not so loud. Sound carries in the night air, you know."

"Ah—" She looked adorably confused. Her mouth was agape—He definitely had to take advantage of such an inadvertent invitation.

He brought his head down slowly; he gave her plenty of opportunity to move, but she didn't dodge out of the way. He saw in her eyes the moment she decided to take the kiss he was offering. He smiled as he closed the last few inches.

Her lips were firm, smooth, sweet. And her mouth! He only used the tip of his tongue, tracing her lips, dipping past them just slightly. He wanted her enthralled, not frightened. She was so still it was clear this was her first time. Gently, he brought her closer until she was touching him from chest to knees.

Who would have thought careful, restrained kissing could be so bloody erotic? He was restricting his lips to her face and his hands to her clothed, corseted back, but he was more aroused than he could ever remember being. And she was so responsive.

Grace panted, making little mewling sounds. Once Lord Dawson's—David's—lips had touched hers, all thought had evaporated, leaving her lost in a whirlwind of sensation. His lips moved lightly, briefly, tantalizingly over her mouth, like a butterfly's wings, teasing. Her own lips felt swollen; his tongue touched them, slid slowly over them.

Heat pooled low in her belly, making everything in that region throb and ache. She wanted . . . she needed . . . what?

His hands brought her body against his. Oh! This. She needed this—and still it wasn't enough.

He cradled her against his chest and moved to explore her eyelids, her cheekbones. Was she moaning? Surely not.

She felt a chuckle rumble through his chest as his hand cupped the back of her head.

"Shh." His lips brushed her earlobe, his words stirring her hair, tickling over her ear, sending shivers skittering down her spine. "Remember, sound travels at night. We don't want anyone to find us."

No, that was right. No one should find them because . . . because they were . . .

They were behaving scandalously in the foliage.

She shoved hard against the miscreant's chest. He loosened his hold immediately.

"What seems to be the problem?" The oaf was grinning.

What wasn't the problem? She, the unmarried daughter of the Earl of Standen, was alone in the garden with a man her father hated. And not merely alone. No. She had allowed the fellow shocking liberties. She had had her person plastered up against his; she had allowed him to kiss her—

She inhaled sharply and covered her mouth with her hand. She had allowed Lord Dawson to give her her very first kiss. Was she mad? Surely that favor should have been reserved for her intended, John Parker-Roth, and not this rogue. Certainly not this rogue. Perhaps Papa was right to hate his family.

"What is it, sweetheart? Cat got your tongue?"

Something about the way he said "tongue" made her flush. She tried to respond, but the noise she made was incoherent—a sound somewhere between a gulp and a growl. She tried again.

"Lord Dawson, I . . . I . . ." What was the appropriate thing to say in this situation?

There was no appropriate thing.

She should slap him soundly, but that seemed unfair. He hadn't been forcing his attentions on her—she had been a very active participant.

"Ohh." The thought caused a slow snake of shame to curl through her stomach. She dropped her face into her hands.

"Grace." She felt his arm come around her shoulders. He pulled her close. She should struggle, but she didn't have the spirit to do so. Besides, his touch was comforting.

"Grace, it's all right. We did nothing wrong. My intentions are honorable."

She lifted her head. "Honorable?"

He grinned. "Definitely. I know it's a bit precipitous, but . . . Will you make me the happiest of men?"

"*What*?" Surely she had misheard.

His grin widened. "Will you marry me?"

She felt her jaw drop. This might be her first time in London, but she could not believe every excursion into the foliage there resulted in a marriage proposal. No one had seen them, and while she most certainly shouldn't have been doing what she'd been doing, no permanent harm had been done. "Are you a lunatic? You've just met me."

He shrugged. "I could tell from the moment you

stepped through the ballroom door, you would be the perfect baroness for me."

The man *was* a lunatic—a very attractive lunatic, but a lunatic nonetheless. Or perhaps he was destitute? "I'm not a notable heiress, you know."

He looked at her as if *she* were the lunatic. "I don't need to marry money—I'm quite plump in the pocket."

"Oh. Well, I can't marry you in any event." And why did she feel a pang of regret when she said that? All she knew of Baron Dawson was that Papa hated his family—and that he was tall, handsome, and skilled in the amatory arts.

He frowned. "Why not?"

"Besides the fact that I don't know you—"

He grinned. "That's easily remedied."

Grace tried not to roll her eyes. "—I already have an understanding with a gentleman." Papa certainly understood she would marry John, and John definitely had his eye on that patch of Papa's land bordering his estate—he wished to plant roses or rhododendrons or something on it.

She started walking back to the ballroom. Lord Dawson fell into step beside her. She had to admit it felt very nice to be beside a man who, well, *fit* her. She allowed him to place her hand on his arm again.

"You didn't kiss me as if you had an understanding with anyone," he said.

She jerked her hand back. "I didn't kiss you at all."

His dratted eyebrow flew up.

"*You* kissed *me*." Her face must be glowing again. She should rent herself out as a lantern.

"That's true. And you struggled mightily to free yourself from my unwanted attentions, didn't you?"

"Er." No, she hadn't struggled; she'd welcomed his

advances in a totally shocking fashion. Yes, that was it. Shocking. "I was so shocked I couldn't move."

"Hmm." Baron Dawson just looked at her. "So, this understanding . . . are you betrothed?"

"Ah, not precisely . . ." And why was she prevaricating? She was as good as taken.

"Oh? What—precisely—are you?"

"Well, er . . ." She just couldn't say the word "engaged." And she wasn't engaged—not quite. Technically, she was free for the moment, for these precious few moments she was in London.

"You are undecided." Lord Dawson took her hand again and raised it to his lips. He smiled slowly. "I shall help you decide."

"No. I . . ."

He picked a leaf out of her hair. She was perfect for him. He was so tired of tiny women. He was always afraid he'd hurt them. Grace on the other hand . . . he would wager she could meet him thrust for thrust.

Zeus, what a thought! His anatomy sprang to attention, eager to begin thrusting posthaste.

He would persuade her to have him. She might think she was committed to this other fellow, but her body told him differently. She would not have kissed him with such innocent yearning if she were in love with someone else.

"You know, you never told me why you came out looking for me," he said. He sent her a sidelong glance. "I suppose it wasn't to drag me into the shrubbery?"

He was rewarded—she stopped. She was almost emitting sparks when she turned to face him. Regretfully, they were now in view of the terrace, so he could not do anything more than admire the sight she presented.

"It was not, you clod pole! I came to ask you about my

aunt and Papa. Do you know why there is such enmity between our families?"

Perhaps it was fortunate Grace's back was to the house. She didn't see her aunt and his uncle slip out the ballroom door. Her aunt didn't see them either, but Alex did. He paused momentarily and then guided Lady Oxbury in the opposite direction. They disappeared behind an overgrown tree.

"Enmity?" He almost laughed. He'd guess hostility was not the motivation urging those two into the foliage. Good for old Alex.

"Yes. Aunt Kate had such a strong reaction when she saw your uncle, she had to withdraw to the ladies' retiring room to regain her composure. Do you know what the connection is between them?"

He could guess what the connection was about to be. "I believe my uncle asked your aunt to marry him the last time she was in London."

Lady Grace gasped. "No! Aunt Kate never mentioned such a thing."

"Uncle Alex never mentioned it, either, until your aunt entered the ballroom this evening." Odd. Why hadn't Alex told him before? They'd certainly got drunk together enough times over the years. And they'd been discussing matrimony—*his* need for a wife and heir—frequently since he'd inherited the title. It would have been natural to bring up a blighted marriage proposal over a bottle of port.

Had Alex suffered a broken heart? Now that he considered the matter, it *was* odd his uncle had never married. Alex wasn't the sort to enjoy casual liaisons—and he was certainly well past his salad days. True, he didn't have a title to pass on, but he did have his own estate—had

had it for years. He should have had a wife and children as well.

Grace's aunt had married Lord Oxbury . . .

Dash it, if Lady Oxbury had been cruel to Alex . . . well, he might have to have a private word with her on that subject.

Lady Grace was shaking her head and worrying her bottom lip with her teeth. It quite sent thoughts of Lady Oxbury and Alex from his head.

"How could that be the reason Papa holds all Wiltons in aversion? A marriage proposal is not an insult—unless your uncle is as busy in the bushes as you are." Grace shot him a most pointed look.

He was willing to bet Uncle Alex was being very busy in the bushes at the moment.

"But an offer would have addressed any question of scandal." Grace frowned. "Are you certain your uncle did actually offer?"

"Oh, yes. And your father turned him down. He hated Wiltons long before Alex asked for your aunt's hand."

"Why? Though if your relatives are all as annoying as you, I quite understand it."

"Very funny. Did your father never tell you about Lady Harriet, the daughter of the Marquis of Wordham?"

She frowned. "No. Who is she?"

"Was. Who *was* she." He smiled slightly. "She was my mother."

Grace's expression changed in a blink. The frown vanished; her eyes and mouth softened. She touched his arm lightly. "I'm sorry."

An odd warmth spread through his chest. Stupid. Grace's compassion was misplaced. He'd had Grandmamma. She'd probably spent more time with him than his mother would have. By all accounts, both his parents had been headstrong and wild, setting things whirling and tumbling like a windstorm, leaving everyone else to clean up the debris.

He didn't have Grandmamma any longer, of course. Riverview was empty now.

But it wouldn't be empty when he married Grace. They would fill it with their children—with their sons and daughters. It would be far livelier then than it had ever been when he was a child.

Grace *had* to accept him . . . and reject the man in the country.

He pushed aside the guilt that threaded through his gut at that thought. He needn't feel guilt. Grace didn't love the fellow.

And was this how his father had reasoned when he'd planned his elopement, stealing Lady Harriet from Standen?

God, no! He was nothing like Luke Wilton.

Grace was frowning again. "Why would Papa have told me about your mother?"

"Ah . . ." He would consider any parallels—and there were none—between his father and himself later. He was alone in the garden with a beautiful woman, even if he was only giving her a history lesson now. "Because thirty-one—well, thirty-two years ago, to be precise— my mother jilted your father to run off to Gretna with the notorious Luke Wilton."

Chapter 4

"I should look for Grace." Kate sounded more than a little hesitant, as if her heart was not in that particular search. Good. Alex had other plans for their brief time together.

It was markedly cooler outside. A scattering of couples dotted the terrace, but Lady Grace was not among them. Alex glanced off to the left and saw her with David in the garden. Should he tell Kate?

"I take it this is Lady Grace's first Season?"

Kate sighed. "Yes. She is a bit old for a debutante—well, more than a bit—she's twenty-five. My brother was planning to marry her off to a neighbor, but his butler's cousin works in the Oxbury dairy and she told my housekeeper who told me. I couldn't . . . I thought I should bring Grace to Town."

"I see." Twenty-five? The girl could manage on her own. As could David. Alex had warned him not to hunt that ground, but if David chose to ignore his sage uncle's advice, so be it. David wouldn't harm Lady Grace. And Alex had his own concerns to attend to.

He placed Kate's hand on his arm. Ah! She smelled

of lavender just as she had all those years ago, when he was young and believed the future was full of promise, not guilt and regret.

Her fingers trembled slightly, but she didn't withdraw.

He smiled. Perhaps the future *was* full of promise. He certainly hadn't felt this hopeful in a long, long time—since he'd last entered this garden with Kate.

He guided her down the terrace steps and off to the right, toward the little bower they'd found that first Season. Was it still there? It wouldn't be surprising if it weren't. Twenty-three years was a long time. The duke—the previous or current titleholder—might well have decided to re-landscape, turning their retreat into a patch of pansies. Or nature's vagrancies could have made it a barren spot of dirt and twigs and dead leaves.

No, his luck held—the alcove was as verdant as he recalled. "Do you remember this place?"

"Yes." Kate's voice wavered ever so slightly. "Of course I do."

Of course she did. Regret darkened his soul again.

She had been only seventeen—but he had been only twenty-two. A man, yes, but hardly more than a boy. He had still believed honor would prevail and love would conquer all.

He'd been a fool, but what else could he have been? He'd been so damn young.

He should have been like his brother, Luke. He should have persuaded Kate to run to Gretna Green on the border between England and Scotland with him. There they could have been married as the Scottish marriage laws were much more flexible than they were in England. Then he would have had twenty-three years of wedded bliss instead of years of solitude, of lonely nights reading by the fire—or, worse, slinking up inn stairs, taking his ease with women he didn't love.

If he had taken Kate to Scotland, he'd have sons now . . . daughters . . . a family.

But no, he was the responsible brother, the thoughtful, cautious, sensible one—and look where the hell it had got him.

Of course daring had gotten Luke dead.

Should he pretend he'd come this way out of nostalgia—pass by, continue through the garden and back up the steps to the terrace, polite, gentlemanly, a pattern card of proper behavior?

No, damn it. He hadn't come all the way to London to be proper. He'd come to misbehave—and he bloody well would do so now. With Kate. He'd woken up hard and aching more times than he cared to count, thanks to her.

He ducked under a low hanging branch to move deeper into the shadows. Kate followed without hesitation or even a whisper of protest.

He held her hand to guide her over the tree roots and down the thin path, a line worn in the grass by other couples. Was anyone else here? He paused, put his finger to Kate's lips when she would have spoken, and listened. He heard snatches of distant music from the ballroom, laughter from the terrace, the rustle of a small animal scurrying through the bushes, but no sound of lovers stealing a kiss in the bower, thank God.

He moved around the high hedge to the small hidden pocket of privacy. Best take no chances. He guided Kate to stand so he blocked the opening in the hedge. If anyone stumbled in, they would see only his back—and hopefully take themselves off immediately.

He didn't want anyone to see them. He didn't want anyone to interrupt them. Hell, he didn't want the party, the *ton*, the whole damn world to exist. He wanted life to be limited to this little patch of greenery, to him and Kate. No time—past or passing; no memories. Just now. Just here.

"We're alone." He barely breathed the words, half afraid anything louder than a whisper would break the spell.

"Yes." She whispered, too. Her head was down; she was staring at his waistcoat.

Moonlight sifted through the tree branches, sliding over Kate's shoulders, over the tops of her breasts, making her skin glow.

He closed his eyes briefly. She was so beautiful, she made his heart—and other organ—ache. He studied the delicate curve of her neck, the soft wisps of hair that had slipped free of their pins. He wanted to hold her close, to protect her from all life's pain—and love every last inch of her perfect body.

He had never thought to stand here with her again. He'd never thought to stand anywhere with her again. When he'd got word she'd married Oxbury, something in him had died. Now it was stirring back to life.

"Kate."

She finally looked up. The tip of her tongue slid out to moisten her lips.

He *had* to touch her, to feel her skin under his. He shed his gloves—he'd like to shed more than his gloves, ofcourse, but not in Alvord's garden—and brushed his fingers over her lips. He felt her breath sigh out, and her eyelids closed. Her face tilted up, her mouth just slightly—but so invitingly—open.

Not yet. He wouldn't kiss her yet. Soon though—very soon.

He traced the swell of her breasts—and watched them swell more as she inhaled. Her top teeth caught her bottom lip. Her hands came up to grip his arms—to steady herself, not to stop him.

He cupped her elegant neck, smoothing his thumbs over her jaw. A small, breathy moan escaped her. Her skin felt hot.

"I've missed you, Kate."

"Ah." Her eyes opened. They were slightly out of focus. "I-I've missed you, too." She swallowed; he felt her throat move. "Terribly."

He traced her mouth with his finger, pulling her lower lip gently down. "Shall I kiss you?"

"Yes. Please."

He bent his head.

How much had she learned from her husband?

He pulled back slightly. No. He would not think of Oxbury. That was the past, and there was no past here. He had left the past behind when he'd slipped into this bower. Here there was only now, only Kate and Alex.

"Please," she whispered. "Please, Alex."

He touched his mouth to hers gently, as he had when he'd been so much younger. Her lips stayed quiet. He brushed over them, moved to her cheek, her forehead, her eyelids. Her skin was so soft.

The scent of lavender teased him, mixing with the rich scents of the garden just as it had before.

He wanted to thread his hands through her hair, but he couldn't. He was still cautious. They had to go back to the ballroom. She could not look as if she'd been doing what they were doing.

He followed the line of her jaw with his lips. She tilted her head back to give him room to explore, and he took the invitation. He brushed aside a tendril of hair, kissed her throat from just below her ear to her collarbone and then down to the delicate mounds of her breasts. She gasped—and then made an odd little noise, a cross between a moan and a breathy pant. He moved back to the pulse in her throat. It fluttered beneath his lips.

He had dreamt for so long of just this—of having Kate back in Alvord's garden, in his arms, kissing her. The dream always ended with her naked under him—that wasn't an option now, of course, but there was one detail he could enact.

He touched his mouth to hers again, but this time he didn't just brush her lips with his. This time he slid his tongue deep into her warm depths.

She stiffened briefly as though startled, and he paused. She wouldn't push him away, would she?

No. She relaxed, letting her body rest against his. Her tongue touched his tentatively, as if she had no notion how to go on.

He cupped her jaw and proceeded to show her. She tasted of mint and lemon and wine. Sweet and tart. Perfect.

He was hard with need. He wanted to free her from the confines of her stays, strip her of her shift, explore her breasts, her belly, her thighs. He wanted more than his tongue deep in her moist warmth.

She was a widow. He was unwed. There was nothing—no one—keeping them from doing what they should have done years ago. They wouldn't even need to fly to Gretna.

He withdrew, rested his cheek against her hair, tried to marshal his thoughts and his breath to ask her to marry him.

She found her composure first.

"Alex, I . . ." She paused.

"Kate—"

She put her finger on his lips, shaking her head slightly.

"No, I . . ." She paused again and seemed to gather herself. A smile wavered over her lips. "Come tonight, to

Oxbury House." Her voice was breathless, nervous. Her gaze dropped to consider his chin. "Will you?"

She couldn't mean . . . ? "You wish me to escort you and Lady Grace home from the ball?"

"No." She jerked her head in a short, negative motion. "No, I wish you . . . I want you . . . to come . . . later." She glanced up to meet his eyes briefly, and then addressed his chin again. "I wish you to come to my room." She was whispering so low he could barely hear her, but her next words were crystal clear. "To my b-bed. I wish you to come to my bed."

"*What*?!"

"Shh! Someone will hear you." Kate bit her lip. Alex's eyes had widened and his mouth had dropped open. He was shocked.

She was shocked herself. A hot wave of embarrassment flooded her. Had she actually just invited a gentleman to her bed?

She had. She stepped away from him and lifted her chin. Alex was frowning at her now. She frowned back. He had better not judge her.

She was an experienced woman, not a debutante like Grace. If Grace had done such a thing, *that* would be shocking. Grace was a virgin, young, and fertile. She was none of those things.

Grace. She should have gone in search of Grace. She should not have come here with this jackanapes.

But she had wanted to come. She had so wanted to go back to that magical time when she was young and in love.

She was an idiot, a complete cabbage-head.

"To how many men have you extended this invitation, Lady Oxbury?"

Oh! She felt as if he had slapped her. How could he think such a thing?

Because he hardly knew her. They had spent only two months of the Season—a few social events—together twenty-three years ago. She had been a child then; she was a woman now. How *could* he know her?

"That is none of your concern, Mr. Wilton."

"I am somewhat particular in my associations, Lady Oxbury."

She should slap *him*. She should certainly disinvite him. She did not want an ass in her bed.

She opened her mouth to tell him exactly that, but the words wouldn't come.

The ugly truth was she *did* want him, had wanted him every day since she'd kissed him in this garden that first Season. She had wished for him on her wedding night after Oxbury had done his duty and gone back to his own bed. She had dreamed of him in the dark—and sometimes at the breakfast table while watching Oxbury read the paper and chew his toast and kidneys. And much as she blushed to admit it, she had often imagined it was he, not Oxbury, above her in bed, working at getting an heir.

She had been fond of Oxbury and had tried to be a good wife to him. She had never taken a lover—but had she been completely faithful?

No, not really. Not in her heart.

Enough! Her husband was dead, had been dead this last year. No one would fault her if she took a lover now—well, no one besides Mr. Saintly Wilton here. She was curious, that was all. She finally had the opportunity to find out what it would have been like if it *had* been Alex instead of Oxbury in her bed.

She thought it would be good. She'd never before felt the sensations Alex had created in her just now. He'd done little more than kiss her—though she'd never before been kissed like that. Where had he learned to be so skilled? *He* had not been married.

"You are particular, are you, Mr. Wilton? I would venture to guess you have associated with more women since last we met than I have men."

Did he blush? Well he might.

"That is a different matter entirely. I am a man."

True, women were supposed to turn a blind eye to men's peccadilloes. If he were her husband—she ignored the pang that thought provoked—she would look the other way. But he was not her husband, and he was taking her to task for the same sin he had doubtless committed too many times to count.

"And I am a widow, Mr. Wilton." She looked away. She couldn't bear to see his expression. "I believe I am free to behave as I see fit. However, if you are not interested in my invitation, we need say no more. Please, forget I ever mentioned the topic."

She would not be embarrassed. He did not know how it felt to be so completely alone. She had no husband, no child—no home. She swallowed a sudden lump in her throat. Well, there was no point in dwelling on things she had no power to change.

So, no, Mr. Wilton had no conception of her plight. He *was* a man. He was in complete control of his destiny. He could choose to marry or remain single. He was the master of his estate. He had not the slightest inkling what her life was like.

"I believe I should like to return to the ballroom now, if you please," she said. "I have been remiss in my duties. I should see if Grace has returned."

The cabbage-headed, cork-brained lobcock stood rooted to the spot, staring at her. Well, she could find her own way back to the ballroom if he did not wish to escort her or was incapable of the task.

"If you will excuse me then, Mr. Wilton? I'm sure you will understand when I tell you I would prefer any future encounters we may have be limited to a cordial nod. I believe we've exchanged all the words we need to for the duration of our separate stays in London."

She was very proud of herself. She had got that speech out without crying or even suffering her voice to crack. She moved to step by Alex.

His hand shot out to clasp her arm.

"Lady Oxbury." He paused. His face was in shadow; she couldn't see his expression. "Kate. My pardon. I meant no insult."

She snorted—she couldn't help herself. Meant no insult? Did the man think she was a complete paperskull?

"No," he said. "I was just . . . surprised."

All right, she could understand that. She'd been surprised herself. She never would have guessed she'd have the temerity to say such a thing.

"Very well. I accept your apology. Now please be so kind as to escort me back to the ballroom."

He looked away. The moonlight glanced along the side of his face—she could see his jaw clench. He made no move to leave nor did he release her.

What was he thinking? Surely he didn't intend to keep her here until Grace came searching? How would she explain her presence in this secluded place? She must go inside now.

She opened her mouth to demand he release her when he turned back.

"Kate." His voice was low and tight.

"Mr. Wilton—"

"Alex, Kate."

He almost sounded as if he were in pain. "Alex, then." She put her hand on his arm. "We should return to the ballroom."

"I . . . may I . . . that is . . ." He took a deep breath and seemed to gather his composure. "If I may, I would like to take you up on your kind offer."

"My offer?"

"Yes. I would like to . . . visit you. Tonight." He was having a hard time getting the words out. "If I may."

Her stomach roiled with nerves and excitement. This was her last chance to change her mind. She should be sensible. She should be cautious.

She should be daring. She had not followed her heart before and had regretted it for years. She would not make that mistake again.

"All right." Now what did she tell him? He couldn't very well knock on the front door—she wasn't that bold yet. But there was a sturdy tree outside her window . . . "Give me half an hour—no, an hour—after I leave the ball. Throw some pebbles against my window—second floor on the northwest corner—and I'll let you in. That is, if you can still climb a tree?"

He grinned then, his teeth flashing white in the moonlight. "I believe I can persuade this old body to do that much."

She frowned. What if he fell? He might do himself a permanent injury. And the scandal! Every last member of the *ton* would be sure to speculate on what Mr. Wilton was doing on the ground outside Lady Oxbury's bedroom. "I'll leave the servants' door unlocked."

"You don't think I can manage the more romantic route?"

She smiled. The teasing note she'd missed was back in his voice. Perhaps this was going to be all right. It wouldn't be love—at least not on his part—but it would be . . . all right. If nothing else, it would satisfy her curiosity. She could finally put her infatuation with him in the past where it belonged.

"I want you to be able to manage other things once you arrive."

"Ha! Ye of little faith. I'll be delighted to show you I have endless stamina." He leaned forward and kissed her nose. "But I believe I will make use of the servants' entrance. No point in wasting energy I can apply to more enjoyable pursuits."

Light and teasing—that was best. Let him think her a merry widow. She ran her hands up his chest to his neck. She would flirt, she would learn to seduce. "I can hardly wait."

She was encouraged by his kiss to surmise that he was as impatient as she.

She was not going to think about Papa and Lady Harriet, Lord Dawson's mother. She was not going to think about the baron's bizarre marriage proposal. She was not going to think at all—she was just going to enjoy fully the one dance she'd ever had when she didn't feel like a lumbering—a *regal*—Brobdingnagian.

Lord Dawson was mad, completely and utterly mad, but he was a wonderful dancer. Grace spun through a turn, tethered by his large, strong hands. She wanted to put back her head and laugh. She'd never felt such joy in movement.

She hated to dance, and she hated to waltz most of all. She always felt so large and ungainly. Most of the time she was taller than her partner and sometimes . . . well, back at Standen she'd been forced to inform Mr. Fenton she would no longer stand up with him—ever. He was almost a head shorter than she and took dancing as an opportunity to get a very close look at her bodice.

But tonight, with Lord Dawson, dancing was an entirely different experience. She felt light and . . . graceful. Her smile widened—and then faltered.

John hated to dance—or at least he hated to dance with her. They plodded around the floor in time to the music, but . . . She sighed. Dancing with John was prosaic at best, but wasn't that the way life was?

This—the dancing, the music, the brilliant colors, and beautiful dresses—this *romance* was merely a moment out of time. A glimmer of magic, impossible to hold. In the morning the elegant members of the *haut ton*, the flowers, the musicians would be gone and all that would be left would be a scuffed floor, a scattering of dead leaves, and a few wilted flower petals.

But that was the morning. Tonight she would revel in the magic; when it was time, at the end of the Season, she would go home to her dull, commonplace life, to Papa and to John.

"Enjoying the music, my dear?"

She would even pretend for the moment that having handsome men call her "dear" was normal. "Yes, I am."

His mouth turned up in a half smile—and her stomach did that odd little flutter again.

It was not fair he was so sinfully handsome. That strong, square chin with its little cleft was completely captivating. And that dimple! Dimples should definitely be outlawed in a face as attractive as Baron Dawson's. He had sun streaks in his slightly shaggy, dark blond hair, and his deep blue eyes glinted with humor—and something else . . . something hot and intense.

She felt rather hot herself. She must be blushing—his smile had grown, damn it.

She closed her eyes, but that didn't help at all. Now she focused on the feel of his hands—firm, yet gentle— as they guided her through the dance. Her bodice brushed against his waistcoat briefly and her breasts felt fuller and heavy. Shocking. She drew in a deep, shuddery breath and inhaled the spicy heat of him.

Her eyes flew open. This was too much. She should have run from him in the garden or at the least fled the moment she'd returned to the ballroom.

She glanced up at his face. His cheeks creased, making the dimple deepen as his smile broadened to a full grin. He knew exactly what she was thinking!

Blast, now her face must really be as red as a fire's embers. She certainly felt as if she were glowing. She frowned again.

He had to swallow a chuckle. Did she think to cow him? That look might work on her not-quite betrothed, but it didn't on him. He could almost feel sorry for the man. If the fellow did wed Grace—an event David was becoming more and more determined to prevent—she would ride roughshod over him. In truth, it would be a charity for David to take Grace off the gentleman's hands. *He* knew how to manage her fire.

Damn. He edged his hips back slightly. Thinking of managing Grace—in his bed, of course—had the predictable effect on his person.

She was still frowning.

"Don't try to look so fierce, Grace. You don't scare me, you know."

Scare him? Grace was tempted to roll her eyes. *He* was the one who was frightening, like a spider sitting in his web of seduction, waiting for her to fall into his trap. "You are absurd. Of course, I don't scare you. I've never scared anyone in my life."

The odd glint in his eyes grew more pronounced. Was he laughing at her? How dare he? She should . . . she should . . .

She should feel angry, but instead she felt hot and unsettled.

"Ah, there I'm certain you're wrong," he said, swinging her through a turn. "I imagine the average male quakes when he sees you."

She snorted. "Only because he fears for his toes. The men of Standen know too well what the *ton* will soon discover—I've sent more men limping home than Napoleon."

He pulled her close to avoid another couple and her bodice brushed his chest again. Her breasts were still extremely sensitive. Her nipples hardened. How mortifying! He couldn't tell, could he?

"Nonsense," he was saying. "I don't worry about my toes at all."

Toes? Damn, she suddenly had salacious thoughts about the man's toes. They were talking about *dancing* not Lord Dawson's bare feet. "You don't worry about your t-toes only because you are an amazingly skilled dancer."

His mouth slid into a slow, knowing curve. He dropped his head and his voice—he had the most wonderful voice, deep and smooth and warm like a cup of the richest chocolate. His words stirred her hair, caressed her ear, sent heated shivers down her back to her—

No. She would not think about such things. No toes, no feet, no secret, wet, aching—No, definitely not. Most assuredly, without a doubt, without question—

"Would you like to see what else I'm amazingly skilled at, sweetness?"

The dark, wet, empty, aching place throbbed with eagerness. Her head snapped away from his lips, and she sent an urgent message to her heart and other organs to behave themselves. She wasn't a child. She knew seduction when she heard it. She gave him her sternest look. "Lord Dawson—"

"Shh, Lady Grace." His eyes were glinting—he was laughing at her again, damn him. "Why are you so agitated? I was merely referring to parlor games—Twenty Questions, Pope Joan, charades, spillikins." One eyebrow arched up. "What did you think I meant?"

Drat her pale complexion! She was definitely burning hotter than the candles now. He was trying to intimidate her. She would not let him do so.

"Seduction, my lord. Do not play me for a fool. You were trying to seduce—"

The orchestra played its last note. Her voice had, unfortunately, got somewhat strident. The ladies and gentlemen near them turned to stare. Lord Dawson raised his other eyebrow.

Damn.

"—to seduce me into the re-refreshment r-room." Please God, let no one be able to see how red she was. Or, if they noticed, let them think it was from the exertion of the dance.

Lord Dawson smirked slightly. "Ah, yes, those lobster patties are so enticing, are they not?"

Thankfully, everyone around them went back to their own conversations. "What?"

"The lobster patties, Lady Grace. The alluring, tempting, *seductive* lobster patties."

"Oh, do stop laughing at me, will you?" And he *was* laughing. Not out loud, of course. He wasn't even grinning, but his damn eyes were positively gleaming.

"But you are so amusing." He took her hand and laid it on his arm. "And the most amusing thing is you have no idea how beautiful, how utterly enchanting you are."

The man was definitely mad. "I am not amusing or . . . or . . . any of that other balderdash." Lord Dawson had started walking, and since he was keeping her hand firmly on his arm, she had to walk as well. "Where are we going?"

"To the refreshment room, of course, and the ravishing lobster patties."

She pulled back. "I'm not hungry." Unfortunately, it was true. Her stomach was too busy jumping and twisting and shivering—all due to his annoying presence—to accept even the smallest morsel of food. A shame, as lobster patties were generally one of her favorite dishes, and she suspected these would be splendid. The Duke of Alvord did not seem the type to stint on his lobster patties.

"Have a glass of lemonade instead, then."

He was very highhanded. "Perhaps I should look for my aunt." Where *was* Aunt Kate? Grace glanced around the ballroom as Lord Dawson stubbornly steered her toward the door to the refreshment room. "And you could look for your uncle."

He smiled and inclined his head toward the garden door. "No need to look. See, they are returning from a promenade in the greenery."

"Well." Grace tried not to stare. "They look as though they are on cordial terms, don't they?"

"Yes, indeed. Perhaps they have managed to deal with their differences."

Grace glanced at the couple again. Aunt Kate was smiling, though she looked a little nervous. And Mr. Wilton appeared a touch stiff. Still, they were together—they were even joining the next set. Was Aunt Kate going to find love again?

Grace grinned. "Perhaps I'll have a glass of champagne."

Chapter 5

She'd actually asked Alex to come to her bed.

Kate gripped her hands tightly together in her lap and pretended to look out the carriage window at the dark London streets.

She must have been mad, that was the only possible explanation. She'd never been so bold before. Bold? Ha! Her action was beyond bold, it was . . .

It was too outrageous to contemplate.

Yet she *had* contemplated it. More than that, she had done it. She had asked Alex . . . and he had said yes.

Oh, dear God. She pressed her hands to her stomach. The damn stays. She could barely breathe.

In just an hour—perhaps less—Alex would be in her bed.

Her stomach twisted. She bit down on her lower lip. At least she had shown one shred of good sense. She had avoided the refreshment room. If her stomach rebelled, she would be saved that humiliation.

What was she thinking? Her stomach was the least of her worries. If Alex actually came to her room—to her *bed*—he would expect her to show some . . . experience.

Some talent. *Something* to make the trip worth his while. She couldn't just lie still as she had with Oxbury.

Oh! She tried to breathe. She must not panic. Oxbury had never complained. He'd seemed to enjoy the exertion. He'd kept at it all those years, even when—

Well, he'd kept at it.

Men needed their release. It probably didn't matter what female was beneath them. In the dark, surely all women were much the same.

Were all men?

No. Alex would not be like Oxbury . . . would he?

She would find out tonight. After all the years of wondering and longing, she would finally know. Perhaps she'd learn what she'd longed for was no different from what she'd had.

Good. The point was she could finally put aside her wondering and move on, unencumbered by the "what ifs" and "if onlys."

Would the experience be different with Alex? Kissing certainly had been. Mmm. She closed her eyes. Just thinking about his lips on hers, remembering the feel of his hard form, the strength of his arms around her started an odd ache in her center.

She flushed. Well, not her center precisely . . .

"That was quite, um, f-fun."

Kate's eyes flew open. Surely Grace hadn't read her mind?

Grace hiccupped and grinned at her—a rather broad, sloppy grin.

Heavens! Kate squinted at her niece in the dim light. Grace's eyes did look slightly glassy, and now that she considered the matter, the girl had stumbled a bit getting into the carriage.

"How many glasses of champagne did you have, Grace?"

"Only t-two." Grace dropped her head back against the squabs and contemplated the carriage ceiling as if the correct number were written there. "Or th-three." She giggled. "I lost count."

"Wonderful." Kate blew out a short, exasperated breath. Obviously she should have been paying more attention to Grace and less—much less—to Mr. Alex Wilton. But how could she have guessed Grace would get brandy-faced at her first London ball? The girl—the *woman*—was twenty-five years old. "Surely you've had champagne before?"

"'Course I have!" Grace snapped her head forward to glare at Kate, but spoiled the effect by losing her balance and slipping sideways. She braced herself on the seat beside her. "Just not s-so much."

"You're going to have quite the head in the morning."

"S-so?" Grace settled back against the squabs again. "I feel sp-splendid now. I've never felt so h-happy."

"Happy's one way to describe it. Jug-bitten is another."

"Oh, pooh. Why are you such a crosspatch? Didn't you have f-fun?" Grace wiggled her eyebrows.

Kate looked out the window in earnest, cupping her hands to block out the dim light of the carriage. Good, she recognized the neighborhood—they were almost at Oxbury House. With luck she would be able to get Grace upstairs and into bed before she fell asleep—or got sick.

"I was not at the Duke of Alvord's ball to enjoy myself," Kate said. "I was there to chaperone you. Obviously, I did not do an adequate job fulfilling my duties."

Grace was contemplating the carriage ceiling again. She giggled and transferred her gaze to Kate. "Is that what you were doing in the g-garden with Mr. Wilton? Chaperoning me?"

More eyebrow wiggling. The girl looked as if she had a pair of dancing caterpillars on her forehead.

The caterpillars would leap off her face if she knew what her aunt had really been up to in the garden.

"I was looking for you." It was only a small lie. And what was it Oxbury used to say? The best defense was a good offense. "And while we're on that subject, what were you thinking, going out into the shrubbery alone? You are not some silly, dewy-eyed debutante." Kate paused. "Well, debutante, yes; silly and dewy-eyed, no—at least I hope not."

Grace actually sniggered. "I wasn't alone."

Good Lord, what *had* Grace been doing? Certainly nothing as scandalous as her own activities . . . No, the situations could not be compared. She was a widow; Grace was a virgin.

Surely Grace was still a virgin . . .

Now she was letting her guilty conscious lead her into the ridiculous.

"Even worse. If you'd been seen, you'd be ruined now. Your Season would be over. London society is full of gossips that delight in shredding young—and not so young—females' reputations."

Grace shrugged. "I wished to speak to Baron Dawson."

"What!" Standen would have Kate's head if he ever got wind of the fact Grace had been talking to Baron Dawson, let alone promenading in the foliage with him. "You went into the shrubbery with Lord Dawson? I don't believe it. I told you to avoid him. You *know* your father does not approve of the man's family."

"Well, P-Papa's not here, is he?" Grace blinked at Kate. "You aren't going to s-snitch on me, are you?" She waggled her finger in Kate's direction. "Because I can snitch, too. You were also in the garden with a Wilton, auntie."

"But you are unmarried. You should have remained sedately on the terrace," Kate said, rather weakly to her own ears.

It didn't matter. Grace was too foxed to concern herself with nuances.

"M-maybe I don't want to be s-sedate. Maybe I want to have some f-fun before I shackle myself to Mr. J-John P-Parker-Roth and his damn roses."

"Grace—"

Grace leaned forward, catching herself on the seat edge before she toppled face first into Kate's lap. "I like Mr. Park—John. I like his mother and his father and his brothers and his sisters. I like the whole blasted lot of them." She waved her finger in Kate's face this time. "But I like Baron Dawson, too. I really, um, *like* him." She sat back, put her head against the squabs again, and wrapped her arms around herself. "He makes me feel all . . . tingly."

"Good God!" Tingly? Tingly would never do. *She* had felt tingly all those years ago. Tingly too often led to thoughts of marriage, and Standen would dance naked at Almack's before he'd let his daughter marry a Wilton. She knew *that* from bitter experience.

Why did Alex and his nephew have to choose this Season to come to London?

Because the old baron had died, of course. So was Lord Dawson in Town for a wife or to lure a few young women—including the daughter of his enemy—down the primrose path?

She straightened. He'd best steer clear of Grace if he had nefarious purposes. If he hurt Grace—

She sighed and collapsed back against the squabs. Even if he meant marriage, the baron must look elsewhere—

Standen truly would never accept his suit. When Alex came tonight, she must have a few serious words with him about his nephew.

If he came. Certainly good sense and caution would convince him, on further reflection, to stay home. He had never been a wild, careless man. Climbing into a lady's bedchamber window—or sneaking up the servants' stairs—was not an activity Alex Wilton would engage in, she was sure.

Or was she? She must remember she'd only known Alex for a few months many years ago. Perhaps he was adept at getting in and out of ladies' bedrooms without detection. And, truthfully, inviting a man to her bed was not something she'd ever have believed she'd do—and yet she had.

But it was Grace's amorous activities—dear God!— that she needed to attend to at the moment.

"Grace—"

But Grace interrupted. "Lord Dawson told me his uncle asked you to marry him before you married Oxbury." Grace frowned, sounding much too sober. "Why didn't you share that bit of information with me, Aunt Kate?"

Thank God for concealing shadows. "It was a long time ago."

"Hmm. The last time you were in London. Is that why you came back, to see Mr. Wilton again? Now that you're free and he's free . . ." Grace sighed. "How r-romantic."

"It is *not* romantic." She didn't need Grace interfering in her . . . in whatever she had with Alex. "Don't be ridiculous."

Grace leaned forward—and almost fell into Kate's lap again. She pushed herself back to a more upright position. "You know, this time Papa can't stop you."

True, Standen *couldn't* stop her. A little thrill of

defiance shivered down her spine. She was no longer seventeen. She was a grown woman—a merry widow. She had lived her life to please her brother and her husband. Now, finally, she could choose to please herself.

Except she couldn't. She wasn't the heroine of a fairy tale, living in a castle by herself. She couldn't marry Alex—even if he asked her, which he wouldn't. It wasn't just that Standen would explode with anger. Society would flock like vultures to feast on the scandalous stories in the Belmont-Wilton past. She couldn't bear that— and she certainly couldn't consider the possibility at the beginning of Grace's Season.

"It's not that simple, Grace."

An affair, though, that would be permitted as long as she was discreet. *Very* discreet. If even a whisper of Alex's visit to her tonight—if he did indeed come— reached the *ton*'s ears, the gabble-grinders would resurrect the stories of Alex's brother and Alex's own ill-considered, short-lived courtship of her.

"Why would Papa want to keep you from marrying Mr. Wilton, Aunt Kate? He must see you'd be vastly more comfortable with a husband than living in the dower house, watching the new Lord Oxbury ruin the estate." Grace grinned. "P-Papa thinks the man's an ass, you know."

"Grace, your language!" Had Standen let Grace grow up like a weed? He should have remarried. Everyone had thought he would after he'd mourned his countess for the requisite year. He'd needed an heir. Still did, but it was unlikely he'd get one now, with fifty-six years in his dish.

"Well, that's what Papa said when your husband died."

"I'm sure he did. He never cared for Oxbury's heir— few people do—but that doesn't mean he would want me to wed Mr. Wilton. Another man—*any* other man—

but not Mr. Wilton. If Lord Dawson explained our history, you must know that." Kate looked down and smoothed her skirt. "And in any event, Mr. Wilton has not mentioned marriage."

"But he will."

Kate snapped her head up and glared at Grace. "He will not."

"Don't be s-silly, Aunt Kate. I saw you waltzing with him. Of course he will."

"You had consumed a significant quantity of champagne by the time you made that observation, hadn't you, Grace?"

"Well . . ."

Kate shrugged. "It makes no difference. If Mr. Wilton offers—which he won't—I must decline."

Grace must still think love conquered all—or perhaps it was only the champagne talking. Real people didn't live happily ever after; they had to face—daily—society's or their family's censure. Love was wonderful, but friendship, respect, and companionship would do, perhaps better than love in a hermit's cave.

"But—"

The coach stopped and Kate was spared further fruitless argument. Her butler-cum-footman, Mr. Sykes, opened the door and peered into the carriage cautiously.

"It's safe, Mr. Sykes. Lady Grace made it home without casting up her accounts."

"Ah. I am very glad to hear it." He extended his hand. "May I assist you to alight, Lady Grace?"

"C-certainly." Grace climbed out of the carriage quickly, but the moment her foot touched the pavement, she collapsed against Sykes.

"Grace!"

"Don't be alarmed, my lady." Sykes slid his arm under

one of Grace's. "If you could disembark and take Lady Grace's other side, I believe we can manage nicely." Sykes was able to brace Grace's not-inconsiderable weight against his body while offering Kate his free hand.

"I'm f-fine, Aunt Kate. I j-just need a minute to get my b-bearings—oh." Grace pressed a hand to her lips.

"I believe the sooner we get Lady Grace to her room, my lady, the less chance we have of a Regrettable Occurrence on the street."

"Very true, Mr. Sykes." Kate scrambled out of the carriage. "Let's get you up to bed, Grace."

Grace nodded and took a step, supported mostly by Sykes.

"The n-night air . . . seems to . . . d-does, actually, have an unfortunate—" Grace paused and pressed her hand to her lips again. She was definitely taking on a greenish cast. "Ohh."

That sounded distinctly like a moan. Kate shot a glance at Sykes. He nodded. "Yes, my lady, I would say time was indeed of the essence."

They hustled Grace into the house and up the stairs, making it to her room without disaster, and propped her up against the bed.

Kate heaved a sigh of relief. She did hope Grace would not be too sick. Now that she thought about it, her one and only episode of overindulgence in spirits had come after her first Alvord ball as well. She'd stolen a bottle of Standen's brandy after he'd enumerated in excruciating detail all the reasons she could not—could never—wed Mr. Alex Wilton. She had never felt so ill—she had never *been* so ill, especially when her brother had bundled her into the carriage at first light. She'd had to ride in the dreadful rocking conveyance all the way to Standen.

She'd best have Sykes fetch their maid. She would

know just what to do to make Grace more comfortable. "Mr. Sykes, will you—"

"Ohh, w-why is the room sp-spinning?"

"What?" Kate whirled around. Grace had decided to try lying down—a poor decision. Her face was now a ghastly shade of white.

"I think I'm going to be—" Grace turned on her side and struggled to push herself up.

Kate grabbed a basin from the cabinet next to the bed. "Get Marie, Sykes—and hurry."

As she thrust the basin under Grace's chin, she remembered one key task she had left undone.

Bloody hell. She hadn't unlocked the servants' door for Alex.

"You don't have to leave on my account, David." Alex watched the Duke of Alvord waltz by, Miss Sarah Hamilton in his arms. Alvord was staring down at his partner as if there were no one else in the room. Miss Hamilton's face was flushed—she looked just as adoringly up at the duke.

There was no question in Alex's mind—or the mind of any other man present, he'd wager—exactly what Alvord wished to be doing at that moment with his American guest. Which was precisely what Alex would like to be doing with Kate. It had been heaven waltzing with her tonight—he hoped his thoughts then hadn't been as apparent as Alvord's were now.

Hell, if the waltz had been danced twenty-three years ago, he'd have been certain to have found a way to get Kate to Gretna, damn the scandal. He would have gone mad otherwise.

And tonight he'd finally be able to—

If he went, that is.

"Why would I wish to stay?" David was saying. "My future wife has departed."

The man was as bad as a terrier with a rat. "I've told you—Standen will never give his consent."

"And I've told you, I don't care. Grace is of age. I don't need the earl's permission."

"You assume Lady Grace is willing."

The cocky bastard grinned. "I assume I can persuade her."

Alex grunted. "Good luck with that. Women's minds are beyond my poor comprehension." Like Kate's. What had she been thinking, inviting him to her bed? Yes, she was a widow, but still, she was *Kate*, shy, quiet, reserved, modest Kate.

Or was she? Twenty-three years changed a person. And truthfully, how well had he known her?

David drained the last of his champagne. "I'm ready. Let's go."

"All right." He wished David would stay. It would make it that much easier for him to slip away to Oxbury House undetected. He didn't want anyone—even David—knowing where he was going tonight.

Was he going?

His head said he shouldn't. The Kate he knew—well, the woman whose memory he'd cherished all these years—would never invite a man to her bed without first securing the church's blessing. If the merest whisper of her indiscretion got out, her brother would be livid . . . and society would feed on the tale like jackals on carrion.

Another organ insisted—strenuously—that he should. Kate had haunted him all these years, her face always lurking in his mind, even when he was busy in another woman's bed. She had stolen a part of his heart and he needed it back.

Kate *was* a widow. For all he knew, she'd been welcoming men into her bed before Oxbury was cold in his grave. Had she even been faithful while the man was alive? Oxbury had been close to seventy when he'd cocked up his toes. Likely he hadn't been able to attend to his marital duties for years.

But this was *Kate*.

And he didn't have to trust his gut. His butler's sister-in-law's cousin worked at an inn near Oxbury's country estate. If Kate had been taking lovers, he would have heard.

Alex collected his hat and cane from a footman and stepped outside with David into the hubbub of horses and carriages and coachmen.

"I'd say Alvord is going to get himself an American duchess, wouldn't you?" David headed down the street toward their townhouse, passing the long line of coaches waiting to pick up their aristocratic owners. Alex fell into step with him, but didn't reply. His mind was elsewhere.

David didn't care if Alvord married a trained monkey, but he had to say something. He was too full of frustrated energy to keep still. Watching the duke waltz with Miss Hamilton had been torture—almost like being forced to watch sexual congress. True, some men enjoyed being spectators to such activity, but he much preferred being an actor—and he'd especially like acting with Lady Grace on a nice, soft bed.

Waltzing with her had been heaven, though not as heavenly as their too-short interlude in the garden. She was just as wonderful to hold and kiss as he'd imagined.

And if he didn't keep talking, he would imagine in painful detail exactly what bedding her would feel like—

and look like and taste like and smell like. He'd much prefer to wait until he reached the relative privacy of Dawson House to indulge in those fantasies. Walking in his damn breeches would become much too uncomfortable otherwise.

"How long do you think it will be before we read of the duke's engagement in *The Morning Post?*"

"What?" Alex looked at him blankly.

Poor Uncle Alex's imagination had clearly wandered in exactly the direction David was trying to avoid, though Alex seemed capable of walking and thinking of Lady Oxbury at the same time. Still, he'd wager the level of sexual anguish in his library tonight was going to be much higher than that of a roomful of randy schoolboys. Fortunately he had a ready and ample supply of brandy with which they could drown their desires.

"The Duke of Alvord and Miss Hamilton—how soon do you think we'll read that they are getting wed?"

"Oh, right—the salacious waltz." Alex cleared his throat. "Very soon." Damn, he'd like to be able to say he and Kate would be wedding soon as well.

Would they be bedding soon? Tonight?

"That'll throw the cat amongst the pigeons. Rothingham's daughter did not look at all happy some colonial upstart might snatch Alvord out of her grasping claws— I suspect she won't give up that ducal prize easily. And Alvord's cousin, Richard Runyon, looked just as evil as the rumors paint him."

Alex tried to control his annoyance. Why was David nattering on about the duke's guests? He wasn't normally such a rattle. "I don't believe I saw Mr. Runyon."

"Perhaps he appeared while you were in the garden with Lady Oxbury."

Alex tripped on some uneven pavement.

"Careful, uncle. You don't want to fall and break something. Might interfere with your courtship."

Alex glared at his nephew. "Courtship? Don't be ridiculous."

"Then what *were* you doing in the garden, Uncle Alex? Examining the flowers? Discussing Plato? You were out there long enough to . . . Well, to do any number of things." Should he tease Alex? If his uncle were anywhere near as frustrated as he was, the man might haul off and darken his daylights for him. Still, Grace would certainly expect him to encourage Alex to pursue her aunt. Teasing might not be the method she'd recommend, but a heart-to-heart talk wasn't his or Alex's style. And in any event, it looked as if no encouragement was necessary.

"Damn it, David, my activities are none of your concern."

David laughed so loudly the stray dog across the street yelped and bolted down an alley.

"Will you be quiet, for God's sake?"

"What? We don't want to disturb the homeless curs or the cutpurses lurking in the shadows?"

"No, we don't—or at least I don't."

David chuckled. "Not up for a fight this evening, uncle?"

"No." Alex did have a quantity of energy to expend, but not on brawling. And Kate would surely not care to have him appear on her doorstep—or windowsill— bleeding and bruised. If he appeared at all, that is.

David laughed again, though a bit ruefully. "In truth, I'm not eager for a fight, myself. I'm already aching enough, if you know what I mean." He winked.

Alex grunted and pretended not to notice, studying the path ahead of him instead. He could almost feel David's thoughtful gaze on him, damn it all.

He hated London. He should go home. If he were at Clifton Hall now, he'd be sitting in his study, a glass of brandy at his elbow, a book in his hands, the fire crackling in the hearth. He'd be calm, tranquil, at ease—not walking a dirty London street, wondering whether he should visit Lady Oxbury's bed, whether he would finally live the dream that had haunted him night after night for year after year.

A warm fire and a good book seemed exceedingly dull.

"If you do court Lady Oxbury," David said, "that would help my cause. You can distract the dragon while I make off with the princess."

"Lady Oxbury is not a dragon, and your cause will only be helped by Standen suffering a complete change of sentiment—an event even the most hardened gamester would not wager on."

Alex wanted to court Kate, but how could he do so in front of the *ton*? All the old gossiping harpies would resurrect the scandals. Zounds, that would be dreadful. No, any pursuit must be conducted in private, away from prying eyes.

What could be more private than Kate's bedchamber?

Kate was expecting him. She was an experienced woman . . .

"Alex, are you attending to me at all?"

But she was not a light skirt. He should marry her before he took her to bed. Still, she had invited him. It would be exceedingly rude not to appear . . .

"Alex!"

"What?" Alex stopped. David was standing on the walk about ten yards behind him. "What are you doing back there?"

David grinned. "Wondering how long it would take you to notice you were alone. You must be immersed in some very . . . deep thoughts." His annoying nephew waggled his eyebrows.

Alex shrugged and resumed walking. David did not.

"What the—" Alex turned again. "Shall I leave you standing there like a lamppost? Come on."

"Alex, look around."

"Why?" Alex looked right and left. He saw a typical London street. "What am I supposed to see?"

"That we're home. This is Dawson House."

"Oh." So perhaps he hadn't been paying attention to his surroundings. He watched David take out his key and unlock the door.

He should follow him into the house, but he couldn't persuade his feet to move. The last thing he wanted to do was go inside—or at least inside David's house. He needed to clear his head, get rid of some of this energy coursing through his veins.

"I think I'll walk for a while. Don't wait up."

David gave him a long look; then shrugged and shut the door behind him.

Alex hesitated. He could still change his mind. He could—he *should*—be sensible. Responsible. He should go up to his room and climb into bed. Alone.

But he wanted to misbehave—thoroughly and utterly misbehave. Proper Alex Wilton wanted to act like a rogue, a rake, a scoundrel.

Well, hardly. But at his ripe old age, he could—he *would*—break, or at least bend, a few rules for once.

He started walking again, this time toward Oxbury House.

Chapter 6

It didn't matter that she'd forgotten to unlock the servants' entrance—Alex wouldn't come. He would never do anything so shocking, certainly not once he'd had the opportunity to consider the matter.

Kate pushed her hair back out of her face as Marie left to empty the basin. Grace had collapsed against her pillows. "Feeling better?"

"A little." Grace closed her eyes briefly. "I'm sorry. I'm afraid tonight was a complete disaster."

"Oh, I don't believe any great harm was done. Lord Dawson kept you from bringing attention to yourself, though it might have been more to the point if he'd kept you from drinking so much champagne."

Grace covered her face. "How can something that tastes so good make me feel so horrible?"

Kate laughed. "I don't know, but if it's any consolation, you're not the first person to run afoul of the drink. The bubbles are very seductive."

Grace sighed. "They are, aren't they?"

"Yes." Kate relaxed a bit. Grace's color was much

improved. A cup of Marie's peppermint tea and Grace should feel, if not right as rain, at least well on the mend.

Kate looked around the room. But perhaps they wouldn't have that tea here. The heavy mahogany furniture and the blood-red curtains were depressing.

This was the master bedchamber. The footmen had taken her things to the adjoining bedroom, even though she was no longer mistress, so she'd had them put Grace's bags in here. With just the two of them in residence, it was silly to stand on ceremony.

This room would suit the new Lord Oxbury—the Weasel—perfectly. He was depressing, too—and any manner of other unpleasant things. She had hated asking him for the key to Oxbury House, and she could tell he'd hated giving it to her. She was convinced he'd only done so in the hope some desperate man would offer for her, freeing him from any further obligation to her.

Yes, this dark room would be perfect for the Weasel, but had it suited her Oxbury? He must have stayed here whenever he'd come up to take his seat in the House of Lords. She didn't know for certain—she'd never accompanied him. She'd always felt she had to stay in the country to see that everything ran smoothly in his absence.

Silly. Critten, the estate manager, was quite competent.

The truth was she'd never wanted to come to Town, and Oxbury had never insisted. Perhaps he knew what she just now suspected—that she'd been afraid she might encounter Alex. How would she have reacted?

Perhaps it was best she'd never know.

"Let's go to my room, Grace—that is, if you feel up to it?"

"Yes. I feel better since I . . ." Grace gestured toward where the basin had been. "You know." She stood, bracing herself on the bedpost. "I'd like to get out of my dress and stays first."

"Of course, I—what *is* that din?"

Grace laughed. "It must be Hermes. He's the only dog in the house, isn't he?"

"Yes, but I was hoping he was asleep."

Marie came in, carrying a pot of tea, a small black and white dog at her heels. "Shh, ye wild doggie. Do nae carry on so. Yer mistress is home now. She did nae desert ye."

"Hermes, you idiot, behave."

Hermes glanced at Kate and gave her a short bark of welcome before turning his attention back to Marie.

"If you can manage it, Marie, will you put the tray in my room?"

"Of course, my lady, as long as this imp of Satan does nae trip me."

Hermes was on his hind legs now, prancing around Marie's skirts, his feathery tail waving as he hopped, his ears flying.

"Yes, and very entertaining ye are, sir. Now move aside, do, so I can get through this door."

Hermes barked and obliged, but still followed Marie closely.

Kate laughed. "You don't happen to have a piece of cheese in your apron pocket, do you, Marie?"

Hermes had been her close companion for the last three years—his presence had helped immeasurably after Oxbury died—but he did have a sad tendency to ignore her when he thought someone might offer him food, unless that someone was the Weasel, of course. He was an excellent judge of character—he knew not to trust the new Lord Oxbury. Any food the Weasel offered was more than likely poisoned.

Marie grinned. "Happen I might. The poor wee doggie

has been so sad with ye gone all evening, I thought he needed a treat."

"Ha! You know he is an accomplished actor, Marie," Kate said. "His skills rival those of Mr. Kean."

"But look at that face." Marie put the tea tray down, and they all turned to look at Hermes.

Hermes barked and lifted his lips in what appeared to be a smile. Then he tilted his head to one side and waved his front paws in the air.

"Oh, give him the cheese, Marie," Kate said, laughing again and sitting down.

"Here then, sir." Marie tossed the treat toward Hermes who snatched it out of the air and swallowed it in two bites. He dropped back to all fours, trotted over to Kate, and lay down by her skirts.

"You know Marie doesn't have any more cheese, don't you, you little beggar?" Kate said, scratching Hermes's ears. The dog merely yawned and put his head down on his paws.

"It's clear what the path is to *his* heart," Grace said, smiling.

"Aye, and it's the same path to many a man's heart, my lady. Keep them fed"—Marie winked—"*all* their appetites, and they're content. Now let me help ye into yer night things, and then ye can have a nice cup of tea and a biscuit or two. It'll settle yer stomach."

Kate poured the tea while Grace went back to her room to change. She inhaled the fragrant steam. The peppermint *was* soothing. She felt some of the tension leave her neck and shoulders. As soon as Marie was finished with Grace, she'd have her loosen her blasted stays and help her into her nightdress. Then she could finally relax.

Unless Alex came.

A hot flush swept up her chest to her neck and on to

her cheeks. She should never have asked him—what had possessed her? He'd been so shocked at her brazenness.

He'd said he would come, but surely he'd changed his mind. Alex had never been one to flout conventions. If he had, perhaps they would have run for Gretna and she would have been married to him all these years instead of to Oxbury. Perhaps they would have had children—

No, they would not have had children.

The thought still sent a sharp pain lancing through her heart.

She was forty years old now, so, of course, she should not be thinking of children. But when she'd been young . . . when she was first married . . .

Each month she had hoped, and each month her hope had leaked from her in red despair. By the end of her second year of marriage, she had finally accepted she was barren.

Oxbury, bless him, had accustomed himself to the truth long before she had. He'd never held it against her, though it had meant his title and all his entailed property would pass to the Weasel—the short, fat, greasy, *annoying* cousin who'd visited twice a year, always looking first at her stomach when he arrived and smiling when he saw it was still as flat as on her wedding day.

She took a large mouthful of tea, but it was too hot to swallow. She spat it back out and put the cup carefully down on the table.

It was a good thing now that she was barren. If she . . . if Alex ever . . . well, there'd be no awkward consequences if Alex . . . if any man . . . ever visited her bed.

But Alex wouldn't come. The risk of scandal was just too great. If he wanted bed sport, he could easily pick from any of the countless young and beautiful London courtesans.

And if he did come, he'd find the servants' door locked. He'd leave and never seek her out again. Which would be a good thing. Very good. Excellent. She exhaled a long, shuddery breath.

She could relax now. She *would* relax. She'd get these blasted stays off and she'd put on her oldest, her most threadbare, most comfortable night clothes.

Marie and Grace came back into the room. "Shall I help ye now, too, my lady?" Marie asked.

"Please." She could hardly wait to be comfortable at last.

This was wrong. He should turn around, go back to Dawson House, go up to his room, have a glass of brandy, and read . . . something.

He'd just finished Byron's *Childe Harold's Pilgrimage*. He didn't feel like starting a new book.

So he was going to screw Kate because he had nothing good to read?

No. He kicked a stone and sent it clattering across the pavement. He was not going to . . . do that to Kate. The word—the thought—was obscene. He was going to . . . going to . . .

He didn't know what he was going to do. He would wait until he arrived at Oxbury House to decide. And he *was* going to Oxbury House. He couldn't help himself. He needed to see Kate. God, he'd spent so many years dreaming of her, wanting her, missing her . . . How could he *not* go to her now?

He crossed the street. It was early for London—the roads were relatively quiet in this part of town. Most of the *ton* were still out at their chosen entertainments—balls, routs, the theater.

It wasn't far to Oxbury House—only a few blocks. It had been farther to Blantrope House. That was where he'd gone the morning after Alvord's ball twenty-three years ago. Lady Blantrope had been acting as Kate's chaperone since Standen's wife was increasing, and Standen had been visiting.

Damn, every detail of that morning was burned into his memory. Thoughts of it bubbled up at odd times— in the middle of the night or the midst of a dinner party—to haunt him. He cringed every time some recollection of it surfaced. He cringed now.

He'd wanted to look precise to a pin, so he'd spent an inordinate amount of time dressing. Sleeping a few hours would have been a good idea, too, but he'd been too nervous to lie still. He'd waited until nine o'clock— an obscenely early hour—and then he'd gone.

It had still been too late. Standen had packed Kate off to the country at first light. Not that it mattered. She was already engaged to Oxbury.

Damn, damn, *damn*. He kicked another stone, sent it ricocheting off someone's front steps. His meeting with Standen had been the most embarrassing, demeaning interview of his life.

When he'd grasped the knocker on Blantrope House's front door, he'd been thinking about Luke and Lady Harriet and the disaster at Gretna Green. He'd worried Standen might still harbor a grudge—and he'd been right, of course. But he hadn't realized Kate had not been honest with him—that she'd been as good as wed when she'd gone with him into the garden.

Why hadn't she told him about Oxbury? More, why had she let him kiss her? Her lack of candor had hurt as much as—or more than—Standen's scathing dismissal.

Alex stopped in front of Oxbury House. He stared at its orderly façade, but in his mind he saw a different building.

The Blantrope butler had left him to cool his heels in a small, dismal antechamber. He could still see the room's hideous red-patterned wallpaper and the disgruntled-looking china cat on the mantel. After waiting almost an hour, he'd been seriously considering flinging the bloody feline into the fireplace.

Or hurling the porcelain beast at Standen's head.

"What are you doing here?" Standen had said when he'd finally stepped into the room. He'd sounded as if he were addressing a cockroach. Still, this was Kate's brother, her guardian. Alex couldn't say exactly what he wanted to to the horse's arse.

"Lord Standen, I came about your sis—"

"My sister has returned to the country."

"I see." Standen's tone had not been at all encouraging, but Alex had been young and stupid. "I came to ask for her hand—"

"Her hand has been given to the Earl of Oxbury. They will wed in a matter of weeks."

"Ah." Alex had felt as if he'd taken a punch to the gut. "But—"

Standen cut him off. "You will have no more to do with her. Do I make myself clear?"

Could the bloody bastard be any clearer? "Yes, but—"

"Good." Standen's lip curled; his nose wrinkled as if he smelled something foul. "I'd drag my sister naked down St. James's Street before I'd see her married to *you*."

Damn it all to hell. He'd left, not really believing Standen. He'd entertained all manner of crazy thoughts on the way home—and then he'd seen the announcement in the *Post*.

He'd been numb at first; once he'd been able to feel again, he'd been overwhelmed by an almost physical pain, as if he'd had an arm or a leg cut off. And in the back of his mind was always the nagging question—if he'd been more decisive, if he'd pressed Kate that night in Alvord's garden to fly with him to Gretna, would she have given up Oxbury and gone?

The man had been thirty years her senior—but he'd also been an earl.

He blew out a long breath. So he was in London again, and outside Oxbury House. Kate was inside waiting for him.

Perhaps tonight he would finally find some peace. That was why he was going to visit Kate. To finish what had not been finished before. To see if he could finally heal this damn wound.

He slipped around the side of the house to the servants' entrance, grabbed the door handle, turned it—

It didn't move.

He frowned and tried again. The knob didn't budge. He took off his gloves and put both hands to the task. Nothing.

The bloody door was locked.

David stretched his long legs toward the fire and wiggled his stocking-clad toes. Mmm. The heat felt good. He took a sip of brandy and savored the liquid's slow slide over his tongue and down his throat. That heat felt good, too. And the heat that would feel the best . . .

He rested his head against the back of his chair, closed his eyes, and finally let his mind go where it wanted. Like a hunting dog slipped from its leash, it flew straight to its quarry.

Lady Grace Belmont.

She was perfect. He would never have guessed he was enamored of red hair—he'd always thought he preferred his women blonde. But he'd never seen hair like Grace's. It wasn't red; it was copper and gold, fire and light. He wanted to bury his fingers in it, let it slide like silk over his palms. Over his chest. Over . . .

He slid lower in his chair, spreading his legs wide so an important part of him could swell with admiration. That part was generating a bit too much heat—his breeches were in danger of spontaneously combusting.

If only Lady Grace Belmont were here.

If Grace were here . . . He took another sip of brandy, rolling it on his tongue. If Lady Grace were here . . .

What would he do if Grace were in this room right now?

What wouldn't he do?

He'd start with her hairpins. Yes. Slowly, one by one, he'd pull each pin out, watching Grace's glorious hair slowly tumble down over her shoulders. Copper over cream—beautiful. Then he'd comb his fingers through it, bury his face in it, inhale its sweet, clean scent. He'd lift a silky handful off her neck, brushing it back so he could kiss the sensitive spot by her ear.

And then? Then he'd explore her face. He'd kiss her jaw, her cheekbones, her eyelids; he'd brush over her lips—he'd not want to get waylaid there so soon—and move down kiss by nip by lick to the pulse at the base of her throat and to her shoulder . . . and then he would loosen her gown.

He shifted in his chair. Could his breeches get any tighter? Doubtful.

Where was he? Ah, yes. Grace's gown. He'd slip it off her shoulders slowly, savoring each inch of perfect skin revealed. Off her shoulders, over her breasts to her waist, her hips, pushing the cloth down to pool at her feet, leaving her in only her stays and shift.

And then he would turn her, push her hair forward so he could kiss the back of her neck, the top of her spine . . .

Would he have the patience to untie her laces?

He snorted. He'd not advise anyone to wager on it. His fingers felt as thick as the organ begging to be released from his breeches. Heh. No, not *that* thick, but still he was certain he would not be able to battle small, knotted laces. He would have to use his knife. Surely Grace wouldn't mind? If he were doing his job correctly, she would be as desperate to be free of her clothing as he was to free her.

He grinned at the fire. Ah, yes, free her—and her lovely, lovely breasts. He would reach around, pull her body against his, and cradle her heavy, round breasts in his hands.

And then he would turn her to face him again. He would trace the delicate curve of her ribcage, of her waist, the generous flare of her hips, her long, long legs down to the hem of her shift. He would kneel so he could better watch his hands move back up, better see them slide up her ankles, her calves, her knees, taking the thin shift with them. He might stop at her thighs, just a little above her knees, to kiss her tender, white skin. Then he would let his lips move upward with his hands, until he cupped her sweet bottom and buried his face in the soft hair at the top of her legs. Would it be red, too?

God, he was panting. He was going to have to open the fall of his breeches. Hell, he wasn't going to be able to walk upstairs unless he took steps to relieve his discomfort. He hadn't had to do that since he was little more than a stripling.

He needed to think about something other than Grace.

Alex. He grimaced. Probably a bad choice. Alex was likely in Lady Oxbury's bedchamber right now, getting to do with his lady everything David had been imagining with Grace. Alex, the cautious, proper Wilton, was participating in what could become a colossal scandal if word of it ever leaked out.

No one who knew Alex would believe it—*he* wouldn't believe it if he hadn't walked home from Alvord's ball with the man.

Or perhaps Alex was just taking an evening stroll through London.

David got up to pour himself another glass of brandy. If he drank enough, he'd not dream of Grace when he managed to drag himself upstairs and fall into bed. He'd not dream at all.

He filled his glass and looked around the library. His great grandfather had been the last Wilton to use this room. Grandda had hated London. Luke, his father, had been only twenty when he'd eloped with Lady Harriet. So young.

Would his parents' love have lasted if they'd lived?

The stories Grandmamma had told him when he was little said yes. She'd created a couple whose devotion would have withstood all tests but death. The tales he'd heard from the innkeepers, stable hands, local gentry, and peers who'd known his father, however . . . well, Grandmamma had always loved fairy tales.

Luke Wilton had not had a reputation that bespoke steadiness and commitment.

He ran his hand along the bookcase. Tomes in Greek and Latin, books on agriculture and horticulture—it was clear the volumes had been purchased solely for appearance.

It had been very easy to make Lord Wordham, his

mother's father, the villain of Grandmamma's fairy tales.
If the man hadn't tried to force Lady Harriet to marry
Standen, his parents wouldn't have run to Gretna and his
father wouldn't have opened his head on a rock in the
stable yard. But now that he thought about it—well, if he
were honest, he would not have wanted his daughter, if
he had one, to marry someone like his father.

But not wanting a thatch-gallows for a son-in-law
didn't justify Wordham's deserting Lady Harriet at the
inn nor did it forgive his shunning her deathbed and ig-
noring her son.

David took a deep breath and another mouthful of
brandy. The spirit's warmth was steadying.

Lord Wordham was dead, but Lady Wordham was
still alive and in London.

He snorted. Why even note that fact? The woman had
never expressed any interest in him either.

He turned back to the fire and poked it, sending
sparks flying.

Alex had been just fourteen when Luke died. Had he
been a model of propriety even then or had he become
one in reaction to his older brother's blatant impropriety?
No matter. Now Alex was finally misbehaving.

David grinned at the fire. If Alex distracted Lady
Oxbury—and she had acted very distracted this evening—
that would give David many opportunities to do many
lovely, scandalous things with Lady Grace.

He would steal her away from this clod in the country.

Just as his father had stolen his mother from Standen.

No. The situations were not similar at all. Luke had
been a niffy-naffy fellow, a scoundrel. David was responsible, like Alex.

Except—also like Alex—perhaps not so responsible
in present circumstances.

Damn it, Grace was meant to be his, not Parker-Roth's. The man had had years to woo her and had obviously failed miserably.

David would court her. If he did not win her heart, then he would withdraw and let Parker-Roth have her.

But he would succeed. He would work very hard to do so—and enjoy every moment of his toil.

He tossed off the last of his brandy and headed for the stairs and bed.

Alex stared at the door. He tugged on the handle again. Nothing happened. It was definitely locked.

Kate had changed her mind.

Bloody hell! He'd walked all this way, struggled with his conscience, and for what? To find the door locked.

She'd been teasing him again, just as she had twenty-three years ago. Was she in her bedroom, laughing?

He wanted to hit something, but he was no longer young and stupid—well, not completely stupid. He certainly wasn't going to pound his fist on a stone wall or a tree trunk. He'd only hurt his hand and call attention to his presence—

Tree trunk. Hmm. Should he . . . ?

No, he should go back to Dawson House. If he were lucky, David could be persuaded he'd merely gone for a long walk. Hell, if he left now and walked briskly, he'd be back in time to join his nephew in the library for a glass of brandy before he headed off to bed.

He was very tired.

He was not *that* tired.

Kate had seemed so sincere in Alvord's garden. Yes, his judgment had been colored by lust, but he'd swear it hadn't been completely obfuscated by his animal instincts.

Perhaps when she'd got home, she'd simply awoken to the scandal his presence in Oxbury House could provoke were it discovered. She'd lost her courage.

He should go home.

He turned and started for the street.

Or perhaps she'd forgotten about the door. Or the butler had come round later and locked up for the night.

He stopped. He couldn't go without knowing.

He was at the northwest corner. She'd said there was a tree. Yes, there it was—a solid tree with plenty of sturdy branches. Very climbable, even for a man of his advanced years. And there was a light in her room.

He was tired of dreaming and guessing. He needed to know for certain if he had a future—or even a present—with Kate.

He picked up a pebble from the garden walkway, hefted it, and took aim at Lady Oxbury's bedroom window.

Chapter 7

Grace cradled her tea cup in her hands and drew in a deep breath. To think she had imbibed so much champagne she'd cast up her accounts! At least Lord Dawson didn't know that detail, thank goodness, though he must have noted her overindulgence.

She muffled a moan, squeezing her eyes tightly shut. How could she have been so buffle-headed? The first glass had gone down so quickly—she'd been thirsty from the dance and a little nervous. She was not used to having such a large, handsome gentleman paying her attention— a gentleman who had already announced he wished to marry her. So when he'd offered her a second glass, she'd taken it gratefully.

And then she'd been so happy seeing Aunt Kate and Mr. Wilton together, she'd had to have a third glass in celebration . . . or was it a fourth?

She took a sip of her tea. She would have been fine if it hadn't been for Baron Dawson. She would have stayed in the ballroom and danced with the men who couldn't find another partner. She would have endured and even been anxious to go back to Standen and listen to John drone on about his plants.

She put her tea cup down so abruptly it clinked against the saucer. She had an odd, very empty feeling in her middle.

Perhaps a biscuit would help. She reached for the plate.

Hermes's ears pricked up as Grace's teeth sank into the crunchy treat. He was at her side before she'd swallowed her first bite.

"Let me guess—you want a biscuit, too?"

Hermes barked twice, wagged his tail, and looked beseechingly up at her, appearing pitifully hungry.

"But you just had some cheese."

The little dog put his paws on Grace's knee and stared intently into her face, his ears drooping. Somehow he managed to convey most eloquently that it had only been a very small bit of cheese, and though he was a small dog, he had the energy and the appetite of a beast twice his size.

"Hermes!" Kate stepped out of her dressing room wearing a voluminous nightdress. "Leave poor Grace alone."

Grace laughed. "But he is so persuasive. Mayn't I give him a biscuit?"

"That will encourage him, you know, but . . . all right. Just one, otherwise he'll beg himself into gluttony." Kate turned to Marie. "Hermes had his walk tonight, didn't he?"

"Aye. Jem, the boot boy, took him out to the back garden."

"Splendid. He should sleep well tonight, then." Kate smiled. "Thank you, Marie. That will be all."

"You don't look terribly sleepy, Hermes," Grace said as Marie left. She held out a biscuit and Hermes snapped it out of her hand, then licked her fingers to get every last crumb. His tongue tickled. "Do you ever feed this dog, Aunt Kate?"

"Constantly. It's a wonder his belly doesn't drag on the floor."

"Yes, I'd say—" Grace examined Kate's nightdress more closely. "Where did you get that? It looks ancient."

"It *is* ancient." Kate sat in the other chair and tucked her feet up under her. "But it's very comfortable."

"And very threadbare. You might want to replace it while you're in Town." Grace couldn't resist; Hermes was dancing at her knee, his eyes so large and pleading. She offered him a bit of her own biscuit. He nipped it out of her fingers and trotted over to eat it by Kate. "Well! Does he think I'll steal it back from him?"

"Perhaps he realizes he's pushed his luck."

"Hmm." Grace cleared her throat slightly. Speaking of pushing one's luck . . . "I should say . . . I mean, well . . ." Best get the words out. She spoke in a rush. "I am so sorry about tonight. I don't understand what happened. I've had champagne before, but I've never been ill."

"A little champagne goes a long way. Did you have anything to eat at the ball?"

"N-no." Her stomach had been far too unsettled to sample the duke's lobster patties.

"And not at the luncheon either."

"I wasn't hungry. I was too nervous, I suppose."

Kate shrugged. "I imagine if you'd eaten, the champagne wouldn't have affected you so much. Next time don't drink on an empty stomach."

The thought of drinking anything stronger than tea was revolting. "You do not need to worry. I'll never touch champagne again." Grace rubbed her forehead. "Did I . . . did I embarrass myself too dreadfully?" She grimaced.

"I should be happy if I am too disgraced to attend another society event."

"No, you did not embarrass yourself at all. I didn't know you'd imbibed too freely until we were riding home in the carriage."

"Truthfully?"

"Truthfully." Aunt Kate put her tea cup down and leaned forward. "However if you are feeling more the thing, we do need to talk."

This did not sound good. Could she plead a recurrence of her indisposition?

"Grace, about Lord Dawson . . ."

Grace's stomach twisted. A recurrence was definitely possible. "W-what about Lord Dawson?"

"He . . . Well, you know your papa would be mad as a buck if he learned you'd been in the baron's company."

Papa . . . Baron Dawson . . .

Grace leaned forward as well. "Aunt Kate, why did Papa never tell me about Lady Harriet?"

Kate's expression suddenly turned guarded. She sat back, putting more distance between herself and Grace. "Lady Harriet?"

"The Earl of Wordham's daughter—Lord Dawson's mother." And the love of Papa's life? But what about Mama? Grace's mother had died in childbirth when Grace was only two. Grace didn't remember her—she'd only seen her portrait in the family gallery—a petite woman with red hair, large brown eyes, and a serious expression. She'd thought Papa had never remarried because his heart had broken when she'd died.

Perhaps his heart *had* broken, but not for Mama.

Grace's stomach twisted again.

Aunt Kate wouldn't quite meet her eyes. "I suppose your papa thought it was ancient history—which it is."

"Except he is apparently still wearing the willow for Lady Harriet." Grace's voice caught slightly. "Didn't he love my mother at all?" She shouldn't care; she knew that, but she still felt betrayed.

Aunt Kate patted her hand. "I'm sure he did, Grace. I always thought he and your mother had a very comfortable relationship. Lady Harriet was just his first love, and"—Aunt Kate blushed—"first loves are very intense. You shouldn't assume my brother still has feelings for Lady Harriet."

"No? Why else would he continue to hate the Wilton family?"

Aunt Kate laughed humorlessly. "Because your father feels his honor was injured by a Wilton, I suppose. He does not forgive or forget, Grace, which is why you cannot cultivate a friendship with Lord Dawson."

Grace sighed. Aunt Kate was right. A wise woman would make a point of avoiding Lord Dawson for the rest of the Season. Besides the fact Papa detested the man, it was clear the baron was a very strong-willed individual, the sort of man who could have the unsuspecting believing that up was down—the sort of man in whose presence she drank too much champagne.

Unfortunately she did not feel at all like being wise. No, she felt like being slightly reckless—though not regarding champagne or any other spirits. But with regard to the baron—and waltzing and lingering in gardens without studying the plantings . . .

This trip to London was a small window—a small interruption—in the gray wall of her existence. A glimmer of magic, a brief portal into fairy tales and happily ever afters. She would enjoy it as fully as she could for as long as she could.

She would be wise and dutiful once she returned to the country and married John.

Grace put the biscuit she'd been nibbling back down on her plate. She suddenly had no room for it—her stomach felt heavy, leaden, as if she'd swallowed a cannon ball.

"You don't need to worry, Aunt Kate. I've already told Lord Dawson his suit is hopeless."

"*Suit?*" Kate shrieked. She fumbled her cup, spilling a little tea on her nightdress. "Surely he hasn't proposed? He just met you."

Right. Grace knew that . . . well, her head knew it. Her heart seemed to have a very different opinion—it felt as if she'd known the baron forever.

"Apparently Lord Dawson is not a man to waste time."

Unlike John. John had never kissed her. That hadn't seemed such an oversight until now.

She hadn't expected John to be amorous. She knew he was more interested in acquiring a bit of Papa's land than in acquiring her. She'd thought he'd be a comfortable husband. Neglectful, perhaps, but she didn't want much attention.

They would have a child or two or three—she couldn't quite imagine the actual getting of those children, but surely John would manage the deed with a minimum of fuss—and she would be content. At least he would never be unfaithful—well, besides his occasional visits to his mistress, Mrs. Haddon.

No, "passion" and "John Parker-Roth" were not usually found in the same sentence unless the subject was vegetative. Roses or gardens evoked John's emotions, not women and weddings.

"You can't marry Lord Dawson." Aunt Kate sounded both stern and worried. She was frowning.

"I know that." Grace frowned back. Grace had not been

the only woman in the garden tonight. "But *you* can marry Mr. Wilton."

"What?!" Aunt Kate squeaked so loudly, Hermes raised his head.

"You can marry Mr. Wilton." Grace leaned forward. "I have no idea why you failed to mention his proposal when we had our little chat in the retiring room earlier, but no matter. You are a widow; he is a bachelor—you are both free. You can marry as soon as you want."

"Ah. Er . . ." Aunt Kate turned bright red. Was that a good sign?

"Did Mr. Wilton propose again tonight, Aunt Kate, when you were in the garden together?" Aunt Kate would have told her already if he had, wouldn't she? Well, perhaps she would have if Grace hadn't been foxed—and then sick. "I saw you waltzing with him. You looked . . . radiant."

"Ah . . . radiant?" Kate looked more horrified now than radiant. "You must be mistaken."

"No, I assure you. I—"

Ping!

Kate bolted to her feet as if electrified. Hermes leapt up and, barking madly, dashed to the window.

"It sounds as if someone's throwing pebbles," Grace said. "Who could it be?"

Ping!

Hermes danced in front of the curtains, then grabbed a mouthful and tugged. Kate stayed frozen in place. She was as colorless as an ice sculpture.

"Shall I see who's there?" Grace started across the room, but Kate's hand shot out to grab her wrist.

"No!" Her calm, self-possessed aunt was acting surprisingly agitated.

"Aunt Kate, what's wrong?"

"Nothing. Everything's fine." Kate tore her eyes away from the window and smiled weakly—but jumped when another pebble hit the glass.

"You know, Grace, this has been quite a comfortable coze"—*Ping!*—"but I'm suddenly very tired"—*Ping!*—"and I do think I'd like to go"—*Ping!*—"to bed"—*Ping! Ping!*—"now." Kate tugged Grace toward the connecting door and opened it. "You should go to bed as well. You need your rest."

That was true. Grace was still feeling a little ill from her encounter with the champagne. "All right." She paused to listen. "And it sounds as if the noise has stopped. Whoever was out there has probably left."

"Yes, I'm sure you're right." Kate literally pushed Grace over the threshold. "Sleep well."

"You, too, Au—"

Slam!

If Grace had been standing any closer, the door would have hit her in the nose. She stared, and then shrugged and turned away. Apparently Aunt Kate did not wish to be disturbed. Just as well. Now that she was alone, she realized she was completely exhausted.

She climbed into bed and lay down cautiously. Thankfully, the room did not start rotating. She glanced at the bedside table. Good. Marie had replaced the basin, so if she should have an unfortunate recurrence of her indisposition, she would not be completely disgraced.

How *could* she have been such a noddy? She should have noticed the bubbles going to her head. To think she—

But she had not been thinking, had she? She'd been feeling. She'd been enchanted by a certain tall, handsome baron.

Oh, dear. She leaned over and blew out the candle.

What was she going to do? Baron Dawson was not a man to take no for an answer, and she must tell him no.

She couldn't break Papa's heart again. She couldn't align herself with a family that had stolen away his first love and caused him such great pain he still ached all these years later. She most certainly couldn't give him grandchildren with Wilton blood running in their veins.

Grandchildren . . . babies . . . her babies and Dav—

No. Not Lord Dawson's babies—John's babies.

Her stomach lurched a little. Was she going to have to use that damn basin?

And she couldn't ignore the effect her actions would have on John, either. He was expecting to marry her. He and his family would be hurt—embarrassed and insulted—if she jilted him. She would hate that.

She turned over on her side. Fortunately, her stomach did not object.

She had to tell David no, but here in the dark, in the privacy of her room, she could dream. What if she *could* tell him yes?

That would be wonderful. She could waltz with him at every ball as many times as she wanted. She could go off with him into society gardens without giving the *ton* anything to gossip about. And once they were in those gardens . . .

She smiled and burrowed deeper into her bed. There would be no botany lectures. No, they would do all the wonderful things they had done tonight—and perhaps a few more. She could tell David was holding back this evening.

His body was so hard and strong—so different from hers. Yet he'd been so gentle. She'd felt sheltered and safe. And the feel of his lips and his tongue and his hands . . . He had provoked so many entrancing, exciting sensations.

The throbbing . . . oh. The throbbing had started again. She was hot and damp and unsettled. She stretched, but even the friction of the sheets against her skin was too much.

She turned over on her stomach and pressed against the mattress, but that gave her no relief.

Thinking about David had been a mistake. She would never get to sleep at this rate. If only she could remember some of John's discourses on plant classification, she would fall asleep in minutes—but she'd never paid enough attention to remember any of his lectures.

There was no help for it—she would have to count sheep.

She turned over on her back, closed her eyes resolutely, and started at "one."

It must be Alex outside—who else could it be?

Kate rushed to the window. *Why* had she chosen to wear her oldest nightdress tonight? It looked like a rag, it had been washed so many times. The lowest scullery maid would be embarrassed to own it. It certainly wasn't an appropriate garment for a seduction. She should change.

There was no time to change.

Had he left? She hadn't heard a stone hit the window for a while. Hermes had stopped tussling with the curtain and had collapsed, panting, on the floor.

Surely Alex hadn't left. Please God, don't let him have left—though why she was asking the Divinity to assist in her liaison—

Hermes jumped up and started barking again as she shoved aside the curtain.

"Shh, Hermes. You'll wake the dead." Alex wouldn't rush off after coming all this way.

All right, so Oxbury House was only a few blocks from Dawson House, but still, he'd made the trip, which must mean he wanted . . .

She wouldn't think about what he must want.

She tugged on the window latch.

There was no real hurry. Alex *must* have left. Why would he stay, after she'd forgotten to unlock the servants' door and then ignored his attempts to get her attention? He likely was halfway home by now.

Damnation, the old latch wouldn't budge. She pulled with both hands. She had to get the window open. He might not have gone far. Maybe if she shouted—

If she shouted all of London would wonder why Lady Oxbury was hanging out her bedroom window, yelling into the darkness.

At least her room was at the back of the building. Perhaps no one would notice.

If she couldn't get this bloody window open, no one *would* notice. She could shout all she wanted—only Hermes would hear her.

She jerked harder on the latch. Was it rusted or painted shut? Surely the blasted window had been opened sometime in the last forty years, or however long it'd been since Oxbury's mother's death. The servants must have aired the rooms before she and Grace arrived. Whatever the case, the damn window wasn't opening now. She pulled one last time, as hard as she could.

Finally! The latch screeched open. She shoved on the window. It protested, too, but went up slowly. She leaned out . . .

She couldn't see a thing—or hear anything, either, Hermes was making such a racket.

"Shh, you silly dog." She held her breath, listened . . .

She heard a low, male chuckle. Where was it coming from? Under the tree? The shadows were too thick to tell.

"Alex?" she whispered urgently.

"Hallo, Kate."

"Alex!" She collapsed against the windowsill in relief. He was still here. "I'm sorry about—"

"Shh." Another low chuckle. "Shall I come up? We can . . . talk then."

She shivered at his pause. Yes, they could talk—and do other things. "Yes, come up. Can you manage the tree?"

"Of course."

There was nothing "of course" about a forty-five-year-old man—even a man in as splendid physical condition as Alex appeared to be—climbing up a tree and through a bedroom window. She bit her tongue and said a few prayers as she watched him shed his coat and waistcoat and make his way up through the branches. She picked Hermes up and stepped back when he reached the window.

"Be careful."

He grinned at her from his perch on a sturdy branch. At least she hoped it was sturdy. She'd be very much happier when he was inside; she did not care to watch him plummet to the ground.

"Fortunately the gardeners have neglected their pruning. This tree grows much too close to the house, you know."

Heavens, did he want to have a discussion of horticulture while he sat in that bloody tree?

"For God's sake, Alex, come in before you fall to your death."

"Very well, since you ask so nicely." He grabbed a branch above his head and swung his legs over the windowsill. In a minute he was standing in her room. He spread out his arms. "Here I am, safe and sound."

"Thank God!" She took a step toward him and froze.

He was so big. She held Hermes a little tighter. It was one thing to imagine Alex, to dream of him here, but a different thing to actually have him in her room.

In her bed? Good God.

"W-would you like some t-tea?" She put Hermes down and turned back to the table.

Oxbury had been forty-seven when they'd married— only two years older than Alex was now. But Oxbury had seemed ancient. Yes, she'd been only seventeen, but that wasn't it, or at least not all of it. Oxbury had been, well, scraggy—only a few inches taller than she, with narrow, slightly bowed shoulders and spindly arms and legs. Back then he'd used stays and false calves and other sartorial tricks to pad his appearance. She'd been startled when he'd come to her on their wedding night. He'd looked like a skeleton in his nightshirt.

She'd be shocked if Alex wore any padding at all, but she'd find out tonight—

Dear heavens. If he actually . . . if they really—

"G-Grace and I were just having a cup of p-peppermint t-tea. It's very s-soothing. And biscuits. There are still some left. Grace didn't have much of an appetite. Nor did I." No need to explain why she'd had no appetite. "They're gingerbread—Hermes's favorite, aren't they, Hermes?"

She turned back to look at the males in the room. Both Hermes and Alex were staring at her as if she were completely addled.

"I didn't come for tea, Kate." Alex's voice was low and warm, but there was a question in it, too—a question she was not quite prepared to answer.

Why couldn't he just grab her, take her to bed, and do whatever it was he did in b-beds? Besides sleep, that is.

"N-no, of course, you don't want tea. I'm afraid—well, I didn't think—I don't have any brandy or—"

He came toward her and took her hands, which had been fluttering around her like drunken sparrows. His clasp was strong, warm, strangely reassuring. Comforting. She took a deep breath and looked up into his face.

"Kate, do you want me to go?"

"Ah." He certainly got right to the point.

"I will if you want me to."

His eyes searched her face. She couldn't bear the scrutiny—she looked away. Hermes had settled down in his bed in the corner. Apparently *he* trusted Alex.

A slightly calloused finger touched her chin, urging her back to meet his gaze.

"The servants' door was locked, Kate. Did you mean for me to leave, then?" He frowned, and she could feel him begin to draw back. "I'm sorry, I—"

She grabbed two handfuls of his soft lawn shirt. "No!" She would have to find the courage to say it. She'd been wrong to hope Alex would take charge. "I-I want you to stay. Please. Don't leave."

He cupped her face in his hands. "You're certain?"

"Yes." She was nervous—terrified, actually—but she was also certain—completely certain—she wanted him here.

Alex looked down at Kate. She was not acting like a woman who made a habit of inviting men to her bed. She seemed agitated. Afraid . . . of him? No. She couldn't be afraid of him. He would never hurt her.

Instead of kissing her, he gathered her close, holding her lightly. After a moment, he felt her arms slide around his waist.

She was so small and delicate.

"Do you miss Oxbury, Kate?"

Where the hell had that thought come from? Was he an idiot? He didn't want to talk about her dead husband, did he?

Her grip on him tightened. "Yes." Damnation, was that a sniff he heard? "Y-yes, I m-miss him."

Hell and blast, all of a sudden she was sobbing. Her shoulders shook; his shirtfront was growing damp. He felt her drawing in deep, shuddering breaths.

"Shh." He cradled the back of her head, his fingers tangled in her hair. "Shh, love."

He knew all about loss, about holes in your life so large you feared you'd fall in and tumble down and down forever. When Da and Mama had died . . .

Damn, his eyes were watering. He must have got a speck in them climbing up through the tree branches. There was a lump in his throat as well. He swallowed.

He was not crying. Only women and dandies cried.

He stroked Kate's hair while she sobbed for Oxbury. It was so soft. It slipped like silk through his fingers and flowed all the way down to her waist. Thank God she hadn't braided it.

She sobbed harder.

Obviously, he was a failure as a rake. He should have kissed her the moment she'd strayed into his arms. He should have tried to stir up her lust—or whatever urge had provoked her to invite him here. He should have got her into bed as quickly as he could. Why the hell did he have to mention Oxbury?

Because the man was only dead a year and had been Kate's husband for more than half her life. There was no escaping those facts. When he took Kate to bed—*if* he took her to bed—Oxbury would be there, too. Hopefully only as a pleasant memory—a pleasant, very faint memory—but from the way Kate was crying . . . well, there just might not be room for a mere mortal in her heart.

If Kate still mourned Oxbury, why the bloody hell had she asked him here?

"I should leave, Kate."

She shook her head and clutched his shirt more tightly. It would take some effort to detach her.

He rubbed her back. Mmm. Her nightgown was worn, the fabric so thin he'd seen the outline of her lovely body—her breasts, waist, hips, even the shadow of her nether curls—when she'd walked over to the tea tray. Now he could feel the warm mounds of her breasts pressed against his chest and the heat of her skin where he stroked her. No dress, no stays, just woman.

A sobbing woman whose mind was definitely not on bed play.

What was he to do? Leave? But she wouldn't let him. Seduce her? Surely even the most hardened rake must hesitate at luring such a tearful female into bed.

He could only try to comfort her. There was no turning back the clock, no uttering a magical incantation to make the last twenty-three years disappear. Kate was who she was. She was not the young girl he'd lost his heart to. That girl was long gone. In her place was this beautiful woman who was . . . who? He didn't know.

He shouldn't have come. He truly was an idiot. He'd wasted half his life dreaming of, longing for, someone who didn't exist.

But she felt so very good. And she smelled just as he remembered. He brushed his lips over her hair, breathing deeply. Whether it was sleight of hand or not, holding her made him feel young again, made him believe anything was possible.

And she seemed to need him. He would give her what he could—whatever she wanted.

"I do miss him," she said. She looked up. Her face was blotchy red, her eyes swollen. She sniffed several times.

He handed her his handkerchief. She wiped her eyes and blew her nose, then looked at the cloth wadded up in her fist. She blushed.

"I'll have Marie launder this and—"

"Keep it. I have others." He should find a way to leave. She had stopped crying. She would want to be alone with her memories.

She dropped her gaze back to his shirtfront and put her hand on his chest. "I'm sorry I turned into such a watering pot. I'm sure that's not what you were expecting."

"Not quite." God, he could feel each one of her fingers through the linen. They burned him, branded him . . .

He should leave.

"Kate, I think—" Damn, her hand was moving lower, over his belly, down to . . . He held his breath.

She stopped at his waist, but her other hand joined the first, the used handkerchief relegated to the floor. Both hands slid slowly up his body, her fingers tracing his muscles through the cloth.

Dear God! He was going to burst into flames, especially the most interested part of him. He moved his hips back to spare her the evidence.

"Kate." Was that his voice, so hoarse and thick? He covered her hands with his, staying their explorations. "Kate, I'm not sure—"

"I am." She looked up at him, her eyes still puffy from her tears. "I wish to seduce you."

"You're lonely."

She hesitated as if she would say something and then changed her mind. She smiled slightly. "So I need company. Will you keep me company?" She leaned forward and kissed the cloth above his heart. "Please?"

He was going to explode. He shouldn't do this. He should climb back out the window, but frankly, he doubted he was physically able to manage the deed at this particular moment. "Er . . ."

She looked up again, a slight frown between her brows, her eyes serious. "I'll be honest, Alex. I know next to nothing about bed play. Oxbury was, well . . ." She shook her head, shrugged, and then smiled slightly. "But I want to learn." She pressed closer to him. "With you."

He tried to think, but all the blood had drained from his head to another organ which was insisting on doing his thinking for him, enthusiastically urging him to get on with it and take the girl to bed. "Kate . . ."

"Please?" Her small hand found the focus of his enthusiasm and gently, almost hesitantly, brushed over him.

"I'm not . . ." Damn, he was panting. "I'm really not, ah." She was tracing his outline now which was growing with each gentle touch. "If you're looking for an expert"— Oh, God. Her fingers . . . if they did that again . . . yes . . . with a little more pressure . . . a little more—no. What was he trying to say? Yes. No. He was trying to say no. Or at least maybe or wait or—what the hell—"If you're looking for an expert, I don't qualify."

Blessedly, her hands moved from their current obsession. He could think again. Or maybe not. Now they were working his shirt free of his breeches and slipping underneath to touch his bare skin.

"I don't want an expert," she said. "I want you."

Chapter 8

Her courage wavered. Had she been too bold? Alex seemed markedly less than enthusiastic.

Well, yes, a specific part of him was very eager, almost alarmingly eager, but the rest of him . . . She started to withdraw her hands from his wonderful, warm skin. She had reached the extent of her limited seduction skills.

His hands slid down to cup her bottom.

"Really, Kate? You really want me?"

She heard hope, need, and a note of pain in his voice that called to her. Perhaps he was as lonely as she was. Perhaps she could offer him something of value besides his physical release.

"Oh, yes, Alex. I've never wanted anything—anyone— as much as I want you." She pushed his shirt up and kissed his hard, lightly-furred chest. Then she pressed her cheek against him and hugged him tightly. She was going to have Alex in her bed. She was finally going to be able to touch him and kiss him, and . . . and do the other thing with him.

She would happily skip the other thing, but that had always been Oxbury's focus, even after it was clear she could not give him children, so Alex would probably be just as interested. It was a male thing, having to do with the male organ. She had spent many nights, especially in the early years of their marriage, lying quietly, making a list of household chores she needed to attend to in the morning while Oxbury worked over her, grunting and sweating and moaning.

No matter. It was usually over relatively quickly. And it was a small price to pay for the chance to touch Alex, to have his attention.

He started to pull up her nightgown. Oh, no. She knew where that would lead. She would be flat on her back in minutes. She was having none of it. Not now. Later, yes. After she did her own exploring.

She pushed back from his chest. "No."

He frowned down at her. "No?"

"Not yet. I want my turn first."

"Your . . . turn?" He sounded—he looked—completely confused. Well, that was all right. She didn't know exactly what she meant, either. But she had asked him here. This was her room. She was going to take charge.

"I want to . . . experiment."

"You do?" His eyes looked distinctly wary. "What exactly do you mean . . . experiment?"

She laughed then. What did he think she meant? She had a very limited imagination. Excitement and an odd recklessness surged through her. She might be forty years old, but she had never felt so young. "I don't know. I'll puzzle it out as I go along." She grinned and spread her fingers over his chest. "You can give me suggestions—as long as you realize I may not take them." She kissed one of his nipples and heard him inhale sharply. "I make the final decisions."

"That is not what I am used to, you know." Was his voice a little breathless?

"I'm sure it is not, but I think I must insist." She traced the line from his chest to the top of his breeches and felt his belly tense. "I don't have any experience to speak of in the arts of seduction, however, so I imagine I will need many suggestions."

"Ah." Yes, his voice was definitely breathless and a little strained. "I . . . see. Well, then, please . . . ah . . . proceed."

She ran her tongue over her suddenly dry lips. There was one other detail she should mention. She watched her finger smooth his soft hair, drawing a little pattern on his stomach. She swallowed. This was rather hard to say. Mortifying. It shouldn't be. He should be happy to hear it.

"Before we . . . s-start . . . ah . . ." She swallowed. "You should know . . . that is, you'll be pleased to know . . . well, you may be relieved to hear you do not need to worry . . . what I mean to say is . . ." She wished she didn't have to say it. He might guess it, of course, due to her age, but age wasn't to blame in this case. The problem . . . the difficulty was . . .

Well, if she weren't this way, she would never have invited him here. There were only so many risks she was willing to take.

"Kate?" The edge of his hand came under her chin. He raised her face.

She met his eyes and looked away quickly. She couldn't be distracted by his touch. She dropped her hands and stepped back. She took a deep breath and stared at his shirt which had now fallen back down to cover his body.

"You need not worry that an unfortunate event will occur in nine months' time." She cleared her throat, swallowed again. Best just to blurt it out. "I'm barren."

"God, Kate."

Was that pity in his voice? She didn't want pity. Not now. For once it was *good* she was barren. And she was far too old for children in any case.

She was going to be a seductress. She was going to play. She was not going to think about children, about a son or daughter with Alex's eyes—

No, she was *not* going to think about it.

"I've had many years to accustom myself to the fact. And it is convenient now, wouldn't you say?" She tried to laugh. "At my age it must be impossible to c-conceive, even if I had ever been f-fertile."

Damn. Her voice broke.

"Kate—"

If they started discussing her failing, they would never get into her bed. She put her fingers over Alex's mouth. She did not want to think about children or Oxbury. She didn't want to think at all.

"We are starting now, all right?" *Please, don't ask questions, Alex. Please just play the game.*

He frowned. She was certain he was going to protest and ruin everything, but he didn't. She felt his lips move against her fingers in a kiss. He nodded. She smiled and stepped back.

"Good. Now, take off your shirt, please."

Alex just looked at her.

Damn. Was he going to insist on talking about children, then? She bit her lip. If he did, she would cry and the whole evening would be a disaster. She would sleep alone again. She would never know what it was like to . . . be with Alex. She would not get the courage to ask him again. She would—

He was reaching for the hem of his shirt. Thank God!

He grasped it in both hands and quickly pulled it over his head, dropping it on the floor by his feet.

Oh. Oh, my. He took her breath away. "You're beautiful."

He snorted, his cheeks reddening. "I am not beautiful."

"You are." She'd known his stomach was flat and hard; she'd just felt it. She'd known his shoulders were broad— but they looked so much broader naked. Muscles curved in his arms—and even in his chest and stomach. He was like a statue of a Greek god, but instead of being cold, white marble, he was warm flesh. She stepped closer and put her hands on him again.

Very warm.

His arms came up to pull her close. She stiffened. Not yet. She wanted to take things slowly, savor every moment. She would not get another chance. This was only for tonight, to satisfy her curiosity. Tomorrow she would be the strait-laced Lady Oxbury again.

"No, Alex. You can only suggest."

"What?"

"You can suggest that you put your arms around me; I'm the one who will decide if you do so."

He looked as if he might argue.

"However, I have decided—for the moment—that this is a good suggestion, so you may keep your arms where they are."

A corner of his mouth turned up. "Thank you."

"You're welcome." She ran her hands over his chest and then followed her hands with her mouth. Her tongue.

She heard a very satisfactory gasp. Alex's hands moved to her sides, slid up toward her breasts.

"Not yet, sir." Though she was surprised to find her body was definitely interested in feeling Alex's touch.

Was that a growl she heard? She laughed up at him

and pushed herself free. "You may remove your breeches next, Mr. Wilton."

He put his hands on his hips. Was he annoyed? Embarrassed? Perhaps this was not such a good game after all.

But she had to do something. She couldn't just climb into bed, stretch herself out, and lie quietly for him to mount her as she had for Oxbury all those years. She didn't want that. Surely there was another way.

"What about your nightgown, Kate? I suggest you remove that."

"I will . . . later." What would she do if he wouldn't play along? Should she give up now? Apparently men were all the same. Perhaps if she were an experienced courtesan, she could seduce Alex, make him so mad with lust he would do anything she said. Not that she wanted to order him around, but—

His hands were at his fall. He was going to play along.

Her entire body flushed, she was certain of it. Heat flooded her face, her breasts, her belly, even the place between her legs that usually winced with the thought of the procreative act. She swallowed. She was even salivating in anticipation of seeing all of Alex's body. Did he know she was so consumed with lust?

She glanced up at his face. His eyes were hot, intense, slightly hooded. A slow smile curved his lips.

He knew.

"I'm having trouble with my buttons, Kate." His voice was huskier than normal, low and deep.

Good heavens, she was actually *throbbing*.

"Oh." The word came out in a shaky breath.

"Yes. Can you help me?"

"H-help you?"

"Please?" He thrust his hips slightly toward her.

There was no hiding that his male organ had swollen to a remarkable size.

She had never considered the issue, but in this case at least, the larger the man, the larger the . . .

"Do you suppose you might undo my buttons for me? I'm sure your smaller fingers are more nimble than mine, and, as you can see"—there was heat and a note of humor in his voice—"I am rather in a state."

"Yes, I can see that." She was the one who'd started this game. She couldn't complain when he came up with his own ideas—she'd said he could suggest things. And the thought of undressing him, while it wouldn't have occurred to her on her own, *was* enticing. "Very well, I will assist you."

Alex inhaled as Kate stepped close to him. She smelled wonderful. The scent of lavender was there as always, but now there was the added scent of heat and need. He wanted to touch her, to kiss her, to strip off her gown and trace that sweet smell of musk and woman to its source.

Her fingers fumbled with one of his buttons, brushing over the hard, aching length of him. "Ah." He closed his eyes briefly. Heaven—or rather, the beginnings of heaven. True paradise would happen shortly, in the bed behind him.

She looked up. "I didn't hurt you, did I?"

"N-no." He could barely get the word out. Hell, he could barely think. He put his hands on her shoulders. He had to steady himself somehow or he would collapse. Thankfully, Kate did not object. She was too busy with her fingers, her wonderful, teasing fingers. Finally she got the last button free.

Ah. He fell into her warm, smooth, delicate hands. Oh, God. He had never felt anything so exquisite.

Until she began to stroke him. Light, tentative touches all along his length.

He was panting as if he had just run a race.

"Are you all right, Alex?"

"No." Was that croaking in his voice? "Yes."

"Am I hurting you?"

"No. God, no."

"May I remove your breeches for you?"

"Yes." He was about to beg her to do so—or to rip them off himself. "Please."

Her hands slid around to push the cloth over his hips and down his legs. Her face, her mouth, was level with . . . dodging, in fact . . .

"May I make a suggestion?" God, he was still croaking like a frog—a lust-maddened frog.

She paused. "What do you suggest?"

"It would be very, *very* pleasant if you . . . kissed me, er, there."

Kate sat back on her heels. "*Kiss* you?"

"Ah." He could feel himself reddening, though how he could feel embarrassment when his emotions were consumed with lust was a bit of a conundrum. Was *all* of him red? He was not about to look. "Kiss. Touch me with your lips . . . there." There could be little question as to where "there" was. "Your lips and perhaps your . . . tongue."

"What an odd suggestion." Kate stared at his cock—he'd swear it grew another inch, though that was clearly impossible. "And you would like that?"

"V-very much."

"Hmm. All right." She leaned forward, and her lips brushed over him. "Like this?"

"Yes." He had never felt anything so wonderful—until her tongue rasped over his tip seconds later. And then her lips fastened onto him. She was a very quick learner.

He was going to pass out. At a minimum, he was going to fall down if he didn't sit down—or better, lie down—immediately. He tugged gently on Kate's hair.

She did not respond. Apparently the woman could be very single-minded when she wished to be. He tugged a little harder.

"Kate, sweetheart, love." He allowed a note of desperation to creep into his voice. Hell, he *was* desperate.

She finally stopped her activities and looked up.

"What is it?" She grinned, the minx. "I am having a splendid time—I do not believe I care to be interrupted."

"And I hate to have to interrupt you, my love, but I do have my physical limitations."

"You do?" She kissed him, and he'd swear the limits of that particular organ expanded again. "Where?"

He choked back a slightly hysterical laugh. "Kate, you are bringing me to my knees—literally. I am a forty-five-year-old man—though I don't know I would fare much better with this torture were I twenty-two again. I suggest—I very urgently suggest—that we adjourn to that lovely bed over there."

Alex did sound desperate, and Kate found she was ready for the next step. She stood, sliding her hands up Alex's sides. She wrapped her arms around his waist, hugging him tightly. His skin was so soft, but his body was so hard. "I think that is a splendid idea."

"I am so glad you agree." He laid his hands on her back and murmured in her ear. "And I have another idea."

"You do?" She wriggled against him, and smiled when she heard his sharply indrawn breath. He was very well-behaved though—too well-behaved. She'd like his hands to move. She'd especially like them to move downward, past her waist. "What is your idea?"

"I suggest you would be more comfortable without this

annoying nightgown. It is far too threadbare to provide any warmth." He brushed his lips over her earlobe. "I think you are generating plenty of heat on your own, but if you feel the least bit cold, I am more than willing to act as your blanket."

"Hmm. You may be correct." She tilted her head back and smiled at him. "Would you care to remove it?"

"Sweetheart, I thought you would never ask."

Alex kissed her once, quick and hard, and then let her go. She felt bereft, but she knew it was only momentary. She watched him strip off his shoes, breeches, and stockings; then he knelt and put his hands on her ankles. She waited, but nothing happened.

"I thought you were removing my nightgown."

"I am." He hands moved leisurely up her ankles to her calves. "Slowly."

"Oh." Slowly was torture—wonderful torture. She grabbed his shoulders. His muscles flexed under her fingers. His hands moved to her knees. "Perhaps you should move more quickly."

"I don't think so. After all, I am only taking my lead from you. You were very slow removing my breeches."

"I'm sure I was mis-GUID-ed." His hands had slid up over her thighs to her hips and his tongue—"Ah!"—his tongue was . . . oh, dear God. She grabbed his head. "What are you doing?"

"What do you think I'm doing? See if you can describe it." He ran his tongue over a very sensitive spot by the place where . . .

She pulled on his hair. She now completely understood his need to assume a prone position. "The bed. You wanted to go to bed."

"Yes. In a moment."

"Now."

"No." He leaned back and grinned up at her. "I strongly suggest that you allow me to take the lead in this game for a while. I'm certain you will enjoy it."

She was certain she would, too, but she wasn't about to say that. "Well, aren't you cocky?"

He laughed. "Indeed. Very cocky. Painfully so, love, thanks to your tender ministrations."

Kate felt her face flush. "I have no idea what you are alluding to."

"No? I shall be delighted to show you in just a very little while." He slid her nightgown higher, over her stomach, over her breasts. She raised her arms so he could pull it off entirely, but he stopped, holding her arms up, the nightgown over her face.

"Come on, Alex. What are you—eek!"

He was kissing her breasts, laving her nipples with his tongue, and then sucking each one into his warm, wet mouth.

Her knees gave out. If he had not been holding her, she would have fallen.

He pulled the blasted nightgown fully off and lifted her into his arms.

"I believe you wished to retire to bed, my lady?"

"Yes, you idiot." Her body was on fire. The place between her legs was wet and throbbing and hot. She had never felt this way before. "Now. Immediately. I need you."

"You do? An old woman such as yourself?"

"Yes!" She half screamed the word. He was not moving quickly enough.

He laughed. "I find this old man agrees with you wholeheartedly."

He finally reached the bed and put her down in the center of it. She didn't want to be apart from him, even for a second. She raised her arms, and he came to her, bearing her down onto the mattress. His weight felt good—so good. There was no need for further play. There was no time. She was mad for him. Desperate for him. She opened her legs, and he slid into her all in one motion. She started to come apart immediately. She grabbed his hips, moaning, twisting, pressing closer. He moved once, and she shattered completely.

In the midst of her storm, she felt him pulse in her, hot and deep.

For a few moments, there was only panting and extreme lassitude. Kate could not have raised her head if her life depended on it. Every inch of her body felt satiated. Sleep beckoned. Then Alex laughed breathlessly.

"Ah, Kate."

She smiled lazily and cracked open one eye. He kissed the tip of her nose.

"I'm too heavy for you."

He was, but she wasn't going to say so. She loved having his body on hers. Breathing was much overrated. She hadn't the air to talk, so she made a low, almost purring sound. He laughed again and lifted himself off her.

She frowned. "I'm cold." She was. Her body, damp from their loving, was chilled by his absence.

"We can't have that, can we?" He pulled up the covers and gathered her into his arms. "Better?"

She closed her eyes again. "Mmm. Much better."

"You are not being very articulate."

What was there to talk about? She was exactly where she most wanted to be—naked, in bed, her head on Alex's shoulder, his arms around her, his hand stroking her back. She was in heaven. She kept her eyes closed, turned her head, and kissed his arm.

"We should talk, Kate."

His voice had a very serious tone to it. Unpleasantly serious.

She didn't want to talk. Talking meant thinking about the past or the future. She did not want to think. She wanted to ignore everything but the present. This perfect moment. She burrowed closer into his warmth.

"Sleep," she murmured.

"I can't sleep, Kate. What if I sleep the night away? What if your maid—or Grace—discovers me here in the morning? Or what if one of the servants finds my coat and waistcoat by the tree? I have to go, sweetheart."

"No. Stay."

"I can't. We have to be discreet, Kate, unless . . ."

She frowned, opening her eyes. Obviously the fairy tale was over. "Unless what?"

"Unless you marry me."

The past and future came crashing in on her. They were far heavier than Alex had been. She sat, pulling a corner of the sheet up to cover herself. She should put on her nightgown so Marie wasn't scandalized in the morning. "You know I can't marry you."

Alex sat up, too, but he didn't bother with the sheet. It pooled below his waist, leaving his shoulders and arms, his lovely chest and belly completely exposed. She reached out to touch him, but he captured her hand in his a little roughly.

His face bore a distinctly mulish expression—eyebrows lowered, lips tight, jaw tense. What was the matter with him? Weren't men supposed to come happily to any widow's chamber, delighted to have some uncomplicated, unencumbered bed play? But Alex was . . . he certainly looked angry.

Well, she was angry, too. She had never given him any

promises, nor had she asked any of him. She'd always known this was to be a one night affair, a secret—a bit of magic—stolen from the very real, completely unavoidable everyday events of their lives.

"I know no such thing." Lud! He was almost growling. "You are of age and a widow. I am not married. What is the impediment?"

Surely he saw the obvious? "Alex, it's Grace's first Season—most likely her only Season. My brother has found her a neighbor to wed—the man's estate marches with Standen—who hates London. When—if—she marries him, she'll be stuck in the country until she dies." She leaned forward. He still had not relinquished her hand. "Don't you see? I want her to have the chance I didn't. I want her to meet other men—"

"You met other men, Kate. You met me."

"Yes, I know, but . . ." It was too hard to explain. Or maybe it was too simple. Maybe she just hoped, if given the opportunity, Grace would have more courage than she had had. Grace was older after all—twenty-five to her seventeen. Perhaps Grace would follow her heart instead of Standen's will.

"Splendid." Alex's hand on her fingers tightened to the point of pain. "So Lady Grace will be able to make some poor idiot like my nephew fall in love with her and then break his heart when she marries another, just like you did."

"No." She felt as if he had slapped her. Worse. As if he had squeezed her heart as hard as he was squeezing her fingers. "I didn't." She sucked in her breath as his grip tightened even more. "Ouch! Alex, you're hurting me."

He almost snarled, but he loosened his hold, moving to put her hand flat against his chest. She could feel his heart hammering against her palm.

"You think you didn't break my heart? God, Kate."

She tried to laugh. The mood definitely needed lightening. "Of course I didn't. It is beating quite vigorously now."

It was as if she hadn't spoken.

"You have no idea, no bloody idea, what I felt when Standen told me of your engagement. I wanted to die." He looked away. His nostrils flared, his mouth formed a thin, white line.

She dropped her eyes to stare at his hand where it pressed hers to his chest. His heart still raced under her fingers.

Her own heart lurched in sickening thuds.

"Why didn't you tell me, Kate? Why did you lead me on, let me hope, let me embarrass myself in front of your brother? How he must have been laughing in his sleeve."

Kate found her voice. "I didn't lead you on."

He skewered her with his eyes. "Damn it, Kate, the bloody announcement of your engagement to Oxbury was in the paper that very morning. I saw it when I got back from my interview with your brother. And then you married so quickly. The gossips dined out on that for weeks, everyone giggling over how Oxbury's lusty passions must have necessitated such a hasty wedding."

"No." How horrible. Thankfully, she hadn't known what tales the tabbies had been chasing. "They weren't actually saying such things, were they?"

"They were."

Kate looked so pale, so shocked, Alex felt a twinge of compassion for her. Only a twinge. She could never be suffering what he had suffered.

He'd been so full of hope when he'd gone to visit her brother that day. He'd known he'd have rough ground to get over—he wasn't a fool—but he'd truly thought love would conquer all.

What romantic twaddle!

And, idiot that he was, he hadn't believed Standen when he'd said Kate was engaged. All the way back to Dawson House, he'd planned how he'd ride to the country and spirit her away to Gretna. He'd marry her over the anvil, officiated by the blacksmith, just as Luke had married Harriet, only he'd be smarter. He'd take her to the Continent until she'd given him a babe, maybe two, so Standen would have to recognize—or at least tolerate—their union.

And then he'd seen the announcement in *The Morning Post*.

Kate was tugging on his hand. She'd let go of the sheet, exposing her beautiful breasts.

He didn't feel even the slightest stirrings of lust.

"Alex, I wasn't engaged when I went into Alvord's garden with you."

He snorted. Did she expect him to believe that Banbury tale? He'd been a fool once—once was enough.

Or had he already been a fool again?

"Why did you come to London now, Kate? To find a wealthy husband—or to be a merry widow?"

"I came to chaperone Grace, of course." Kate hesitated. Her face went still, as if she was coming to some decision—and then she smiled. God, she was so damn seductive, he felt her siren call even through his pain and anger.

"But I find I like being a merry widow as well." She ran her hand down his chest. "I liked what we just did very, very much. Shall we do it again?"

He stared at her. How could she say that so lightly? All that had just happened between them—it must have been only physical for her, only bodies joining, his body as good as any other man's. He *was* a fool.

Damn it all, the pain was unbearable, worse even than when he'd learned of her engagement. He wanted to hurt her back.

"No, once was enough for me." She flinched—good. "I came just for old time's sake, you know. To scratch an itch—see what I'd been missing. I've satisfied my curiosity, thank you. I've no need to repeat the experience."

He made himself climb out of the bed when he wanted to fling himself out. He ignored her shocked expression as he pulled on his clothes. Even knowing she didn't have a functioning heart, it hurt him to hurt her. He was most definitely an idiot.

He went out the window in a blur of agony. He was never going to speak—he was never going to see— Lady Oxbury again.

Chapter 9

"Where is your uncle?"

Lord Dawson choked on a mouthful of champagne. He muffled his coughing with his handkerchief as he peered around a pillar to locate the source of the hissing. Lady Grace Belmont glared at him.

Damn. He felt like he'd been kicked in the gut. She was so beautiful—so . . . vivid. She made all the other girls back in Easthaven's ballroom fade completely from his thoughts—not that any of the insipid misses had managed to find a foothold in his brain box anyway.

Grace was looking especially alluring tonight in a green dress with a deeply plunging neck that admirably emphasized her very large, very lovely—

Her fan appeared to block his gaze. A pity, but just as well. He could not allow himself to be seduced. He was not in charity with her at the moment. He sent that thought directly, with emphasis, to his most argumentative organ.

He might never be in charity with her again. He'd come tonight with the firm resolve to put her behind him and start his bloody matrimonial hunt all over. He was just having one more glass of champagne here in the refreshment room before venturing back into the terpsichorean fray.

"And a very good evening to you, too, Lady Grace."

Her frown deepened—she had detected his sarcasm. Not surprising; it had been thick enough for the most obtuse member of the *ton* to perceive—and Grace was not obtuse.

Damn. He would not think of Alvord's garden and the way her expression had softened when he'd mentioned his mother. So the woman had a heart, unlike her father. Most women had hearts . . . though not encased in such lovely, sumptuous packaging.

There, it was much easier to tame lust than . . . another emotion.

Grace thrust her jaw forward. "I asked you a question, my lord."

"Did you? Then perhaps you noticed I did not answer it."

He thought for a moment she would haul off and punch him. No ladylike slapping for his—

No, not his. Never his. He could not marry her; he could never marry a woman so closely related to the female who'd wounded Alex. He didn't know the details, of course. Alex hadn't said. Alex wouldn't talk, but the look in his eyes the morning after Alvord's ball when he'd left London had spoken more eloquently than any words. David hadn't seen that look since Grandda and Grandmamma had died. Something—someone—had hurt Alex deeply.

Lady Oxbury.

It could not be a coincidence Alex had left Town the morning after he'd spent the entire night . . . where? David would wager his estate Alex had been with Grace's aunt. The woman was as cruel as her brother, Standen.

Was Grace that cruel as well?

No. That he couldn't believe. Grace had been only kind to him—

Blast it, was he flushing?

"Don't be a complete ass." Grace was still hissing like a snake. "We have to talk. Your uncle has hurt Aunt Kate horribly."

He almost dropped his champagne glass. "My uncle has injured your aunt?" He pressed his lips together. He was close to shouting. Two elderly women—Lady Amanda Wallen-Smyth and Mrs. Fallwell—stopped their conversation to look at him. He forced himself to smile politely until they moved off, then adopted his own serpent-like sibilance. "Are you insane?"

"I most certainly am not. I—"

"Here is your lemonade, Lady Grace."

They both turned to stare at the new arrival. Mr. Belham was not a feast for anyone's eyes. His face was all nose. He had no chin to speak of, and his eyes were small and sadly dwarfed by his overwhelming snout.

Grace snatched the glass from Mr. Belham's hand.

"Thank you, sir. If you will excuse me now, I have matters of importance to discuss with Lord Dawson."

Mr. Belham's small chin dropped.

"Go on." She made a shooing motion with her hands. "You are very much in the way here. Go back to the ballroom and ask some poor miss to stand up with you."

"Ah." Mr. Belham's tiny eyes almost started from his head. "Er, yes. Of course. I'll just be on my way then."

"Splendid. Do enjoy yourself." Grace turned back to Baron Dawson as Mr. Belham stumbled out of the refreshment room. She was delighted to get rid of the annoying little man. He would never have trapped her into accompanying him if she'd had all her wits about her.

But she'd been looking for Lord Dawson and so had missed Mr. Belham's approach.

It was just as well. The man had helped her find her quarry—her very angry quarry. What reason had he to be in such high dudgeon? It was her aunt who was suffering.

She looked up at him, and her heart stuttered. He was so large and so incredibly handsome, even with a pronounced scowl twisting his features.

When Papa got so angry, she always tried to placate him, even while her own anger twisted in her gut. She felt like a dog with its tail between its legs, cowering from the blows of his harsh words. She never argued with him, never defied him. The only time she'd ever let him see her temper was when she'd decided to come on this trip to London. Even then he hadn't believed she'd actually go until she was seated in the carriage with the steps up and the door closed.

But she didn't feel like cowering before Lord Dawson. No, she felt like going at him hammer and tongs. Instead of anger or fear, she felt an odd thrill, a shiver of excitement. She wasn't at all worried he would hurt her verbally or physically. Rather, she thought they would . . . after a healthy argument they would . . .

Of course they wouldn't! She ducked her head and took a sip of her drink.

David smiled slightly. After riding roughshod over Belham, was his—no, not his—was the lady suddenly turning shy? It really was unfortunate he could not pursue her—she was such an enticing mix of fire and diffidence.

It was so damn good to see her. He should be furious— he *was* furious—but he was also bloody delighted to be standing just inches from her.

"Lemonade, Grace?"

She flushed. "I find champagne does not agree with me."

"Shot the cat, did you?" He'd wondered if she'd had too much to drink at Alvord's ball.

She shot him a very quelling look. "You could have prevented me from consuming so many glasses."

"If you'll remember, I did try to dissuade you, but you insisted you would be fine, that you had drunk champagne before."

"And I had. Just not in that quantity, apparently." Grace shuddered slightly. "Well, it will not happen again. I am foreswearing the drink for as long as I live."

"Oh, I hardly think you need to take so extreme a course."

"*You* were not the one emptying—well, enough of that. As I said, Lord Dawson, we need to talk. It is vitally important." She glanced around the room, her eyes pausing when they touched upon Lady Amanda and Mrs. Fallwell. "Somewhere more private, I believe."

"You are not afraid to be private with me?" He was teasing her now. He couldn't help it. He'd work on being angry later, when he didn't have her enticing, lovely, lush, wonderful body before him—and her delightfully prickly personality. Now he couldn't help but be happy, couldn't keep lo . . . lust from blooming in his . . . heart.

And what if Grace had something truly important to say? Then perhaps he wouldn't have to be angry at all. He could just be . . . hmm. In a nice private location.

Grace flushed, her eyes wavering slightly before she straightened her spine, lifted her chin, and gave him a scornful look. "Don't be ridiculous. I'm certain your poor male mind can focus on something other than seduction for a few minutes."

He coughed. Poor, naïve girl.

She put her hand on his arm and tugged. "Come. Let's find a place where we can have a serious discussion."

"Very well." He nodded at Lady Amanda and Mrs. Fallwell as he walked past them. The ladies nodded back, their eyes gleaming with suspicion.

He should not go with Grace. He was opening himself to malicious gossip. It would not help his matrimonial prospects. He wanted an unexceptional bride, didn't he? Going off into a private room with another woman would certainly compromise that goal.

And yet . . . Gossip be damned. He didn't really want an unexceptional bride—he wanted Grace. If Grace had a rational explanation for whatever had transpired between Lady Oxbury and Alex, he wanted to hear it.

She peered into a small room and nodded. "This should suit." She pulled him over the threshold and shut the door.

"Aren't you being a bit indiscreet, Lady Grace?" Not that he was complaining. The room was hardly more than a closet. There was a single, uncomfortable-looking chair, a small table, and a bookshelf with excruciatingly boring titles such as *A Discourse on Crop Rotation* and *Some Thoughts on the Topic of Sheep Shearing*. It must be the room where unwelcome guests were deposited.

The limited space meant he had to stand very, very close to Grace.

"Aren't you being a bit idiotic, Lord Dawson? As I said, we have a serious issue to discuss. Are your animal instincts so strong you cannot control them long enough for rational discourse?" Grace hoped her voice didn't waver. This room was smaller than she'd thought—and Lord Dawson was so large. He filled the space rather alarmingly.

David confined himself to a noncommittal grunt. The

air was rapidly filling with Grace's scent, a mix of soap and lemon and . . . Grace. His animal instincts were urging him to engage in some truly idiotic behavior. Frustration made his voice harsher than he intended. "Get to your point, Lady Grace."

"Very well." Grace pulled her thoughts away from Lord Dawson's shoulders and pointed her fan at him. "Something is seriously amiss with my aunt, and I firmly believe your uncle is the cause."

David crossed his arms to keep from grabbing Grace and pulling her against him. "Can you be more specific?"

"Yes, I can. I will grant you my powers of observation the night of the Alvord ball"—Grace flushed—"were not at their sharpest, but I would swear my aunt and your uncle were getting along famously. Remember their waltz?" How could anyone forget? Watching them had been extremely disconcerting. Had she and Lord Dawson looked so scandalous when they'd been waltzing?

Grace shivered slightly. She had certainly felt scandalous. Well, not scandalous precisely. She hadn't been giving their appearance one second's thought. She'd been too busy feeling, enjoying having Lord Dawson's arms about her and his chest so close . . .

She unfurled her fan and plied it vigorously. It was very warm in this tiny room.

David nodded. He, too, had thought all was well with Alex and Lady Oxbury when they were waltzing. Extremely well, if Alex's woolgathering on the walk back to Dawson House was any indication. The problem must have occurred later.

"Aunt Kate was very distracted on the ride home," Lady Grace was saying. "Almost agitated. But the next morning she was different. She was still agitated, but, well—"

Grace frowned, idly tapping her fan against her hand in thought. David contemplated that movement. She just happened to be holding her fan near her lovely breas— dress. Her lovely dress that so delightfully revealed her large, well-shaped—

Focus. He needed to focus on the question at hand— not the lovely—the things he would most like to have in hand. If he and Lady Grace could mend the rift between her aunt and his uncle—if it were indeed just some silly misunderstanding—he would be free to lust after Grace again with a clear conscience. That would make him very, very happy.

"Pay attention, Lord Dawson." Grace poked him with her fan; he forced himself to look at her eyes, not her . . . right, not her, hmm. She had very nice eyes, too. Green with flecks of brown and yellow.

"Aunt Kate has periods when she is pleasantly be-mused. I'll be talking to her and realize her thoughts are miles away. She'll just stare off into space, with this funny, dreamy sort of smile. Other times I'll come upon her and it's clear she's been crying. Whenever we're out in society, she keeps glancing around as if she's looking for someone. And then when we saw you here alone, she turned white as a ghost."

David wanted to ask if *she* had been looking for *him*, but he stopped himself in time.

Grace frowned. "I think your uncle must have come by Oxbury House after the ball. Someone was throwing pebbles at Aunt Kate's window, though how Mr. Wilton knew which window was my aunt's . . ." Grace shrugged, caus-ing her lovely shoulders—and, well, other things—to move delightfully. "But who else could it have been? And they must have spoken, don't you think?"

He grunted. He'd wager they'd done a lot more than

speak. Alex would not have looked so stricken—would not have fled London—if he'd simply engaged in conversation.

Grace poked him with her fan again. "So, my lord, tell me where your blasted uncle is."

He pushed her fan aside and stepped back—as far as the tiny room would allow him. "Home at Clifton Hall."

Grace gaped at him. "What? He's left London entirely?"

"I've just said so, haven't I?"

"But that's ridiculous. How could he have done such a thing?" She brandished her fan, but he caught it and took it away from her. He was tired of being poked.

"Very easily. He packed a bag and saddled his horse. I sent the rest of his gear along later."

"Later? How long has he been gone?"

What harm could there be in telling her? "He left the morning after Alvord's ball."

She snapped her jaw shut. "I knew it! The man is a rake, a rogue, a . . . a complete scoundrel."

How dare she say such things about Alex? For once the passion he felt had nothing to do with lust. "If you were a man, Lady Grace, you would be naming your seconds."

Grace bit her lip. Lord Dawson had stiffened up like a poker. She could tell he was going to storm out of this little room at any moment, all high in the instep.

Well, she was angry, too, but that wasn't going to solve Aunt Kate's problems. She needed to calm down and calm this glowering man down as well.

She held up a hand—and then two as Lord Dawson approached her, clearly intent on getting to the door as quickly as possible. She pushed against his chest. He would have to knock her down to get out—which was beginning to look like a distinct possibility. He grabbed her hands as if he would remove two cockroaches bold enough to sully his person.

"Lord Dawson, storming off like this will do no good." He was not listening to her. He'd already discarded her hands and was stepping around her. She lunged and grabbed his lapels. "My lord, wait. I apologize. I spoke in haste. I retract, most humbly, my comments about your uncle."

He finally paused. He was still looking at her as if she were the lowest class of vermin, but at least he was looking at her.

She loosened her grasp, smoothing his lapels where she'd wrinkled them—but she was careful to keep her body between him and the door.

"Let's be rational. I love my aunt, and you love"—He was glaring at her again. Apparently "love" was not a manly enough word to use—"hold your uncle in high esteem." Better. Lord Dawson relaxed, at least slightly. "I'm sure we both want them to be happy." He nodded. Good.

"It also seems clear they cannot address the problem, whatever it is, dispassionately."

He snorted at that. "Bloody right." He grimaced. "Pardon my language."

She waved her hand. "Please, don't refine on it." He was talking to her, which was all that mattered at the moment. "It's equally clear to me that your uncle's chosen method of dealing with the issue"—Lord Dawson straightened, his face darkening. Oh, dear, she was going to lose him—"which is *perfectly* understandable" —he softened slightly—"will not result in a satisfactory solution."

"I don't see what is unsatisfactory about it."

Grace kept herself from rolling her eyes, but just

barely. Of course he didn't see the problem—he was a man, and most men were completely blind to the many emotional facets of an issue. They saw only the one side that was right under their nose. Look at her father—no, she would prefer not to look at him.

"Is your uncle happy, Lord Dawson?"

He frowned. "Well . . . no."

"Has he been happy—really happy—recently, or for as long as you can remember?"

"N-no."

"Does his unhappiness have something to do with my aunt?"

"Damn right, it bloody well does."

"Exactly. So how will hiding away on his estate make him happy?"

"He is not hiding."

She could argue with that, but she did not care to get into a spitting match with the baron. His lowered brows and set chin did not bespeak an open, conciliatory mind. "Well, perhaps not. Yet don't you agree that while leaving London allows him to avoid whatever—"

Lord Dawson snorted and raised a very obnoxious eyebrow.

"—all right, *whoever* is causing his pain, it won't make the pain go away. He has to address the root of the problem. He needs to meet with my aunt—"

"He did meet with your aunt. I believe it was that meeting that sent him back to Clifton Hall."

"Pardon me, my lord, I mean no disrespect, but that's ridiculous! How could a conversation, a *short* conversation, carried on between my aunt in her room and your uncle outside—are you all right?" The man had turned red and was making a choking noise.

"Yes. I'm fine." He cleared his throat. "I believe the . . . conversation . . . was a little more intense than that."

"Were you there?"

"Good God, no!"

Why was he so appalled? "Well, then you can't know, can you?"

Lord Dawson made some odd, sputtering sounds and wouldn't meet her eyes. Very strange.

"And even if they *had* had a very complete discussion, which we do not know that they did—"

Lord Dawson was now making strangling sounds.

"—running away"—He glared at her—"that is, leaving Town so that they cannot meet again indicates the issue has not yet been resolved."

"You don't know that."

She did roll her eyes then. "I do know that his flight—um, departure—means your uncle still feels pain. Do you deny that?"

He certainly looked as if he would like to, but honesty won over loyalty. "No."

"Exactly. And I'm certain my aunt is still hurting."

Lord Dawson made a very rude noise. Her fingers itched to wrap themselves around his neck and squeeze. She took a deep breath—and noticed his gaze drop to her chest.

The man was absolutely maddening. She'd told Aunt Kate she needed a fichu for this dress, but Aunt Kate would not listen to reason—and Grace hadn't had the heart to argue with her, her aunt had been so despondent. She snatched her fan off the table where Lord Dawson had placed it and unfurled it, directing his attention back to her face.

"My lord, your attitude is not helping matters. You have apparently taken a dislike to my aunt." He made another derogatory sound. She pressed her lips together and counted to ten. She must remain calm. She could not let her infernal temper get the better of her.

"That is your prerogative. However, it has nothing to say to the problem at hand. You need to put aside your personal prejudices"—another scoffing snort. She was about ready to kick the nodcock in the shins . . . or some softer, more sensitive location—"to focus on what is best for your uncle." No need to mention Aunt Kate as well; she'd heard enough disparaging sounds for the time being.

Lord Dawson's nostrils flared; his lips formed a tight, thin line. He was not persuaded, but at least he was listening.

"I firmly believe your uncle and my aunt need to come to some understanding so they aren't tortured by their past." She stepped forward, laid her hand on Lord Dawson's chest, and looked up at him, hoping he could discern the sincerity in her eyes.

"And if they cannot manage to see that, then the people who care for them—you and I—need to. I think we should find a way to bring them together physically"—now why did the man's face turn red?—"so they cannot run from each other. If they are stuck in the same place, they may have a rational, thorough discussion. They are both intelligent adults. They must realize it would be much more comfortable if they could move about in society without constantly fearing they might encounter one another."

"You may have a point." Lord Dawson gazed down at her, his eyes hooded. She could not read his expression, but at least the anger had left his face. He seemed relaxed.

His gloved hand covered hers where it rested on his waistcoat, his fingers almost absentmindedly stroking the back of her glove. Even through the layers of cloth she felt . . . something. Strength. Heat. Possessiveness? Her other hand came up to join its mate. Heat curled low in her stomach.

He smiled slightly.

No, he was not relaxed. There was a . . . not tension, exactly. An energy. That was it. An air of expectation, of watchfulness about him.

Suddenly the passion between them was no longer anger.

She wet her lips, and his eyes followed her tongue. Her mouth felt swollen, hot. She opened it slightly. Was she panting?

Now she knew the look in his eyes. He was a cat playing with a mouse—and she was the mouse.

Oh, how she wanted to be caught.

His face moved down toward hers. His lips were so close . . . She tilted her chin—

"Grace!"

"Ack!" She jumped back and tripped on her skirt. She would have crashed into the bookcase if Lord Dawson hadn't caught her. "Aunt Kate, what are you doing here?"

"Acting as your chaperone." Aunt Kate quickly stepped into the room and shut the door behind her.

It was very crowded with three adults in such a small space, especially when one of them was glaring at the other two.

"How did you . . . er." Grace cleared her throat and looked at Lord Dawson.

Lord Dawson examined the ceiling.

"How did I find you? I asked Mrs. Fallwell and Lady Wallen-Smyth. They thought you had come this way. They were correct." Aunt Kate looked pointedly at Grace. "Mrs. Fallwell, by the bye, is a noted London gossip."

"Oh."

"Oh, indeed. Fortunately tonight she is much more interested in the Duke of Alvord and Miss Hamilton, so I think your"—Aunt Kate sent Lord Dawson a scathing look. He received it with a completely bland expression—"little indiscretion will go unnoticed if we proceed directly to the ballroom."

Grace frowned. But she and Lord Dawson had yet to come up with a plan to mend the rift between her aunt and Mr. Wilton. "You go ahead, Aunt Kate. I'll be along in just a minute."

"What?" Aunt Kate's mouth dropped open.

"There's no need to look so shocked. Lord Dawson and I merely have a few things we still need to attend to."

"I'll bet you do. Things like the things you were attending to when I entered this room?"

"Ah." Grace felt her cheeks burning. "No, er, that is . . ." She looked at Lord Dawson. He was examining a gouge in the room's pitiful little table. "I'm sure Lord Dawson—"

"Exactly. I am very sure Lord Dawson . . ." Aunt Kate stared at the baron. The baron stared at his fingernails. "Good evening, sir."

Lord Dawson inclined his head as Aunt Kate yanked Grace out of the room.

Damn. David collapsed—carefully—onto the room's lone chair. It was just as uncomfortable as it looked, but he didn't plan to stay long. Once he gave Grace enough time to get to the ballroom and perhaps join a set, he could leave this infernal room.

Well, he also had to give a certain organ time to resume its normal proportions.

Blast it all, why did Lady Oxbury have to arrive at just that moment? A second later and he would have had Grace in his arms, his mouth on hers, his tongue deep . . .

All right, so it was probably best Lady Oxbury had arrived when she did. Best, but damn frustrating.

He dropped his head back against the wall and let out a pent-up breath. He should think about Grace's words not her—Right. Think about what she'd said.

He hated to admit it, but Grace was correct. Alex wasn't happy, and he likely wouldn't be happy until he resolved his issues with Lady Oxbury. But how to get him to accomplish that feat? When the man had left for Clifton Hall, he'd acted like he never wished to see Grace's aunt again.

David turned his head to look at the bookcase. A small, black spider dangled from one of the shelves. It appeared to be floating in air until you stared closely enough to see the thin strand of silk supporting it.

Grace was correct about another point as well. The first step to getting Alex and Lady Oxbury to discuss their differences had to be getting them in the same location. Alex was not going to come back to Town, but with all the gossips in London, it wouldn't be a good choice anyway. Some other—any other—location was preferable. The last thing Alex needed was the gabble-grinders sniffing around him. He valued his privacy too much.

So if Alex would not come to Town, Lady Oxbury would have to go to the country. But she couldn't very well visit Clifton Hall, and Riverview was now a bachelor establishment as well. Neutral ground would be better in any event, but where? Whom did he know who would be willing to host a house party and who had a wife or mother or other suitable female to act as hostess?

His mind was a complete blank. He couldn't think of a single name.

The spider slowly drifted down to the next shelf and

started crawling over the books. He watched it scale *A Few Theories on Household Management*.

He didn't know many of the *ton*. He'd never been to Eton—Grandda and Grandmamma had thought it better that he be schooled at home. He'd spent a few years at Oxford, but all the other men there had seemed little more than boys, more interested in pranks and whoring than their academic studies. He'd had very little in common with them.

Perhaps Lady Grace knew a likely host.

The spider moved on to *Several Highly Efficacious Tonics and Cordials*.

They definitely needed to arrange a house party. The country with its greater privacy—and more opportunities for assignations—would be a far more likely location for Alex and Lady Oxbury to effect a reconciliation. And if Alex and Lady Oxbury were no longer estranged . . . He smiled at the spider. He could build his own little web to catch a certain spirited young lady.

There were so many delightful spots in the country to steal a kiss or two. Picnics by the lake, strolls through the gardens, a ramble through the woods. Rules were always more relaxed there and, in any event, Grace's meddlesome chaperone would be too busy with his uncle to be popping into every secluded room or leafy bower. He should be able to have Grace saying "I do" to any number of delightful activities.

He would be certain to procure a special license before they left just in case he could persuade her all the way to the altar.

He consulted his pocket watch. Had enough time elapsed since Lady Grace departed? Surely so. He would go out into the ballroom—

Wait a minute. He'd forgotten Viscount Motton. He'd seen him here tonight.

The viscount was around his own age and brilliant—he'd been involved in a few investments with him. Even better, his estate was a long day's ride from Clifton Hall—close enough to be almost in Alex's neighborhood, but far enough that Alex would have to stay over. Hmm. And if he were not mistaken, Alex had spent part of the trip up to Town nattering on about some crop rotation scheme Motton was trying at Lakeland that he might want to implement himself. He'd even been talking about stopping by Motton's estate. Perfect.

Now he only had to come up with some subtle way to suggest a casual acquaintance hold a house party in the middle of the Season for his benefit.

Right. That would be easy.

He stood and straightened his waistcoat. Best be—

The door swung open with an inordinate amount of giggling. Two very surprised people stared at him. He bowed.

"Good evening, Lord Featherstone; Mrs. Fallwell."

"Ah." They gaped at him, apparently unable to compose a coherent sentence between them.

"I was just leaving."

"Ah."

He bowed again, stepped around them, and walked briskly toward the ballroom. He did not look back.

He did not want to know . . . he did not want to think about anything concerning the old roué, the society gossip, and that very small room.

Chapter 10

Hermes was barking . . . in her ear?

Kate cracked open an eye. Hermes's large orbs stared back at her. She groaned.

"Go back to bed. It's the middle of the night."

Hermes begged to differ.

"Ow!" He brushed up against her breast. It was uncommonly sensitive, perhaps because her courses were a few days late.

Her courses were never late.

She must have some odd malady. She was so tired, and she felt bloated and out of sorts all the time.

Hermes was still staring at her; absently, she stroked his ears.

It wasn't surprising she was tired. She'd been keeping most irregular hours, and when she did find her bed, she didn't sleep well.

She sniffed, wiping away a sudden tear as she pictured the primary reason for her lack of sleep. Damn it all, men were supposed to want bed frolic without any emotional complications. Alex should have been *happy* she wasn't demanding anything of him.

She'd had a wonderful time, and then he'd had to go and ruin it by asking her to marry him. She couldn't marry him. He must know that. Why had he teased her with the offer?

She smiled slightly. But oh, what he'd done with her in this bed. His touch had been magical. There was no resemblance—none at all—between bed activities with Alex and with poor Oxbury. Just thinking about Alex made her body throb in embarrassing places. She craved his touch . . .

But she could never have it again. She couldn't flirt with scandal by carrying on an affair with him—and, in any event, he'd said he never wanted to repeat the experience. And then he'd left her—and London—so abruptly.

He had hurt her—but she had hurt him. Why had she played the merry widow then? She should have given him the truth.

Had she broken his heart? Well, they were even. Her heart was in pieces as well.

She sniffed again. She was crying far more easily these days, too. She must get more rest.

Hermes licked her face.

"Stop it, you silly dog." She lifted the covers. "Here, as a special treat you can sleep next to me. But this is a once in a lifetime opportunity, you know, so do not get used to it." She was very fond of Hermes, but she'd learned early on that letting him sleep in her bed gave her uncontrollable sneezing fits.

She closed her eyes to give him the proper example.

His very wet tongue accosted her cheek once more.

"*Please* go back to sleep. It's too early to get up."

"But it's not, my lady." Marie pulled open the bed curtains.

"Wha—?" Why was Marie here? And her bedchamber was full of light . . . but it faced west. "What time is it?"

"Almost two o'clock."

"In the *afternoon?*" She'd never slept that late. She prided herself on being an early riser. She must definitely be sickening.

"Aye. Jem took Hermes for his morning walk, but I thought ye'd want to take him out now."

It was two o'clock! How was that possible? She'd dragged Grace away from the Wainwright ball early last night because she'd been too exhausted to stay another minute.

"I brought ye some chocolate."

"Ah." Chocolate. A nice cup of chocolate would settle her nerves. She struggled to sit up—and inhaled the thick, sweet scent. Ohh. She put her hand over her mouth. "I don't want any chocolate this morning—I mean afternoon. Take it away. Please."

Why was Marie giving her that look? And why was she staring at her chest? She looked down at her thin nightgown. She'd become attached to the old thing in the last few weeks since—she blushed . . . and saw her breasts darken slightly.

Obviously the garment was too threadbare.

Were her small breasts looking a little larger? And a little . . . different?

Ridiculous. She crossed her arms over them and winced. They were definitely sensitive.

"Yer courses are late, aren't they, my lady?"

Marie would know since she collected the soiled laundry. "A little late."

"How late?"

What was this, the Grand Inquisition? "I don't know.

A few days. Perhaps a week." She was feeling nauseous. Was there a basin handy? She might have need of it.

Marie was frowning at her. "If I did nae know any better, I'd say ye were increasing."

"*What*?!"

"Increasing. Ye know. Breeding. In the family way. With child."

"Ga." She dove for the cupboard by the bed and flung it open. Thank God! She grabbed the basin and emptied her stomach. "Ohh." She wiped her mouth with the back of her hand.

Marie gave her another look. Kate clutched the basin more tightly. At the moment it seemed like her sole anchor to reality.

"But I couldn't . . . It's not p-possible . . ."

"Aye, I know."

"I'm forty years old."

"*That's* not the impossible part. Many a woman past forty finds herself with a babe. As long as ye still get yer courses, ye can still get a child."

"Oh." Surely she knew that—she just hadn't thought about it. She'd been so regular all these years. And Oxbury had exercised his marital rights several times a month—almost daily when they were first married— yet she'd never conceived. "But I'm barren."

Marie shrugged. "Perhaps the fault was with yer lord. I've seen more than one barren woman bury her first husband and have a quiverful of children with her second." Marie fixed her with a penetrating gaze. "And *that's* the part that makes it impossible for ye to be increasing—ye have no husband." Her gaze sharpened. "Or do ye?"

"Of course not. You know I'm not married. Don't be ridiculous."

"Ah, but church vows aren't needed for a babe. It just takes a man in yer bed with lively seed and a strong plow."

She must be as red as a beet. She could barely get her breath. Could she be . . . had she and Alex made . . . but they had only done it once . . .

"Had ye a man in yer bed, my lady?"

"Ah . . ."

"And it needn't be a bed, ye know. A quick poke in the garden will do the trick as well."

"But . . ."

Marie crossed her arms. "Ye may as well tell me, my lady. There's no point in lying. I'll know soon enough when yer courses don't come and yer belly swells."

"Ah. Ah. Oh." She threw up again and then burst into tears.

Marie took the basin carefully from her hands, sat down on the bed next to her, and gathered her into her arms. Kate hugged her and sobbed into her sturdy shoulder.

"Ye know, my lady," Marie murmured in her ear, "ye need to send a note to Mr. Wilton."

She was increasing.

What in God's name was she going to do?

Hermes tugged on his leash, pulling Kate down the hall. It was a good thing he knew the way to the park. She couldn't find her way out of her room at the moment. She was locked in a nightmare.

Could she be increasing? After all those years with Oxbury, month after month of disappointment . . .

Marie must be wrong.

But her courses were over a week late and they were never late. And she'd never felt this way before—so tired and . . . odd.

It could be the strain of coming to Town, couldn't it, and of seeing Alex again?

Alex. She had done much more than see him. She had tasted him and touched him and felt him deep inside her . . .

Dear God. She *must* be increasing.

She grabbed hold of the banister before she pitched down the stairs. If she fell, she might hurt the baby.

The *baby* . . . ohh.

"Are you all right, Aunt Kate?"

"Wha—?" Grace was standing next to her. Where had she come from? "Yes. No. Ah."

Grace and Hermes stared at her.

"Perhaps you're sickening." Grace laid her hand on Kate's arm. "I was worried when you slept so late, but maybe . . . do you think you need to go back to bed? I'll take Hermes out for you."

Going back to her room, pulling the covers over her head, hiding from . . . No, that would do no good. Even if she hid in her room for all nine months, she'd still have a baby at the end . . .

Dear God, a baby! How was she going to tell Alex? Marie was right. He deserved to know. But the man was forty-five years old. He could not want a child. And she'd promised him she was barren before he'd even ventured into her bed. Would he think she'd lied to him intentionally? He thought she'd lied about her engagement to Oxbury.

This wasn't the sort of news one put in a letter. She should tell him face to face—but he had left London.

And if Marie knew Alex was the father, would all the *ton* guess as well?

She wet her lips and swallowed. "N-no. It will do me good to get out, I'm sure."

Grace was still frowning at her. "Why don't I accompany you then? You still look pale."

"All right. Yes. That would be fine. Delightful."

"Let me just go get my bonnet. Wait for me in the entry hall, all right?"

Kate nodded. Grace gave her another worried look and then hurried to her room. Kate stumbled down the stairs.

Sykes was standing by the hall table. "Good afternoon, my lady."

"Good afternoon, Mr. Sykes." She clutched Hermes's leash more tightly. Mr. Sykes looked unpleasantly serious. Surely he didn't know about the scandalous state of her womb? "Do you have something to say?"

Sykes let out a gusty, rather depressing sigh. "Unfortunately I do, my lady. The new Lord Oxbury has sent word he is coming up to Town. He should be arriving shortly. I'm sure you understand, but the staff will need to move you and Lady Grace to other accommodations as Lord Oxbury"—Sykes swallowed as if he'd just had to down a draught of extremely nasty medicine—"will expect to be occupying the master suite."

"Of course, Mr. Sykes. I understand completely." Dear heavens! The situation had just got horribly worse. Why was the Weasel coming to Town? He was certain to note the moment her waist got half an inch larger—though he shouldn't care. Oxbury had been dead over a year. There was no chance anyone would think the baby legitimate.

She let herself down slowly onto a handy chair.

If she didn't marry, her baby would be a bastard.

"My lady, are you feeling quite the thing?"

She couldn't meet Sykes's eyes—she merely nodded and waved a hand in his direction. Hermes came over and put his paws on her knees, barking and waving his tail in an encouraging fashion.

He was a dog. He did not understand the depths of her despair.

What would the Weasel do when he discovered she was increasing? Would he throw her out into the street?

Of course, she *was* forty years old. It was possible she would miscarry . . . She put a protective hand over her middle. She didn't want any harm to come to her baby—hers and Alex's.

She sniffed and searched for her handkerchief.

"Lady Grace, please, look to Lady Oxbury," she heard Sykes say. "I fear she is unwell."

"Aunt Kate." Grace put a hand on her shoulder and bent to look searchingly into her face. Kate focused on Hermes. "Are you certain you're all right?" She dropped her voice. "Is it that time of month, perhaps?"

Kate's head shot up. *That* time of month? She began to laugh, she feared a touch hysterically. "No. It's not. Definitely not."

Grace stepped back, looking hurt. Thankfully, Sykes—probably assuming her malaise was a female complaint—had taken himself off.

"I sometimes get weepy at that time," Grace said.

Kate stood. She had to get out of this house and into the park, into the open, the fresh air. She had to get a grip on her emotions. "Yes, I know. I thank you for your concern, it's just . . ." She let out a long breath. What could she say? "Mr. Sykes just told me the Weasel is coming to London."

"Oh." Grace grimaced. "I see why you might be crying."

"Yes, well, I am better now, and Hermes has been very patient. Shall we go?"

* * *

"Did you see Miss Hamilton dancing with Mr. Dunlap at the ball last night? Or, more to the point, did you see the Duke of Alvord watching Miss Hamilton dancing?" Grace was grasping for conversational straws. This was her fifth attempt; if she met with as little success this time as she had with her previous efforts, she was going to give up and just sit quietly on the park bench next to Aunt Kate watching Hermes chase squirrels.

"Hmm?" Aunt Kate fiddled with Hermes's leash and stared off into space.

"Alvord did not look at all happy—not that I blame him. I had one set with Mr. Dunlap. I grant you, he's very handsome, but . . . well, I found him unsettling. He reminds me of a rotten apple—big and red on the outside, but brown and soft and nasty on the inside."

"If the apples are rotten, tell cook to throw them away."

Grace rolled her eyes. It was hopeless.

Hermes, barking maniacally, dashed after another squirrel. This one scampered back toward Oxbury House and dove into some large, dense bushes. Hermes followed in hot pursuit.

Grace jiggled her foot; Aunt Kate frowned at Hermes's leash.

Hermes's barking faded.

"I think I'll go see what happened to Hermes, Aunt Kate."

Aunt Kate did not reply—she probably hadn't even heard. She was sniffing again and dabbing her eyes with her handkerchief.

Something was seriously wrong.

"I'll be right back." Grace spoke a little louder. Aunt Kate nodded and blew her nose.

Grace strode across the lawn. What could be the

problem? Aunt Kate had been fine last night. Well, not fine. A little sad—she'd been sad ever since Mr. Wilton had left London—and tired, but not the watering pot she was this afternoon.

She reached the bushes. She was not going to plunge into the greenery. "Hermes?" No response. The stupid dog. Where had he got to? Surely Hermes had the sense to turn around and come back once the squirrel took to the trees. She walked around the shrubbery—

"Oof!" Her stomach collided with a masculine shoulder. A masculine hand shot out to grab her hip.

Her heart flew into her throat; she opened her mouth to scream—and then saw who was crouching in front of her.

Lord Dawson.

Oh. Her heart paused, took stock of the situation, and changed from the rapid tattoo of panic to the slow thud of something else entirely. It dropped from her throat to her stomach. Lower even. To . . . She flushed.

The last time she'd seen Lord Dawson, they'd been standing very, very close together in Lord Easthaven's tiny waiting room. He had been on the verge of kissing her. If only Aunt Kate had not arrived at precisely that moment—

No. It was very good Aunt Kate had arrived. If she hadn't, who knows what might have happened.

A little shiver ran up Grace's spine. *She* knew what would have happened—exactly what had happened in the Duke of Alvord's garden.

She should not be hoping for a recurrence of such activities, but part of her was—the odd, daring, hoyden part that had emerged when she'd defied Papa to come to London and which was insisting she gain a few adventures during her stay. The other part—the dutiful daughter, the well-bred lady of quality—was suitably shocked by her behavior.

She pushed the prim Grace to the back of her consciousness.

Lord Dawson was looking up at her now. Well, not looking *up* precisely. Looking *at* would be more accurate. His head was on level with her—

She turned even redder and tried to step back, but he wouldn't let her go. "What are you doing?"

He grinned at the parts of her by his face and then finally tilted his chin to look into her eyes. "I'm making the acquaintance of this friendly dog."

She looked past Lord Dawson's large body. Hermes was lying on his back, an expression of canine ecstasy on his face as the baron gave his belly one more scratch. "Hermes!"

She swore the beast grinned.

"Ah, is he a friend of yours as well?" The baron stood, but did not step back nor allow her to move to a more appropriate distance. The hand that had been scratching Hermes moved to join its fellow so he now had his fingers on both sides of her waist.

Prim Grace tried to get her attention. She ignored her.

"He's Aunt Kate's dog." She was having a difficult time drawing breath. "I'm sure she is missing him." She glanced back down at Hermes. He yawned and chewed on a stick.

"We won't be long." Lord Dawson slid his hands higher.

Grace glared up at him, but she was certain she failed miserably to look stern. It was very hard to feel any kind of righteous indignation when one was unable to breathe—and when the hoyden Grace was urging her to grab Lord Dawson's face and pull it down to hers.

His blue eyes lit with a spark of . . . what? Something very hot. As she watched, the spark spread. It must have jumped from him to her because she was suddenly extremely overheated.

"I have good news."

She saw his lips move. She remembered so clearly how his mouth had felt on hers in Alvord's garden. She wanted to feel it again . . . She moistened her lips and watched his eyes follow the path of her tongue.

"What?" She was as bad as Aunt Kate. She couldn't make herself focus on what the man was saying. If only he would bring his lips closer . . .

He did. He brought them very close indeed. He brushed them over her forehead, her cheek . . .

She tilted her head, parted her own lips. Her eyes drifted shut.

No, no, no, prim Grace was shouting, but it was difficult to hear her over the pounding of her heart—and very easy to ignore her.

Lord Dawson's mouth touched hers—just the barest glancing contact. Oh! His hands wandered almost to her breasts and then back down to her hips. They stroked over her skirt, pressing, bringing her up against his hard body.

She was panting—quietly, discreetly, she hoped, but definitely panting. She wanted to be even closer.

Hoyden Grace slid her hands around to Lord Dawson's back and tightened her arms. Mmm. He felt so good.

His mouth had returned to hers. She felt him smile, then his lips moved again in light little kisses. Too light. She made a mew of annoyance and opened her mouth wider.

He chuckled. She felt a moment's doubt, a slight whisper of embarrassment, and then all was forgotten as his tongue slipped between her lips.

To say she was shocked would be to understate the case.

His hands kneaded her derriere while his tongue swept through her—over the roof of her mouth, over her tongue, over her teeth. She felt so full. A heavy, damp ache throbbed low in her belly . . . no, lower than that . . . between her legs. She needed something—

Dear God, what was she doing?

She shoved against Lord Dawson's chest. He withdrew his tongue into his own mouth—where it belonged—and loosened his hold on her.

"Lord Dawson—"

"David."

"What?" His voice was husky and lower than usual, and if his eyes had looked hot before, they were blazing now.

"My name is David." He leaned forward and ran his tongue over her lower lip. "You cannot go back to 'Lord Dawson' after this very intimate encounter."

She was certain she flushed so red she might burst into flame. "I shall call you Lord Dawson if I like."

His lips slid into a very salacious grin. "All right. That might be fun. And you can call me 'my lord' when I slide between your beautiful milky thighs on our wedding night."

Her jaw dropped. If she'd been red before, she was now whatever was redder than red. How did one respond to such an outrageous comment?

Simple. One did not. One pushed one's hoydenish side to the far back of one's mind and let Prim Grace out of exile.

"I believe you said you had good news, *Lord Dawson?*"

"Indeed I do, *Lady Grace.*" Lord Dawson raised an eyebrow as he leaned back against the tree trunk. "I was able to get us an invitation to Viscount Motton's house party." He smirked. "In fact, I was able to persuade, very subtly, if I say so myself—"

"I'm sure you are the only person who would say so. You do not strike me as the epitome of subtlety."

"On the contrary, Lady Grace, I am exceedingly subtle"—he waggled his eyebrows—"in many endeavors."

Grace crossed her arms and snorted. She was completely in control of herself now. Lord Dawson gave her a challenging look, but she was not going to accept any challenges from this man. She had the distinct notion she would lose.

He waited a moment and then shrugged. "I was able to persuade Motton to hold the house party. He hadn't had a thought about having one before I suggested it."

Grace merely raised her eyebrows. Lord Dawson was obviously looking for plaudits. Ridiculous! The man was cocky enough as it was. She was definitely not going to stroke him—

She flushed. *Verbally* stroke him, of course. She was not going to tell him how wonderful he was. She cleared her throat. "And that is good news because . . . ?"

"Because Motton's estate is not far from Uncle Alex's, and Alex has a particular interest in the viscount's cultivation theories. I think he can be persuaded to attend. If you can get your aunt to come, they will have many opportunities to address their differences in relative privacy."

Grace nodded, though the opportunities springing to her mind were those she could have with Lord Dawson. Obviously she was a candidate for Bedlam.

"I see your point—and I do think I can get my aunt to come. We just learned the new Lord Oxbury will be arriving shortly—I'm certain Aunt Kate would rather be elsewhere when he reaches Town." Perhaps that was the problem. Perhaps her aunt was behaving so oddly because she was tired of London. She had spent her life in the country, after all. She was not a young woman. Perhaps she just needed to get away from the hustle and bustle of Town. "Let's go ask her."

"Good afternoon, Lady Oxbury." David executed a short bow and felt a twinge of compassion. The woman looked terrible. She'd obviously been crying—her nose was red and her eyes were swollen.

Perhaps she wasn't the harpy he'd been imagining.

"Good afternoon, Lord D-Dawson." She tried to sound cold, but the effect was spoiled when her voice cracked on his name.

"Aunt Kate! What *is* the matter?" Grace sat down on the bench next to her aunt and put an arm around her.

"Nothing." Lady Oxbury wadded her handkerchief into one hand, raised her head, and lied. "I'm perfectly fine."

"You are not perfectly fine. You've been crying."

Grace had as much finesse with her aunt as Hermes had with squirrels. Lady Oxbury glared at her.

"I have *not* been crying."

"You have. Your face is all red and blotchy."

"I got a speck in my eye. It is out now. I am *fine*."

This speech was accomplished with more glaring and some teeth gritting.

"But—"

It was definitely time to interrupt Grace before her aunt strangled her with Hermes's leash. "Lady Oxbury, as it happens I was in search of you. I stopped at Oxbury House, and your butler directed me here."

"Oh?" Lady Oxbury gave Grace one last glare, and

then turned her attention to him. She smiled tightly. "And what did you wish to speak to me about, Lord Dawson?"

"He has an invitation to the country, Aunt Kate."

He would have to muzzle Grace once they were married to keep her from putting her foot into her mouth constantly. She was rather like a bull in an emotional china shop. He smiled slightly while Lady Oxbury glared at Grace once more.

"You are interrupting Lord Dawson."

Grace frowned and opened her mouth to argue, but she didn't have much of an argument—she *had* interrupted him. She must have realized it as well; her frown deepened, but she remained silent.

"Lady Grace is correct, Lady Oxbury." David grinned as Grace finally snapped her mouth shut. "Viscount Motton is getting up a house party. I have an invitation and I believe you will be receiving one soon . . ."

It was Lady Oxbury's turn to frown and open her mouth.

". . . as will my uncle."

Lady Oxbury's mouth hung open for a moment. She blinked. "Mr. Wilton will be in attendance?"

"Perhaps. He is being invited, but, as you know, he's down at his estate, so I can't say for certain whether he will be there or not." Mentioning Alex had been risky. If Lady Oxbury held his uncle in extreme aversion, knowing he might be a guest would surely convince her to stay in London. But if she were not averse to Alex's presence, if she actually wanted to see him . . .

He trusted his gut—it had never steered him wrong in all his investment decisions—and his gut told him Lady Oxbury wanted to—was desperate to—see Alex.

"Why is Viscount Motton having a house party now?"

Because he'd been carefully maneuvered into doing so. No, he couldn't say that—and, on second thought, Motton was so canny, he probably just let David think he was maneuvering him. "Motton said he was ready for a respite from the noise and dirt of London."

"Exactly." Grace beamed up at him and then turned to her aunt. "I'm ready, too, Aunt Kate—aren't you?"

"Well . . ."

If Lady Oxbury was hesitating, they had won the field. David allowed himself to relax slightly.

"Wouldn't you like to be back in the country for a week or two, Aunt Kate? Breathe clean air, take long walks, admire the scenery . . ."

David admired Grace's scenery while she continued to try to persuade her aunt. She had the loveliest breasts he'd ever had the pleasure to see. Not that he had seen enough of them. He could only imagine how they would look freed of dress and stays.

And he *had* imagined it. He'd spent hours last night picturing Grace's breasts—how they would look when she stood naked in his bedchamber or lay on his sheets or sat astride him. He'd imagined how they'd feel in his hands, how her nipples would taste . . .

He'd spent the night tossing and turning, aching to see how accurate his imagination was.

It had certainly been a pleasant surprise when Grace had collided with him just a few minutes ago. How fortunate he had come upon Hermes in a relatively private location. The greenery had shielded them admirably. The foliage wasn't dense enough for a longer, more thorough interlude, but it had been completely adequate for the abbreviated encounter they'd just enjoyed.

In the country though . . . He'd never been to Motton's estate, but the man must have plenty of land—and trees and leafage. House parties provided a multitude of opportunities for amorous explorations. He was looking forward to exploring more of Lady Grace Belmont's glorious person. It would be beyond wonderful.

"Don't you agree?"

"Yes, definitely. Without a doubt. I've never . . . ah, what?" He looked blankly at Lady Oxbury. Surely she hadn't been asking if he would enjoy fondling—well, rather more than fondling—her niece? "I'm sorry. I'm afraid I wasn't attending."

He would not look down at his breeches to determine if an astute observer could tell to what he *had* been attending.

"Don't you agree Grace should not miss any part of the Season?"

"Oh, no, indeed. If you've been to one ball or Venetian breakfast or rout, you've been to them all. You see the same people over and over." It was true. He'd been disappointed, when he'd decided, at the time that, he could not marry Grace, to find he'd already met all the other eligible ladies.

Lady Oxbury sighed. "Very true."

"Exactly true," Grace said. "And it's not as if I'm in the market for a husband, is it, Aunt Kate?"

"Well, as I believe I've said, I did hope you would look around you, Grace."

"I have looked around me."

Was Grace flushing? She had glanced very briefly his way, hadn't she?

"And I can look more at this house party."

Oh, sweetheart, I'm hoping to keep you too busy to look anywhere but at me.

"And you don't want to have to share Oxbury House with the Weasel, do you?"

"*Very* true." Lady Oxbury looked at him again. "Does Lord Motton have a suitable hostess?"

"I believe he said his Aunt Winifred would fill that role." What Motton had actually said was *Crazy old Winifred will come if I let her bring her damn menagerie.* David looked down at Hermes who, apparently having had his fill of squirrel chasing, was resting on the grass. "I'm certain you can bring Hermes as well."

Hermes, hearing David say his name, immediately rolled over and presented his stomach for scratching.

Lady Oxbury sighed. "Very well, then, I guess we will go."

Chapter 11

"Ah, Lady Grace. This came for you in today's post."

"Thank you, Mr. Sykes." Grace took the letter and examined it.

"Who's it from, Grace?" Aunt Kate removed her bonnet and unfastened Hermes's leash.

"Papa."

"Oh? I'm amazed your father could find paper and pen—he is not a correspondent. Thank you, Mr. Sykes." Aunt Kate took the rest of the letters from the butler. "I don't believe I got a single missive from him in all the years of my marriage."

"Hmm." Grace stuffed the letter in her pocket. She had a bad feeling about this. "Papa hates to waste time or money on things he views as unnecessary." So why would he write to her?

"You are his daughter; I am merely his sister. I'm sure he wants to know how you are enjoying your Season. Have you written him yet?"

"No." The thought had not occurred to her. As far as she knew, all correspondence went directly to Papa's estate manager; Mr. Boothe hated London almost as much as Papa. He would not be amused by her stories of Town. "I can't imagine Papa would like an account of the balls and parties we've attended or the sights we've taken in. Perhaps he is looking for some household item." Though then he would have just asked Mrs. Drexel, their housekeeper. Her stomach twisted. "Or perhaps he is summoning me home, but I would have thought he'd have written you. Do you have a letter from him?"

"No." Aunt Kate leafed through her pile. "Ah, but here is something from Viscount Motton."

"It must be the invitation to the house party."

"Yes, it is." Aunt Kate skimmed the sheet of paper and then looked up and frowned. "It's in two days' time. Do you really think we should go?"

"Yes." Grace would wager a hefty sum that if she could only get Aunt Kate and Mr. Wilton together, give them some privacy, and allow them to talk, the two would resolve whatever issue was troubling them. "Definitely."

"But I've already accepted the Palmerson invitation for next week."

"Send our regrets. I can't imagine Lady Palmerson will be devastated by our absence."

"Well, no, of course not, but it will be one of the bigger events of the Season. You'd be able to meet so many eligible men."

"The men will still be here when we return, Aunt Kate. We will not be gone that long."

Aunt Kate bit her lip. "And this excursion will put you much in the way of Lord Dawson. I cannot like that."

Anticipation shivered up Grace's spine. Nothing could come of her time with Lord Dawson—she knew that—but she wanted it anyway. It was simply one more adventure, one more taste of freedom and excitement before she had to return to her normal life.

"That will not be a problem. You know I've already explained matters to the baron. And he won't be the only man attending the house party. The viscount must be inviting a dozen or more people, don't you think?"

"Well, yes, but—"

"So there is no need to decline Lord Motton's kind invitation. In fact, I would like to attend. I miss the country—and I've never been to a real house party. It should be entertaining."

"Well . . ."

"And frankly, Aunt Kate, you are looking a trifle out of curl. A few days in the country would do you good."

"I don't—"

Hermes, apparently of the opinion that he was being ignored, stood on his hind legs and waved his front paws.

"Hermes, do you think we should go to Lord Motton's country estate?" Grace asked.

The little dog barked enthusiastically.

"See, Hermes agrees with me."

Aunt Kate laughed. "Oh, very well, I suppose it can't do any great harm. And you are right. I could stand to get away from Town for a while."

"Exactly." And Aunt Kate could stand to see Mr. Wilton again. She hadn't mentioned him as a reason not to attend, and surely she would have if she was determined never to encounter him again. "You should send word now, shouldn't you?" No point in delaying and letting her aunt come up with more arguments against the trip.

Aunt Kate nodded. "Yes. I'll pen our acceptance and ask Mr. Sykes to have one of the footmen take it over— and I'll send our regrets to Lady Palmerson. And then I think I'll take a little nap." She blushed. "I'm, er, uncommonly tired these days for some, ah, reason."

Why was Aunt Kate embarrassed by being tired?

"You just need to visit the country. London is so noisy; you probably aren't sleeping well at night."

Aunt Kate turned even redder, if that were possible. "Yes." She cleared her throat. "I, ah . . . Yes, you are p-probably right. If you'll excuse me, I'll just go up to my room now, write these notes, and lie down for a while. Come, Hermes."

Grace watched Kate and Hermes climb the stairs. Why did it feel as though her aunt was running away? Well, no matter. At least she had convinced her to accept the house party invitation. Hopefully Lord Dawson would be as successful getting his uncle to attend.

How was he going to persuade Mr. Wilton, given the man had already left London? She was not certain a simple letter would be enough. Hmm. She had best discuss it with him tonight. He should be at Lord Fonsby's soiree. They could step into the garden, find a secluded spot, and . . .

Talk. Nothing else. There would be only talking with Lord Dawson from now on.

She could stand to take a turn about the garden— she was feeling markedly overheated. A breath of cooler air would be just the thing.

The Oxbury House garden was sadly overgrown; a caretaker had been in charge for far too long. Certainly Aunt Kate had never lived here when Oxbury was alive, and she'd said Oxbury had only come up to Town when Parliament was in session—and not even then the last few years when his health had been failing. The big tree by Aunt Kate's room was in desperate need of pruning. Its branches almost touched the window.

Grace sat on a bench by a bush with small white flowers. She should know what it was called—John certainly would. Whenever she'd made the mistake of admiring some foliage at the Priory, John's home, he'd given her a long, boring discourse on its history and variations. She'd soon learned not to comment on anything vegetative. But this specimen must be as common as any weed if it was flourishing in this poor, neglected patch of earth.

It was rather pretty, but unfortunately it seemed to make her sneeze. She reached for her handkerchief— and found something in her pocket . . . ah, Papa's letter. She'd forgotten. She pulled it out and broke the seal.

You will be happy to learn—Papa didn't bother with a salutation—why should he? The letter was addressed to her—*that Parker-Roth and I have reached an agreement.* An agreement? Her heart started to pound. *The wedding is set for next month. You may inform your aunt. Plan to return shortly to prepare for the occasion.* He signed it "Standen."

She gulped air. Black specks danced before her eyes. She fisted her hands, crushing the letter in her fingers. She would not faint.

The wedding was to be next month?!

She wanted to scream, but she couldn't draw in enough air. She wanted to hit something—someone.

Papa and John—how could they do this to her?

Yes, she had expected to wed John some day—but not next bloody month. And it would have been nice if he had bothered to propose.

She uncrumpled the letter. Perhaps she had missed something . . . No, she'd read all her father had written, but there was a short note from John, scribbled at the bottom of Papa's sheet.

Lady Grace, I hope you are enjoying London. As you know, I do not see the attraction besides the periodic

*meetings of the Horticultural Society. Mother and
Father send their regards.*

> *Your obedient servant,*
> *John Parker-Roth*

Bah! She wadded the paper up once more and threw
it on the ground. Such passion! If she were an exotic
rose, now, or a . . . a . . . oh, damnation. She didn't even
know a proper plant, but if she were an unusual bit of
greenery, John would be in raptures. Common, boring,
known-her-forever Lady Grace Belmont, however, certainly couldn't get his heart to race.

Well, she very much doubted *he* could get *her* heart
to race, not like Baron Dawson could. It was racing now,
just thinking of their heated encounter in the park.

She pressed her hands to her cheeks. What had she
been thinking, to allow the man such intimacies? It was
completely shocking—but it had felt completely right.

Was Lord Dawson a wizard? She had never before
experienced the urge to get so close to a man, to touch
him or be touched by him.

Most males were slightly repulsive. She'd discovered
that as soon as she'd grown from girlhood—as soon as
she'd grown breasts. That was when every male of her acquaintance had become incapable of directing his attention to her face. John had been one of the least afflicted;
she had caught him studying her chest surreptitiously, but
at least he'd had the courtesy to look her in the eye when
he spoke to her.

But Lord Dawson was different. Oh, he noticed her
breasts, all right—and, they, to her extreme mortification,
noticed him. They felt swollen and sensitive now, just
thinking about him. As if they would gladly leap from her
stays . . .

She was losing her mind. Or perhaps the man *had* put a spell on her. Why else would she be wondering how his hands would feel on her naked skin? What sensations his mouth, his tongue, his teeth would evoke if they encountered her nipples, which were now hard, pointed, and aching.

She pressed her hands against her bodice.

She should be incapable of imagining such bizarre activities, and yet, here she was, in the Oxbury garden, imagining all kinds of salacious things and causing various areas of her body to throb. If only Lord Dawson were here—

No! Having Lord Dawson here would be a disaster. Her malady was all his fault.

She bent over to pick up her discarded letter.

At least the baron didn't focus solely on her breasts. Oh, no. She could still feel the imprint of his hands on her derriere, the heat of his mouth on her lips, the wet fullness of his tongue . . .

Heavens, she was panting! She had to get control of her thoughts. She needed to lock this new hoydenish side of herself away for good; prim and proper, that's what she should be.

She smoothed out the letter and looked at John's addendum once more. There wasn't a single thing in it to make anything but her head throb.

Lord Dawson *had* mentioned marriage, more than once. Surely sharing a marriage bed with him would be much more interesting than climbing into one with John . . .

What was she thinking? She couldn't marry Lord Dawson. John would make an adequate husband. He was just more restrained than Lord Dawson, and restraint was a very good thing. Much more restful. All this throbbing and aching must be tiring after a while.

She stuffed the letter back in her pocket. It was time to go in. She would write a few lines to John. She could tell him about the Wainwright ball.

No, he wouldn't be interested in that at all.

Hmm. Would he be intrigued by the gossip swirling through the *ton* that the Duke of Alvord might wed Lord Westbrooke's American cousin if the duke's cousin, Richard Runyon, didn't kill him first?

No. John didn't approve of gossip, and she had to agree that all the tittle-tattle concerning the duke was rather farfetched, almost like a bad gothic romance. This was London in the nineteenth century, after all.

She could write about their plans to attend Viscount Motton's house party. He might have heard of the viscount—Lord Dawson did say Motton was employing some new cultivation theories. Cultivation theories sounded like something John could get very excited about. Perhaps he would even be moved to visit . . .

She did not care to have John attend this gathering. If—*when*—she married him, she would be stuck—well, compelled—*delighted*—to spend the rest of her days with him. She just was not ready to do so now—especially now that she knew her wedding was so soon. She very much needed her few more weeks of freedom.

Lord Dawson's face and figure popped into her mind. Damn. She could not be entertaining thoughts of the baron.

But she wanted to. She wanted to entertain much more than thoughts.

Perhaps she could strike a bargain with herself. She would be a little daring at this house party. It would be her last opportunity before she became Mrs. Parker-Roth.

She wouldn't do anything too dreadful—just steal a kiss or two. Get this out of her system.

Didn't men sow their wild oats? Well, this would be her one very minor scattering.

John should be pleased—she was actually thinking in vegetative terms.

She stepped through the garden door into the library.

"Is it warm outside, Lady Grace?"

"Eek!" She pressed her hand to her heart. "Don't sneak up on me like that, Mr. Sykes."

Sykes raised an eyebrow. "My apologies. Next time I shall be certain to drop something when you enter a room I am already occupying; however, I do think it is a good thing I did not do so today."

"What?" She looked around. Sykes had a bottle of brandy in his hand. "Are you . . . ?"

"Imbibing? No. I am ascertaining that Lord Oxbury will have a sufficient quantity of spirits should *he* wish to imbibe when he arrives."

"Oh. Of course." Lord Oxbury was coming. His arrival was reason enough for their departure.

"*Is* it warm out, Lady Grace? You look a trifle flushed."

"Warm? No, actually, it's cool." As long as she didn't think about a certain baron.

She would be spending days in the man's company, days with hours of free time and acres of secluded places.

She shivered.

"I see. You aren't ill, are you?"

"Of course not, Mr. Sykes. I am feeling fine. Wonderful." Especially when she considered all the interesting things Lord Dawson could do in the secluded spots of Lord Motton's estate.

She felt herself flush again. She should not be considering such a subject. But she was. Given the opportunity—

and she suspected the baron would give her plenty of opportunities—she was going to do far more than consider the subject.

Mr. Sykes was observing her closely. "Are you certain you don't have a touch of the ague, Lady Grace?"

"No, I am perfectly healthy." Mr. Sykes did not look convinced. Well, she could stand a few moments of privacy. "But maybe I should go lie down as a precaution. If you'll excuse me?" She hurried out the door before he could make any more observations.

They had to go to this gathering for Aunt Kate's sake, but that didn't mean Grace couldn't get some . . . enjoyment from the excursion as well. She pushed open the door to her room and looked at the writing desk. She should answer Papa's letter. She should send a few words to John.

She should, she should, she should. She was so tired of "should."

When she went to Lord Motton's estate, she was going to do a few things she shouldn't.

Kate lay on her bed, curtains drawn, staring up at the canopy. What should she do?

Her thoughts had been flapping wildly like birds in a net ever since she realized . . .

Oh, God, oh, God, oh, God . . .

There were herbs she could take, things she could do to . . . It was early days. No one would ever know . . .

She would know.

But she wasn't married. If she did nothing, if she grew round and heavy, everyone would whisper. More than whisper. The *ton* would gossip, laugh, mock her. Give her the cut direct. Her brother would berate her; the Weasel would call her a harlot, toss her out on the street . . .

If the Weasel tossed her out, would Standen take her in, let her live in his home and give birth to her bastard under his roof?

No. How could he? He would tell her she had besmirched his name and he would be right. And then where would she go? To the workhouse?

She turned onto her side. What was she going to do?

Damn it all, this wasn't supposed to happen. She was too old to be enceinte. She'd never thought . . . well, why would she? She'd had regular congress with Oxbury for over twenty years and had never conceived. Of *course* she thought she was barren.

She was an idiot, a bloody sapskull. Widows, experienced women, women who took lovers were supposed to be smart about these things. They were supposed to know what precautions to take. Mistakes like this didn't happen.

Dear God. She had finally conceived—and it was a mistake.

She covered her face with her hands to muffle her sobs, but she didn't have to worry Marie would hear her. She was crying too hard to make a sound.

They were leaving for Lord Motton's estate the day after tomorrow. Alex might be there. She might see him.

Did she have to tell him? Maybe she could go away somewhere, say she had a friend in Yorkshire, leave before she started to show, stay away for nine months, have the baby, and give it away—

Oh! Give her baby away? How could she do that?

How couldn't she? She couldn't raise a child by herself, in poverty and disgrace.

She wiped her face on her sheet and rolled onto her back again. Marie was right. She had to tell Alex—he deserved to know. But would he even listen to her? She had stupidly hurt him badly, so badly he had fled her room, fled London.

She would have to apologize first. Grovel. Beg his forgiveness—and then tell him she had lied to him.

She squeezed her eyes shut. How could he ever believe her, believe she was sorry, that she hadn't intended to mislead him?

Was it a lie when you told a falsehood you sincerely believed was true?

She stared back up at the bed canopy. She shouldn't try to make excuses for herself. All Alex needed to know was that she was sorry, but he had a child growing in her womb.

She laced her hands protectively over her stomach. But that wasn't true, either. She wasn't sorry. Oh, yes, she was, because it was all such a terrible mess, but if Alex had loved her, if he had wanted to get her with child when he'd come inside her . . .

If, if, if. The truth was what she needed to face, not her wishes, not her dreams.

"My lady?" Marie's hand appeared on the bed curtain. Kate turned over quickly, so Marie saw her back and not her tears when she let the light in. "It's time to get ready for the soiree."

"Psst!"

Lord Westbrooke raised an eyebrow. "Do you suppose you should see why that potted palm is trying to get your attention, Dawson?"

David repressed a sigh. Lady Grace would never make a competent spy. At least he hoped it was Lady Grace.

It must be. The Addison twins were normally not so discreet.

Come to think of it, where were the Addison twins? He hadn't seen them at the Wainwright ball or any of the recent society events—and he had been looking. Was it too much to hope they had decamped and returned to the country for good?

"If you'll excuse me, Westbrooke?" How to say this diplomatically? "I'm certain I don't need to suggest that it would be best not to mention the, um, furtive vegetation?"

"My lips are sealed." Westbrooke grinned. "But you might tell Lady Grace that if she wishes to hide in the greenery, she shouldn't wear blue. The gown is lovely, but rather noticeable, don't you agree?"

"Definitely. I'll put a word in her ear." David nodded and turned to stroll past the palm. Surely Lady Grace would have the sense to come out of the vegetation on her own. If he was compelled to haul her out, the gabble-grinders certainly would notice.

"Why didn't you come talk to me when you arrived?" Grace sounded very disgruntled. And she had a leaf in her coiffure as well. He had best take her somewhere private where he could remove it for her. He put her hand on his arm.

"And good evening to you, too, my love."

"Shh." She darted a glance to either side. "Do you want to set the prattle boxes to chattering?"

"No, which is why I didn't dash to your side the moment my foot crossed Fonsby's threshold."

"Oh. Yes, well, I see your point."

He saw that she looked adorably confused. She flushed all the way down to . . . hmm. Her breasts were displayed in all their glory.

Well, not *all* their glory, of course. She did have a bodice to her dress, but at least it was cut low enough to display her beauty as fully as was allowed by society's dictates.

He guided her toward a door he had already determined led to a less crowded part of the house.

Now that he considered the matter, perhaps he should suggest she reclaim her modest fichus. He found he did not care for the thought of other men observing her charms.

"What I wished to tell you is Aunt Kate has agreed to attend Lord Motton's house party. She sent our acceptance this afternoon."

"Splendid." And this small chamber led out onto a rather isolated, dark section of the terrace. "Do you think it is stuffy in here?"

"Yes, I suppose so. I don't know. What does it matter?"

"It matters not the slightest. Let's just step out this door and enjoy the cool night air."

"All right." Grace went into the dark with him. "So have you got your uncle to agree to come? It is most important. Aunt Kate is still not herself."

He'd noticed. Lady Oxbury had been standing on the other side of the room with a group of chaperones that included Mrs. Fallwell, Lady Amanda Wallen-Smyth, and Lady Gladys, the Duke of Alvord's aunt. She'd seemed to be staring off into space while the other women conversed. At least she'd paid scant attention to Grace's whereabouts and the nefarious men who might be luring her charge astray.

No matter. He had been paying careful attention. He intended to be the only nefarious man to tempt Lady Grace into misbehavior. He maneuvered her so her back was to the balustrade and his back was to the door, his body shielding hers from anyone who might venture onto this little corner of the terrace.

"So, what has your uncle said?" Grace frowned at him, but didn't protest her location. Had she not realized his intentions?

He smiled slightly. She looked especially alluring tonight. Her skin—her lovely, wonderful skin—was an enticing play of cool, creamy paleness and seductive shadows.

"Lord Dawson, what did Mr. Wilton say? Is he coming?"

"Hmm?" He could not help himself. He'd surreptitiously removed his gloves and stuck them into a pocket; now he put his hands on her upper arms. His fingers smoothed her silky skin. He heard her breath catch.

"He didn't say anything. I didn't ask him."

She had looked slightly alarmed and slightly expectant when he'd touched her. Those expressions vanished and she glared at him.

Would she slap him if he tried to kiss her?

"Why didn't you ask him?"

"Besides the fact he is not in Town at present—"

"I *know* that!"

"—I thought it inadvisable to push him too hard. He may smell a rat, you know, and refuse to set foot on Motton's estate."

"Oh. Yes, I see." Grace put her hands on his waistcoat and looked up at him. Her voice held sincerity and a touch of pleading. "That would be terrible. I'm convinced he is the author of Aunt Kate's discontent. He *must* come."

Did she know she was driving him mad? He covered her gloved hands with his bare ones. "I think he will come, but if he doesn't, his estate is not so far from Motton's. I will devise a way to get him and your aunt together."

"You promise?"

Zeus, she was looking up at him as though he could work miracles. He was only a man. He could not decide the future; he could not determine anyone's fate.

But he wanted to. He wanted to work miracles for her.

He would find a way. He could not promise Alex and Lady Oxbury would reach the accord Grace so obviously hoped for, but he could promise to bring them together. He *would* succeed, even if he had to knock Alex out and abduct him to do so.

He bent his head toward Grace. Her eyes grew wary; she started to draw back. He slid his hands up her lovely arms to her beautiful shoulders.

"I promise." He moved closer. She stayed still, like a frightened rabbit, frozen, ready to bolt. He would not let her bolt. He was her fox; he would consume her.

"I promise," he whispered again, against her mouth. He traced her lips with his tongue. She sighed softly and he slipped inside.

She was hot and wet. She was his. Her body sagged against him—her lovely, soft, rounded body. Her hands moved up to his neck; his hands moved down to her hips, urging her even closer, pressing her against his need. He could not get enough of her. He plunged his tongue into her sweetness . . .

She pushed against him. Had she been struggling for a while to get free? No, he would have noticed, even through his madness. He raised his head.

"Lord Dawson." She was panting, her lovely breasts heaving, but she still clung to him. His cheek had not yet felt the sting of her hand. "You go too far." She spoke in a breathy whisper.

He smiled and kissed the tip of her nose.

"Sweetheart, believe me, I intend to go a lot farther."

She inhaled sharply, but still made no move to slap him. How far could he go? Regrettably, it would be inadvisable to investigate on Lord Fonsby's terrace.

"Just not tonight." Did she look disappointed? Splendid. He put her hand on his arm and headed back inside. He could barely wait until he had the time and privacy to see just how far Lady Grace would permit him to venture.

Chapter 12

Alex stared out at the rain. It splashed in the puddles on the terrace and ran like tears down the Coade stone statue of Hermes he'd purchased in a moment of whimsy.

Funny, Kate's dog's name was Hermes.

Damn. He turned away from the window. He should light some candles—it was too dim in the library to read.

He didn't want to read.

He walked over to his desk. Windom, his estate manager, had been after him to work on his accounts ever since he got home. Something about a drainage problem in the south fields and a new kind of seed . . .

Blast it all! He left the desk and went back to the window. He'd tried to work on the damn accounts almost every day since he'd fled London. Windom was getting impatient with him. He didn't blame him. He was getting impatient with himself. His attention was shot to hell. Nothing interested him any more.

What the blazes was he going to do? He had to put Kate behind him. He couldn't spend the rest of his days drifting from room to room, staring out windows.

The rain continued to fall. It had been misting or

pouring every day since he'd got back to Clifton Hall. Everything smelled musty. He could feel the damp in his bones.

It had been too wet to work in the fields or take Lear for a good long gallop, but he had the sinking feeling those activities would no longer cure him of the dismals.

He shouldn't have left London. Hell, he shouldn't have left Kate's room, but something in her glib tone had shot straight to his heart like a well-aimed arrow.

Maybe if he had stayed and simply enjoyed what she was offering, he would have cured himself of this infatuation. Perhaps they could have had an enjoyable liaison for the Season. He might have got tired of her—or she of him, of course. In any event, he could have finally put this longing to rest.

He rested his forehead against the windowpane. God, could he ever fill the hole she'd torn in his heart? He had lived for years with the emptiness of loss, but he'd still had a vague sense of hope. Now that was gone and in its place was this bleak ennui. He felt as if he were dead, but had just forgotten to lie down in his coffin.

He closed his eyes, then opened them again and straightened. No, he was not some silly fribble to be brought low by love. The very thought was nauseating. Damn, he was acting like some court-card, some mewling dandy *poet*. Disgusting.

And what if David actually married Lady Grace? It would have to be over Standen's dead body, but stranger things had happened. If he did not want to cut all connection with his nephew, he would have to learn how to meet Lady Oxbury in social settings. At David's wedding, the christening of his first child—

He squeezed his eyes shut again. God, the pain that

thought caused him. But he had to get over it. He wanted David to be happy.

He would stop this ridiculous moroseness immediately. Lady Oxbury was just a woman, and there were plenty of women in the world who would be happy to spend time with him—women who were younger, more beautiful—

No, he was not ready for comparisons. He would not think of Ka—Lady Oxbury. He would not think at all. He would just do. He would start slowly. There was no hurry. Just taking the first step to free himself from this awful gloom was—

"Sir?"

His butler was at the door. He'd been so lost in thought, he hadn't heard the man approach. Well, that would change right now. "Yes, Grant? What is it?"

"This just arrived from Viscount Motton." Grant handed him a note. "The footman is awaiting your response."

"I see." He pulled his spectacles from his pocket and glanced over the text.

Motton was having a house party at Lakeland, was he? Splendid! What could be a more perfect first step out of his misery? True, sometimes the viscount allowed his odd sense of humor to rule his better judgment—one of his gatherings reportedly included a competition to determine who possessed the worst singing voice—but a little screeching was a small price to pay to get out of the dungeon Clifton Hall had become.

If the planned festivities were too wearing, well, he'd been wanting to talk to Motton about the viscount's new cultivation scheme and to view his fields firsthand. And if that failed to amuse, Lakeland was only a day's ride away. It would be easy to come home.

"Grant, tell Lord Motton's footman I shall be delighted to attend."

* * *

"Lord Dawson has arrived, my lady."

"Oh." Grace's heart almost leapt from her bodice. She stopped packing to press her hand to her chest. Just the man's name made her stomach flutter as if it housed a flock of sparrows. "I'm not quite ready. Is my aunt packed, Marie?"

"No. Ye both are taking forever. Yer just going for a few days, ye know, not weeks."

"Yes, I know. It's just, well, I'm not certain what to expect . . ." She glanced around the room. Perhaps she should just pack her entire wardrobe and be done with it.

"I'll put him in the blue parlor and have some brandy sent in."

"Perhaps that would be best. I won't be too much longer."

Marie laughed. "My lady, any time waiting is too long for most gentlemen."

Grace let out a long breath once the door closed behind Marie. How was she going to survive this house party? She'd be spending days in close proximity to Lord Dawson with hours free to wander the estate in relative— well, perhaps actual—privacy. Many opportunities for him to do exactly what he'd done at Lord Fonsby's soiree . . . and more.

Ooh. Her knees gave out and she sat down abruptly. Fortunately, the bed was there to receive her. She was throbbing again.

She'd decided she was going to sow a few wild oats, yes—but only a few. Not a crop. She was still marrying John Parker-Roth in a matter of weeks; in fact, she was leaving for Devon after the house party to make the final preparations. She was not at heart—could not be—a hoyden.

Where was the proper, prim, always-follow-the-rules Grace when she needed her? She was only the veriest whisper in the farthest, darkest recesses of her mind.

She must get herself under better control. Once she wed John . . . well, she could not be lusting after another man.

But she *was* lusting after another man right now. She covered her face with her hands. Dear God, she was. How was she to stop?

She should have slapped Baron Dawson there on Lord Fonsby's terrace. He'd expected her to do so, she could tell. He had put his tongue in her mouth and had run his hands over her person, pressed his body against hers—ohh . . .

She hadn't wanted to slap him, she'd wanted to tell him to do it again. And when he'd said he intended to go a lot farther, she'd almost begged him to do so immediately—sooner than immediately if possible—there on Lord Fonsby's terrace. She'd wanted to cry when he'd taken her back inside.

Was she mad?

She *was* mad. She was also in serious, serious trouble.

It was all very well to have an adventure or two, but John would expect her to be a virgin on their wedding night. She wasn't familiar with all the particulars—usually the discussion of a woman's marital duties happened on the night before she was expected to assume those duties—but she'd be willing to bet the odd sensations she felt with Lord Dawson were closely linked to the marital act. They certainly were linked to nothing she'd ever experienced before.

She rubbed her forehead. Perhaps she should discuss the problem with Aunt Kate. Her aunt had been married.

By all accounts, she'd been faithful to Oxbury, so she must also know how to control these peculiar urges.

Grace put her last few items in a valise and went to her aunt's room. Hermes met her at the door, barking and dancing on his hind legs.

"Sorry, Hermes. I don't have any treats."

Hermes paused, gave her a long look, and then sneezed and trotted over to the hearth to lie down.

"Are you ready to go, Grace?" Kate stood by her bed, surrounded by portmanteaux. "As soon as Marie makes Lord Dawson comfortable, she's coming back to help me finish packing."

"You look as if you are taking as much as I am."

Kate pushed her hair back off her face. "It's ridiculous, isn't it? We will only be gone a short while. I'm sure I am bringing far too many things." What was the matter with her? She wasn't usually so indecisive.

It was nerves, of course. She was hoping Alex would be at this house party.

No, she was dreading it.

It made no difference what she felt. If he was there, she would have to tell him about his child.

Dear God! She sat down quickly. A child. *Alex's* child.

"Aunt Kate, I need to ask you something."

Grace was looking down at her skirt, twisting the fabric with her fingers. Something was obviously amiss. "Yes? What is it, Grace?"

"I'm a little concerned . . . That is, I should probably tell you . . . Well, as you know, Lord Dawson will be at this house party . . ."

"Of course I know—he's downstairs waiting. As he was kind enough to offer us his protection on the drive out to Lord Motton's estate, we should not keep him waiting."

"Yes. Well, the thing is . . ." Grace finally met Kate's gaze. "I might need protection from him."

"What?!" She knew she should never have accepted this invitation. "I will have a word with him immediately. If he thinks—"

Grace flushed. "Or he might need protection from me."

Kate's jaw dropped. For a moment she couldn't muster a single sound. "I-I don't think I understand."

"I thought you might know what to do. I mean, you've been married. You must know all about the urges one feels."

"Ah . . ." Urges? Grace hadn't said urges had she? "Er . . ." What should she answer? Just a short while ago, she would not have known what Grace was talking about, but unfortunately now she was all too familiar with urges—and not very familiar with controlling them. "What you should do—"

"I'm back." Marie bustled into the room. Kate could have fallen on her neck and kissed her. It was cowardly of her, she knew. Grace had asked for advice, but she had no advice to give her. She laid her hand over her stomach. Look where *her* urges had led her.

"The footmen are on their way up to get these things," Marie said, putting the last dress into a portmanteau. "Why don't ye both go down and wait for the carriage?" She looked up and grinned. "Ye can keep his lordship company. He's wearing a hole in the rug with his pacing."

Kate bent and put on Hermes's leash. "That's a good idea, Marie. Are you ready, Grace?"

She bolted out the door before Grace could answer.

Kate stopped at the stairs. That was not well done of her. Grace deserved an answer—needed an answer if she was going to get through this house party without putting herself in Kate's position—enceinte, but unwed. That would indeed be horrendous.

She hoped Grace had more control than she, but the Wilton men were devilishly seductive. And it was Kate's job as chaperone to see that Grace didn't go astray.

"I'm sorry," Kate said as Grace caught up. "I shouldn't have hurried away like that."

Grace smiled slightly. "That's all right, Aunt Kate. I'd thought these feelings must be common, but I guess I'm—"

"They *are* common, Grace." Kate wasn't entirely certain of that, but she suspected it was so—and she couldn't bear the distress she heard in Grace's voice. She put her hand on Grace's arm. "That's why girls are told to avoid being alone with a gentleman—and why chaperones are there to be sure they follow that rule. I have been sadly remiss, but I promise I will stick to you like a burr at this house party."

"Oh, no." Grace looked completely appalled. "You can't do that!"

"But, Grace—"

"Grr."

Kate glanced down. Hermes was literally bristling, his teeth bared.

"Good heavens, Hermes, what is the matter?"

Hermes barked vociferously and lunged, jerking Kate's arm forward. She grabbed for the banister to keep from going head first down the stairs. "Hermes! Will you—oh."

She saw what had disturbed Hermes. The Weasel was standing by the front door, handing his hat to Sykes. He looked up at the commotion. Good God, his eyes were going for her stomach. She scooped Hermes up and held him in front of her.

"Cousin," he said in his annoying, nasal tones, "how . . . nice to see you again."

Nice? Yes, he probably did think it was nice to see her—just as he must think it nice to see a cockroach right before he heard the crunch of his heel flattening it.

Hermes gave another low growl. Kate kissed the top of his head and strove to sound polite.

"I trust you had a pleasant trip, Horace?"

The Weasel shrugged, his bony shoulders shifting his shabby, cheap coat. He hadn't yet spent Oxbury's money on a new wardrobe.

The man was most unpleasant looking. He had all of Oxbury's less favorable traits plus a few of his own. He truly did look like a weasel—thin with a narrow face, long pointed nose, and small beady eyes.

Her Oxbury had not been much to look at, but at least he had not been pompous and obnoxious.

She descended the stairs, Hermes held shield-like in front of her stomach. When she got within five feet of the Weasel, she stopped. One step closer and Hermes would start barking. Here, he only growled menacingly.

"Have you met my niece, Horace?"

Horace smiled in his usual oily fashion. "I don't believe I've had that pleasure."

Kate nodded and gritted her teeth. It had to be done.

"Lady Grace, Lord Oxbury. My lord, as I'm sure you know, Lady Grace is the Earl of Standen's daughter."

"My pleasure, Lady Grace." Oxbury bowed slightly.

"Lord Oxbury." Grace gave the barest curtsy and offset that little politeness by lifting her chin and peering down her nose at Horace—not hard for her to do as Horace was a good four inches shorter than she.

"I shall check on the carriage." Sykes, the coward, handed Lord Oxbury's hat to a footman—one of the many new servants hired in the last few days to support Horace's substantial self-importance—and dashed out the door.

Horace sniffed and looked back at Kate. "You are leaving?"

"Yes." Hermes wriggled, indicating his wish to be set down. Kate hugged him tighter and stroked his ears. There was no way she was going to expose her torso to Horace's scrutiny. "We have been invited to a house party at Lakeland, Viscount Motton's estate. We are on the verge of departure."

"I see. I wonder—" Horace's eyebrows—well, in his case eyebrow was more accurate as there was no demarcation between the two—shot up. He was looking at a spot just behind them. "And who might this gentleman be?"

Horace's tone suggested the gentleman might be a pimp or debaucher. Kate turned to see what nefarious blackguard had slipped by Mr. Sykes's guard.

Lord Dawson stood scowling in the doorway to the blue salon. "I am Baron Dawson. Who are you?"

Horace puffed up like an angry cat. Hermes must have thought so, too. He started growling again and struggled to be let down.

"Shh, Hermes."

"I am the Earl of Oxbury, of course—the owner of this magnificent house."

If Horace got any more self-important, he'd explode.

Kate glanced at Lord Dawson. Oh, dear, it looked as if he was going to say something cutting. Not that Horace didn't deserve it, but there was no need to brangle. They were leaving momentarily.

She spoke before the baron could vent his spleen. "We are in Lord Dawson's debt, Horace, as he has kindly offered to escort Lady Grace and me to Viscount Motton's house party."

Lord Dawson came over to stand next to Grace. Kate had never noticed before—obviously, she had been too focused on the man's uncle—but the baron was a very large and intimidating man. He clearly could pick Horace up in one hand and break him in two.

Even Horace seemed to realize this truth. His tone was almost polite. "Ah, I see. Very kind of you, Dawson."

"My pleasure, Oxbury."

Lord Dawson was still glaring at Horace. Surely he would refrain from baiting the man for a few more minutes? Where in God's name was the blasted coach?

Mr. Sykes appeared at the door. "The carriage is ready."

Alleluia! "Well, we must go. Don't want to keep the horses waiting. So glad we had a moment to see you before we departed, Horace." May God forgive her that lie. "I'm sure you'll find all to your liking here. Mr. Sykes is very efficient." Kate grinned like an idiot and edged toward the door. "And here comes our luggage." A procession of footmen, directed by Marie, streamed down the stairs. "Do have a pleasant time in London." She paused to let the luggage precede her. "Did you have a particular reason for coming to Town at this moment, Horace?"

She hadn't expected a real answer, just a polite—or as polite as Horace cared to manage—platitude. She was halfway out the door when she heard his response.

"Actually, yes, I did. I've come to acquire a wife."

"Oh." Grace and Lord Dawson were gaping at Horace, just as she was certain she was. Even Hermes seemed stunned by this pronouncement—he stopped growling. The Weasel, a man with close to sixty years in his dish, a man she had always assumed was a confirmed bachelor . . . the skinny, oily, annoying, pompous Weasel was going wife hunting? "Well, good luck to you."

Horace chuckled and smoothed back his few stringy gray hairs. "I doubt I'll have to rely on luck."

"Ah, right." She was going to burst out laughing or cast up her accounts on the marble floor. "Of course. Exactly. Yes, indeed. Good-bye then."

"Good-bye." Horace smiled slightly—at least that was what she thought the twisting of his lips meant, but perhaps he just had a touch of indigestion—and waved. "Don't hurry back."

Poor Lady Oxbury. David rode behind the coaches as they pulled away from Oxbury House. He certainly would not want to have any extended contact with Lord Lobcock. The few minutes he'd been forced to endure the man's company had been too many. What a bloody coxcomb!

Zeus took exception to a vegetable cart and tried to bolt. He reined him in, and then had to avoid a cowhanded idiot in a high-perch phaeton who was attempting to take a corner too fast. Fortunately the Oxbury carriages were far enough ahead they missed everything. He swallowed his curses and urged Zeus to pick up his pace. He would be very happy to shake London's dirt from his boots—and his breeches, coat, and hat—for a while.

Once they got free of Town, he moved up past the baggage carriage to ride alongside the coach carrying Grace and her aunt. He tilted his head from side to side, stretching out the kinks in his neck, and let out a long breath.

God, he'd forgotten what quiet sounded like. London was never quiet. Even at night, there was constant din—the rattle of wheels against cobbles, the clop of horse hooves, the shouts of drunken, young—and not so young—bucks. He'd got so used to the noise, he hardly noticed it any longer. Until now, that is, when it was absent.

Now he could hear birdsong and leaves rustling in an errant breeze. And the air! He could take a deep breath again without falling into a coughing fit.

Mmm. He was looking forward to this house party, to taking Zeus out for a gallop without worrying about carriages or other riders, to strolling along peaceful, tree-shaded lanes—with Grace on his arm, of course—and wandering off into a secluded corner to steal a kiss . . . or more.

He had taken the liberty of procuring a special license. It was burning a hole in his pocket, actually. As soon as he persuaded Grace to have him, he need only find a minister, a pair of witnesses, and then, after the vows, a nice, soft bed.

He shifted in the saddle. Too much musing on *that* subject would make for a very uncomfortable ride. He'd best direct his thoughts to a less stimulating topic—like Lady Oxbury and Alex.

He glanced at the carriage. What *had* happened between them?

Zeus shook his head, making the bit jingle. David leaned forward and patted him on the neck.

It must have been something momentous. Alex had looked like hell the morning after Alvord's ball. David snorted, causing Zeus's ears to twitch. No, Alex had looked like he was *in* hell. He'd only seen the man that haggard when they'd found Grandda's and Grandmamma's carriage crumpled by the big oak.

David sighed, shaking his head. He'd expected his uncle to be disgustingly cocky at breakfast that morning, if he put in an appearance at all. He'd assumed the man had been frolicking all night in Lady Oxbury's bed—it had been close to daybreak when he'd heard him come in.

So what had happened? Had Lady Oxbury refused to see him? But then where had Alex been—walking the streets of London all night?

Damn it, Alex deserved some happiness. Not that he ever appeared unhappy—he was not a man to wear his heart on his sleeve—but there was always a slight air of melancholy about him, as if he saw the world's colors dimmed by a thin layer of gray, a thin covering of London's soot, if you will.

When he'd seen Alex that morning, he'd decided Lady Oxbury must be a cold-hearted bitch, but now that he saw how much she was suffering . . . well, he didn't know what to think.

"Lord Dawson!"

He snapped his attention back to the coach. Grace had opened the window and was leaning out. "What is it, Lady Grace?"

"It's my aunt. She is feeling most unwell. Can you ask John Coachman to stop, please?"

"Of course."

The coachman had heard Lady Grace and was already pulling back on the reins.

"And if you could come help her down." Grace glanced back at her aunt, and then looked up at him. "It's rather an emergency."

"Certainly." He vaulted from his saddle and jerked open the carriage door. Grace had not overstated the case. Lady Oxbury's face was as white as a sheet—the parts that didn't have a pronounced greenish tinge, that is.

"Would you like to get down, Lady Oxbury?"

She nodded frantically, her hand pressed tightly to her mouth.

He half lifted her out. She leaned against the side of the carriage while he helped Grace and Marie. Then he grabbed Hermes while the women hurried away from the road. Lady Oxbury made it only a few steps into the grass before she cast up her accounts.

Grace braced her while she finished. "Are you feeling more the thing now, Aunt Kate?"

"Ooh." Lady Oxbury shook her head. "I still feel . . . I still think . . ."

Grace wrapped her arm around her aunt's waist and urged her toward a sturdy tree. The three women disappeared behind the trunk.

David heard the sound of retching.

John Coachman pushed his hat back with his whip and scratched his forehead. "Shall we bide here a while, yer lordship?"

"I think that would be wise." He should offer his assistance, but he didn't wish to intrude on Lady Oxbury's privacy. He took a few steps into the grass toward the tree—being careful to avoid one particular spot—and cleared his throat. "Lady Grace?"

Marie emerged from behind the trunk first. "My lord, could ye get the wicker basket from the carriage? I packed a few things that might help, but a woman in my lady's condition . . . well, I think we'll be stopping a few more times afore journey's end."

"I see." There went his hope of making good time. At least Lakeland was not far—they should arrive by dark, even with frequent stops. "I will fetch it immediately."

He handed Hermes to John Coachman. Fortunately, the basket was in plain sight. He gave it to Marie and watched her hurry off behind the tree. In a moment Lady Grace appeared.

"How is your aunt?"

"Better, I think." Grace frowned. "I wish I knew what was wrong."

"Marie mentioned a condition . . . ?"

"A condition?" Grace's brow wrinkled. "Aunt Kate isn't prone to carriage sickness, if that's what you mean."

"No. But her maid said—" His jaw dropped.

Good God. Alex . . . Lady Oxbury . . .

Was it possible? *Had* Alex spent the night in Lady Oxbury's bed with interesting results? And now it was imperative the lady see his uncle because the man was about to be a father?

David snickered.

Grace frowned. "What's so funny?"

"Oh, nothing." He pressed his lips together, but that didn't quite contain his mirth. "N-nothing at all."

"You should not be laughing. Aunt Kate is very sick."

He nodded. "I'm n-not l-laughing."

Grace gave him a very nasty look and went back to help Lady Oxbury. Thank God.

He walked carefully to the other side of the carriage and then collapsed against it, howling with laughter— as quietly as he could—until tears ran down his cheeks.

He could hardly wait to see Alex.

Chapter 13

Alex let Lear choose his own path up the drive to Lakeland, Motton's manor house.

He was tired, but satisfied. It had been worth leaving home before daybreak; he'd already had time to take a preliminary look at Motton's cultivation techniques and chat with Watkins, Motton's estate manager. The man was a genius. There were definitely a number of improvements he'd seen that he could implement at Clifton Hall. Hopefully he would have time during this house party for some rational conversation with Motton on the topic.

Lear's ears twitched. Yes, he heard it, too. Carriages were approaching from behind. He reined up, glanced back, and frowned. The man accompanying the coaches looked familiar. He was too far away to be certain . . .

His eyes dropped to the man's horse. Damn. He'd recognize that stallion anywhere. What the hell was David doing here—and, more to the point, who was he escorting?

Only one possibility came to mind. Alex jerked, causing Lear to back and toss his head in protest.

"Sorry, boy." He patted his horse's neck. David must

have caught sight of him then, because Zeus broke into a canter, covering the ground between them in minutes.

"Alex! Well met!"

"Is it?" He could be wrong. Please, God, let him be wrong. But the person—or persons—in the carriage must be female, and the only females he could think might be in David's company were Ka—Lady Oxbury and Lady Grace.

Perhaps Lady Oxbury had stayed in Town. Lakeland was only a short trip from London. A maid would suffice as Lady Grace's companion for such a brief journey; perhaps the girl was meeting a suitable duenna here.

Right. And perhaps he would sprout wings and fly.

He wished he could fly, if not through the air, then on Lear's back. Ride like the wind home to Clifton Hall and hide behind a locked door.

He blew out the breath he hadn't realized he'd been holding. He was being absurd. He was not a frightened little boy, and Lady Oxbury wasn't some hobgoblin. They were two adults. They could behave as adults, surely, and get through this damn house party politely.

And he could manufacture an excuse to run—*head*—for home tomorrow morning.

"Who's in the carriage?" He braced himself for the answer. The vehicle was traveling very slowly, as if its contents were exceptionally fragile.

"Lady Grace." David paused and gave him an odd look. "And Lady Oxbury."

Did David think he was communicating something significant with his bobbing eyebrows? It was not a secret Alex had made a fool of himself over the woman.

"I see." He sounded nonchalant, if he said so himself. He was surprised Motton knew Ka—Lady Oxbury.

Did Motton know her? It would be somewhat unusual. She had been out of society for a long time, and Motton was around David's age . . . He frowned. "You didn't happen to have anything to do with the invitations to this gathering, did you, David?"

David grinned. "Perhaps."

"Damn it, you know I parted on less than cordial terms with Lady Oxbury."

"Actually, the last time I saw you with the lady—at Alvord's ball—you looked to be on exceedingly cordial terms with her. I could only speculate as to why you left London so precipitously."

The coaches were getting closer. *Why* were they moving so slowly—to prolong his agony? "You aren't an idiot, David. You might have put two and two together."

"I might have." David gave him another odd look. "If we are doing sums, you might wish to do a few calculations of your own."

Alex tore his eyes away from his approaching doom to glare at his nephew. "What the devil are you talking about?"

"You haven't had any communication with Lady Oxbury since the morning after Alvord's ball?"

"No. Of course not."

"Then you might wish to have some communication with her in the next day or so."

"Why?"

There went David's damn eyebrows again. "Lady Oxbury is not feeling at all the thing. We had to stop frequently on our trip from London."

"I'm sorry for her indisposition, but what does that have to do with me?"

"That's the question, isn't it?"

What was wrong with David? "Are you suggesting I gave her this illness?"

David choked. "I'm not certain Lady Oxbury is ill precisely." The man was laughing!

Had the world gone mad? Alex glanced at the carriage again. In just a few moments, *he* would go mad. "I'm as healthy as a horse, and, more to the point, I haven't been in London for weeks."

David nodded. "Lady Oxbury's stomach was most unsettled the entire trip. Fortunately her maid had come prepared—nausea is not unusual for someone in Lady Oxbury's condition."

"Lady Oxbury's condition?" The coach was only twenty yards away. "What condition? Why the hell are you talking in riddles—"

Good God! Alex gaped at David. David shrugged.

"As I say, you might wish to have a serious conversation with Lady Oxbury. In fact, I strongly recommend it." David smirked. "I imagine you might find it life-changing." With that the blasted man turned and rode back to the coaches.

Alex stayed rooted to his spot. Condition. Nausea. Not ill . . .

But she had said she was barren. She had been married to Oxbury for twenty-three years and had had no children. She was forty years old. She couldn't be . . .

He couldn't be . . .

Damn. He stared like a complete cods-head as the coach lumbered by, Kate's pale face visible in the window.

She couldn't be pregnant with his child, could she?

A surprising possessiveness surged through him. He could barely breathe. Lear shifted under him, uncertain what his frozen body meant.

He had dreamt of having a child with Kate. Of being a father . . .

But what if she still wanted to live the life of the merry widow, inviting man after bloody man into her bed?

Lear jumped under him as his knees tightened with rage. He forced himself to relax his body, but he would not relax his resolve. If Kate did not want him, so be it. But he would have his child.

He took a calming breath. *If* there was a child. He must not leap to conclusions. David could be wrong—most probably was wrong.

In any event, it looked as though he'd be staying for the whole damn gathering.

He turned Lear toward the house and urged him into a gallop. He might as well catch up with the carriage; there was no point in putting off his meeting with Kate.

He rode up just as the footman was letting down the steps. David helped Lady Grace from the coach and then a smaller woman—by her dress, the maid.

Lady Grace looked over as he approached. "Mr. Wilton,"—they both heard a gasp from the carriage—"how nice to see you."

The maid gave him a hard look that promised serious repercussions—drawing and quartering at the least—if he did anything to harm her mistress. He stepped cautiously past her, and she, David, and Lady Grace continued toward the house, leaving him alone with Kate.

He looked into the coach—he'd swear his heart lurched.

Kate was so beautiful, sitting in the shadows, staring down at her lap—so pale and delicate. So prim—but she had been anything but prim in her bedchamber that night.

A rush of desire swamped him. He wanted her. No matter what she said to him, how she felt about him—he wanted her. But he wanted her love, too. And if she were indeed enceinte . . .

"Kate." He extended a hand.

She pressed her lips together while she looked at his gloved fingers. Then she emitted a little sigh and laid her hand in his. "M-Mr. Wilton." There was a slight catch in her voice. She kept her eyes lowered.

He helped her down. When her feet reached the drive, she glanced up at him briefly. Her color fluctuated from white to red to white again. Was she going to faint? He put a hand under her elbow.

"Kate," he said, his voice low so none of the servants could hear, "are you all right?"

She nodded. Her tongue slipped out to moisten her lips. "Yes." She swallowed. "Yes, I am all—all right." She looked up at him again. "Alex—Mr. Wilton—I—" She stopped and smiled weakly. "I had better go lie down. I find I don't travel well these days."

She was a coward. She should speak to him now. Tell him she needed to have a private word with him at his earliest convenience. There was no point in putting it off.

But she *was* a coward. And she was bone tired. She had not realized how exhausting travel would be. And how mortifying! How many times had they been forced to stop the carriage on her account? After the first few times, she'd had nothing left in her stomach to lose.

A growl emerged from the coach.

"Oh, poor Hermes." She turned back. Hermes was glaring at her from the carriage seat. He expected to be lifted out, not forced to scramble down the steep stairs.

"Let me get him for you." Alex's broad hands reached for the dog. Hermes yelped once, sniffed Alex's gloves, and then consented to being picked up. "Does he have a leash?"

"Oh, yes, I—" She looked inside the carriage. Where had she put the leash? She had been in and out of the coach so many times on this dreadful trip. "I—I don't know . . ."

Alex smiled at her and she wanted to melt into a puddle at his feet or throw herself into his arms. Fortunately his arms were already occupied by Hermes. She clasped her hands together so they couldn't misbehave.

"Don't worry," Alex said. "I can carry him for you if you think he'll stray on his own."

"That might be best, if you don't mind, it being a strange house, you know. I don't usually take Hermes about, but I couldn't leave him behind with the Weasel in residence."

Alex raised an eyebrow as he tucked Hermes under his arm. "The Weasel?"

"The current Lord Oxbury." She flushed. Her stomach was fluttering, but she didn't feel as though she would be sick again. "I know I shouldn't call him that. I don't usually, in public, that is. It just slipped out."

He was frowning now. "He is not kind to you? I had heard rumors, but I'd hoped they were unfounded."

Now she felt as if she would burst into tears. Heavens, she wasn't usually such a watering pot. All this emotional turmoil must be related to her condition.

Dear God, her "condition"! She had to tell Alex—but how on earth was she going to do it? She couldn't just blurt it out here. He might drop Hermes in shock. Or fury.

Should she tell him when there were people around to defend her should he turn ugly?

She was being ridiculous. Alex wouldn't harm her.

"Lady Oxbury, *are* you all right?" Alex was scowling now. "You know you can call on me if that blackguard shows you any disrespect."

"Oh, no, I'm fine. Well, I'm not fine, but . . ." She

smiled weakly up at him. "I'm so sorry. I'm not making any sense. I'm just tired."

"And here I am, making you stand and converse when all you must want is to find your b-bed"—Did Alex blush? If so, he recovered immediately—"and rest. Take my arm." He smiled. "The arm that is not already full of dog, of course."

She loved him. Oh, God, how she loved him.

She was in serious trouble. She took his arm, repressing a slightly hysterical giggle. Her feelings for Alex were the least of it. She was unmarried and increasing, carrying the child of a man her brother detested, a man she had misled into believing she was barren.

She glanced up; Alex smiled reassuringly down at her.

But perhaps a man who didn't hate her—yet. His feelings might change when she revealed her secret.

She bit her lip, swallowing more tears. She *must* get her emotions under better control.

Lord Dawson and Grace had waited for them. As soon as they approached, the footman rapped on the front door. It swung open on his second knock; his fist almost collided with a large, gray parrot.

The parrot emitted a loud squawk. "Hey, mate, watch wot yer doin'!"

The poor footman jumped back, tripping over his own feet. Hermes, taking instant exception to the bird, struggled to get free of Alex's grasp. He barked vehemently.

The parrot leaned forward and barked back.

Hermes yelped and gazed up at Alex. Alex shrugged.

"Theo, your manners!" The gray-haired woman on whose shoulder the parrot was sitting looked sternly at her pet. "Apologize immediately."

Theo bobbed his head. "Aw, Theo's sorry, Theo's sorry."

"I apologize as well," the woman said. "Theo was

raised on a sailing ship. Sometimes his conduct is not all one would wish." She smiled and stepped back. "And where are *my* manners you may ask? Please, come in. I am Edmund's—Lord Motton's—Aunt Winifred, Miss Winifred Smyth. This, as I'm sure you've surmised, is Theo. I inherited him when my uncle Theo, God rest his soul, passed on."

"Your uncle named his pet after himself?" Grace asked as they stepped into the grand marble entranceway.

Miss Smyth laughed. "Oh, no, I did that. Theo's original name was quite inappropriate."

"Heh, heh," Theo said, "name was—"

"Theo!"

"Aw, Theo's sorry, Theo's sorry."

"And you must be . . . ?"

"Baron Dawson," David said, "Lady Oxbury, Lady Grace, and my uncle, Mr. Alex Wilton."

"I am so delighted you could come. Edmund would be here to greet you, too, but he is, unfortunately, dealing with an . . . issue in the rose parlor."

A loud crash emanated from a room down the hall, followed by a man's voice.

"Damn it, you hairy little—"

Miss Smyth raised her own voice. "I'm certain you are tired from your travels and would like to rest, so if you will just come this way?"

She led them up the stairs just as another crash and fresh cursing erupted.

"Good to see you, Dawson. Sorry for the confusion when you arrived."

David grinned. Motton looked so calm now. He hadn't sounded so calm earlier.

"Sherry?"

"Thank you." David took the glass from the viscount. "What *were* you doing when we arrived?"

"Chasing Aunt Winifred's bloody monkey." Motton grimaced. "He is not the best behaved beast in Christendom."

David snorted. "Miss Smyth's parrot has a few etiquette issues itself."

Motton rolled his eyes. "I believe I mentioned Aunt Winifred had a menagerie, did I not?"

"You did." David took a sip of his sherry and glanced around the room. He was still the only guest to arrive at the pre-prandial gathering. "Where is everyone?"

Motton cleared his throat. "Actually, I wished to have a moment to speak to you alone."

David's attention swiveled back to Motton. "Oh?"

"Yes." Motton studied his sherry glass. "The thing is, Dawson, I delegated most—well, all, actually—of the planning for this house party including the, ah, guest list to my aunt."

"Yes?" That was completely reasonable. Why did Motton seem uncharacteristically perturbed? "Is there a problem?"

"Well . . ." Motton cleared his throat again and took a large swallow of sherry. "I'd say, wouldn't you, that Aunt Winifred seems like a nice, normal older lady . . . er, that is if you subtract the parrot and the monkey?"

"Yes . . . if you subtract the parrot and the monkey."

"Unfortunately, looks are deceiving. Aunt Winifred, though she rarely frequents London or attends any *ton* events, knows exactly what the latest *on dits* are—and how to, ah, use them."

"Use them?" Whatever was Motton getting at?

"Yes. She has an unusual sense of humor. She enjoys stirring up trouble, setting the cat amongst the pigeons, if you will, though I do believe she is always good hearted about it."

"I'm afraid I don't follow you."

Motton examined his sherry. "You noticed how Lady Oxbury and your uncle are both here?"

"Yes. I tried to hint to you that would be an excellent outcome."

Motton shook his head. "No hinting was necessary. I merely mentioned Lady Oxbury to Aunt Winifred and she immediately added Mr. Wilton to the guest list."

"Splendid."

"You may not think so shortly." He smiled ruefully. "Lady Oxbury and Mr. Wilton are not the only individuals Aunt Winifred invited with ulterior motives."

David heard female voices approaching. Was Grace's among them? He thought so. Yes. There she was—and behind her were the Addison twins. He turned to glare at Motton.

Motton shrugged. "And that's not the worst of it."

Not the worst of it? What could be worse? The twins almost bowled Grace over in their dash to get to him. Well, Motton could pay part of the price for this appalling development. David nodded at the girls, then stepped behind Motton and over to Lady Grace, leaving the viscount with the matching pair of matrimonial barracudas.

"How is your aunt?" David asked. Grace looked beautiful, as usual, in a celestial blue gown with a neck that displayed a lovely expanse of skin and mounded breasts.

"Resting. I think she'll be down shortly." Grace glanced around. "I don't see your uncle."

"I'm certain he'll be down shortly as well." He saw one of the Addison twins looking in his direction. He took Lady Grace's elbow and directed her toward the windows. There was no time to waste—no time for roundaboutation. "May I ask a boon of you?"

Grace looked startled. "Yes. Well, I think so. What is it?"

"Do you see those two young women talking to Lord Motton—the twins?"

Grace glanced over. "Yes, of course. Miss Amanda and Miss Abigail. I met them in the hall just now."

"Can you please see that I am never alone with either one of them?"

"Why?"

"They are trying to catch me in parson's mousetrap and I don't wish to be caught"—he smiled down at her—"at least by one of them."

She opened her fan and fluttered it in front of her face. She had reddened again. Her beautiful skin showed her every emotion.

Damn, he had a sudden overwhelming desire to see how it responded to intense bedroom pleasure. Not an appropriate thought for Motton's drawing room.

"Will you help me, Grace? Protect me? Please?"

The fan moved more quickly. Grace glanced at the Addisons once more. "You are being absurd."

"I am being truthful. Painfully truthful."

She smiled slightly and shook her head. "Absurd, but yes, I'll do my best to see you aren't trapped by one of the Misses Addison."

"Thank you. I—"

"I'm sure he's here, Cordelia." Miss Smyth entered the room, an older, white-haired woman with a cane at her side. "He's a big, strapping fellow."

Miss Smyth surveyed the few people assembled. Her eyes hit upon him—he *was* the tallest person in the room—and lit up. She grabbed her companion's arm and started dragging her in his direction.

Hell. There was something about the woman with Miss Smyth . . . Was she why Motton had said the Addisons weren't the worst of it?

Miss Smyth reached him and smiled.

Bloody hell.

"Lady Grace, if you'll excuse me for interrupting, I have someone who especially wishes to meet Lord Dawson."

Dread exploded in his gut. He looked at the white-haired woman. Were there tears in her eyes?

Good God, it couldn't be . . .

"Lord Dawson," Miss Smyth said, "I'd like you to meet Lady Wordham." Her smile grew. "Your grandmother."

Kate sighed. She couldn't delay any longer. She was dressed; she had dismissed Marie.

She should have gone down with Grace when Grace had looked in a little while ago, but she'd lost her courage. She'd even considered pleading fatigue and hiding in her room. But she couldn't do that—she couldn't hide away for the entire house party. She had to face people—Alex—eventually.

She studied her reflection in the cheval glass, turning sideways to scrutinize her profile. Thank God for the current fashion of high-waisted gowns. Her middle had begun to look larger—well, perhaps that was her imagination. Marie *had* been lacing her stays more loosely, but more from an excess of caution than need.

Her breasts, however, were another matter. They were most definitely larger—they were barely contained by her bodice. Marie had already talked about making an alteration or two.

Would Alex notice? Surely not. Her breasts were large for her, but she had been rather small-breasted before. They weren't beacons of her condition . . . were they?

She would take a shawl down with her. It might be drafty. Where had Marie put her Norwich shawl when she'd unpacked? She opened the wardrobe; pulled out a few drawers . . . Ah, there it was. She draped it over her shoulders and finally acknowledged she had run out of ways to put off the inevitable. She took a sustaining breath and stepped out of the safety of her room.

She need only follow the sound of conversation to find where everyone was gathering before dinner. From the volume of noise, many more guests had arrived.

She paused outside the room. Was Alex there? He should be; she was coming down quite late.

She took another deep breath, gathered her shawl around her, and nodded to the footman who'd been waiting to open the door. Perhaps she could find a nice corner to hide in . . .

What was she thinking? She needed to watch over Grace. Lord Dawson was here.

She stepped over the threshold and surveyed the room. Her eyes found Alex immediately, as if he were a magnet. He was talking—well, listening—to one of the Addison twins, his back to the door. She moved to the other side of the room. Yes, she had to discuss the . . . situation with him, but not here amongst all these people. And she felt completely incapable of discussing any other subject with the man.

She did not immediately see Lord Dawson. Since he would tower over all the guests except Alex, he could not be hiding in the crowd. Had the other Addison twin cornered him? No, there she was, conversing with a very young gentleman.

And where was Grace?

"Looking for your niece, Lady Oxbury?"

"Oh!" She hadn't noticed Miss Smyth approaching. Fortunately the woman was not accompanied by Theo. "Yes. Do you know where she is?"

Miss Smyth smiled. "Lord Dawson dragged her out into the bushes not five minutes ago."

"*What*!?"

The people around her stopped their conversations to stare. She tried to smile for their benefit while her heart lurched in her chest. It was beating so hard, she feared it might push her newly oversized breasts right out of her bodice.

Miss Smyth took her arm and led her toward an elderly woman on a settee. "Now don't be concerned, Lady Oxbury. I'm certain Lady Grace is completely safe in the garden with Lord Dawson. He was understandably upset, and I'm afraid it was my fault."

"Upset? Your fault?" Whatever was the woman talking about?

Miss Smyth nodded. "Yes. I happen to be good friends with"—she paused and frowned at Kate's shawl. "Aren't you overly warm, Lady Oxbury?"

It *was* a trifle stuffy in the room. Actually, she was quite warm indeed. She was warm all the time now that she was—

Kate pulled her shawl closer. "Oh, no. I'm perfectly comfortable. I believe there's a slight chill in the air."

Miss Smyth lifted an eyebrow, and then gave a small shrug. "Very well. As I was saying, I am good friends with Lady Wordham, Lord Dawson's maternal grandmother."

"Oh." The mother of the woman Standen had loved and apparently never quite got over.

Kate slipped her hand under her shawl to rest on her stomach. Alex hadn't talked about his brother's death. Did he blame Standen? If Lord Wordham hadn't promised his daughter to Standen, if the young couple hadn't been pursued . . .

She'd been all of nine then. Standen had been twenty-five—Grace's age now. He'd come home from that Season different. But what had Lady Wordham felt? Standen had lost the woman he thought he loved—though she, obviously, had not loved him. Lady Wordham had lost a daughter.

"Lord Wordham died last year, you know, probably close to the time your husband passed." Miss Smyth paused, took Kate's hand in hers, and patted it. "My sincere condolences, dear Lady Oxbury, on your loss."

"Why, ah, thank you, Miss Smyth."

"You, of course, are much younger than Cordelia. You may marry again."

Good God, did Miss Smyth have a knowing gleam in her eye? Surely not!

"Cordelia, however . . ." Miss Smyth shrugged. "She is not in the best of health, I fear. I tell her she'll live another ten or twenty years, but I don't think she believes me. I mean, look at me. I'm almost seventy and in fine fettle. I feel as if I'll live forever—well, except for my rheumatism . . ."

Kate wasn't sure what to say. She needn't have worried. Miss Smyth didn't need any encouragement to continue.

"Cordelia wishes to tidy up, as it were. Attend to unfinished business. So when she told me she'd always re-

gretted she'd never even met Harriet's son, I knew I had
to do something. I do so like bringing people together."

Surely Miss Smyth hadn't winked? And when was
she going to give her her hand back? It seemed rude to
just pull it away.

There was a disturbance at the door. They both looked
over. A tall, broad-shouldered, very angry-looking man
and a slim, equally angry-looking woman had just entered.

"Oh, dear," Miss Smyth said. "That's Lord and Lady
Kilgorn. Scots, you know. Rather hotheaded. I'd best go
help Edmund deal with them." She smiled and patted
Kate's hand again. "You will go sit with Cordelia, won't
you, dear? And look, here is Mr. Wilton to keep you
both company."

Alex! No. She wasn't ready . . . She felt cold and then
hot. Clammy. Certainly she wasn't going to faint, was she?

"Dear Lady Oxbury, you look so pale. Mr. Wilton, I
think Lady Oxbury should sit down, don't you? Why
don't you take her to the settee over there?"

She heard his deep voice, a note of concern evident,
and felt his strong grasp on her elbow.

"My pleasure, ma'am."

Chapter 14

"What am I going to do? I can't go back in there."
David ran his hand through his hair.

"Why not?" Grace tried to catch her breath. She'd had
to almost run to keep up with David, he'd left the drawing room so quickly. "What is the problem?"

The problem obviously had something to do with Lady
Wordham. Miss Smyth had barely got the name out of her
mouth before David had grabbed Grace's hand and pulled
her out the door and into the bushes. And this trip to the
vegetation had nothing to do with seduction. David wasn't
even touching her now. His hands were fisted at his sides.

"Didn't you hear? That woman is my grandmother."
He looked away, his jaw tense.

She wanted to wrap her arms around him, hold him,
comfort him . . . but what was she comforting him for?
Lady Wordham had looked harmless. More than that,
the poor old woman's eyes had been full of longing and
regret. And tears.

There was something here she didn't understand, so
she must tread cautiously. "She's your mother's mother?"

"Yes."

David still stared off into the distance. A muscle jumped in his cheek. He looked as taut as a bowstring.

"Have you met her before?"

"No, God damn it. Why would I?" He glared at her, but she wasn't convinced he saw her. "She and her husband never came to visit—they never even sent me a note on my birthday. In all my thirty-one years, this is the first time a member of that family has acknowledged my existence."

Grace laid her hand on his arm. For a moment, she thought he would jerk it away, but he didn't. He looked down at her.

"Perhaps Lady Wordham wanted to see you, but her husband wouldn't let her. She is recently a widow. Perhaps this is the first time she has been free to do what has been in her heart all these years."

David snorted derisively and looked away again—but he didn't move away. She put her other hand on his arm as well.

"Or perhaps she was as bad as her husband, but now sees that such malice and pettiness is wrong. Perhaps she regrets her actions—or lack of action—and wishes to make amends."

He looked back down at her. "Why should I think that?"

"Why shouldn't you? She has come all this way; she looked so eager—so happy—to see you."

He snorted again. She shook his arm slightly.

"What have you got to lose, David? If she is as unfeeling as you say, you have had your opinion confirmed. You can avoid her—or even cut her—for the rest of the house party and feel justified in doing so. But if she has had a change of heart—or if she has always had a good heart—you've gained a grandmother and lost this anger and pain you've been carrying all your life. It must weigh you down terribly."

He stared at her, his face expressionless. Was he going to cling to his hatred, tell her to leave him alone?

It would be best if he did. She was going to marry John, not David. She should not be out in the garden with him. She should have refused to come.

But she could not bear for him to hold onto this pain any longer. He needed to get rid of it—to talk to his grandmother. But he needed to choose that. She could not do it for him.

His hands came up and covered hers, and she felt his body relax.

"Will you come with me? Will you stay with me while I talk to Lady Wordham?"

She should say no.

"Yes, if you wish me to."

"I do." He wrapped his arms around her. "How did you get to be so wise?"

She laughed. "It is easy to be wise when it is someone else's problem you are solving."

He kissed her lightly on the nose. "Then I hope I can be wise for you, when you have a difficult problem to solve."

She ducked her head so he could not see her eyes, see the pain and longing she knew were there. If only he *could* help her solve her problems—but that would be John's place.

He put her hand back on his arm. "Let's go in, and I will apologize to Miss Smyth and Lady Wordham for my rude and precipitous exit."

"I don't have to apologize to you, too, do I?"

"What?" Alex's teacup clattered in its saucer and he felt his ears burn as he turned to look at his host. Had

Motton noticed he'd been staring at Kate, watching her converse with Lady Wordham and Lady Kilgorn?

He'd intentionally chosen a spot on the other side of the room from her when the men returned to the drawing room after port. For some reason she'd acted nervous earlier when he'd sat with her. She'd used Lady Wordham almost as a shield.

What did she think he would do? Pounce on her? They definitely needed to have a frank conversation, but Motton's drawing room was not the proper place.

The viscount shrugged. "I seem to be apologizing to everyone tonight. I hope you don't mind that Lady Oxbury is here?"

"No, of course not. Why should I mind?" Not only was Kate here, her room was next to his—with a connecting door. Someone—Miss Smyth?—had a very twisted sense of humor. He did not expect to get a wink of sleep tonight.

Motton smiled slightly, almost slyly, and took a sip of his tea. "Why indeed?" He looked over at Kate. "Aunt Winifred tells me you and Lady Oxbury were acquainted before her marriage."

Alex stiffened. "Only slightly. I believe we crossed paths once or twice when she was in London. She left to marry Oxbury before the Season was over, so she wasn't in Town long."

"Hmm."

Dash it, what did Motton mean by hmming that "hmm" in just that tone?

"Oxbury was many years her elder, wasn't he?"

"Yes." Did the cur think Kate had been unfaithful? "By all accounts, she was completely devoted to him."

"Oh, I'm sure she was. Lady Oxbury is above reproach." There was that damn smile again. "It is . . . nice that she's come back to London now that her period of mourning is over. Do you think she'll wed again?"

What *was* the man getting at? "It would not be a surprise if she did."

Motton nodded. "And if she did marry, she might even have a child or two."

Alex's teacup crashed into its saucer.

Motton raised his eyebrows. "I'm sorry." He chuckled. "There I go, apologizing anyway. But did I say something to offend you, Wilton?"

"No. Of course not. Just my own clumsiness. I am the one who should apologize. I must still be tired from my travels—got up very early this morning, you know." It was past time to change the subject. "I say, I thoroughly enjoyed talking to your man Watkins. Very knowledgeable."

"Yes, he is, isn't he? I—oh, blast!"

Miss Smyth had appeared in the drawing room, accompanied by Theo on one shoulder and a small monkey dressed in the black and silver of Motton's livery on the other.

"I'm going to kill her. I swear I'm going to kill her." Motton forced a smile. "If you'll excuse me, Wilton?"

The viscount headed toward his aunt.

"Avast! Trouble on the portside!" Theo flapped his wings, disarranging Miss Smyth's hair and disturbing the monkey.

The monkey screeched.

The Addison twins screamed.

"Aunt Winifred, I believe we had a discussion earlier today about the livestock."

"Oh, pooh, Edmund. Theo is perfectly well-behaved, and you'll see I have your namesake on a leash." She flourished a red leather strap she had tied to the monkey's leg.

Alex heard a choked laugh behind him and turned. He had the very odd feeling that his heart had jumped in his chest. Kate was standing there grinning.

His heart wasn't the only organ jumping.

"She named the monkey after Lord Motton. Can you believe it?"

"No." He grinned back at her. He hadn't seen this uncomplicated glee on her face since she was seventeen. If only she hadn't married Ox—

But she had.

It didn't matter. That time was in the past. She was here now, unwed, and . . . increasing?

Would she tell him? Should he ask?

How do you ask such a question?

He cleared his throat and gulped down the rest of his tea. This time he managed not to make the teacup clatter, though only just. Kate was watching him, a small frown between her brows. What was she thinking?

"Would you like another cup of tea, Mr. Wilton?"

He wouldn't, but if he said yes, she would take his cup and go away, giving him a moment to get his heart and other organ under control.

"Thank you, Lady Oxbury. That would be very kind."

She carried Alex's cup back to the tea tray. She needed to get her nerves under control. She took a deep breath and then another as she poured the tea carefully into the cup. Her hand only shook slightly.

She had to tell him about the child.

The cup rattled in its saucer. She put it down quickly and glanced around. No one was paying the slightest attention to her; they were all transfixed by Miss Smyth, Lord Motton, and the monkey. Well, and the parrot, too.

She took another breath, smiled slightly, and picked up the cup again, starting back across the room to Alex. How difficult could it be? She would just smile coolly and say, "Mr. Wilton, do you recall the evening you spent in my bed? Well, I need to inform you there has been . . . you will be . . . in less than nine months' time . . ."

Her hand shook so badly, she had to grasp the cup in both hands.

She couldn't do it. She couldn't tell him.

She *had* to tell him. He deserved to know he was going to be a fath—She swallowed. That he was going to have a chi—

She couldn't do it. There was no way she could get the words out.

"Are you all right, Lady Oxbury?"

"What! Oh, oh yes." She'd managed to navigate the room without noticing. "Yes, thank you, Mr. Wilton." She handed him his cup.

He took a small sip and looked at her. She looked at him. She moistened her lips.

"Mr. Wil—"

"Lady Ox—"

They smiled at each other.

"Go ahea—"

"You fir—"

Kate laughed, it was too absurd. She heard Alex's deep chuckle echo her—and then felt his hand on her arm.

"You first, Lady Oxbury," he said, smiling down at her. "I insist."

She couldn't find the breath to speak. "Ah . . ."

"Aunt Winifred!"

She turned to look back at Viscount Motton. Now Edmund the monkey had jumped to the decorative lintel above the door and was screeching down at Edmund the viscount.

"Get that bloody beast!"

"Theo!" Miss Smyth frowned at her parrot. "Your language!"

"This is one time Theo and I are in perfect agreement, aunt. Will you curb that animal?"

"Very well. Come, Edmund." Miss Smyth tugged on

the monkey's leash. The leash dropped out of her hands. Edmund-the-monkey screeched again and leapt for the curtains. Edmund-the-viscount looked as if he, too, would like to screech, or at least curse freely.

Miss Smyth smiled brightly at the gathering. "Who would like to take a brisk turn about the terrace?"

"Lady Oxbury?" Alex offered his arm. She took it and let him lead her toward the garden and darkness, where she could tell him . . .

She wasn't ready.

Lady Kilgorn was standing by the door, watching Lord Motton and her husband try to catch the monkey. Poor woman. She'd been estranged from Lord Kilgorn for years, but now found herself sharing a bedchamber with him. It must be very uncomfortable. According to Marie, no other accommodations had yet been arranged. Surely she would enjoy a turn about the terrace.

"Lady Kilgorn, would you like to join us?"

She laughed. Kate guessed she was not yet thirty. She had beautiful creamy skin, jet black hair, startling blue eyes, and a ready smile—when she wasn't glaring at someone.

"Well, I'd like to stay and watch Ian scamper after the wee monkey, but I doubt he'd thank me for it—I'd be laughing too hard, it is so funny." She looked from Kate to Alex. "Yes, I'd like to join you, if I won't be in the way?"

"No, indeed. We were just going to invite Lady Wordham to come with us as well, weren't we, Mr. Wilton?"

"Of course, Lady Oxbury." Alex's expression was unreadable. Was he annoyed or relieved? She couldn't say. It didn't matter. With Lady Kilgorn on her one side and Lady Wordham on the other, she was safe. She could put off the inevitable just a little longer.

* * *

"Lord Dawson, would you be so kind as to escort me around the terrace?"

"Oh, Lord Dawson, please, surely you would prefer to take a turn around the terrace with me?"

David looked at the Addison twins and hoped his mouth wasn't agape. Did they not see Lady Grace on his arm? He was certain he still felt her hand.

He glanced down. Yes, there she was, biting her lips to keep from laughing, he was sure.

He drew his arm closer against his side, trapping her hand securely. He was not letting her stray an inch while these man-eating maidens were in the vicinity.

"I'm sorry, but as you can plainly"—he tried not to put too much stress on that word—"see, I am already committed to Lady Grace."

"Oh, but surely she will give up her place," Abigail— or perhaps it was Amanda—said.

"Won't you, Lady Grace?" the other twin said. "Won't you give up your place to me?"

"To *me*." Abigail glared at Amanda—and vice versa.

David squeezed Grace's hand even closer against his side, and turned to look at her. He was certain his eyes held groveling entreaty and abject terror. She couldn't desert him now—she couldn't be that cruel.

She smiled slightly. "I'm sorry, but Lord Dawson and I have matters to discuss. I'm afraid I can't cede my place to either of you."

Thank God! David struggled to look and sound pleasant. "And since I am completely incapable of choosing between you"—*ever*—"I regretfully cannot offer my other arm. And as Lady Grace says, we have matters to discuss that would certainly bore you"—*since they don't deal solely with your narrow little concerns*—"so if you will excuse us?"

He dashed out the garden door while the twins were still sputtering.

"My heartfelt—my *very* heartfelt thanks, Lady Grace, for not deserting me in my hour of need."

She laughed. "They were rather forward, weren't they?"

"Rather. I have been dodging them ever since their come-out; they live near my estate. I thought I'd escaped them when I came to Town—I was not very pleased to see them in London, and I was even less pleased to see them here."

They strolled along the terrace. Fortunately, it was an unseasonably warm evening—a little chill, but the ladies appeared to be comfortable without their shawls. Except for Lady Oxbury—she still clutched hers; she had not shed it since she'd appeared in the drawing room.

"Is your aunt feeling quite the thing?" Was this another sign that Lady Oxbury was increasing? *Was* she increasing? He had indicated to Alex that she might be, and Alex had acted as though it were a definite possibility.

Grace frowned. "I don't know. I confess I've been worried about her. She's been behaving so oddly."

"Oddly? How so?" Not that he knew what behavioral signs indicated pregnancy. He only knew the behavior that precipitated the state—a behavior he would most dearly like to engage in with Grace. And if that behavior resulted in Grace growing big and heavy with his babe?

A part of him grew big and heavy at the thought. Good God! He'd never considered children, certainly never thought he'd want one or two or more.

Oh, of course, he knew he needed an heir, but that had been, well, just a word. He hadn't thought of an infant, a small person with his blood flowing in its veins, a being made through a very intimate act with . . .

Bloody hell, the thought was physically painful in its intensity.

Grace sighed. "Well, you saw how weepy she was in Town. I don't think she's usually that way at all. And she's been so tired even though she's sleeping more than usual."

Grace was frowning, obviously sincerely puzzled and distressed. She was a female—wouldn't she know the signs of pregnancy? Perhaps he was mistaken. But then why had Lady Oxbury's maid referred to her "condition"?

Whatever the situation, Grace obviously had not been told anything. He would not mention his suspicions. Alex was here now. He was a responsible adult. Adult? The man was forty-five. Well, and Lady Oxbury was forty. One would think they were too old . . .

In any event, Alex was here. This was his concern. If Lady Oxbury carried his child, Alex would not rest until he had addressed the situation to his satisfaction.

But would it be to Lady Oxbury's satisfaction? There were two people involved here . . . but, thankfully, he was not one of them. He had his own somewhat difficult female to deal with.

"At least Mr. Wilton is here," Grace was saying. "I am so glad. Thank you for persuading him to come."

Should he lie? No, he couldn't, even by omission. "I have to confess I didn't persuade Alex. He came to see Motton's cultivation techniques, I suspect. He was rather surprised"—shocked would be a better adjective—"when I met him on the drive and he discovered you and Lady Oxbury were going to be guests as well."

"Oh?" Grace frowned for a moment, then shrugged. "Well, it doesn't signify. He's here, that's all that matters. Aunt Kate has the opportunity to talk to him. They can resolve any problems they have with each other."

Easier said than done, if the problem was the one he thought it was. The only resolution for that was a special license and vows before the parson as quick as may be. People might still count on their fingers the months between church and birth, but that couldn't be helped. It would be vastly better for Lady Oxbury to walk down the aisle in her current state than a few months further along when she was bulging with child.

And, of course, there was no question they must marry. Alex's baby could not be born a bastard.

Miss Smyth poked her head out the terrace door, her parrot still on her shoulder. "You can all come inside again," she said brightly. "Lord Kilgorn caught Edmund—my monkey Edmund, I mean."

"Caught 'im good. Put 'im in chains."

"Oh, stop, Theo. They merely tied the leash more firmly to his leg so he couldn't get into mischief again." She turned to address everyone on the terrace. "Do come in. It is quite safe—but you know, it was quite safe before as well. Edmund is rather high spirited, but he wouldn't hurt a flea." She stepped aside to let Lady Kilgorn and Lady Oxbury pass. "Edmund the monkey, that is, though I assume my nephew wouldn't hurt anyone either. Still, you can never be sure with men, can you, Mr. Wilton? Here, let me help you, Cordelia. Yes, thank you, Mr. Wilton, you take Cordelia's arm. That's the way."

Everyone started back into the drawing room. Grace stepped forward as well, but David stopped her. "Not yet," he whispered.

Fortuitously, they were in a darkened portion of the terrace, in a patch of shadow cast by a large tree. If they were quiet, everyone would go inside without noticing they were not among the crowd. They could have a few moments of privacy.

He found he was very anxious for a few moments alone with Lady Grace. All this thinking about infants had heated his blood. He needed to take a few moments to cool down—and for one of his organs to calm down—before he went back into the light and heat and prying eyes of the drawing room.

"It's a beautiful evening, don't you agree, Lady Grace?"

"Um, yes. Yes, it's very beautiful." Grace was just as happy to have a few more moments away from the drawing room. It was overwarm and stuffy there—and she did not like those Addison girls one bit. What shockingly bold hussies, the pair of them!

She drew in a deep breath of the cool, night air. A breeze rustled through the treetops and somewhere off in the distance, an owl hooted.

It was very dark in this corner of the terrace, and Lord Dawson was standing very close. She took a few steps away to rest her hands on the balustrade. Was he going to kiss her?

She should insist on going back inside immediately.

He had not followed her. He was still standing where she'd left him. Perhaps he was only interested in enjoying the night air and avoiding the stuffiness—and the Addisons—inside.

She was relieved. Of course she was relieved. She was virtually married to John Parker-Roth. She should not want kisses from another man.

But she *wasn't* married, not quite yet.

"You are going to talk further with your grandmother tomorrow, aren't you?"

"Yes, after breakfast." He made a noise, not quite a laugh, not quite a sigh. "I confess I'm more than a little nervous. Perhaps we should have left the drawing room to have our conversation this evening, but I don't believe either of us wished to bring attention to ourselves."

"You are wise. People are so interested in everyone else's business." Why did society have to be so hungry for gossip?

He shifted slightly. "I don't know what we will say, but I do believe you were right. Even if I wished to continue avoiding the situation, Lady Wordham—"

"Your grandmother." She looked over her shoulder. He should learn to say it. He nodded.

"My g-grandmother seems to feel a need to address the issue."

"She is getting older. She is just out of mourning for her husband. Perhaps she is feeling that time is precious and limited."

"Perhaps."

She felt him move. She turned to see what he was about, and found herself quickly trapped between his hard body and the balustrade. They were alone and in the very darkest spot of the terrace. She should have been extremely alarmed.

She *was* extremely something, but it wasn't alarmed.

"Thank you, Grace."

"For what? I did nothing."

"You listened." His lips turned up ever so slightly. "You asked the right questions." There was enough light from the moon—and they were standing so close together—that she could see the softening in his eyes. "You gave me courage when I needed it."

"No, I—"

He silenced her with his fingertips. The sly man had removed his glove; his skin was warm and slightly rough as he stilled her lips and then slowly traced their outline.

What was he doing? Why did her lips feel suddenly swollen? She parted them slightly.

"Yes." He pulled her lower lip down just a little with his thumb. "You did give me courage."

His lips touched hers as lightly as his fingers had. The briefest brush and then brush again.

"Oh." She inhaled. His scent was all around her—the scent of soap, linen, and . . . him.

His arms gathered her close—a good thing as her knees had chosen that moment to turn to water. His lips kept playing with her mouth, teasing her with fleeting brushes. She moaned.

That must have been the sign he'd been waiting for. His mouth finally came to rest on hers, and his tongue traced where his finger had earlier. She moaned again, opening wider, and he slipped inside.

Heaven. He was stroking deep and wet, over her tongue, over her teeth, over the roof of her mouth—filling her.

Causing another emptiness to open. An aching, throbbing emptiness, a heat, a madness.

He moved his mouth to her cheek, and all she could do was cling to him, panting, mindless.

"I need you, Grace."

Yes, need. That was right. He needed her. She needed him.

No . . .

"I need you, Grace. For this"—he returned to her mouth and leisurely, thoroughly, filled her again—"but also for your wisdom"—he brushed his lips over her forehead—"and your strength."

He pulled back, cupping her face in his hands. "Marry me, Grace. Please?"

He was asking her to marry him again. Lord Dawson— David—was asking her to become his wife, live in his house, sleep in his bed. Bear his children.

She could say yes and have his wonderful, amazing mouth on her skin, everywhere on her skin, doing things she could barely imagine . . .

She couldn't say yes. There was John. There was Papa. There was the history of their families.

Why did none of those things seem particularly persuasive at the moment?

"Grace? Will you marry me? Will you be my wife?"

"I . . ." Could she say yes? "I—"

"There you are, you naughty children!"

Grace tried to jump back and slammed into the balustrade. Miss Smyth and Theo had stepped out onto the terrace. They strolled toward them.

Dear God, could she be more embarrassed? At least all her clothing was in order.

Of *course* her clothing was in order! What was she thinking?

"Naughty children. Naughty, naughty."

"Shh, Theo."

David cleared his throat. "Miss Smyth, I—"

"Oh, you shush, too, Lord Dawson. It's a house party. The rules are a little looser. Everyone expects young people to have a little fun."

"Fun! That's wot we're 'aving. A spot o' fun. Naughty—"

"Theo! Behave yourself." Miss Smyth smiled at Lord Dawson and Grace. "Do I have to say the same thing to you?"

"I—" Grace's mouth was so dry she couldn't get any more words out.

"Miss Smyth—" David did not sound the least bit alarmed.

Miss Smyth laughed. "Don't say another word. You wouldn't be young and lusty if you didn't try to steal a kiss in the moonlight. Now come in and join the others. We are trying to get up tables of cards, and we need you to make the numbers even."

Chapter 15

It was a glum group at the breakfast table. Alex chose some kidneys and toast and took the seat next to David.

David glanced at him, grunted what must have been a welcome, and returned his attention to his plate. Kilgorn didn't even look up from his coffee.

Damn Miss Smyth. What had she been thinking? Why in God's name had she put him in the room next to Kate—a room connected to Kate's by a blasted interior door? An *unlocked* door . . . and yes, he had checked.

Did she *wish* to torture him?

He'd barely slept a wink; he'd kept thinking of that damn door. It would take but a moment to open it. If he waited until their servants left, no one need know he was visiting Kate in her bedchamber.

He had a good reason to seek her out. He needed to talk to her. He had to find out if David's suspicions were true. If she was carrying his child . . .

His knife slid on his plate, making a hideous scraping noise. The other men flinched and glared at him before returning to their own private gloom.

Talking was not the only thing he needed from Kate.

His lust was almost unbearable. He'd spent years trying not to imagine her in bed, especially in bed with Oxbury. Now . . . He stabbed a kidney. Now he knew she was lying in bed alone, just steps from him.

Bloody hell.

He had cured himself of the woman. He had been ready to be finally free of her when he'd come to Town with David. And then he'd seen her at Alvord's ball—and at Oxbury House.

He'd done more than see her—he'd touched her, tasted her, taken them both to the most amazing climax he, at least, had ever experienced.

Now when he thought of her in bed, he thought of the silky smoothness of her breasts, the slightly tart taste of her nipples, the musky scent of her . . .

Damn it all, he was as hard as a poker here in Motton's breakfast parlor with only two other men for company. Thank God his lap was shielded by this sturdy table.

The fact of the matter was he was going to go mad. Even the pain of her rejection had left him, burned away by this all-consuming lust. Did she have the slightest clue what he was suffering? Did she feel it, too?

No. She looked so cool, so self-possessed.

He should leave Lakeland and go home to Clifton Hall.

He couldn't leave. He had to find out if Kate was increasing.

Damn it all. He shifted position and tried to contemplate Motton's cultivation techniques.

Cultivation. Planting seeds in well-tilled soil, in fertile fields . . .

Motton had a lake. He'd seen it when he'd ridden up. With luck, it was cold, ice cold. He would test it after breakfast. Perhaps a plunge into freezing water would cool his damn ardor.

"Good morning, gentlemen!"

He groaned—and heard David and Kilgorn echo him as they all struggled to come to their feet.

"Good morning, Miss Smyth." Fortunately David was able to locate his voice. Alex merely nodded, as did Kilgorn. Also fortunately, there was no livestock accompanying Motton's demented aunt.

"I'll just join you, shall I?" Miss Smyth made a noise that might have been intended as a giggle. "Though I'm certain it's not *my* company you've all been longing for."

Alex clenched his teeth to keep from agreeing aloud. David was stricken with a coughing fit; Kilgorn simply glared.

"Be sure I will take the ladies to task for abandoning you."

All three men came down with coughs.

"My, my, gentlemen. I'll have to see if Edmund has any horehound tablets or licorice for your throats. Where is my nephew, by the by?"

"He was here earlier," Kilgorn said. "He left to attend to some estate business. Ye might find him in his study, if ye look."

Kilgorn sounded as hopeful as Alex felt. He looked at Miss Smyth's plate—it was piled high with eggs, toast, sausage, kidneys, and ham. No, she wasn't going anywhere for a while.

"Thank you, my lord. I should have guessed. Edmund is very conscientious, you know. He would never let a little fun and frolic distract him from his duty."

Kilgorn snorted. "And speaking of fun and frolic, where's your wee monkey this morning, Miss Smyth?"

"Oh, *that* Edmund is still sleeping." She tittered. "Edmund the monkey is nowhere near as industrious as his namesake. But don't worry, I'll bring him down later. He does enliven a party, does he not?"

"In a manner of speaking." Kilgorn carefully arranged his knife and fork on his plate. "Have ye managed to find me proper accommodations yet, Miss Smyth?"

"Oh, my lord, I am so sorry, but I haven't. You'd think in a place this size, there would be rooms to spare, but . . ." She sighed. "Well, and you'd think I'd have remembered that you and your lovely wife have an . . . unusual domestic arrangement, but . . . well, I do apologize."

Alex could swear he heard Kilgorn's teeth grinding across the table. The man did have dark circles under his eyes. Obviously he wasn't getting much sleep—and not for the reasons a man would hope. Miss Smyth had put him in the same small bedroom as his estranged wife. A bedroom with only one bed.

Frankly, it was hard to believe Miss Smyth was being completely honest about the situation. Even he, who hadn't been to Town in twenty-three years, knew the Earl of Kilgorn and his countess had lived apart for the last decade. He'd never met Kilgorn before, though. The man was only David's age—he must have married very young.

"I sent word to the inn, Miss Smyth, but I was told it was full up."

"Yes, I know. It's not a very large place, and I believe there's some . . . some event or something going on. There is no space to be had."

"I could sleep in the stable."

"Oh, don't be silly, Lord Kilgorn. You'd have all the stable boys in a dreadful pother. No, no. Please be patient just another day or two. Mrs. Gilbert, the housekeeper, is working on the problem. I'm sure she'll have a solution as soon as may be."

Kilgorn shifted in his chair and cleared his throat.

"It is not very . . . comfortable for Lady Kilgorn, ye understand."

"Oh, yes, I understand completely. I have apologized to her most sincerely. As I say, I'm sure Mrs. Gilbert will have a solution shortly." Miss Smyth smiled brightly and popped a forkful of eggs into her mouth.

Lord Kilgorn nodded. He clearly had more to say on the subject, but just as clearly recognized any further discussion was futile.

"I believe I'll take a bit of a walk. If ye'll excuse me?"

"But have you looked outside, Lord Kilgorn? It's rather nasty—damp and drizzly."

Kilgorn grinned. "Aye. It reminds me of Scotland."

"Oh, well, do enjoy yourself then." Miss Smyth waited until Kilgorn was out of the room to shrug and say, "Those Scots. They are a bit different, aren't they?"

Alex felt Kilgorn had dealt with Miss Smyth in a remarkably restrained way. Having to share quarters with your estranged wife must be exceedingly awkward. He chewed thoughtfully on a mouthful of kidneys.

He'd give anything to be forced to share a room with Kate. To be forced to share a bed with Kate. All night, every night. To—

"Now, Mr. Wilton, what is putting such a smile on your face?"

David helpfully thumped him on the back as the kidneys tried to go down his windpipe. At least Miss Smyth must think his heightened color was due to his choking.

"N-nothing," he gasped. David stepped in to rescue him.

"Miss Smyth," David said, "I have an appointment this morning with Lady Wordham. Do you happen to know if she's come down yet?"

Miss Smyth clapped both hands to her cheeks. "Oh, dear, my dreadful memory. Yes, indeed, Lord Dawson, she came down when I did, and she particularly instructed me to tell you she'd be waiting for you in the yellow parlor. I'm so sorry. Please apologize to her for me and tell her it's all my fault you didn't appear sooner."

"I'm sure she'll understand." David stood. "I'm afraid I must leave you two alone."

Over his dead body. Alex leapt to his feet. "Regretfully, I, too, have to go."

"Oh? Where are you off to?"

Trust Miss Smyth to ask awkward questions. He looked out the window for inspiration and saw a dog run by in the wet. Dogs. Wet.

"I thought I'd see if I might be of assistance to Lady Oxbury. I might walk her dog for her, so she doesn't have to go out into the damp."

Miss Smyth beamed at him. "How chivalrous. That is an excellent idea, Mr. Wilton. Don't let me detain you."

Lady Wordham was on the settee staring out the window at the rain.

David stepped into the yellow parlor. She didn't turn. Did she not know he was there? Perhaps she was as hard of hearing as Grandmamma had been. She must be about the same age, though she looked very little like Grandmamma.

Grandmamma. Damn. Thinking of her still opened a gaping emptiness in his chest. Ridiculous. He was a grown man. It had been a year. He should not still feel this . . . loss.

She had been old; old people die.

But not so suddenly, not when they were healthy—laughing and teasing and gossiping one day and gone the next, caught in the twisted mess of a wrecked carriage.

For weeks—months—afterward, he'd expected to see her or Grandda every time he turned a corner at Riverview. Every time he entered the library or the breakfast parlor or passed their favorite bench in the garden.

He sniffed and pulled out his handkerchief. He'd got a speck in his eye.

"Lord Dawson." Lady Wordham must have heard him then. Damnation. He stuffed the handkerchief in his pocket.

"My pardon. Got a bit of soot in my eye." He cleared his throat. "It's rather dark in here, isn't it? I'll just light a few candles."

Hell, she was watching him as if he were a bloody miracle or something.

She had disowned her own daughter, for God's sake, and her own grandchild. Him.

Well, perhaps she had not done so, but she had allowed her husband to do so. She'd never written, never marked a single one of his birthdays, never given the slightest indication that she knew he was alive.

"Thank you for consenting to meet with me, Lord Dawson."

"My, ahem, my pleasure, ma'am." God, he wished Grace were here now. It was her fault he was facing this uncomfortable interview.

Lady Wordham smiled slightly. She looked rather familiar all of a sudden, rather like . . .

Like the person who stared back at him from the mirror every morning.

No. There was no family resemblance whatsoever. He'd always been told he looked just like his father and just like Grandda's younger brother who'd died of smallpox.

"Well, I know it can't be a pleasure, but I do appreciate you doing so. I also know it must have been a very nasty surprise seeing me here. I told Winifred you would not like it, but I was desperate to meet you and I wasn't certain you would agree to visit me if I extended the invitation. After all, you had not sought me out when you came to Town."

He cleared his throat again. Good God, this was worse than he'd imagined. He should feel righteous anger, but Lady Wordham just seemed so old and sad.

She shook her head. "Do not prevaricate. I understand, I think, why you would not wish to see me. Well, why would you? I am a stranger to you—"

"Not just a stranger—" He pressed his lips together. Surely he hadn't sounded as hurt as he feared?

Lady Wordham sighed. "Will you please sit down, my lord? I promise to be brief, and if you do not care to hear from me again—"

Lady Wordham's voice caught, and she had recourse to *her* handkerchief. Could this get any more awkward?

"Lady Wordham, it isn't necessary—"

"Yes, it is." Her voice was surprisingly firm. "I am seventy-five years old, my lord. My husband has recently died. It is very clear to me that I shall not live forever. It is time—past time—to address a few . . . regrets while I still can. Please, sit down."

He sat. This interview could not last forever, and then he could spend the rest of the house party avoiding Lady Wordham. If it was as embarrassing as he feared, she would probably wish to avoid him as well.

He could manage it. She didn't look much like Grandmamma. Grandmamma had been plump and soft, always smiling. Lady Wordham was almost gaunt and serious. Sad.

Why should she be sad?

He pushed the thought away. Her happiness or sadness was none of his concern.

Lady Wordham sighed again. "This is harder than I expected."

"Don't feel—"

She held her hand up to stop him. "Hard, but necessary, Lord Dawson, if not for you, then for me. Please indulge an old woman."

"Of course."

She smiled at him. "Thank you." She closed her eyes for a moment and then leaned forward. "Harriet, your mother, was our youngest and somewhat spoiled, I'm afraid. She was too much like her father—very strong-willed and stubborn. She was also a little wild."

He caught himself nodding and stopped. He had surmised as much, but he didn't wish to give Lady Wordham the impression he was agreeing with her about anything.

She studied her hands. "I've thought about this over and over, why Harold—my husband—insisted Harriet wed Lord Standen, when anyone with half a brain could see they were not well matched." She looked up. "And yes, I saw it, too, and tried to reason with Harold, but he would not be swayed. I did say he was strong-willed and stubborn, didn't I?"

David smiled slightly. "Yes, I believe you did."

"I think Harold was of the opinion Standen would settle Harriet down. Harold had just celebrated his fiftieth birthday that Season, and it hit him hard. His father had died at fifty-one. I believe he was all too aware of his mortality and wanted to ensure that his baby, his pet, would be taken care of."

"His pet?" David swallowed. He would not shout at the old woman. "And so he disowned his pet and left her in an inn yard with her dying husband?"

Lady Wordham gaped at him. "What? What do you mean?"

What did *she* mean? This odd act was most distasteful. "You must know Lord Wordham tracked my parents to an inn."

"Yes, of course."

"And that he was dragging my mother away when my father came back from the village."

"I don't believe he was dragging Harriet anywhere . . ."

"When my father tried to defend my mother, he tripped and hit his head on a rock. He died after your husband left."

Lady Wordham frowned at him, anger clear in her eyes. "Who told you that? Surely not your other grandparents?"

"They did . . ." Or had they? Had he actually heard that story from Grandda or Grandmamma? He'd grown up with it, but he might have heard it from Alex or even one of the villagers. Now that he thought about it, neither of his grandparents had talked much about his father's death. Grandmamma had told him wonderful tales about how beautiful and spirited his mother was and how clever and bright his father was, but had she actually told him what had happened at the inn and what Lord Wordham had or hadn't done?

"No, I'm not certain . . . I don't know where I heard that story. But if it isn't true, why didn't my mother go home to you? Why did she come to my father's parents? And why didn't you come to her funeral or ever visit or write me?"

Damn. He sat back and took a breath. He sounded much too emotional.

"I said Harriet was strong-willed and stubborn, and I've admitted my husband was as well." Lady Wordham shook her head. "I don't know exactly what did happen, only that when Harold came home, he was a broken man. He told me Harriet had disowned him—disowned us— that she'd said she wanted nothing more to do with us, that she held us responsible for your father's death. And he *felt* responsible. No, he hadn't laid a hand on the boy, but he knew if he hadn't pursued them, Luke would not have fallen and died."

It was exactly what he'd thought, too, but now it seemed slightly unfair. If he ever had a daughter—he and Grace—he would damn well pursue her if she ran off with some man.

"I do know Harold stayed away a week," Lady Wordham said. "He told me he stayed near Harriet—she wouldn't let him stay *with* her—until your parents arrived to take her and your father's body to Riverview."

"All right, I suppose I believe that. At this point it is only hearsay."

"As is the story that Harold deserted Harriet."

"True." He could stop now—he *should* stop now. A portion—a large portion—of the wound had been healed; he could part on cordial terms with Lady Wordham. But if Grace were here, she would not let him stop; he knew it. She would insist he try to heal the whole wound. And she would be right.

"But why did you not come to my mother's funeral?" He gripped his hands tightly together. "Why did you never come see *me?*"

"I wanted to; dear God, I wanted to." Lady Wordham reached forward as if to touch him, but stopped herself and dropped her hand back into her lap. "Emotions were raw then, Dav—Lord Dawson. I believe your grandparents did blame Harold for causing their son's death and, as I said, we agreed they had some basis for that belief. And Harold and I—well, if your father had not gone off with Harriet, none of it would have happened. She would not have died, either."

David opened his mouth. How dare she lay any blame on his father?

She rushed on. "Even though we knew Harriet was equally at fault—we never thought your father had taken her against her will. But we were not totally rational at the time." She leaned forward again. "Can you understand at all, Lord Dawson? Can you imagine having a daughter, having her run away, having . . ."

Lady Wordham used her handkerchief again.

Yes, the damnable thing was he *could* imagine it—now that he had met Grace, he could imagine it very clearly.

"As to why we did not visit you, we never felt we would be welcome. And we could understand that, too. Your grandfather had lost his son; you were now his heir. You needed to be at Riverview to learn to manage the estate. You were happy—we did ascertain that."

She paused and took a shuddery breath, glancing at him and then down to her lap where her fingers twisted in her skirt. They were so thin and fragile looking.

She spoke very softly, her voice fragile as well.

"Now, with Harold gone . . . I just had to see you. Ask you to forgive me; see if we could . . . We've both lost people special to us . . ."

She was right. She'd lost a daughter and a husband; he'd lost parents and grandparents. What would be served by refusing to recognize that fact?

He still had one grandparent left.

He felt a burden shift, lighten. He smiled. "Well, Grandmother . . . should I call you Grandmother? I'm afraid I've already had a Grandmamma, but—"

"Oh, yes. Oh, please. I would love it if you would—"

His grandmother dissolved into tears. He hesitated a moment, then sat down beside her and gathered her into his arms.

Grace sat on the window seat in her room and stared out at the wet lawn. A very tall figure with a short, moppy dog came into view. She smiled. Was that Mr. Wilton with Hermes? They made a very odd pair.

Hermes took off across the grass after a squirrel. He chased it up a tree, barked vociferously for a few minutes, and then trotted back to Mr. Wilton.

Aunt Kate should be with them. Why wasn't she? Was she still feeling poorly?

What *was* the matter with her? She'd been an early riser when they'd first got to London; now she didn't get out of bed until almost noon and more times than not greeted the day clutching a basin, her stomach sadly unsettled.

She *must* be ill. She should see a doctor, yet when Grace had suggested as much, she'd turned very pale and had refused, insisting it wasn't necessary.

What could Grace do? She'd been so certain the problem was somehow connected to Mr. Wilton. She'd thought once she got the two of them in the same place, everything would be resolved, but so far that plan hadn't worked. Aunt Kate was still not in plump currant. Mr. Wilton must have had nothing to do with the problem.

Well, they had only been here a short while. She might be too impatient. She needed to give it time—but not too much time. If Aunt Kate were not better by the house party's end, Grace was going to insist a doctor be called. She would go and fetch one herself, if need be.

Mr. Wilton and Hermes had moved out of sight. She should go downstairs. She would like to go for a walk herself, but it was too damp. She was not as intrepid as Lord Dawson's uncle. Well, and the rain was starting to come down harder now.

She would go out later, when the weather had cleared. Perhaps she would look for Lady Kilgorn. How tragic that she and her husband had been estranged so long. They had married very young . . . had they wed for love or for duty?

Hmm. Thinking of estrangement, had Lord Dawson met with Lady Wordham yet? She hoped so. It was wrong to maintain such enmity for so many years. Perhaps the sin had been great, but it had happened over thirty years ago. And Lady Wordham was old and frail—she didn't have many more years left to her. It was time to find a way to forgive.

It was time for Papa to forgive, too.

Mr. Wilton and Hermes came back into view, moving at a brisker pace. She grinned. Perhaps the man was not *that* intrepid.

She should go downstairs. She would, in just a minute.

Could Papa forgive the Wiltons? He was not the forgiving sort, but maybe he could find enough charity to accept Aunt Kate marrying Mr. Wilton. If Mr. Wilton would bring Aunt Kate pleasure in her declining years, surely Papa would not begrudge her that comfort? He knew the Weasel would not take good care of her.

And if Papa would not object to Aunt Kate marrying a Wilton, how would he feel about . . .

No. She would not consider it. Her situation was nothing like Aunt Kate's. Aunt Kate was Papa's widowed sister; she was Papa's only child. It had been just the two of them for so long—as long as she could remember. Much as he might bluster, much as he might drive her to distraction—to anger, even—she loved him. She could not marry his enemy. She could not leave him all alone.

John Parker-Roth would make a fine husband. She liked him well enough. He was intelligent, even interesting if one were interested in plants. His family was very congenial, though his mother's paintings were a bit . . . It wasn't as though Mrs. Parker-Roth hung her artwork throughout the house. As long as Grace avoided her studio, she could avoid embarrassment.

And once they were married . . .

Perhaps John was merely reticent. Once they were married, surely he would . . . After all, he *was* a man. He had a mistress. He must know how marital relations were conducted. Surely he would be able to perform adequately. Perhaps he was even more skilled than David in the amorous arts.

She closed her eyes and rested her head against the window glass.

No. It had been one thing to consider marriage dispassionately when she had never experienced passion, but now . . .

Last night on the terrace had been wonderful—the solid strength of David's arms surrounding her, the hard security of his chest, the touch of his lips, the sweep of his tongue. He'd made her feel sensations she'd never felt before—and not just physical sensations.

Men might find women interchangeable, but she was not a man. And David had not made her feel interchangeable. He'd made her feel loved—not just wanted, not just lusted after, but *loved*. She'd never felt so cared for, so valued, so cherished before.

Tears leaked out and ran down her cheeks as the rain ran down the window glass.

Dear God, what was she going to do?

Chapter 16

Kate looked out her bedroom window and saw Alex and Hermes walking across the lawn—Alex so tall and straight, his long legs eating up the ground, Hermes scurrying to keep up.

She leaned forward. She loved watching Alex. As silly as it was to say it, her heart leapt whenever she saw him. She felt a thrill, a surge of pleasure and happiness . . . until she thought about what she had to tell him.

She closed her eyes briefly. How *was* she going to tell him?

She pressed her forehead against the cool glass of the window. She saw a squirrel run past Hermes; the demented dog took off after it, barking wildly. The squirrel scampered up a tree trunk and high into the branches, yet Hermes still barked at it. She smiled slightly. What went through that little canine head?

Her eyes traveled back to Alex where he stood watching Hermes. He had such broad shoulders and such small, tight a—

She pressed her hands to her flaming cheeks. Where had that thought come from?

Still, it was true—Alex might be forty-five, but he carried himself with the vigor of a man half his age.

He did other things with youthful vigor as well—

Her cheeks were burning again. She turned away from the window.

It was kind of Alex to take Hermes out. She had been indisposed again or she would have braved the wet to go with him.

Perhaps.

If she'd gone with him, she should have felt compelled to tell him . . .

She pressed her hand to her lips. The thought made her stomach twist.

When would this nausea end? Surely she would not be condemned to spend nine months worshiping at the basin every morning. Didn't most women feel better once the first few weeks were past?

She stood sideways in front of the looking glass once again, spreading her hands over her stomach. *Was* there a slight bulge there?

No, it was her imagination. Her stomach was just as flat as always . . . for now. But eventually . . . perhaps soon . . .

She had to tell Alex. This wasn't a secret she could keep for long.

She went back to the window. Alex and Hermes were out of sight.

Would Alex get angry when she told him? Standen certainly would, and she would have to tell him, too. She didn't relish listening to him bellow at her, but the thought didn't twist her heart the way the thought of Alex's anger did.

She sat down heavily on the window seat. Alex had good reason to be angry. She had tricked him, though not intentionally. But he already doubted her veracity. More than doubted—he was certain she was a liar. He'd spent all these years thinking she'd been engaged to Oxbury when she'd gone with him into Alvord's garden. She hadn't been, of course. Standen had made that deal behind her back. She hadn't even seen the announcement in *The Morning Post*—her brother had bundled her into the carriage for home long before the paper came out. She didn't discover she was engaged until Reverend Posten read the banns at church the next Sunday. She'd almost fallen out of her pew.

But Alex thought she had tricked him—and now she had to tell him she had tricked him again—that he was going to be a father when she'd promised him she was barren.

She smoothed her skirt over her lap. What would he do when she told him? Would he wash his hands of her—or would he ask her to marry him?

He might propose. He was honorable, chivalrous. He'd mentioned marriage that night at Oxbury House.

So what would she answer if he did ask?

She didn't know. She'd imagined the scene too many times to count since she'd realized she was increasing. Sometimes she was brave and told him no. He should not be penalized for her mistake. But other times she was a coward and said yes. The thought of being pregnant and unwed was terrifying. She would be cut by society, and her child would be a bastard, always living on the fringes of the polite world.

Her palms were clammy; her breath came in short gasps—

She must not panic. She forced herself to inhale and exhale slowly. She would talk to Alex. Soon. She could not put it off much longer.

She would need somewhere private. Once she finally mustered her courage, she would not wish to be interrupted. An isolated spot somewhere on Lord Motton's estate might serve, but she would have to first persuade Alex to go with her. And she would have to wait for a sunny day; today was far too damp . . .

She was procrastinating again. It might well rain all week and then where would she be? Heading back to London without having discussed the issue with Alex at all.

Surely there was some place in this very large house where she and Alex could be assured uninterrupted privacy.

Her eyes went directly to the door by her bureau. It connected her room with Alex's. She'd assumed it was locked. Was it?

Alex was still out with Hermes. This would be the perfect time to find out.

She put her hand on the knob, turned, and pushed carefully. The door swung open on well-oiled hinges. Holding her breath, she peered inside.

"Aunt Kate—"

"Eek!" Kate banged her head against the doorjamb.

"Oh, dear. Are you all right?" Grace hurried toward her from the hall while Kate slammed the connecting door closed and stepped away from it. She did not want Grace speculating about that other room—or, more precisely, the room's occupant.

"I'm fine. You just startled me." Kate steadied her voice. "Did you want something?"

Grace frowned at the door, a puzzled expression in her eyes, but then shrugged and turned to Kate. "I came to see if you wished to go downstairs." She smiled slightly. "I found I was getting tired of my own company."

Kate forced herself to smile as well. "How fortunate, because I, too, am tired of my own company. Shall we go downstairs and see what mischief Miss Smyth's monkey has got into?"

Grace laughed. "Or what outrageous things her parrot has said?"

"Yes." Kate took Grace's arm. "Miss Smyth's pets do enliven the party, don't they?"

She would go downstairs now, but tonight . . . Tonight she was going to open that connecting door.

"So what do you think I should do, Hermes?"

Hermes tilted his head as if giving the question careful thought and then barked enthusiastically.

Alex nodded. "Yes, I think I agree. I must take the issue up with Kate as soon as possible. Today. Tonight at the latest."

Hermes wagged his tail and then took off after a squirrel.

If only his life were so simple. Well, he didn't really wish to be a dog—at least not a silly little lapdog like Hermes—but he did wish things were less complicated.

He should not have accepted Kate's invitation to come to her bed. He'd known it was wrong at the time. He should have stayed home with David, had a glass of brandy in the study, and gone up to bed early. His own bed.

But, damn, it had been good. So good. Even now, standing in the damp, in the middle of Motton's lawn, he could get lost in the memory.

He closed his eyes and saw her again—as he'd seen her every single night since he'd scrambled out that damn window at Oxbury House. It was a wonder he ever got any sleep; he'd been reduced to relieving his . . . tension the way he'd done it as a boy, with his hand. It was that or lie stiff, hard, and sleepless all night.

He felt himself growing hard now. How could he not? She'd been so beautiful—hair tumbling over her bare shoulders, her lovely small breasts almost glowing in the candlelight, their sweet nipples taunting him. And her graceful waist, her flat belly with its delicate navel, the sweet nest of curls between her lovely, white thighs . . .

And the feel of her . . . her hair, like silk; her skin, like rose petals. Her breasts fit the palms of his hands perfectly, her nipples pebbling so sweetly when his fingers . . . and then his lips . . . brushed them.

She'd grown hot and damp at his touch. Her scent had surrounded him. Her mouth had tasted like heaven, and when he'd come inside her . . .

He'd dreamed of her, of being with her—in her—for twenty-three years. Even when he'd tried not to, when he'd told himself she was married to Oxbury, she would never be his, still his dreams took him to her bed.

How could he regret finally being there in truth?

And damn, if anyone walked by now, they could not fail to notice his breeches were bulging in a very obvious fashion. Thank God Hermes was his only companion.

Did the dog actually think that squirrel cared he was at the foot of the tree, barking—if you could call the little sound he made barking? Hermes certainly didn't look very intimidating—the squirrel was almost as big as he was.

Hermes gave one more bark and then trotted back to him. Alex turned up his collar against the damp and resumed their walk.

In a few months' time, would Kate's belly still be smooth and flat or would it be rounded by his babe?

He should feel a stab of panic at the thought, but all he felt was lust and pride and something else, something gentle and warm. Something he couldn't remember feeling before.

He wanted to protect Kate from the gossips, to keep her safe . . . and in his bed.

He had to talk to her today, but where? He couldn't very well take her for a tramp across Motton's estate, not in her condition . . . that is, if she *was* in a condition. And anyway, it was too damp. It was actually raining now.

"Come on, Hermes. Time to go in."

He turned and headed back the way he'd come. Hermes must have had enough of the weather as well, because he didn't protest.

Could he find a quiet corner in the house where he and Kate could have a private conversation? This was not a chat he'd care to have interrupted—or overheard, even by the servants. If the word got passed around that Kate was increasing . . .

No, there was only one place for a discussion of such a sensitive nature. The place where the . . . problem had started—Kate's bedroom.

He would use that connecting door tonight, and if by some chance the conversation moved to her bed . . . well, he wouldn't complain at all.

David looked warily around the blue drawing room. Was this a safe place to read? The library had too many shadows and not enough escape routes.

He could go hide in his bedroom.

No, he wouldn't put it past the Addison twins to corner him even there.

He chose a chair that faced the door so no one—no young lady, no husband-hunting Addison—could creep up on him unawares. At the first sight of a feminine slipper, at the first sound of a female voice, he would bolt. He could dash out through the other door to the hall or head for the terrace via the French windows.

He was in a particularly precarious position at the moment. Motton's butler had informed him most of the men had gone out riding. He would have gone as well if he hadn't been talking to Lady Wordham. To his grandmother.

He smiled. He owed Lady Grace a large debt of gratitude. She'd been completely correct. There was no point in carrying a grudge—and now that he'd given it up, he realized what a heavy burden it had been. His whole life had been shadowed by a vague feeling of anger and abandonment, an ever-present niggling sense of unease. Half of his heritage had been obscured by a dark cloud.

Now, thanks to Grace, a fresh wind had dissipated the gloom. He'd learned about his mother's family—and he had a grandmother again. Lady Wordham would never replace Grandmamma, of course. Grandmamma had raised him, she and Grandda, and he had loved her as a mother. He would always miss her.

But Lady Wordham was tied to him by blood as well, and it felt good to know about that side of his family. He had an uncle, two aunts, and various cousins whom he'd never met. He'd always known *of* them, of course—his uncle was now the marquis; he couldn't live in England and be completely unaware of the man—but that was different. He just might see about paying a visit or two when he returned to Town.

But first he had to be certain he left the house party a free man—or, better, a man betrothed to Lady Grace, not a devious Addison twin.

He opened his book, but kept an eye on the door. He must remain alert. He was alone and unprotected. His grandmother had gone upstairs to lie down, and Grace was not in evidence. Where could she be? Didn't she understand that her absence put him at grave risk?

If she *were* here . . . Ah, he'd happily be found in a compromising position with Lady Grace. He would dearly love to initiate a compromising position. A *very* compromising position. A nakedly—

"Lord Dawson!"

He shot to his feet. Damn! One of the Addison girls

had appeared in the doorway. Had she taken her shoes off and arrived on tiptoe so as to make no sound?

He should not have allowed himself to become distracted by thoughts of Grace.

"Ah . . . Miss . . . ah . . . Addison." Which of the bloody little ferrets was she—Abigail or Amanda?

"What a pleasant surprise, finding you here. I thought you'd be out riding with the other men." Good God, was the woman actually batting her eyelashes? "Did you stay here hoping to encounter me?"

"No!"

Perhaps he had been a little too forceful in his reply. Miss Whichever Addison blinked, but rallied quickly.

"Oh, Lord Dawson, you are so droll!"

He was going to be so absent the moment she took one step closer. It might be hard to explain such a precipitous exit, but he didn't care. He'd plead a sudden, urgent need to visit the privy, if he had to.

Hell, she'd probably follow him into the damn jakes. The girl knew no shame. He cleared his throat.

"Sorry to have to leave you so quickly, Miss, um, Addison, but I'm afraid I must go—"

"No, you don't, you cheeky little devil."

He blinked. Surely Miss One-or-the-Other Addison hadn't said that? There was shameless and then there was . . . He couldn't think of an adjective extreme enough to convey his sentiments.

"Stop, thief!"

No, now that his brain wasn't completely frozen by panic, it was obvious who the speaker was—Miss Smyth's parrot.

"Eek!" Miss Addison-in-the-Room screeched and grabbed at her skirts, revealing a significant quantity of ankle had there been anyone in the room who cared to see. Miss Smyth's monkey darted across the floor by her feet.

"Edmund, you bad creature, come here!" Miss Smyth followed, her parrot on her shoulder.

"Bad creature! Stop, thief!"

"Oh, hush, Theo, do." Miss Smyth smiled at David, then turned to Miss Still-Screeching Addison. "Please, Miss—which one are you?"

"Abigail."

"The older one?"

"By five minutes."

"Well, good for you—you elbowed your sister out of the way from the very beginning, didn't you?"

"Ye—no." Miss Abigail Addison frowned. David swallowed a laugh. He could come to like Miss Smyth very well.

Miss Amanda Addison put in her appearance then, pointing a finger accusingly at Miss Smyth's monkey. "That creature stole my plume!"

The monkey, attired today in a bright red coat and matching hat, was indeed clutching a pink plume. It screeched at Miss Amanda, scrambled up the curtains, and swung onto the mantel. A porcelain shepherdess, accompanied by two sheep, toppled to the hearth, shattering into hundreds of pieces.

"Oh, dear," Miss Smyth said, "I hope Edmund wasn't especially fond of that knickknack."

"Yer in big trouble, matey."

Surely it wasn't possible for a parrot to gloat? David bit back a smile. Theo seemed uncommonly pleased with the monkey's misbehavior.

"Oh, Lord Dawson, can't you please rescue my plume from that, that . . . creature!" Miss Amanda was gazing at him beseechingly. He was not impressed.

"I'm certain Miss Smyth can get your plume for you better than I can." He grinned. "I don't want to risk my fingers—the animal might bite."

This unchivalrous reply seemed to give her pause for a moment, allowing her sister the opportunity to push into the exchange.

"Quite right, my lord. You can't be too careful. Who knows what diseases that beast might carry?" She batted her eyelashes at him again.

Apparently his barony outweighed his lack of bravery, at least on Miss Abigail Addison's scale.

Miss Smyth's mouth was opening and shutting, but no sound was emerging. She pressed her hands to her breast and took a deep breath. "Diseases? Diseases!"

"Scurvy dog."

"You are quite right, Theo, but not about Edmund." Miss Smyth took a step closer to Miss Abigail and waggled her finger right in front of the girl's nose. "I'll have you know, miss, that my Edmund does not carry diseases. How could you even think so? The very idea! He's never been sick a day in his life. I'm sure he does not care to be so insulted."

Miss Amanda made the ill-considered decision to enter the fray. She laughed. "But he's a monkey, Miss Smyth."

Motton's aunt rounded on her new target. "I am well aware that he is a monkey. He is a very intelligent monkey—certainly more intelligent than a pair of young women I could mention"—Miss Smyth sniffed—"but won't."

Two identical jaws dropped. Four identical eyebrows snapped into two identical frowns.

David stepped forward. Surely the girls wouldn't harm Miss Smyth, would they?

They were not given the opportunity. Lady Kilgorn, Lady Oxbury, and Lady Grace fortunately stepped into the room then.

Lady Kilgorn laughed. "Where did the wee monkey get that feather, Miss Smyth?"

"From me, Lady Kilgorn." Miss Amanda sounded exactly like the spoiled four-year-old daughter of one of David's friends. "And I want it back."

"Well of course ye do." Lady Kilgorn walked over to Edmund and extended her hand. "Here, sir, give me that feather, if ye please."

Edmund screeched. He did not seem inclined to comply.

"Ah, ye drive a hard bargain, do ye?" Lady Kilgorn looked around the room and picked up a small, silver snuff box. "Will ye trade me then, sir?"

Edmund looked at the shiny object in Lady Kilgorn's hand for a few seconds; then he dropped the plume and grabbed the box. Lady Kilgorn picked up the feather and handed it to Amanda. Miss Smyth clapped.

"Well done. You have quite a way with animals, Lady Kilgorn." She beamed at the woman. "I was obviously very wise to include you in this house party." She glared at the Addison twins. "Though clearly I did make a few mistakes on the guest list."

The Addison twins gasped in unison.

Grace had stepped away from the fracas and closer to David.

"Come with me into the garden?" he asked. She seemed to hesitate. "I'd like to tell you how my interview with my grandmother went."

She smiled then. "Of course."

They stepped out the French windows. The other women were having a spirited discussion about pets and appeared not to notice their departure.

The air was fresh, damp, and a little chill, but invigorating. Grace let Lord Dawson put her hand on his arm. They walked across the terrace, down the steps, and along a path.

"How did your conversation go, my lord?" She was so glad he had spoken with Lady Wordham. It had been obvious to her that the elderly woman needed to make peace with her past, but men could be so obtuse sometimes, so *pigheaded*. Just look at her father. Once he got a notion in his brain box, it was almost impossible to shake it loose.

"It went very well." David grinned. He looked so happy and . . . young. "Thank you for urging me to talk with her. I think it helped us both."

She squeezed his arm and smiled back at him. "Of course it did. And you were very kind to meet with her."

He shrugged. "I don't know about that. I was not very eager for the interview—and it was not pure charity by any means. I did gain something important—I learned about my mother and her family—my family."

"Yes, of course. But you could have lived your life adequately without knowing those things. Something would be missing, yes, but nothing crucial to your happiness. Lady Wordham, however . . . Well, I think she needed to be forgiven. Whether she was truly at fault or not, I think she felt the burden of the past."

He nodded and they strolled in silence for a few moments. Grace tried to memorize every detail—the feel of his arm under her hand, the height and breadth of his body next to hers, the way the sunlight gilded his hair. All too soon, she would be returning to Standen and walking down the aisle to an altar where John Parker-Roth waited.

Could she hold these impressions in her heart, clear and sharp and alive, so she could relive them in the years to come? No. They would fade like a painting hung in the sunlight or subjected to the inevitable dust of time.

It was just as well. She would have John. She should not be keeping another man in her heart.

They had strayed into an overgrown section of the garden. The air was heavy with the scent of wet dirt and leaves.

"Grace."

"Hmm?" It was so quiet here, so private. Almost as if she and David had managed to walk into another world, a world blessedly free of practicalities.

David stopped and put his hands on her shoulders. He had a very intent look in his eyes. He was going to kiss her. Good. She tilted up her face, parted her lips. She wanted this. It was another memory, another sensation to store away for as long as she could.

His mouth touched hers, gently at first, asking, not demanding; giving, not taking. It moved to her eyelids, her cheeks, light touches that burned into her heart, heated her, made her melt with need.

She whimpered softly and his mouth returned to hers. This time its touch was not light. It was wet. Deep. Consuming. His tongue swept through her until she was certain he knew every corner of her soul.

She put her hands round his neck and let her body sag into his, soft to his hard. Madness burned in her; hunger; desire.

"Grace?"

"Hmm?" She blinked up at him. She didn't want to talk. Talking meant thinking. She didn't want to think. She wanted to feel.

She cupped his face, kissed his jaw, urged him to come back to her.

He did. His hands moved to her hips. She wanted them on her breasts . . .

He pulled his head up, laughing, panting slightly. "Grace, stop."

She didn't want to stop; she never wanted to stop. She reached for him again, but he grabbed her by her shoulders and set her away from him. His touch was gentle, but unbreakable.

"Grace." He was grinning. "This is lovely, and I

would definitely like to get back to such activities very soon, but first I have an important question to ask you."

Oh, dear God. She should turn away. She should make an excuse to go back to the house.

No, running away did no good. Just as she had urged him to talk to his grandmother, now she must talk to him.

She couldn't talk. Her throat was clogged with tears.

How could she explain her loyalty to her father? Her duty to honor his need above hers—above something as transitory as lust? She could tell by looking in David's eyes he would not understand, and she did not want to see the joy in his face drain away.

But he was relatively young, and they had only known each other such a short while. He would find another woman to love. Her father had only her.

"Grace, will you marry me?"

She didn't have to watch his face; she couldn't see it, she was crying too hard.

"No, David. I'm sorry. I can't."

Chapter 17

"You're retiring early, are you not, sir?" Roberts put Alex's coat in the wardrobe.

Alex swallowed a sigh. His valet could be damn annoying sometimes. "Not so early."

Roberts raised an eyebrow. Alex contemplated planting his fist in the man's eye socket just under that obnoxious brow.

His valet was a moderately perceptive man. Both eyebrows shot up, and then he bowed hurriedly. "I take it that will be all for the night?"

Did the man's glance dart toward the connecting door? Alex strove for an impassive—a phlegmatic—demeanor. Roberts probably knew exactly what he was contemplating—servants knew every blasted detail of one's life—but he need not acknowledge that fact out loud. "Yes, thank you. That will be all."

Roberts headed for the door. Alex couldn't help himself—the words were out before his brain fully realized he was speaking.

"Ah, one more thing . . ."

Roberts stopped with his hand on the doorknob. "Yes?"

Alex's brain finally caught up to his tongue. Was he a complete idiot? He couldn't ask that. "Never mind."

Roberts smirked. "I noticed Lady Oxbury also sought her bedchamber early. The gathering must be very tiring."

He'd so enjoy throwing a shoe at the coxcomb's head. "Exceedingly tiring. So tiring I may sleep late tomorrow. Do not bother to come until I call for you." Ha! Let Roberts make what he would of that.

It was obvious what Roberts was making of it. The man grinned at him. "Very good, sir." He waggled his blasted eyebrows. "And may I say I wish you the best of luck?"

Damn it, he was flushing. He could feel the heat flood his neck and face. "Why would I need luck?"

Roberts' eyebrows moved faster. "I have no idea, sir." He slipped out, closing the door quietly behind him.

Bloody liar. Roberts had a crystal clear idea of what he thought Alex intended—only he was wrong.

Well, partly wrong. He would love to love Kate, to take her to bed and do what he'd done to her back in London.

Ah, there was the rub. What *had* he done to her in London?

He reached for the brandy decanter and poured himself a full glass. Was he going to be a father? Have a child—a son . . . well, or a daughter. A baby.

In the first year or two after Kate had married Oxbury, he'd been tortured by the thought of her growing round and heavy with Oxbury's brat. It wasn't well done of him, he knew that. He'd known it even then, but he hadn't been able to help himself. In his mind, having Oxbury's child made Kate's marriage irrefutable. When the years passed and she stayed slim and childless, he could fool himself that she didn't share Oxbury's bed, that she wasn't tied to the man.

There might be some truth to that. Oh, not that Kate

was a virgin—she'd clearly not been one when he'd climbed into her bed in London. But her ties to Oxbury . . . for better or worse, they hung by a thread— or by the new Lord Oxbury's whim.

If she'd had a son, things would be very different. She'd be the earl's mother. And even if she'd had a daughter, there would be that life she and Oxbury had created together.

Alex sat down heavily in the brown leather wingchair and stared at the fire, cradling his brandy in his hand. He'd thought a lot about children, about legacy, in the year since Da and Mama died.

When *he* died, there would be no one to mourn his passing. Oh, David would—and perhaps David's children would miss old Uncle Alex—but that was different. He would have no direct descendent; no son to carry on his name; no daughter with his blood. And no one to inherit Clifton Hall. He blew out a long breath. Perhaps he would leave it to David's second son.

If David had a second son.

Nonsense. David had to marry and have children— he had a title to pass down. It looked a bit uncertain at the moment that his bride would be Lady Grace, however. Something had happened this afternoon to cause a falling out. At dinner tonight, the two would not let their eyes meet. If by accident their gazes did connect, they looked away as quickly as they could. When David had entered the drawing room after dinner, he'd looked for Grace—and then gone to the other side of the room. Grace had retired shortly afterward.

It was unfortunate, but David was only thirty-one, still relatively young to be considering matrimony. And, given Standen's dislike of all Wiltons, choosing a different bride would probably increase David's domestic harmony.

But *he* was not young.

He swirled the brandy in his glass. He'd seriously considered marriage a few years after Kate's wedding. He'd wanted children, and he'd found a lady who seemed congenial. But he'd vacillated and she'd married someone else.

That was the story of his life—he failed to act decisively and he lost the prize. If only he'd flown with Kate to Gretna Green twenty-three years ago, just as Luke had taken Lady Harriet . . .

He took a sip of brandy. All that was water over the dam. History. This was today. He had a decision to make now.

If Kate indeed carried his child, there was no decision to be made. He would not let his child be born a bastard.

He put down his brandy, rose, and strode toward the connecting door. It was time to put an end to his uncertainty.

"That will be all for tonight, Marie. Thank you." Kate rubbed her temples. She was developing a crushing headache.

"Would ye like a spot of tea, my lady?"

Kate's stomach twisted. Regretfully, tea would not help in this instance. "No, thank you."

Marie made a small huffing sound and lingered by the door. Kate looked up. It was obvious the woman would burst if she didn't open her budget. Unfortunately, Kate was certain she knew exactly what Marie wished to say—and she did not want to hear it.

She could ignore her—she *should* ignore her.

Whom was she fooling? That tactic had never worked

in the past; there was no indication it would work this time. Marie was capable of standing there until tomorrow.

She sighed. "Did you have something else to say, Marie?"

Marie's chin came up. She looked quite pugnacious. "Happen I do."

Kate nodded; Marie glared.

Zeus! If Marie wanted to ring a peal over her head, she should just do so and be done with it. It was hard to imagine she could say anything Kate had not already said to herself.

Kate looked down and pressed her fingers to her forehead. It didn't help. "Yes? And you wished to say . . . ?"

"Ye know ye have to tell him soon, don't ye?"

Kate didn't need to ask who "he" was. There was only one male in attendance whom she needed to tell anything. She had decided earlier she would do so tonight, but now that tonight was here . . . She glanced at the connecting door. Perhaps tomorrow.

She looked back at Marie. Her maid actually appeared sympathetic. Damn. Tears pricked her eyelids.

She would *not* cry.

"I will get to it, Marie."

All trace of sympathy vanished; now Marie merely looked exasperated. "And when will that be, my lady? Ye said the same thing last night."

She had, hadn't she? "Well, yes, but the house party has just begun."

"And it will end all too soon with poor Mr. Wilton no more the wiser, I fear."

Poor Mr. Wilton? What was poor about Mr. Wilton? He didn't puke his breakfast up every morning. He wasn't worried people were looking at his stomach; he didn't wonder if it had begun to protrude, if everyone would guess . . . exactly the truth. And in just a few months—perhaps a few weeks—no one would have to guess. It would be painfully obvious to anyone with eyes in his—or her—head that an interesting event was expected.

She pressed the heels of her hands into her forehead. What if Alex laughed at her when she told him? What if he washed his hands of her, said she'd seduced him so now she could pay the price?

No, he would never do that. He might be very, very angry, though, and she couldn't blame him. He'd gone all these years without any encumbrances, and now she had to tell him . . .

She couldn't do it.

She *had* to do it.

"I've hardly had time—"

"Ye've had plenty of time." Marie clicked her tongue. "I see how it fashes ye. Ye've nae been eating or sleeping well. That canna be good for ye or the wee bairn."

"Well . . ." Certainly worry was contributing to this blasted headache.

"It's nae gonna to get any easier, my lady. Just think if ye wait till ye are showing, how awkward that will be. I canna think Mr. Wilton would like to find out then that he's the cause."

"Nooo . . ." Where was that basin? She was going to be ill.

Marie crossed her arms. "If ye do nae tell the man tonight, I will tell him in the morning."

Kate's head snapped up. "You wouldn't!"

"I would." Marie looked exceedingly mulish.

"But I should go to Lady Grace. She appeared very upset in the drawing room this evening."

Marie just stared at her.

"And I'm not dressed." Kate spread her arms. "See, I am already in my nightgown."

Marie snorted. "The man has seen ye in yer nightgown afore, my lady. He's likely seen ye without yer nightgown—or any gown at all. I do nae think he'll be complaining of that when ye walk into his bedroom."

Dear God! Walk into Alex's bedroom . . . she could not do it. It was as simple as that.

"I'll speak to him tomorrow morning, I promise." She could meet him in the garden. That would be private enough.

"Ye'll speak to him tonight, my lady, or *I'll* speak to him tomorrow morning." Marie slammed the door behind her for emphasis.

"Ohh." Kate covered her face with her hands. What was she going to do?

She was going to tell Alex . . . somehow. She had to. Marie was a woman of her word; if Kate did not find the courage tonight, Marie *would* march up to Alex tomorrow.

When had she so offended the Fates? She had lived a good life. She had done as her brother insisted and married Oxbury. She had been faithful to her husband. She gave alms to the poor, visited the sick, said her prayers every night . . . almost every night.

Other widows entertained gentlemen in their beds, and they did not become enceinte. And she had only done it once. It was not fair.

"What do you think, Hermes? What should I do?"

Hermes yawned and put his head down on his paws. He appeared completely unmoved by her troubles.

She blew out a long breath and looked at the connecting door. How difficult could it be? She and Alex were both mature adults. They could discuss this rationally, couldn't they?

Panic grabbed her throat so tightly she could barely breathe.

Perhaps she should practice. She walked over and stood in front of the looking glass.

"Mr. W-Wilton—" She cleared her throat and took a few deep breaths. "Mr. Wilton, I wish to . . . to . . ."

She could not sound frightened. There was nothing to be frightened about—

Of *course* there was something to be frightened about . . . it was growing in her womb right now. She put a shaking hand on her stomach.

What did she want from Alex? A marriage proposal? How could she accept? She would be making him pay for her folly. She was too honorable for that. Perhaps a proposal of a different sort? But men did not want pregnant mistresses and squalling brats.

She put both hands over her abdomen. Her baby would not be a squalling brat. He or she would be loved and well cared for . . . if they both weren't starving in the workhouse.

She leaned on the dressing table and took some more deep breaths. This was not working.

The important thing was to tell Alex that she was . . . that he was . . . that there was a child on the way. Once that basic task had been accomplished, she could address all the other issues. With luck—a commodity that had been sadly lacking in her life of late—Alex would not totally desert her. He might even have some constructive thoughts on how to address the problem.

Yes, of course. Two heads were better than one . . . She touched her stomach once more. Not two—three . . . Oh, dear.

She squared her shoulders and stepped up to the

connecting door. Enough. It was time to find some courage—past time.

She put her hand on the knob and took one more sustaining breath. She could—

She was jerked forward as the door opened from the other side.

"Eek!" She reached out with her free hand to brace herself and encountered a hard, male chest. "Oh!"

"Kate! Are you all right?" Alex grabbed her shoulders to steady her.

"Um." He smelled of brandy and linen and . . . Alex. He'd taken off his coat and waistcoat. His fine lawn shirt was so soft under her fingers.

His skin was softer. She remembered the feel of him very clearly . . .

She snatched her hand back as if burned. He frowned down at her.

"*Are* you all right?"

"Yes, of course, I'm all right. Why wouldn't I be?" She bit her lip. She hadn't meant to sound so sharp, but her stomach was jumping around like Miss Smyth's monkey. She cleared her throat—her mouth was suddenly as dry as the Sahara. "May I come in?"

The right corner of his mouth slid up into a half smile. "You already are."

She flushed. "Well, yes, but may I come farther in?"

The left corner of his mouth turned up to match the right. He stepped aside. "Of course. Would you like a glass of brandy?"

Brandy was not one of her favorite drinks, but it might help steady her nerves now. "Yes, thank you. That would be very pleasant." She stepped past him. She glanced briefly at the bed—she was already as red as a ripe tomato, so her added blush would surely go unnoticed—and then focused on the chair by the fire. The single chair.

She stopped. Where should she sit?

"What's the matter?" Alex looked up from pouring the brandy.

"I, er . . . nothing." She would stand.

His brow furrowed. "You don't look very comfortable."

She was not very comfortable—in fact, she was exceedingly uncomfortable. She was nervous. And he wasn't helping matters.

A man should not be so handsome. Alex had discarded his cravat. The neck of his shirt was open, revealing the strong column of his throat. She remembered exactly how he'd looked with no shirt at all, how broad his shoulders were, how soft the hair that spread over his chest, trailing down to . . .

She turned away quickly to stare at the fire. She was certainly hot. And . . . damp. Wet. Achy and . . .

"Go ahead and sit in the chair, Kate."

She clasped her hands tightly together. Kate. She loved it when he called her Kate instead of Lady Oxbury. She was tired of being Lady Oxbury. She wanted to be just Kate, just herself, and to hear her name in his voice. It was so intimate. Just the two of them, just Kate and Alex. No interfering brothers, no obnoxious cousins-in-law, no gossiping *ton*—just them.

And one other. She put her hand over her stomach. She had to tell him.

She looked back at him. "Where will you sit?"

He waved his hand vaguely. "Somewhere."

Mmm. His hands. He wasn't wearing gloves; his long, broad fingers were naked.

She remembered exactly how those hands had felt on

her skin. Slightly calloused; strong but gentle; sure and tantalizing; teasing; promising . . .

Her knees felt weak. She definitely needed to sit. She lowered herself into the chair—and shot back out of it. It was still warm from Alex's body.

"What's the matter?" Alex's voice roughened with concern. "Did you sit on a pin or something?"

"N-no."

He came over, handed her the brandy glasses, and bent to run his hands over the seat. She had a glorious view of his breeches stretched tight over his muscular arse.

She wet her lips. And she remembered exactly how his naked arse had felt under her hands as he'd pumped his seed into her . . . his seed which had taken root, his seed whose fruit was the impetus for this visit.

She had to tell him she was increasing.

She took a swallow of brandy.

"I don't feel anything sharp." He straightened. He was so much taller and larger than she. "I think it's safe for you to sit now."

"I . . . I think I'd prefer to sit on the ottoman, if you don't mind." She suited action to words. Unfortunately, this brought her eyes directly on level with Alex's fall. If she raised her hand, she could touch him there. If she leaned just a little forward, she could kiss . . .

Did she see a more pronounced bulge?

Alex sat down abruptly and took his brandy back from her. "Did you have a particular reason for . . ." He cleared his throat. "I mean, why did you come . . ." He shook his head. "No matter." He smiled. "I am delighted to see you, Kate." He leaned forward and combed his free hand through her hair. "I've missed you." His thumb stroked her cheek.

She swallowed. Her condition was making her very

weepy. "Ah . . ." They had just seen each other downstairs, but she knew that was not what he meant. "I've missed you, too."

The last time they'd been together in a bedchamber, he'd left so abruptly—both her bed and London. That had been her fault—it was the first thing she should apologize for. "I'm sorry for what I said. I never meant to hurt you."

He did not pretend to misunderstand. "What *did* you mean, Kate?"

She pulled back a little and looked down at her brandy. "I-I'd dreamt of you for years, Alex, all the years of my marriage. And then, when I saw you in the Duke of Alvord's ballroom . . ."

She paused. She wanted to say something that sounded like the truth, but wasn't quite. She couldn't. Alex deserved to hear all of it, the carnal with the sweet.

She tried again. "I wanted you, Alex. I've wanted you all these years. I wanted to see if . . . loving you would be as good as I'd dreamt. But I didn't want you to feel compelled to offer more than a pleasant romp in the sheets." She smiled briefly. "I thought a single romp would be enough to satisfy my curiosity. The actual act . . . with Oxbury, it hadn't been . . . well, I could have lived without it. But with you . . ."

His hands gently tilted her face up so she had to meet his eyes. "It was never about a romp in the sheets to me, Kate. Never. Was it really that for you?"

More truth. She bit her lip. "No." The word came out in a whisper. "No, it was never that."

"What was it then?" He took the brandy glass from her fingers. His hands slid down to her shoulders and then her upper arms. He urged her closer. She half stood and he swept her forward onto his lap. "If it was not purely physical, what was it, Kate?"

"Um." He expected her to think, sitting on his lap in her nightgown, unprotected by stays or shift?

She didn't need to think—she knew it was love, on her part at least, but she didn't have the courage to say so.

"One chair is enough, don't you agree?" he said.

"Ah." One chair seemed more than enough. She was overwhelmed by sensation—his thighs pressing against her bottom; his arm firm around her; his chest cradling her; his fingers stroking her jaw. She tilted her head to rest on his shoulder.

She should tell him now. "Alex."

"Hmm?" He had that very intent, very hot look in his eyes. His mouth was coming closer. She let her eyes drift shut as his lips touched hers.

She would tell him later.

His fingers left her jaw to cup her breast.

"Eep!" She'd swear a jolt of energy shot from his fingers directly to the aching place between her legs.

He chuckled. "I'd rather make you sigh than squeak, my love. Let me try again."

His tongue slipped between her lips and stroked deep into her mouth. His thumb found her nipple. Thankfully, her breasts were no longer sore.

She had to tell him.

She would tell him later when she could think of something other than the feel of his tongue sliding over hers. He was working loose the little buttons that ran up the front of her gown. His large male fingers were taking much too long with the task. She would be happier if he would just rip the gown open.

He'd called her his love. Had he truly meant it? Or was that just a casual endearment, something he said to any woman he had panting in his hands.

She was definitely panting. Ah. He finally had the

nightgown open. He was touching her, his fingers sliding over her skin. It felt so very good. And . . . oh. His mouth left hers to move to her jaw and then to the sensitive spot right below her ear . . .

Yes. He was moving in the right direction. She arched a little to encourage him.

"Eager, Kate?"

She would think him exceedingly obnoxious, cocky even, if she hadn't heard the catch in his voice, the slight breathlessness.

She shifted on his lap. Hmm. Perhaps he *was* cocky. Very cocky. There certainly was a large ridge growing under her—

"Ohh." His mouth, his tongue, had reached her nipple.

Alex smiled. He'd made Kate moan. He wanted to moan, too. His . . . desire was becoming a very large, throbbing ache.

He laved her nipple and made her moan again.

Why *was* Kate in his room? Did she have the same purpose he'd had when he'd opened her door?

Well, there was no rush. They had all night. Mmm. All night. He could think of a number of things he would like to do to pass the time.

He moved to her other breast. He needed to get her out of this nightgown. He wanted to see every beautiful inch of her as he had at Oxbury House. He'd dreamt of that night so many times.

He returned to her mouth and skimmed his free hand over her hip, down her leg, to the hem of her nightgown. This chair was all very well, but he would prefer the bed. He wanted to stretch her out naked on the sheets and have both hands free to explore her thoroughly. Very thoroughly.

He started sliding his hand back up her leg, taking her gown with him.

At some point she would come to the reason for her visit. If she did not, he would initiate a conversation. One way or the other, she was not leaving this room without telling him whether he was going to be a father or not.

God! The thought that his child might be growing in Kate's body . . . it was terrifying and awe-inspiring. His babe at her breast . . . a son or daughter with his blood and Kate's. It was a dream he'd not had the courage to dream for years.

He kissed her slowly and thoroughly, pretending it was true, praying it was true.

He would ask her if she did not tell him, but it would be better if she told him. Perhaps she would find it easier to talk in bed . . . naked in bed . . .

He now had her skirt up to her knees. He could not proceed farther without a bit of contortion. It was time to move this interesting activity to a more congenial location.

He slipped one arm under Kate's knees and the other around her back and stood up.

"Eek!" She flung her arms around his neck. "What are you doing?"

He grinned. "Taking you to bed. Does that meet with your approval?"

"Yes." Some of the lust cleared from her eyes and she frowned. "No."

"No? I promise sharing a bed will be far more comfortable than sharing that chair—though that was very nice and I will return us there, if you insist." He bent his head to kiss her again, but she put her fingers on his lips before he could reach her mouth.

"No, Alex. Put me down."

She hated to say those words, but she had to. If

she went to bed with him now, she would not find the presence of mind to tell him what she had come here to say, at least not until long after they had done what she most wanted to do in that lovely bed. She might even persuade herself to put off telling him till the end of the house party.

He shifted his hands and slid her down the length of his body. She felt the hard ridge of his erection. He was as eager to go to bed as she was.

Would it be so very wrong? The damage—would he see it as damage?—was already done; he couldn't get her with child again. They would both enjoy the interlude. They could spend the remaining nights of the house party pleasuring each other. It would be wonderful.

It would be wrong. By keeping her child—their child—a secret, she would be lying to him, and she wanted only truth between them from this moment on. When she opened her body to him this time, she wanted to open her mind and heart as well. If he wanted no part of her once he knew—well, so be it.

She took a deep breath, gathered her courage, and looked directly into Alex's eyes.

Chapter 18

"There is something I must tell you."

Kate looked so serious. Her eyes were huge; her face was still; there wasn't a hint of a smile anywhere in her countenance. She was still standing in the circle of his arms, but she had withdrawn completely.

He fought the urge to pull her close. "Yes, Kate?"

"I . . . I . . ." She swallowed. There was a tight, almost panicked look about her eyes now. Should he help her, tell her he already knew?

But did he know? Perhaps she was trying to tell him something else. "Just say it, Kate. It can't be that bad."

"But it is!" Her voice was almost a wail. She must have heard it, too, because she pressed her lips tightly together and closed her eyes. Was that a tear shimmering on her cheekbone? He brushed his thumb over the dampness, then wove both hands through her hair to cradle her head. He kissed her gently, briefly on the mouth.

"Tell me, sweetheart. Trust me, please?"

Her eyes flew open. "But you can't trust *me*!"

Can't trust her? He felt as though he'd been kicked in the gut. Had she been entertaining other men in her bed—

is that what this was about? But why would she feel the need to tell him that?

This time he was not going to jump to conclusions.

"Kate, you are making me anxious. Just say the words. We'll deal with the message once it's out, all right?"

"All right." She stepped back; he let her go. She clasped her hands tightly in front of her and stared at his chest.

"Do you remember what I told you when you"—she cleared her throat—"visited me at Oxbury House? When we . . ." She gestured toward the bed and then glanced up at Alex.

His face took on a cautious expression. "You told me many things. Which particular bit are you referring to?"

"I—" He must think her a complete ninny. She was not normally one to beat around the bush. She would take his advice and just say it. "When you came to Oxbury House, I told you I was barren."

"Yes, I believe you did."

"I'm sure I did. That's why you agreed to . . ." She gestured at the bed again. "You know."

He was frowning now. "I do know, but you are wrong. I did not take you to bed because you'd told me you were barren. I took you because I couldn't help myself. I wanted you more than food or water or air."

"Oh."

His eyes were so intent, so clear and honest—but she still hadn't told him about the baby. She couldn't entertain any other thoughts until she told him that. She dropped her gaze back to his chest and forced the words out.

"I lied. I'm not barren. I did think I was, because after all those years of marriage, I never conceived. It's true Oxbury didn't try often or at all at the end, but when we were first married, he was very assiduous in his efforts to procure an heir."

She looked back up at his face. Was he paler than before? She saw a pulse beating in his temple. He must hate her.

"Kate, why are you telling me this? How do you know now you aren't barren?"

"Because—" She stared at his chest again. No, she should look him in the eye when she told him. She wrenched her attention back to his face. "Because I am . . . with child—with *your* child."

His eyes widened. He looked shocked for a moment, and then his face lit up. He grinned and grabbed her shoulders.

"You are? Are you certain?"

"I-I think so. Marie seems certain. And there are signs that I am."

He pulled her into a tight hug. "I had hoped as much—David had hinted at it, but then, what does he know about such things?"

She wrapped her arms around his waist. This was not the reaction she'd expected.

"I'll get a special license—Shall I leave tomorrow or wait until after the house party?—and we'll be married as soon as may be."

She felt as if she were being swept along by a flood, unable even to grab for a low hanging branch to stop her progress. Still, she had to make the attempt.

"You don't have to marry me, Alex."

He held her away from him and frowned fiercely down at her. "Don't be ridiculous. Of course, I have to marry you. I will not have my son or daughter born a bastard."

"But—"

"No." He put his finger on her lips. "If you do not care for me, you should never have invited me into your bed"—his voice dropped—"and into your body."

"But I feel like I've trapped you."

"Kate, I've never wanted to be trapped more in my life. I've dreamt of marrying you for twenty-three years and now that you are carrying my child I will not be denied." His eyes turned guarded. "Is it you who feel trapped?"

She sighed. "I did when I thought I would bear this baby and face all the scorn and condemnation alone. When I imagined what my brother and the Weasel would say."

Alex pulled her against him again. She rested her cheek on his chest. She felt so relieved.

"They will say 'congratulations' and 'best wishes.' And if they are silly enough to count the months on their fingers, we will ignore them."

"Mmm." She rubbed her cheek against his chest. "I love you, Alex. I tried to be a good wife to Oxbury, but I never stopped loving you."

"And I love you, Kate." His hand stroked her hair. "I have missed you, you know. For twenty-three years." He laughed. "And I've missed you even more these last few weeks, when I knew *exactly* what I was missing."

She felt safe and protected—no longer alone. It was wonderful. But something else would be even more wonderful. "Do you suppose we might go to bed now?"

She felt his chuckle rumble in his chest under her cheek. "To sleep?"

She started to pull his shirt out of his breeches. "Eventually." She ran her hands over his belly. In place of fear and worry, she now felt an overwhelming . . . lust. And love, of course. But right now she wanted him inside her as quickly as possible. She slid free one of the buttons on his fall.

"Eager, are you?"

"Yes. Very." She got the fall open and almost sobbed

with pleasure. He was not wearing drawers. She wrapped one hand around his thick warm shaft. "Take your shirt off."

"So demanding. Is this what motherhood does to you?" Alex's voice sounded breathy and a bit strained. "Careful, Kate, or you'll unman me."

"I don't want to wait, Alex."

"An understandable sentiment."

"I've waited too long."

"I couldn't agree more, but you will have to wait a moment more or you will have me spilling my seed in your hand."

"Oh." She sighed and regretfully let go of her prize. She stepped back. "Very well."

Alex wasted no time. He grabbed the hem of his shirt and hauled it over his head in one deft motion. Then he shoved his breeches down over his hips and kicked them out of the way.

"Ah." She'd thought she'd remembered every detail of his body, but she had not. Or perhaps it was just that memory could never do reality justice. Naked, his shoulders and chest seemed impossibly broad—much broader than when they were confined by shirt and coat. His arms bulged with muscle and sinew. Dark hair dusted his chest, trailing down to . . . Mmm.

She reached for him. He grabbed her hands.

"No, you don't. No touching until we remove this voluminous nightgown."

She flushed. "I wanted something more seductive, but this was all I had."

He grinned. "The only problem with this nightgown is that it is still on your body. It will be lovely in a heap on the floor, I promise you." He grabbed the skirt. "Raise your arms."

She raised her arms, and he pulled the nightgown up and off her as quickly as he'd disposed of his shirt. Another night he would move slowly, teasing her, but not tonight. Tonight he felt like a starving man who suddenly finds himself at a banquet. He was too hungry to savor the feast.

Zeus, she was beautiful. Lovely, small breasts—though perhaps not as small as they had been—Was that another indication of her condition?—flaring hips, gently curving belly . . . He put his hand over the place where his child grew. *His* child. To have Kate and a babe . . . It was almost more joy than he could bear.

He grinned again. Ah, to have such problems. He bent to flick one of Kate's nipples with his tongue. She squeaked and grabbed his shoulders. He was delighted to be burdened with such happiness.

He lifted her onto the bed and scrambled in after her.

Kate reached for him, but he evaded her grasp. "Not so fast, my love."

She grabbed for him again. Didn't he realize she was desperate? "Yes, Alex. Now. I need you now."

He held her arms above her head with one hand. "Soon, I promise, but not quite yet."

He kissed her forehead, her cheek, her jaw, the base of her neck. She twisted her hips, spread her legs, arched her back. His light kisses were teasing her to the point of madness.

Ah. He finally reached her nipples. They were so tight and hard. His tongue flicked over each in turn, and then he latched on and sucked.

It was good—it was wonderful—but it was not enough.

"Please, Alex." She would beg, cry, scream, whatever it took to get him to go where she most needed him.

He freed her hands so he could stroke her breasts, while his mouth at last moved lower. He paused to leave a lingering kiss on her belly.

"Do you suppose it's a girl or a boy?"

"Huh?" For the first time since she'd realized she was increasing, she was not thinking about the baby. "I don't know."

She tried to feel warm and maternal, but all she could manage was hot and carnal. "Could we talk about this later? I need you to attend to something else first." She flexed her hips.

Alex laughed. "You know, I think that is probably a good idea. I find I'm slightly distracted myself." He grinned rather wolfishly up at her and then dipped his head again. He had moved from her belly to her—

"Eep!" She sat up, the sensation was so exquisite.

"What? Do you like this?" His tongue flicked over the very sensitive little spot between her legs.

"Yes. Oh, yes." She lay back and opened her legs wider. His hands cupped her bottom and lifted it slightly. His tongue probed delicately, teasing . . .

She was going to explode. She was going to die. She was going to—

"Alex! Oh, please . . ."

"Kate." His voice was tight. He sounded almost as desperate as she felt. "Yes. Now."

He put her down and came over her. She felt his heavy erection touch the point that so ached for him. She almost sobbed with desire. She wanted him; she needed him inside her like she needed air to breathe.

She tilted her hips, and he slid in deep.

"Ah." She shivered as he stretched her—and then he started to move. "Alex. Ah. Oh, Alex. Oh."

She gripped his hips and shuddered, sensation washing through her. And then a heartbeat later, he stilled and she felt the warm flood of his seed.

They stayed that way for minutes—he, heavy on her; she, hugging him tightly. They were joined by his body, but also by the peace of completion. The loneliness of all the years of her marriage—and the year of her widowhood—was gone.

"Mmm," he said, rolling to his side and taking her with him. "That was nice."

"It was beyond nice. It was marvelous. You were marvelous."

He smiled. "Pretty good for an old man, eh?"

"Not so old." She ran her hand over his hip. They were still joined. "And soon to be a father."

"Yes. A husband and a father."

"Did I actually say I would marry you, sir?"

He raised an eyebrow. "Well, I'm not certain these lips"—he kissed her briefly—"said yes, but these"—he flexed his hips. He was growing inside her already—"definitely did." He drew a lazy circle around the tip of her breast with his finger, skirting her nipple. "Are you inclined to dispute it, madam?"

"N-no." Her nipple was again a small, hard bud. If only he would touch her there . . .

"Now that I think about it, I believe I'd best keep you in this bed until I have your complete and utter agreement." His hand moved to slide down her back and massage her bottom. "I imagine this old brain can come up with a number of persuasive arguments. What do you think?"

"I think I am very eager"—she rolled her hips and was delighted to see Alex's gaze sharpen—"to be persuaded."

* * *

"Fetch Lady Grace immediately, man. Tell her her father is waiting."

Oh, no. Grace stopped in the hall, a hollow feeling suddenly opening in her stomach. Not Papa! What was he doing here? He was bellowing loud enough to wake the entire house party. She hurried down the stairs to intercept Lord Motton's butler. "It's all right, Mr. Wilks. I'll deal with Lord Standen."

"Grace," Papa said, "pack your things. You are leaving."

"Hallo, Papa. Why are you here?" How did Papa even know she was at Lord Motton's estate? She had purposely not written to tell him.

"To bring you home, of course. Go pack your things."

Anger warred with embarrassment in her breast. The other house party guests were beginning to gather in the entryway. "But Papa, the party isn't over yet."

"It is for you." Papa's jaw was set; his eyes had their stony expression. "We are leaving as soon as you are ready. I hope you don't have too much frippery with you."

Didn't these onlookers have something better to do with their time? The Addison girls, with their mouths agape, closely resembled beached fish.

"What about Aunt Kate? I think she's still asleep."

Was Papa grinding his teeth?

"Let her sleep. She is not coming with us." He snorted. "Her chaperoning duties are ended. Let us hope she is not forced to earn her keep as a duenna, since she certainly did a terrible job bear-leading you."

How dare Papa speak of Aunt Kate so dismissively? And in any event, Grace did not want to leave now, even though things were vastly uncomfortable with Lord Dawson. She would go home and do what Papa wished, but when the party was over. Not now. She needed her last few days of freedom.

If only all the people staring at her would go off to the breakfast parlor or the garden. She'd been able to stand up to Papa back home, when she'd decided to go to London, but here . . .

And perhaps the trip to London had not been a good notion. Her life had been much simpler before she'd come to Town.

"How did you know we were here, Papa?"

Papa scowled. "Oxbury wrote me. The man's an ass, but at least he had the sense to warn me my daughter was going off with a Wilton. Unlike my blasted sister."

He said "Wilton" in the same tone he'd use for "vermin." Anger twisted in her stomach. She wanted to shout, but shouting at her father never did any good, and it would just add to the spectacle they were presenting. The Addison twins were whispering to each other now.

Perhaps she could reason with him.

"You are not still bearing a grudge, are you, Papa? The scandal with Lady Harriet happened over thirty years ago."

Papa's lips drew into a tight, thin line—the corners of his mouth grew white and his nostrils flared. "And how do you know that story, miss? I've never told you it, I'm certain of that."

"I—"

"What's going on here?" Lord Dawson pushed his way past the Addisons and strode over to stand next to her. "Is this man bothering you, Grace?"

Grace closed her eyes briefly. Could the situation get any worse? David looked ready to flatten Papa—and Papa looked equally inclined to fisticuffs. That would certainly add to this raree-show—the two of them pummeling each other in Lord Motton's entryway, though Papa would be the one getting pummeled.

She struggled to breathe. She'd almost forgotten this feeling of walls closing in, of being trapped and helpless. She hadn't felt it since Lord Alvord's ball—since her . . . friendship with Lord Dawson. Her friendship that was shortly to end.

She sighed. "No, everything is fine, Lord Dawson." Fine? Ha! As fine as a sunny day in Hell. "This man is my father, Lord Standen. Papa, Lord Dawson."

David's eyebrows shot up; then he smiled slightly and extended his hand. "Ah, my apologies, Standen. I misunderstood the matter."

Papa's expression became even stonier. He looked down at David's hand as if it were a rotting fish and then turned away, giving him the cut direct.

"I told you to get ready, Grace."

David's brows snapped down. "Now see here—"

Grace put out a hand to stop him. Even Lord Kilgorn, Lady Kilgorn, and Lady Wordham had joined the crowd. Those obnoxious Addison girls were hanging on each syllable, memorizing every mortifying aspect of the scene so they could recount it later to all and sundry.

If only she knew a magic word to make herself disappear. She should have gone up to gather her things the moment she'd seen Papa. If she had, she'd be out in his carriage by now, rolling down the drive. She'd already decided she had to go home after the house party, hadn't she? It was not such a great tragedy to leave early.

"It's all right." She took a deep breath. She hated it when she sounded so breathless. She wasn't frightened. She was embarrassed. She just did not like being the center of attention. "I'll go—"

"Lord Standen!" Miss Smyth hurried in from the breakfast parlor, Theo perched on her shoulder. "How nice of you to stop by. Come into the red drawing room and I'll

get you a pot of tea. I'm sorry I wasn't here to greet you."
She frowned slightly. "Did I know you were coming?"

"Tea! Man wants ale, matey."

Papa glared at Theo and then at Miss Smyth. "This is
not a social call, madam. Thank you for your kind offer,
but I will be staying only as long as it takes my daughter to pack her belongings." He turned his glare back to
Grace. His very limited patience was obviously reaching its end.

"Oh." Miss Smyth blinked. "But the party isn't over
yet." She looked at Grace. "Do you wish to leave now,
dear?"

"No. I mean, yes." Grace took another breath. "I mean
my father's here now. It's convenient for me to leave."

No! David wanted to shake Grace. What was happening to her? Where was the fiery woman who'd fought
and argued with him, who'd insisted they find a way to
bring Alex and Lady Oxbury together? Where was the
girl who had bullied him into meeting with his grandmother? She had gone and left behind this beautiful
shell, this pale, cringing shadow of his Grace.

This was clearly Standen's doing. He'd like to throt-
tle the bloody bastard.

"Party's not over." Theo cocked his head, and turned
one eye to examine the earl. "Spoil-sport."

Standen's face turned red and his fists clenched as if
he was only a hair's breadth from grabbing Miss
Smyth's parrot and wringing its neck.

"What seems to be the difficulty, Aunt Winifred?"
Lord Motton came out of his study and surveyed the as-
sortment of people gathered in the entryway. "Hallo,
Standen. You just arrive?"

"Yes. And I am just departing, as soon as my daughter

gets her things." Standen turned to Grace, his nostrils flaring. "You are keeping the horses standing, Grace."

"But the house party isn't over yet." Motton smiled. "Why don't you join us? I'm sure we can find you a room."

Miss Smyth coughed significantly.

"Ah, so there are extra rooms, are there?" Lord Kilgorn said, his voice rather quiet and dangerous-sounding.

Motton looked at his aunt. "Would you care to answer that question, Aunt Winifred?"

Miss Smyth smiled brightly at Lord Kilgorn. "Extra rooms, my lord?"

"Aye."

She glanced at Lord Standen. "Well, there might be one, but only in a manner of speaking, you know."

Lord Kilgorn raised an eyebrow. "In a manner of speaking?"

"Yes. You know how it is."

He shook his head. "Nay, I canna say I do."

Miss Smyth kept smiling. "Ah. Well, I suppose it *is* a bit complicated, what with this and that. And the other."

"Madam." Lord Standen bit off each word. "Do not concern yourself. I am not staying." He almost shouted at Grace. "Get your things now."

"Yes, Papa."

"But—" David choked down panic. He was not going to let Grace go without a fight—he *could* not let her go. Yes, she'd rejected his suit yesterday, but he'd sensed regret and sorrow in her answer. She cared for him, he knew it. He just needed to overcome her scruples, whatever they might be. He'd counted on having a few more days to persuade her. She couldn't leave now.

Standen was white with rage. David didn't care; he wasn't afraid of the earl. It was Grace's look that stopped him. Her eyes held pain and entreaty. She did not want him to say more, so, much as it went against the grain, he held his peace. Grace gave him a fleeting smile and hurried upstairs.

With her departure, the gawkers dispersed. David kept a close eye on the Addison twins. It looked as if they might approach him, but thankfully, they changed their minds and headed off toward the music room. With Grace gone, he would have to be extra cautious around those two.

Hell, if Grace left, he wouldn't stay either. He'd head back to London as quick as may be.

"Why don't you come into my study, Standen?" Motton said. "You may as well be comfortable while you wait."

"I'll be comfortable standing right here."

"Nevertheless . . ." Motton stepped aside to usher Standen into the study. The earl went reluctantly. As soon as the door closed behind the man, David took the stairs two at a time. He hurried down the hall and rapped on Grace's door. He wouldn't be so bold normally, but desperate straits called for desperate measures—and fortunately everyone was either still asleep or already downstairs. There were no gossips in evidence.

"My lord." Marie opened the door. "Please come in and see if ye can talk some sense into my lady."

Grace whirled around. "Lord Dawson! What are you doing here?"

David stepped into the room and closed the door behind him. He had no time for roundaboutation. "Grace, don't leave."

Grace's eyes dropped from his. She stared at her portmanteau as she stuffed a handful of clothes inside it. "I have to leave. Papa is here."

"No, you don't. You are of age. Your father cannot order your obedience."

She glanced up. "It is not a matter of obedience. I love my father. I do not wish to hurt him."

"But what about me?" Desperation trumped pride. "Do you not care that you hurt me?"

She straightened, pushing her hair back off her face. "Of course I care, but you will get over it."

Good God! Her words turned like a knife in his gut. "How can you say that? How can you dismiss what I feel out of hand?"

Grace's eyes were strained, but dry. "How long have you known me, Lord Dawson? A few weeks?"

"Yes, but—"

"What can a person really feel—really know—about someone in such a short time? Attraction, yes. You are attracted to me. If circumstances were different, that might be enough. But circumstances are not different. There is too much history between our families for us to overcome. And Mr. Parker-Roth expects me to meet him at the altar." She closed her portmanteau. "You will find some other girl who will suit you as well or better than I. You will get over me."

"I won't." He swallowed. He finally understood how his father must have felt, faced with the threat of losing his love to another man. Society and reputations be damned. David would grab Grace right now and flee for Gretna if she were willing.

If she were willing. But she wasn't willing. She obviously didn't feel for him what he felt for her.

So now he also knew how Standen had felt when Lady Harriet chose his father over him—and that pain had stayed with the man through a marriage and Grace's childhood, year after year, even till today.

"Your father didn't get over losing Lady Harriet."

Grace stared at him, her mouth slightly open, as if his

statement had caught her unawares. Was she going to change her mind?

No. She shook her head, a wooden, determined expression on her face.

"The situations aren't the same," she said. "If anyone is in my father's position, it is John Parker-Roth. If I were mad enough to run off with you, he would be left standing alone at the front of the church, jilted as my father was."

David had little sympathy for a man who had so failed to woo Grace he hadn't even kissed her. "But does Parker-Roth love you, Grace? He may like you; he may find you a comfortable—a safe—option for marriage, but does he love you? Does he ache for you and dream of you? Does his heart leap when he sees you? Is he always listening for your voice, waiting for your smile?"

David clenched his teeth. He had to stop blathering on so—he was making a fool of himself. He couldn't force Grace to love him. Love was a gift that must be given freely.

Grace bit her lip and stared at him. He thought he saw uncertainty in her eyes again. He started to open his arms to welcome her back, but she shook her head and turned away.

"My father is waiting for me, Lord Dawson, and as I'm sure you discerned, he is not a patient man. I must go."

"Very well." The searing pain of her rejection made it hard to breathe, but he would not fall apart—he would keep a stiff upper lip. He extended his hand. "I wish you the best, Lady Grace."

She put her smaller hand in his. "As I wish the same for you, my lord."

Did he feel a trembling in her fingers, see moisture in

her eyes? Before he could be certain, she'd left, closing the door quietly behind her.

Marie stood, hands on hips, and looked him up and down. She made a guttural sound that spoke volumes.

"Och, my lord, and here I was thinking ye actually had something in that brain box of yers."

Chapter 19

"David, we wanted you to be the first to hear our good news."

David looked up from the desiccated earthworm he'd been studying. The sun was out, the flowers were in bloom, but the only thing that seemed real to him at the moment was this poor dead creature that had been stupid enough to venture out of the safe, dark earth.

Alex was grinning. Hell, Alex and Lady Oxbury were positively glowing. He'd never seen Alex so happy. If he could feel anything, he would feel delighted for them. "So I see you've ironed out your differences?"

"Yes. I'm getting a special license and we'll be married as soon as possible."

David forced himself to grip Alex's hand. "Congratulations." He looked at Grace's aunt. "And best wishes, Lady Oxbury." He tried for a touch of levity. "Or should I say good luck? You are taking on a formidable chore, ma'am. Everyone thought my uncle a confirmed bachelor."

"Oh, I'm not worried." She looked adoringly up at Alex, then glanced around the garden. "But where is Grace? We thought she'd be out here with you."

Just hearing Grace's name caused a stabbing sensation in his gut. "Didn't you hear? Lady Grace left."

Lady Oxbury's eyes widened. "Grace left? When? How? Why wasn't I told?"

David clasped his hands behind his back. "Lord Standen arrived about an hour ago. Apparently the current Lord Oxbury alerted him to the fact Lady Grace was attending a house party that included members of the nefarious Wilton family." He meant to sound self-mocking, but he feared he merely sounded bitter. "I regret to say I believe the earl is not very pleased with you, Lady Oxbury. He seems to feel you should have prevented the situation."

"I can't believe it." She looked at Alex. "Could my brother be that stupid?"

"Apparently he could." Alex frowned at David. "And you let her go?"

"Of course I did. What did you expect me to do? I have no influence with Lady Grace."

"No? I would have thought otherwise." Lady Oxbury worried her bottom lip with her teeth. "My brother must have forced her."

"No, Lady Oxbury, he did not. Your niece went willingly, I assure you."

"Don't be ridiculous. Grace wouldn't have returned home without complaint."

"Well, she did." He took a calming breath. There was no point in snapping at Lady Oxbury. "She is betrothed to a neighbor."

"Mr. Parker-Roth. Yes, I knew there was an understanding of some sort, but I also know she doesn't love him." Lady Oxbury shook her head. "She couldn't be repeating my mistake, could she?"

"It sounds as if she is." Alex turned to David. "And so you must not repeat *my* mistake."

"What are you talking about?" David was not in the mood for riddles.

"Twenty-three years ago," Lady Oxbury said, "I did what my brother wanted me to do. I left London and married Lord Oxbury. I let family loyalty separate me from your uncle."

"And I should have come after you." Alex kissed Lady Oxbury's fingers. "Or I should have persuaded you that night in Alvord's garden to flee to Gretna with me immediately. I should have anticipated how Standen would react."

"Nonsense. Who could have guessed my brother would bundle me off to the country? More to the point, who could have imagined he would marry me off so quickly? One does not expect such behavior in this day and age—even the day and age of twenty-three years ago. It is positively barbaric."

"I'm afraid your brother *is* barbaric, at least where my family is concerned, Kate."

Lady Oxbury sighed and shook her head. "I don't understand it. I can't think his heart was broken when Harriet ran off with Luke—he did marry Margaret a few years afterward and they seemed to have had a comfortable enough arrangement."

"Whatever the reason," Alex said, "we know he is capable of rushing Lady Grace up the aisle. You can't delay, David."

Lady Oxbury nodded. "At least Grace has attained her majority. You don't need her father's consent to wed."

David wanted to laugh, though he'd never felt so humorless. "But I do need Grace's consent. Your niece has no interest in wedding me, Lady Oxbury. She's content with this neighbor."

Lady Oxbury snorted. "I don't believe that for an

instant and neither should you. Did Grace say she didn't love you?"

"Not in so many words, perhaps."

Lady Oxbury frowned at him. "Don't assume you know Grace's mind, Lord Dawson. I have observed her closely—I had to; I was her chaperone. I would say she is very much in love with you. I spent many a sleepless night worrying about it, since I knew my brother would not be pleased with the connection."

"You need to go after her, David," Alex said. "You can't let one short conversation determine your life. You may not be as lucky as I." He wrapped his arm around Lady Oxbury's shoulders. "You might not get a second chance."

"And a second chance is not the same as the first chance, Lord Dawson. You need an heir; you should marry Grace now, while she is most capable of giving you several children." Lady Oxbury blushed.

Alex grinned. "We have some other good news. Kate is . . . well, we are anticipating an interesting event in a few months' time."

So he had not misunderstood—Lady Oxbury *was* breeding. It was odd to see a couple of such advanced years beaming over such a thing, but they were obviously delighted. David shook Alex's hand again and gave Lady Oxbury a kiss on the cheek.

"Splendid! I will not only have a new aunt, but a new cousin as well."

Alex gave him a pointed look. "Go after Lady Grace, David. Give our baby a cousin more his—or her—age."

Lust and regret flooded him at the thought. He would love to give Grace a baby, but that would never happen. Alex and Lady Oxbury were blinded by their own love. They hadn't seen Grace take her leave of him.

Grace was on her way to Devon to wed her neighbor

and he—he was going back to London tomorrow to start the search for a wife all over again.

Zeus, what a depressing thought.

Grace stared out the carriage window at the trees and grass and shrubs. Every moment put more distance between her and—

She would not think of him.

"Thank God Oxbury wrote to tell me you'd gone off with Dawson. I never thought I'd be beholden to that horse's arse, but there you have it." Papa shook his head. "I should have warned you to give the Wiltons a wide berth, but it didn't occur to me. They don't frequent London, as a rule. I swear this must be the first time they've come to Town in years."

"Yes, I think you are right." Why did they have to come this Season? If only . . .

No, she was glad she'd met David. He'd made her feel so many new things. And she was certainly glad Aunt Kate had met Mr. Wilton again. Had they worked out their differences? She wished she could have stayed to find out, but surely Aunt Kate would write. Well, she'd come to the wedding . . .

Grace bit her lip hard. The next time she saw Aunt Kate, she'd be preparing to walk down the aisle at the village church to marry John.

She felt like a noose had dropped over her head.

"Even though you didn't know about the Wiltons," Papa was saying, "Katherine certainly did. I'm shocked she didn't tell you to avoid them. It was to save her from Dawson's uncle that I married her off to Oxbury, you know. The woman must be dicked in the nob if she thought I'd countenance any sort of contact between you and a Wilton."

"But, Papa, I don't understand." Grace studied her father. He looked smaller than she remembered. Older. Had he changed so much in the short time she'd been gone—or had she changed? "Why do you dislike the Wiltons so intensely? Surely it is not merely because Lady Harriet preferred Lord Dawson's father to you? That happened so long ago."

Papa scowled at her. "I do not choose to speak of it. It is enough for you to know that I do dislike them."

Grace should have felt anger, but she had no room for any emotion besides the deep, leaden sadness of leaving David. Still she was not going to let her father hide in silence.

"No, Papa, it is not enough. Your hatred of the Wiltons ruled Aunt Kate's life and now it is ruling mine. You owe us—you owe me—an explanation."

Papa frowned and dropped his gaze to study his hands. He said nothing for so long Grace gave up hope he would respond. She swallowed her annoyance and turned her attention back to the scenery.

"I was young and in love," Papa said finally. He spoke so quietly, Grace hardly heard him over the creaking of the carriage.

"Yes. You were young—it was over thirty years ago."

"Some things aren't changed by time, Grace."

Some things—like her feelings for David? Would they never fade? They must. She couldn't live forever with this heavy black cloud shrouding her heart.

"I understand that, Papa, but this was hardly more than a brief dream, wasn't it? You only knew Lady Harriet for part of one Season. A few dances, a handful of conversations. You didn't know her at all."

Just as she hardly knew David.

And Aunt Kate had hardly known Mr. Wilton, yet their love had endured.

Papa spread his hands. He looked almost helpless. "I loved her."

"You were infatuated. You were only . . . what? Twenty-five?"

"Your age."

"Yes, but now you are fifty-six." She wouldn't still pine for David when she was so old, would she? She pushed down the panic that threatened to overwhelm her. She would get over her feelings. She would marry John, have children. She would remember David fondly, without rancor.

"It doesn't matter," Papa said. "It doesn't matter how old I am. It's like it happened yesterday."

Oh, God. Grace squeezed her eyes shut. No. She rested her head against the squabs, turning slightly so he wouldn't see her tears.

She would *not* think of David, she would not—but memories of him were all that filled her heart: his eyes crinkling when he was amused; the warm, deep sound of his voice; the touch of his lips. But even more than those things, she remembered his concern for his uncle, his willingness to put his past hurt aside to bring some peace to his grandmother, the way he'd held his tongue when she had so needed him to do so in Lord Motton's entryway.

He understood her as no one had before.

"Lady Harriet was everything I wasn't." Papa spoke quietly again, almost as if he were talking to himself. Grace turned her head to watch him. He was looking out the window, a slight smile curving his lips.

"She was lively and inventive. Quick and bright. Everything sparkled when she was present. She was like a star, fallen to earth—and I was a lump of coal." He sighed and shook his head.

"Wilton was much the same. It was clear why they were attracted to each other—like to like. But they were too much alike. Wordham—Harriet's father—thought Harriet needed steadying; Wilton was too flighty. Wordham wanted Harriet to marry me." Papa at last looked over at Grace. His eyes were full of pain. "But Harriet wanted Wilton."

He leaned toward her, his voice growing more forceful. "If Wilton hadn't convinced Harriet to run away with him, she would have married me. She'd be alive today."

Grace leaned forward, too. "You don't know that, Papa. Lady Harriet died in childbirth. If you had wed her, she might have died with your child . . . as Mama did."

Papa looked startled, as if that thought had never occurred to him.

Grace reached out to touch his knee. "Didn't you love Mama at all?"

He cleared his throat. He looked flustered. "Your mother was a fine woman. Very pleasant. We rubbed along tolerably well."

Grace sat back. "But you didn't love her."

"I was fond of her."

"But you didn't love her."

Papa hunched a shoulder. "Love causes no end of pain and turmoil. Affection—or respect—is a better sentiment for marriage. Compatibility, such as you have with Parker-Roth, will get you through the years."

Until death do they part. The words popped into Grace's mind unbidden. She had always thought they were sad; now they sounded like a goal. After year upon year of polite, boring matrimony, finally a release.

"I do wish you would visit Standen, Lord Dawson. Talk to Grace."

"I can't see how that would help, Lady Oxbury." David had been on his way to take his leave of his grandmother and had interrupted Alex and Lady Oxbury in the green parlor. Fortunately they'd been exchanging only a kiss—a rather heated kiss, true, but at least all their clothing was still properly fastened.

"I just cannot believe she is consenting to marry her neighbor. There must be some misunderstanding."

"Believe me, Lady Oxbury, there was no misunderstanding." And Grace had been correct. They *had* known each other only a very short time. They were just caught up in lust; the feeling would wear off in a month or two.

"Still, it would be worth a trip to see her, David," Alex said. "Likely she spoke in haste and almost immediately regretted her words."

"Yes, I'm sure that's it." Lady Oxbury smiled up at Alex as though he'd just said something brilliant. "Grace can be somewhat impetuous at times. With her father surprising her like that, showing up on Lord Motton's doorstep with no warning, who knows what odd thoughts were going through her head?"

"You should go, David. What can you lose? If Lady Grace is adamant, at least you'll know beyond a shadow of a doubt that she does not wish to wed you. But if you discover she regrets her decision or that it was all a misunderstanding, then you've won years of happiness." Alex grinned down at Lady Oxbury in a completely besotted way.

David closed his eyes briefly to keep from rolling them. Why did he have to be subjected to such a large dose of April and May today of all days? Not that he wasn't happy for Alex and Lady Oxbury. He was. He just didn't care to feel that happiness right now. He had too much misery to occupy him.

"Yes, well, I'll think about it."

"You'd best not think long, Lord Dawson. My brother can be very determined when he has a mind to be."

Alex nodded. "It would be hell to arrive just moments after the vows were said to discover Lady Grace had been pining for you and had wed the neighbor in despair."

"Yes, of course. I promise to give it serious thought. At the moment, however, I am in search of Lady Wordham. I wish to bid her farewell; I'm off for London today."

"London?" Alex frowned. "It should be Devon."

"Yes, well, I have some business to attend to in Town that cannot wait."

"I think you're making a mistake, David, but if you insist on doing so, I'll ride with you. I'm leaving shortly myself."

Now that he made note of it, he saw Alex was dressed for travel. If he went with him, he'd be badgered every step of the way to alter his course for Devon and Lady Grace.

"You go ahead, Alex. I don't want to delay you. I'm not certain how long I'll be with Lady Wordham."

Lady Oxbury smiled. "It is so wonderful you've reconciled with your grandmother, Lord Dawson."

"You should call me David, Lady Oxbury, since we are shortly to be related. And yes, it is wonderful. I can thank your niece for pushing me toward that reconciliation." No matter how much pain he was in because of Grace now, he couldn't forget she had helped him see the futility of clinging to old hurts.

And clinging to new hurts? *Should* he put aside the pain of his last interview with Grace and ride for Devon?

Ridiculous! He did not care to ask for her rejection again. He was not a complete fool.

"You don't happen to know where I might find Lady Wordham, do you?" The sooner he spoke to his grandmother, the sooner he could leave this benighted house party.

"I think she's in the rose garden, David." Lady Oxbury smiled. "And, please, you must call me Kate."

"Not Aunt Kate?"

She laughed. "I think Kate will be sufficient."

"Very well, Kate. Thank you, I will go look in the rose garden and leave you two to resume the activity you were engaged in when I arrived—though I would suggest you close the door this time."

Lady Oxbury—Kate—flushed. Alex laughed.

"Good idea," he said. "You may close it behind you when you leave."

David smiled as he pulled the door shut. At least one Wilton had benefited from this infernal Season.

Lady Wordham was sitting on a bench in the rose garden, her face turned up to the sun.

"Careful, Grandmother. You'll ruin your lovely pale complexion."

Lady Wordham laughed and patted a spot on the bench next to her. "Come sit, David. I promise to be good and put up my parasol, even though the mid-afternoon sun feels wonderful on my old bones."

David sat and smiled at his grandmother. "Is that why you are sitting out here by yourself—to enjoy the warmth of the sun?"

She reached over and patted his hand. "That and to have some quiet in which to think." She leaned closer. "Do be careful of those Addison girls. One or the other of them means to trap you into marriage."

He laughed. "I think the only thing that has kept me safe so far is the fact they both wish to compromise me. They keep foiling each other's plots."

"Well, I must tell you, I don't care for either of them." Lady Wordham looked away to examine a rose. "Lady Grace, now . . . she seems like a very nice girl."

David repressed a sigh. First Alex and Kate, now his grandmother. Was everyone at this gathering—aside from the Addison twins, of course—trying to match him with Grace? "Lady Grace left, Grandmother, did you not hear? Her father came and took her back to Standen."

"I did hear, of course. When are you leaving?"

"Now. I only tarried to say good-bye to you."

Lady Wordham grinned. "Don't waste time sitting with an old woman, boy. Go on." She patted his hand again. "Go after the gal. I want another great-grandbaby before I die."

He coughed, hoping to dislodge the sudden lump in his throat. "I'm leaving for London, Grandmother. Lady Grace made it clear before she left that she wasn't interested in my suit."

His grandmother's mouth hung open for a moment. Then she snapped it shut, sat back, and frowned. "Balderdash. I've never heard anything so ridiculous in my life. The girl is obviously madly in love with you."

He shrugged. What was he to respond?

Lady Wordham leaned forward and tapped him on the knee. "No. No, you must be wrong. I've observed you both. By my age, one has learned a thing or two. I *know* she feels something for you."

He tried to laugh. "Annoyance, perhaps."

"Don't be an idiot. The girl loves you. Go after her. Find out what the problem is. You can't let silly pride stand in the way of happiness."

He was not going to argue. He leaned over to kiss her weathered cheek. "I'll see you in London."

She grabbed his hand and looked intently into his eyes. "David, I know the pain of letting pride keep me from someone I love." She laid her hand along his jaw. "Don't be a fool like me, grandson. Go to her."

"It's not that easy."

"It *is*. Well, it may not be easy, but it is simple. Just go."

He stood and tried to smile. "I will think about it."

"But will you do it or will you be pigheaded like your grandfather and deny yourself this love?"

There wasn't an answer that would satisfy them both, so he just bowed and left.

He was waiting for his horse to be brought round when Miss Smyth found him in the entryway.

"Not you, too?" He bit his lip, but the words had already been said.

"Et tu, Brute?"

He scowled at Miss Smyth's parrot. "I didn't know Theo had studied the classics."

"He has a very eclectic collection of phrases; he's rather like a magpie that way, hoarding odd bits of things. Well, he's very like my Uncle Theo, of course. That's where he learned it all." She looked at his greatcoat, then glanced at the door. "You're leaving?"

"Yes. I've said good-bye to Lord Motton and thanked him for his hospitality; I thank you, as well, of course, for acting as his hostess and organizing . . . everything."

He suspected Miss Smyth had organized a few too many things. Frankly, he'd been hoping he could sneak away without attracting her attention. He was sure what she would say, and he was rather tired of being urged to go to Devon. Couldn't people comprehend that Grace's father had given him the cut direct and that Grace herself had indicated her wishes concerning him very clearly, so clearly even a dunce such as he could understand?

Miss Smyth was frowning. "You should go to Devon, you know."

"Miss Smyth, you do understand Lord Standen would probably have me shot on sight?"

The woman snorted. "I'm sure that's illegal. You're a peer."

"*And* Lady Grace informed me in no uncertain terms

she has absolutely no interest in furthering our acquaintance."

"Oh, she didn't mean that."

He was sorely tempted to tear his hair out by its roots. "She is marrying her neighbor."

Miss Smyth waggled her finger at him. "Only if you don't get on your horse and ride posthaste to the rescue."

"She doesn't *wish* to be rescued."

"There is no need to shout, my lord."

"Sorry." He took a sustaining breath. "The fact of the matter is Lady Grace is content with her situation."

"And if you believe that, you are a bigger dunderhead than I thought."

"Dunderhead! Numskull! Blockhead!" Theo apparently was full of synonyms for idiot.

He was not going to shout at a parrot, so he contented himself with a glare. Theo fluffed his feathers and glared back at him.

A footman stepped inside. "My lord, your horse is ready."

He nodded at the man, keeping himself from falling on him in gratitude only by an extreme exercise of will. "Ah, yes. Well, I must be going. Thank you again, Miss Smyth, for your hospitality."

"It won't have done any good if you let Lady Grace marry her neighbor. Go to Devon for God's sake, man! Show some backbone."

Arguing with Miss Smyth—and her parrot—was clearly futile. Retreat was his best course of action.

David nodded politely and fled.

Chapter 20

"Papa, I cannot marry Mr. Parker-Roth."

Papa looked up from *The Morning Post*, a forkful of poached eggs suspended halfway between his plate and his mouth.

"Ridiculous." He completed the fork's trip, chewed his eggs, and washed them down with a mouthful of coffee. "Of course, you'll marry Parker-Roth."

"No. I cannot." Grace pushed her plate of cold toast away from the edge of the table. She couldn't eat; her stomach was in far too much turmoil to even consider ingesting anything. "I thought I could when I left Lord Motton's estate. I thought I could when we rode over to the Priory yesterday to see John. I even thought I might be able to go through with the wedding after I took a turn about the garden with him and listened to him drone—I mean discuss all his infernal—that is, interesting plantings."

Grace paused. She was breathing so quickly she was making herself dizzy.

"But I can't. I just cannot do it."

"Nonsense. You are merely experiencing maidenly

nerves. Once the wedding and the bedding are behind you, you will be fine."

Her stomach lurched, threatening to disgorge its limited contents onto the breakfast table. She pressed her hand firmly to her mouth and breathed steadily through her nose. She moved her fingers far enough away from her lips to allow a response.

"No."

"No what?" Papa had gone back to his paper as if the subject were closed.

"No, I will not be fine." There. Her stomach had subsided to a slow churn. She lowered her hand and focused on her father. "I have thought about this all night, Papa. I hardly got a wink of sleep. And I have come to the firm conclusion I cannot marry John. It would not be fair to him."

Papa waved a hand in her direction and turned to a new page in the newspaper. "Don't worry about that. I'm sure Parker-Roth doesn't care."

"I cannot imagine John doesn't care that I'm in love with another man."

"You'll get over that."

Could she be hearing Papa correctly? A man who had harbored a grudge against an entire family for over thirty years because the woman he'd loved had rejected him, the man who had told her as recently as a few days ago that he still loved that woman—this man was telling her she would get over being parted from her own love?

"You never got over it, Papa."

"What?" He pulled his nose out of the paper long enough to frown at her. "What do you mean?"

"You never got over Lady Harriet."

He scowled at her and returned to the newspaper. "I married your mother, didn't I? I . . . adjusted. You will, too."

"But you had no choice. Lady Harriet was beyond your reach. She was dead. Lord Dawson—"

He glared at her. "Do not mention that name in my house."

Grace threw down her napkin and stood. "Why do you insist on clinging to this animosity? I'll wager you'd never even met Lord Dawson until he walked into Viscount Motton's entryway."

"What has that to say to the matter?"

"What? Everything! How can you hate someone you've never met?"

"Easily."

She grabbed onto her temper with both hands. She knew it would do no good to shout at Papa. Instead she leaned on the table and looked him in the eye.

"Right. You're right. It is even easier to hate someone you've never met. You don't know all the good things about him."

"There are no good things about a Wilton." Papa's mouth was set in a white line. He snapped his paper and turned away from her to read it. "You're allowing yourself to become hysterical."

"I am not." She was shouting. She swallowed and tried to rein in her anger. "You are not allowing yourself to hear the truth in what I am saying." She straightened, clasping her hands together to keep from wrapping them around Papa's neck. She must try to remain calm. Rational. "Lord Dawson was the same way. He'd decided he hated his grandmother until I was able to persuade him to talk to her. If you would only meet—"

"No!" Papa slapped his newspaper down on the table and surged to his feet. "I will not meet with Dawson. I have no need to meet with him. I will not see the man again."

"You will, unless you wish never to see me again." She raised her chin and hoped David had not changed his mind about matrimony. "I intend to marry the baron."

"Oh, really?" The veins in Papa's forehead were pulsing—never a good sign. "And how are you going to manage that? You have no way of traveling to Motton's estate—if Dawson is even there still—as my carriages are *not* at your disposal. But, more to the point, you will not be free to wed the baron as you are marrying Parker-Roth tomorrow."

"No!" She grabbed the back of her chair. In less than twenty-four hours . . . "I thought the wedding was not for days yet. You said—"

"I prevaricated."

Married in less than twenty-four hours . . . dear God! "I never actually agreed. John never actually proposed." He certainly had never kissed her. The man couldn't want to wed her. She would be doing them both a favor to decline.

"That doesn't matter. You will actually marry."

"No. I will go now and tell him that I must cry off. It will be awkward. It will be embarrassing, but in the long run, it will be better. He cannot want an unwilling bride."

Papa crossed his arms, his face stony. "None of that matters. He has agreed to marry you. It is a good match. You will be close to home, among people you know. You *will* marry him. There is no more to be said."

She gripped the chair back harder. She wanted to pound her hands on her father's chest. "No. I will *not* marry him. I can't."

"You *can*. You were willing enough before you went up to London. Damn it all, you were willing enough when you left Motton's estate."

"I was not willing—I was resigned."

"Bloody hell." Papa threw his hands up in the air, and then leaned toward her, his right index finger stabbing at her. "You listen to me, miss. You will marry Parker-Roth. I am your father, and I order you to do so."

She stabbed her finger back at him. "You can't order me. I am of age. I will not marry the man, do you understand?" She tried to get her voice under control. "I am sorry, Papa, but what you ask is impossible."

Papa was shouting now. "You are not going to do to Parker-Roth what Harriet did to me. You are not jilting the man, do you hear me?"

"The entire house hears you, Papa."

"Good. Go to your room, you ungrateful girl. I will see you again in church."

"When the vicar asks if I take John as my husband, I will say no, Papa."

His face was the color of a furnace. His veins looked like they would burst. Surely he would not suffer an apoplexy?

"Go!" He roared the word.

Grace went.

So he'd taken the road to Devon. So he was an idiot.

David looked at the inn's bed and sighed. It was too short for someone his height, but at least it looked like the sheets were relatively clean.

He should have taken the road to London. He'd certainly decided to do so when he'd left Miss Smyth in Motton's entryway. But when he'd come to the crossroads . . . well, somehow his horse had headed toward Devon.

If he'd taken the road to London, he'd have been home days ago, sleeping in his own roomy bed. He'd have gone to a number of balls and routs already and started his marital search over.

Damn.

He couldn't muster any enthusiasm for sorting through the giggling debutantes, the coy young misses, the slightly desperate maidens beginning to wilt on the vine.

He wanted Grace. He *really* wanted Grace. If there were any chance in hell he could still have her . . . well, it behooved him to leave no stone unturned.

So here he was, pausing at The Blue Heron before going to Standen tomorrow morning to turn over the last stone. He'd arrived at the inn just before dinner. Had a nice chat with a Mr. and Mrs. Weyford, a young couple, rather newly married . . . well, all right, it wasn't so nice a chat. Oh, the couple were perfectly pleasant. The problem was he kept thinking of Grace, imagining it was they, not the Weyfords, exchanging fleeting glances full of promise of what they would do once they got upstairs to bed.

He'd preferred his conversation with Reverend Barnsley, the other guest at the inn. The reverend was on his own, on his way to take up a living in Cornwall, and an enthusiastic angler. A well-placed question here and there kept the man discoursing on fish and bait and tackle all evening.

And now he was in his room with this lonely, short, uncomfortable-looking bed. Tomorrow he'd reach Standen. He'd know for certain whether there was still a chance to make Lady Grace his baroness. Maybe he'd discover she'd already wed her boring neighbor.

God, that thought was beyond depressing.

He climbed into bed and tried to find a comfortable position. It was impossible. The mattress was stuffed with rocks.

It was going to be a very long night.

* * *

Dear Papa,
  I am sorry I must disappoint you now, but I cannot disappoint myself—and John—for years. Please tell John that I love him, but as a brother, not a husband, and extend my sincere apologies and regrets to him and his family.
  I love you, even though I cannot do your will in this regard.

                                        Grace

There. Grace sanded the letter and stood it up against her pillow where the maid would find it when she came in to wake her. It had been another long, sleepless night, but finally she felt at peace. She'd made her decision. She was leaving. Now, before the sun was up. If she left when it was still dark, no one would see her.

All she had to do was get to The Blue Heron. She had enough pin money left to buy a seat on the stagecoach to London. It wouldn't be a comfortable trip, but she would manage. She would go to Aunt Kate . . . if Aunt Kate were in London.

Surely she would be. Though the Weasel must still be at Oxbury House . . .

But Lord Motton's house party was over; everyone must have returned to Town. And if Aunt Kate wasn't in London, Lady Wordham would be. Grace would find *someone* to help her.

She had no choice. She couldn't marry John. He deserved a woman who would love him with her whole heart, but Papa seemed incapable of understanding that. She wouldn't put it past him to tie her up and throw her in the carriage to get her to the church. Then her only recourse would be to refuse to say her vows, and she couldn't do that to John and his family. No, she had to go now.

She put all the money she had as well as her few small pieces of jewelry—to be pawned in only the most desperate circumstances—into her reticule and stuffed it into the pocket of her cloak. Then she blew out the candles and opened the window. There was enough moonlight to see the branch of the big oak tree that grew by her room—and the long way down to the ground.

She hadn't climbed a tree in years. The worst part was getting out her window, leaving the safe, solid building to swing over to a shaky, swaying branch. Then it was a matter of inching her way carefully backward, feeling for solid footing, untangling her skirts from branches, pushing her hair out of her eyes as the tree plucked her pins out. Thankfully there was no one to observe her awkward escape.

She leaned against the tree trunk for a moment when her feet finally touched the ground and blew out a long breath of relief—as well as a short prayer of thanksgiving. She'd made it safely to earth without killing herself, though she was rather a mess. She picked a few twigs out of her hair and then twisted it into a knot at the back of her neck, marshalling her remaining pins to restrain it as best she could. Next time she had to escape down a tree, she would be sure to add extra hair pins to the contents of her reticule.

A cloud drifted over the moon, plunging her into darkness. Thank God that hadn't happened a few moments earlier.

She waited for her eyes to adjust, and then started

carefully across the lawn. With luck no one would look for her until long after she was gone.

She stumbled in a rabbit hole and almost fell. Damn it! She couldn't risk turning an ankle.

She slowed her pace. Once she reached the road, the ground would level out and she'd be able to move faster, but for now it paid to be cautious. She would not worry—even at this rate she should reach The Blue Heron in an hour or two, well before the stagecoach pulled in. And then she would leave Standen—her home—for good.

She sniffed. Blast. She couldn't cry. Papa truly had left her no choice.

She concentrated on picking her way across the lawn.

The sun wasn't up yet, but he was.

David sat on the edge of his bed and rubbed his face. Enough tossing and turning. He'd go out for a ride, clear the cobwebs from his brain and the cricks from his back. Maybe he'd head toward Standen just to get the lay of the land.

He met Reverend Barnsley in the corridor. They walked together down the stairs.

"Up early, Lord Dawson?"

"Couldn't sleep. And you? Did you also find your bed a touch lumpy?"

"No, slept like a rock. I'm out to commune with God's creation—and see if the fish are biting. I left my gear outside—just ran back to get my prayer book." He grinned. "Forgot it at first."

"Ah. Good fishing hereabouts?"

"Indeed. I had the great fortune to strike up a conversation with the innkeeper after you went upstairs last night. He said there's a smashing fishing hole within walking distance. Care to join me?"

David needed to move, not sit. "No, thanks. I'm off for a short ride."

They stepped outside. There was Barnsley's pole, leaning against the wall. The reverend nodded and picked up his gear. "Enjoy your ride," he said and strolled off toward a line of trees.

David headed for the stables. It was cool and damp, with a touch of mist lingering on the ground. He drew in a deep breath. He felt better already.

"Morning, milord." The stable boy jumped up from the pile of hay he'd been lounging on. "I'll be getting yer horse—"

"No, thanks. I'll saddle him myself."

"As ye wish, milord."

Zeus nickered a welcome. He seemed eager to get out and stretch his legs. As soon as they reached the road, David gave him his head. They thundered over the ground, the damp wind blowing some of the dark cloud from his soul. He wasn't hopeful, but he felt less blue-deviled.

He saw a figure trudging toward him—a figure in skirts. The woman looked up—she must have heard Zeus's hoof beats—and then dashed off into the trees.

Odd. Did she need to answer a sudden call of nature? He would give her her privacy. He rode past at a gallop . . . and slowed.

It was early and somewhat dark. She was a woman alone. It was unlikely she was in any danger, but one never knew what riffraff might be lurking in the woods.

He looked back. She was walking again, moving like someone who needed to be somewhere quickly. Surely he could help her. He turned and started to gallop toward her.

She glanced over her shoulder—and darted back into the trees.

What the hell? He slowed. Was she afraid of him? She couldn't be—at least, she couldn't be afraid of him personally. No one but Grace would recognize him in this part of England—and, in any event, he'd never had a woman fear him. Was someone—some man—tracking this poor girl? She must think herself in danger to hide at the first sign of a fellow traveler.

He urged Zeus forward, peering into the trees as he approached the place where she had disappeared.

"Madam," he called out. "Please don't be alarmed. I would like to help you, if I may."

He saw movement a little farther ahead. He kept Zeus to a walk, staying on the road.

"I promise I won't harm you. I'm Baron Dawson of Riverview. Please tell me how I might assist you."

Had he heard a gasp?

The girl peered from behind a tree and then stepped out of the foliage. She was tall and . . . familiar.

"David? David, is that really you?"

"Grace!" He swung off Zeus's back.

She ran toward him and he opened his arms. He took her lush body against his, holding her tightly while he kissed her.

Her mouth was wet and hot and wonderful. Her breasts were so soft against his chest—she must not be wearing a corset. It would take only a moment to have this cloak off her, and just a moment more for her dress to follow. And then his shirt and breeches . . .

Was he dreaming? If he was, he never wanted to waken. He moved from her mouth to her cheek.

"Oh, David, I'm so glad to see you."

This dream just got better and better. "And I'm very,

very glad to see you, Grace." He lifted her silky, long hair to nuzzle her neck.

"Oh, please . . ."

He kissed a spot right under her ear and started moving down her neck.

". . . please stop."

What? He raised his head. This couldn't be his dream. He would never have Grace telling him to stop. This was either a nightmare or it was actually happening.

"You want me to stop?"

"Yes. You must." She looked up at him, but kept her lovely, soft body exactly where he wanted it—plastered against his. He ran his hands down her back and pulled her wonderful derriere closer. She didn't resist at all.

"Why?"

"I must get to The Blue Heron. I am running away from home."

"Oh." A horrible thought struck him. "You haven't married the neighbor, have you?"

"No." She rested her head against his chest. "I couldn't do it, David. But I'm supposed to marry John this morning. That's why I'm running away. Papa refused to see reason. He'll force me down the aisle if I don't escape. I have to make it to the inn in time to get a seat on the London stagecoach."

"No, you don't."

"Yes, I do. You don't know Papa."

"Well, he can't force you to marry this neighbor if you're already married to me, can he?"

"What?" Grace gaped up at him so deliciously he had to kiss her again—and run his hands over her enticing body as well.

"Marry me. Please, Grace? You truly would make me

the happiest of men. I came all this way in the hopes of persuading you."

"But—"

"I tried not to come, even though Alex and your aunt and my grandmother—even Miss Smyth—urged me to do so. I was intending to return to London. But they all assured me you loved me—and I finally realized you'd never said you didn't."

"Ah."

It was a small point, perhaps, but it was enough to have given him courage. He cupped her face in his hands and looked into her eyes. He wanted her to see the truth of what he was saying.

"I love you, Grace. I know that beyond a shadow of a doubt. And I will never get over this love. If you won't have me, my life will go on; I might even marry someday, but I will never stop loving you. Just as Alex never stopped loving your aunt."

"And Papa never stopped loving your mother." She was crying a little and smiling—and still leaning against him. That must be a good sign.

"I have a special license. I got it before we left for Motton's house party. And there just so happens to be a minister at The Blue Heron who will, I'm sure, be delighted to marry us, and a very nice couple who I'm equally certain would be willing to act as our witnesses. We can be married within the hour—within the half hour." And in bed moments later, but he wouldn't say that. No need to push his luck.

"Well . . ."

"Please, Grace? I love you to distraction." And he was especially distracted at the moment by her scent and her taste and the heavenly feel of her curves against his chest and his hips and his—

Good God, he was panting. He took a deep breath—which only pushed his body tighter against hers. "I would love to spend my life loving you, Grace. Please say you'll marry me."

"Oh, David." She was crying more than smiling now. "I do love you so much. I was miserable as soon as the carriage pulled away from Viscount Motton's estate, and I've been miserable every day—every hour, every minute—since. I was foolish and wrong when I left you. I love my father, but you are my life, my future. Of course, I will marry you."

"Huzzah!" He picked her up and twirled her around. He had never, ever been so happy. "Then let's go find Reverend Barnsley and the Weyfords." He took her hand and pulled her over to Zeus. She stopped suddenly.

"I can't ride with you! Your poor horse will collapse under our weight."

"No, he won't, will you, Zeus, old man?"

Zeus snorted and shook his head. Grace laughed.

"See?" David said. "Zeus thinks you are being ridiculous, and I agree. Come on." He grabbed Grace around the waist and lifted her onto Zeus's back; then he swung up to sit behind her, wrapping his arms around her to hold her securely. If he enjoyed the feel of her curves . . . well, it was all in the name of safety.

Grace settled back into David's arms. She was finally where she belonged—where she most wanted to be.

The walk from Standen had been nerve-wracking. It had been so dark. She'd tripped over every rock and root and jumped at every animal call, every rustle in the bushes. The back of her neck was stiff from worry—she'd been terrified someone would come after her and take her back to Standen. And the thought of traveling alone all the way to London . . . Well, she was very glad she wouldn't have to endure that experience.

She tensed. She wasn't safe yet. The moment Papa discovered her missing, he would turn the house upside down and scour the countryside looking for her. If he found her with David, there was no telling what he would do. And when they got to The Blue Heron . . .

"David, Mr. Timms, the innkeeper, thinks I'm marrying John this morning. If he sees me, he'll wonder . . ."

"Don't worry. I think we can avoid Mr. Timms."

She saw The Blue Heron ahead of them now. David turned, taking them into the trees a short distance from the inn. He dismounted and helped her down.

"Stay here while I put Zeus back in the stable and find the Weyfords."

She watched him lead his horse away. There was no good place for a woman her size to hide. What would she do if a servant came by? Most, if not all, of the people who worked at the inn would recognize her. She could crouch in that thicket perhaps—

"Grace—"

"Eek-ahem." She tried to turn her squeak into a cough.

David raised his eyebrows and grinned. "Grace, this is Mr. and Mrs. Weyford from Kent. They are on an extended wedding trip. Mr. and Mrs. Weyford, my very-soon-to-be bride, Lady Grace Belmont."

"How nice to meet you, Lady Grace." Mr. Weyford bowed.

"And how romantic—a wedding in the woods." Mrs. Weyford smiled.

David put Grace's hand on his arm. "Let us hope Reverend Barnsley will consent to take a break from his sport to perform the ceremony."

Reverend Barnsley—at least, that's who Grace

assumed the man standing on the riverbank holding a large fish was—grinned at them as they approached.

"Will you look at this beauty?" he said, holding the fish higher. "It must be close to a foot long, don't you think?"

"At least a foot," David said. "Reverend, may I present my fiancée, Lady Grace Belmont?"

"A pleasure to meet you, Lady Grace." Reverend Barnsley transferred his fish to his left hand before taking Grace's fingers in his right.

"And you, Reverend Barnsley." She tried to keep smiling. If the man would perform the wedding ceremony, she couldn't cavil over a bit of piscine odor. "That's a very fine fish you have there."

"A trout, Lady Grace. A very fine trout."

"Indeed." She looked at David. The annoying man was struggling not to laugh.

"I say, that *is* a fine trout, Reverend." Mr. Weyford stepped closer to examine the catch. "What are you using for bait?"

Before Reverend Barnsley could launch into a dissertation, David cleared his throat. "Reverend, if I might interrupt, I was hoping you could do me a small favor."

"A favor? Of course, Lord Dawson. How can I help?"

David pulled a sheet of paper out of his pocket. "I have a special license here, and Mr. and Mrs. Weyford have agreed to act as witnesses. Lady Grace and I would like you to marry us."

Reverend Barnsley examined the paper. "It seems to be in order." He looked up and smiled. "I'd be happy to officiate. Where and when did you wish to marry?"

"Here and now," David said.

Reverend Barnsley's eyebrows shot up. "By the trout pool?"

"Can you think of a better spot?" David asked.

Grace looked at the grass, the trees, the water. It was a beautiful place for a wedding.

Reverend Barnsley grinned. "No, by Jove, I can't. Here, Weyford, if you would be so kind?" The minister handed Mr. Weyford his trout to hold, then bent to pick up his prayer book.

Chapter 21

"What a stroke of good luck that the Weyfords are trout-mad, too." David hauled Grace across the lawn to the inn.

"Why?" Grace dug in her heels. "*Will* you slow down? What is the rush?"

He stopped and grinned down at her. She was flushed and her wonderful bosom was heaving. In just a few moments, he would see every inch of that lovely, large . . .

Something else was growing painfully large.

"Because I should probably buy breakfast for everyone to celebrate our marriage, but I am very—*very*—anxious to celebrate in an entirely different, extremely private manner, if you get my meaning." He brushed her breast to help her comprehend.

"Oh." Her color deepened to bright red. "Is it . . . I mean, do we have to . . . so soon? It's daylight. I thought that . . . activity was something one did at night."

"Oh, no, I assure you, it can be accomplished at any time or place." He felt absurdly cheerful. "Even here, now."

"What!?" Grace's voice actually squeaked. "Out-side?" She looked around rather wildly. "Here?"

"Well, yes, though I personally don't like the public

nature of this specific location. But it is certainly physically possible. Still, I think a bed and a locked door would be better for your first time, don't you think?"

"Ah. Er. Um."

Obviously, Grace was too overcome to express her opinion.

"And I did think it best, given our situation, that we consummate our marriage promptly. It makes it so much more . . . final, don't you think, if your father should happen to stop by the inn looking for you? I assume we have not passed the time when your wedding to Parker-Roth was to take place?"

"Oh. Yes. You're right." Grace darted a glance toward the road, then grabbed his hand and started almost running toward the inn.

He did like an eager bride.

Grace felt her heart pounding just like it had when she'd first launched herself out her bedroom window. It must be too late for Papa to make her marry John. She was already married. But David was right. Best to be *very* married.

She pulled the hood of her cloak low so it shaded her face as they got closer to the inn. She would prefer the servants not recognize her sneaking up the back stairs into a man's room.

Heavens, what was she doing?

She hesitated, but David did not. He yanked open the door and pulled her in after him, up the narrow stairs, down the corridor to his room. She slipped inside and he followed her, closing the door and locking it securely behind him.

Thank God. She released her breath in a sigh of relief. She was finally—

Her eyes found the bed, and her heart started thudding in her chest again.

"Don't be nervous, Grace." David's fingers found the clasp on her cloak and opened it.

"I'm n-not n-nervous." She stepped away as soon as her cloak came off in his hands. "Well, m-maybe I am."

She looked horrible. She should have taken the time to put on her corset. What had she been thinking? Now her overlarge breasts were hanging and jiggling in a most distressing way. And her hair had long fallen out of its pins.

"I don't have a nightgown."

David laughed!

"Grace, love, a nightgown would be very much in the way."

"It would?"

He nodded.

She thought about that. Of course, she knew a bed was involved in marital relations, and she didn't usually climb into bed with her dress and shift on, but there was no reason why she couldn't. In this case, with inn sheets involved, perhaps it was just as well. She would . . .

David was unfastening her dress.

"What are you doing?"

His lips curved in a slow smile and his eyes were positively hot. "I'm getting you completely, utterly, wonderfully naked."

"Eek!" She wriggled free. "Surely that is not a good idea."

He followed her retreat across the room. "On the contrary, it is a splendid idea. A brilliant idea." He smiled again. "An idea I've thought about and dreamt about since I first saw you enter Alvord's ballroom."

"You're jesting." Oh, dear. His smile . . . she was *throbbing* again in that very embarrassing place. "Stop that."

"Stop what?"

"Stop looking at me that way. It makes my stomach feel all fluttery."

"Really?" He looked at her stomach—

She covered it with her hands. Thank God she still had her dress on. "Yes, really."

"You know, I think that is probably a good thing." He'd stopped trying to touch her, but now his fingers were working on his own clothes. He flung his greatcoat and coat in a corner and started on his waistcoat.

"What are you doing?"

"I've decided perhaps you are shy because I am fully clothed, so I'm rectifying that situation."

"Oh."

The waistcoat and cravat went flying. Then he loosened the neck of his shirt and grabbed its hem.

"Ah, do you think . . . I mean . . . um, well . . . are you sure that is wise?"

He raised an eyebrow. "Wait a moment." He lifted his arms, pulling the shirt up and over his head. Then it, too, flew off to the side.

Oh. Her mouth went suddenly dry. Her heart felt as if it had stopped, but the lower place was throbbing wildly enough for two hearts. She grabbed a chair back. Her knees were threatening to give out.

He was beautiful. His arms curved with muscle, his shoulders were huge—amazing they had fit in his coat. His broad chest was covered with golden hair. Was it as soft as it looked?

"Like what you see?"

"Hmm."

Suddenly he was close enough for her to touch. She put her hand on his chest. Yes, the hair was soft, but his body was hard, like warm marble.

"Then let me see, too." He reached for her dress.

"No." She snatched her hand—regretfully—back to hold onto her bodice. "You don't want to see. I'm much too large."

David's gaze narrowed, becoming hotter. "You cannot be too large."

She shook her head. What did men know? "Oh, yes. I am . . . huge. Not ladylike at all."

She watched him swallow. His voice sounded strained.

"Grace, listen to me. I like large. I love huge." He laughed, an oddly shaky sound.

"But ladies are supposed to be small and delicate."

He rolled his eyes and stepped back. "Look at me. Do I look small and delicate?"

She looked at him. He was magnificent . . . and very, very large from the top of his head to his broad shoulders and chest, his flat, muscular stomach, his . . .

She blushed. There was a very significant bulge under the fall of his breeches. "N-no. You are not s-small."

"Of course not. And I don't want a small woman. I would crush her. I need—I want—a large woman. You, Grace. I want you."

He put his hands on her shoulders. "Please don't hide from me. I want to see—I'm *dying* to see—every glorious inch of you." His hands moved, slipping her dress off her shoulders. "Please? Please let me see. Let me touch." His hands moved lower. "Let me taste."

How could she say no? Her body ached for him. She wanted him as much, or more, than he wanted her. It was a madness, but one she felt powerless to cure.

Or perhaps he was her cure.

"Yes," she whispered as her dress whispered over her breasts and down to her waist. She heard David suck in his breath; she felt her nipples peak, pushing against the thin covering of her shift.

And then her shift slipped down to her waist as well.

"God, Grace, you are so beautiful."

"No, I . . . ah."

His hands were on her breasts now, stroking their sides. His fingertip traced a circle around one nipple. He was . . . looking at her.

She should have been mortified. She *was* mortified, but she was also . . . excited. Her breasts felt so sensitive.

And then his thumb flicked over the hard nub of her nipple.

"Eek!"

"Do you like that?" David murmured.

"Y-yes." It felt wonderful.

His mouth moved to cover her nipple and suck. Ah! She felt the pull all the way to the achy, wet, empty place between her legs. It was beyond wonderful. And then his hands brushed her waist, and her dress and shift slithered the rest of the way to the ground.

She was completely naked and shockingly happy to be so. She felt so alive and . . . powerful. David was staring at her with an almost worshipful expression.

He pulled her against his body. His lips teased her neck, her ear. His chest, with its lovely soft hair, felt splendid against her breasts—but his breeches were too rough on her other tender flesh. She pushed away from him so she could solve that problem. She reached for the buttons on his fall.

"Huh?" David raised his head. Grace's breasts were truly the most beautiful, most glorious breasts he had ever seen, and the taste and scent of her skin were beyond intoxicating, but the sensation of her fingers brushing the front of his breeches made even those delights fade. He was going to explode—hopefully not literally—with happiness.

"You have too many clothes on." Grace laughed. She felt so free—free to please herself for the first time— well, and to please David, too, she hoped. His love had given her this heady, wonderful, overwhelming feeling. She could be angry or happy; she could cry or laugh; she could be serious or silly—he would still love her, and she would still love him.

"If I am completely naked, you should be, also." She worked loose the first button. She was thankful, too. She had barely escaped disaster—and marrying poor John would definitely have been a disaster. She would have locked herself—locked them all—forever in the dark prison of duty.

If she'd wed John, she would never have known this heat, this life that was surging through her. She hadn't known it existed when she'd defied Papa and gone with Aunt Kate to London. Its first whisper had teased her when she'd seen David in the Duke of Alvord's ballroom, and it had grown in her with each kiss, each touch, each word exchanged. It was lust and it was love, and she was now finally—finally!—going to discover its depth and breadth. She laughed and stroked David's growing bulge through the cloth of his fall.

David bit his lip. Ah. Grace shy was adorable, but Grace bold was incredibly erotic. She was killing him— in the best possible way—as she worked on opening his breeches. He felt each brush of her fingers on his cock, yes—that was wonderful—but in his heart also. Seeing her beautiful, red-gold hair cascading over her creamy, lush breasts with their delicately tinted nipples, inhaling the sweet scent of her heat and desire . . . well, he'd almost wager his cock would tear his buttons free by itself if Grace didn't manage to slip them from their holes.

But she did. Finally she opened the last button and his fall fell away. He'd dispensed with drawers this morning, not knowing at the time what an inspired decision that was, so his heated flesh sprang naked into the cool air of the room and Grace's gentle touch.

"Oh, my." Grace stared at the prize in her hands. So *this* was the male member. She ran her finger carefully from its root to its tip. It jumped . . . with delight? David sucked in his breath sharply. She glanced up at him. His face looked strained, but in a good way.

His voice sounded strained, too. "You can"—he swallowed—"touch . . . me . . . all you want, love. You won't hurt me."

"No?" She wrapped her hand around him. He was large and warm, soft and hard. Quite different from her.

"No." He was almost panting. "N-not at all."

"I see." She grinned and moved her hand up his length. He groaned. Her fingers flew away as if burned. She frowned at him. "You said I wouldn't hurt you."

"And you didn't." He moistened his lips. A bead of sweat slid down his face. He seemed to be having difficulty forming sentences. "That was a groan of pleasure."

"A groan of pleasure?" She looked extremely skeptical. And, God, she wrapped her lovely fingers around him again. Some day he would love to play this game— let her take the lead entirely—but not today. Today he needed to get to the . . . point before he collapsed or spent himself ignobly in her hand.

"Indeed. Here, I will make you groan, too."

She snorted. "No, you won't."

Zounds, he loved her. He would never have guessed this kind of love existed. He'd made love to enough females—but he now realized it had never been love he'd been making.

He grinned. "Would you care to wager on it?"

"Well . . ." Grace hesitated—and then grinned back at him in a delightfully shy, mischievous fashion. "Yes. What shall be the stakes?"

"Hmm. If I make you groan, you will do one thing in bed that I ask you to do."

She frowned. "What kind of thing?"

"Something you will enjoy, I promise."

She laughed. "All right. And if I win?"

"Well, I'm not sure you'll have won if you don't groan—and I shall be very disappointed with myself—but if you don't, I will do one thing you ask me to do—in bed."

She chewed on her lip for a moment. "Very well, I accept your terms." She held out her hand to seal the agreement.

He clasped it and pulled her against him. Wonderful—but his breeches were still in the way. He wriggled out of them and picked Grace up.

"Oh! Be careful. I'm too heavy."

"No, you aren't." He lifted her higher, so his mouth could reach one of her nipples. "You don't seem at all heavy to me." He flicked her nipple with his tongue and she squeaked.

"I should have bet I could make you squeak." He carried her over to the bed and dropped her onto the mattress, making her squeak again. "But that would have been too easy."

He joined her. The mattress must still be lumpy, but he didn't feel it now. Grace wasn't complaining either. She was spread out on her back, looking trustingly up at him.

God, he felt such love. He wanted to make Grace groan, yes, but he also wanted to make her laugh, keep her safe, give her children, entwine his life with hers year after year after year until they were truly inseparable.

He kissed her forehead, her eyelids, and her mouth—quite thoroughly. He explored her neck, her breasts, her belly, and her lovely, soft thighs. He—

She pressed her legs together before he reached his goal.

"*What* are you doing?" She sounded quite alarmed.

He looked up at her. "Kissing you. Isn't that obvious?"

She struggled onto her elbows. "I-I am certain what you are doing is inappropriate."

"Indeed?" He brushed his lips over the reddish curls at his end of her lovely body. "In which book of manners did you find a list of appropriate forms of marital kissing? I've not seen that tome."

She flushed—all of her flushed. It was a truly delightful display. "I have not read it in a book, of course."

"No? So which patroness of Almack's made this pronouncement?"

"Don't be absurd. The patronesses don't discuss such things."

"They've ruled on the appropriateness of dances. And, now that I think on it, they have approved the waltz, so I believe they would definitely find this form of kissing unexceptional."

"David, you are being absurd."

"Not at all." He stroked her thighs; she sucked in her breath and opened them for him. "But I'm not certain they would approve of *this* type of kissing. You must ask them when next we are in Town."

"What are you—eek!"

She closed her knees again in shock as he flicked his tongue over the hard little nub hidden in her curls. How delightful—she'd trapped him exactly where he wished to be. He licked her again.

"Oh! Oh!" Her hands gripped his head, her fingers weaving through his hair. "D-David."

"I think that was more of a wail than a groan."

"What?"

"I must make you groan, remember?"

"What are you—oh!"

He smiled as his tongue slid over and around her. He breathed in her musky scent, tasting her deeply. Her hips bucked and shifted. She made lovely little sounds—definitely squeaks and gasps and moans . . . but did she groan?

No matter. He was about to groan. He was so hard, and she was so wet and ready. It was time, but first . . .

He felt the tension in her body build, heard her breath catch . . . and then he touched his tongue delicately once more to her hard little pleasure point. She made an odd sound—a soft scream—and sat up. Then she groaned—definitely a groan—and fell back onto the mattress.

He followed her, slipping into her body, thrusting through her barrier as quickly, as gently as he could, and holding, surrounded by her wet heat. He had never felt anything so wonderful in his life.

"Did I hurt you?"

"Yes." She sounded very annoyed.

"I'm so sorry. It won't happen again."

"It had better not."

He kissed the tip of her nose. He wanted to give her time to adjust, but his body was clamoring for release.

"The first part was lovely, though." Her hands slid down his sweat-slicked back to his buttocks.

Her touch was exquisite. And her body under his . . .

heaven. So soft and hot and wet. He couldn't wait another instant. He moved as cautiously as he was able.

"Is . . . is that all right?"

"Mmm." She gripped his arse harder, pulled him toward her, and wiggled her hips.

"Ah." It was too much. He thrust again.

Gentle. Careful. Not too hard.

He was fighting a losing battle. At least he was going to be fast—not usually a good thing, but with this being Grace's first time, probably a blessing.

Blessing or curse, it was the way it was going to be.

He managed to hold onto a thin thread of control until the final glide through her tight heat. He stopped deep inside her, suspended in anticipation, and then his seed leapt into her welcoming body.

He collapsed as carefully as he could onto her. He felt her arms go round him, hugging him close.

Grace closed her eyes. It had all been so overwhelming. She ran her hands up his back and breathed as deeply as she could. Her legs cradled his hips. She was surrounded by his heat and scent. It was wonderful.

She felt very, very married.

"I'm too heavy for you," he murmured by her ear. He moved off and out of her.

She shivered. Without his body covering hers, she was chilled—but not for long. David pulled the covers up and gathered her close. She nestled her head in the crook of his shoulder.

The place between her legs was sore and wet—and empty now. Had she really felt . . . what she'd felt?

"Are you all right, Grace?"

"Mmm."

"Is that a yes?"

"Mmm-hmm." She smoothed her fingers over the hair

on his stomach. Words were beyond her abilities at the moment.

David ran his hand up and down her side. "Where were you going to take the stagecoach if I hadn't found you?"

"London." She licked his skin. Mmm. Salty. "To Aunt Kate." She pressed herself closer. She would like to do what they'd just done again.

"I doubt she's there. I didn't get a chance to tell you, but when you were packing and leaving with your father, my uncle and your aunt were . . . having a frank and thorough discussion."

"Oh?"

"Like the frank and thorough discussion we just had."

"Oh." Aunt Kate had done . . . this? Surely she was too old.

"Alex left Motton's estate shortly before I did to procure a special license. He and your aunt are probably married and on their honeymoon now."

"Aunt Kate didn't wait for me?" She should feel offended—would feel offended when she could feel anything beyond this overwhelming languor.

"Well, they were in a bit of a hurry. Your aunt is carrying Alex's child."

That news broke through her lassitude. She sat up. "What?!"

"Your aunt is going to be a mother." He cupped her breast, stroked it. "And my uncle is going to be a father."

"Oh." David's touch felt so good; it was completely distracting. She should think about her aunt, but later. Now desire curled low in her stomach; the sore spot between her legs started to throb. *Could* they do what they'd just done again?

Another thought managed to drift through her heated consciousness.

"If I hadn't run away, I'd probably be at church now."

David leaned forward and licked her nipple. "I'm glad you're not."

"So am I." She arched her back, trying to encourage him to keep doing what he was doing. For the first time since she'd reached womanhood she wasn't embarrassed by her breasts. She was almost proud of them. She frowned. "I do hope Papa spoke to John."

David pulled her onto his chest. "Stop worrying. Parker-Roth's a grown man. He should have realized he didn't have your love." He cradled her head and kissed her very thoroughly. "Frankly, your passion would have been wasted on him."

"And it's not wasted on you?"

"Of course not. I made you groan, didn't I?"

She grinned down at him, mischief in her eyes again. "I'm not so certain you did."

David's eyes widened. "What do you mean? I had you writhing and moaning."

"Ah, but was I groaning? Moaning, yes, I'll grant you moaning. But groaning . . . I'm not so certain."

David shrugged, causing his skin to slide in a very delightful way across her nipples. They peaked at once—and the bold man noticed. His hand came up to play with one hard nub.

"I see you are a difficult woman, Lady Dawson. And I, being the gentleman I am, do not wish to dispute a lady—especially my lady wife. I will concede to you this time." His thumb pressed on her nipple, and she drew in a sharp breath. "What is my penalty?"

"That was an easy question to answer. She knew exactly what she wanted. "You must do what you just did—everything you just did."

"Everything?" He pressed her nipple again, and she

felt his touch all the way to her womb. "You mean from the time your lovely back first hit this not-so-lovely mattress?"

"Yes." Grace smiled in anticipation. She wiggled slightly and felt a specific part of him grow. "Everything."

David grinned. "My pleasure, Lady Dawson." He flipped her onto her back and kissed her, his free hand sliding over her body to the place that most ached for his touch. "My very, very great pleasure."